THE
SECRET
KEEPER

BOOKS BY SIOBHAN CURHAM

Beyond This Broken Sky

An American in Paris

The Paris Network

Sweet FA

Frankie Says Relapse

The Scene Stealers

Non-Fiction

Antenatal & Postnatal Depression

Dare to Dream

Dare to Write a Novel

Something More: A Spiritual Misfit's Search for Meaning

THE
SECRET
KEEPER

SIOBHAN CURHAM

bookouture

Published by Bookouture in 2022

An imprint of Storyfire Ltd.
Carmelite House
50 Victoria Embankment
London EC4Y 0DZ

www.bookouture.com

ISBN: 978-1-80314-575-4
eBook ISBN: 978-1-80314-574-7

For Jack Curham and Maria Rasulova

To know your enemy, you must become your enemy.
Sun Tzu, *The Art of War*

Even if I knew that tomorrow the world would go to pieces, I would still plant my apple tree.
Martin Luther

1

AMERICA, 1942

A year after the war started, my beloved Grand-mère Rose wrote me from her home in France. *I might not be able to contact you for a while,* she informed me in her elegant, looping script, *so I have condensed everything I need to say to you into nine words—which will hopefully be easier for you to remember!*

Love your fear
Seek the wonder
Embrace the mystery

I think of her words now, as he passes me my martini. How on earth am I supposed to love this terror that threatens to floor me? I imagine giving myself a hug, but that only makes me feel weaker at the knees.

"Thank you," I say, praying my voice doesn't waver.

"You're welcome." Steve takes off his jacket and I see dark patches of sweat creeping from the armpits of his shirt. Could it be that he's as anxious as me? As he turns to survey the bar, I also notice a bump just above his waistband—the unmistakable outline of a pistol tucked into the back of his pants. My mouth becomes so dry I'm barely able to swallow.

"Gee, it's hot in here!" I exclaim, fanning my face with my pocketbook.

"Perhaps we could go somewhere a little cooler," he replies.

"How about over there, by the terrace?" I nod to the archway at the end of the bar, which opens onto a panoramic view of the ocean and the dark, flat silhouettes of palm trees.

"Sure."

As he follows me, I try to tune out the people at the other tables and focus on my posture instead. *Just imagine you are walking with a pumpkin on your head.* I hear Gran-mere Rose's lilting voice in my mind, and I pull my shoulders back and straighten my head. The skirt I'm wearing feels too tight, the heels on my shoes too high. What if I stumble?

Keep focused! He's a snake-in-the-grass enemy operative and you're about to expose him, I remind myself as I sashay through the bar, hips swinging from side to side.

When I reach the terrace, I take a moment to compose myself, then turn to meet his gaze, smiling in what I hope is a provocative manner.

"I think you're very beautiful," he says, placing our drinks on the table.

"Why, thank you," I reply breathlessly.

"I'd love to get to know you better."

"I'd love that too." I place my hand on his shoulder, hoping he can't feel my fingers tremble.

He moves in slowly and I mentally prepare. *Don't go for his gun too soon. Start with both hands on his shoulders. Work your way down. Make it look like a caress.*

As he pulls me into an embrace, I can smell the stale onion on his breath. My heart pounds so violently I'm sure he can feel it reverberating through him too. I let my hands trail down his back until they reach the cold, hard outline of the pistol. I smile coolly over his shoulder—

"And cut!"

We release our embrace and turn to look at the director, Joel. This is it, the moment of truth. Have I done enough? Was I convincing enough? Or is my acting career over before it's even really begun?

"That was awesome," Joel says. Then he turns to his left, where the narrator is standing off camera. "OK, Ron, wanna run your lines?"

"Sure thing." First Lieutenant Reagan clears his throat and looks down at his script. "Oh, Steve," he reads. "The small of the back may be a good place to hide a pistol, but not in a tight squeeze. And now Steve is in a very tight squeeze—he's ended up with an appointment with the enemy's secret police."

The camera that had been focusing on my face moves back and the studio lights come up.

"The camera loves her," I hear the assistant director say to the murmured agreement of another member of the crew. "Great presence."

I glance around for my screenwriter friend, Mike—or First Lieutenant Michael Ryan as he's now known—and spot him hovering in the wings. He gives me a reassuring thumbs up. I know he pulled a lot of strings to get me this part. I hope I haven't let him down.

I glance back at Steve—or rather, the actor William Holden. If all else fails, at least I can now say that, at the ripe old age of twenty-one, I've performed with someone who's starred in a movie with my hero, Barbara Stanwyck. And last year, the narrator, First Lieutenant Ronald Reagan, was voted one of Hollywood's most popular new young actors.

But I'm tired of clinging to tenuous connections like this. I've been doing it ever since I've been trying to catch a break in this town. Every time I wait on a producer or a screenwriter in the diner, every time I've been given a non-speaking role as a maid, or a helpless Indian girl in a Western, I've snaffled it up like a mouse grateful for crumbs. But I'm sick of crumbs; now I long for a meatier role.

I gaze around the set at the extras sitting at the tables with their pretend drinks in front of the painted backdrop of the trees and sea. "WELCOME TO ENEMYAREA," a sign on the wall behind the bar proclaims. This part isn't exactly a starring role, but at least I had a couple of lines, and it's for a training video for American undercover operatives who'll be going to Europe to fight the Germans. At least I'd be able to say that I played a small part in the war effort—literally!

A bulky man in a sharp suit and fedora hat steps from the shadows and mutters something to Joel. They both turn and look at me. I pull myself up tall, aware that I might still need to perform.

"Good work, Elena," Joel calls over to me.

"Thank you." I hold my breath.

"No need for any more takes," he adds. "You nailed it first time."

"Yes!" I exclaim with the unabashed excitement of a child, instantly destroying the cool Hepburnesque façade I'd been trying so hard to cultivate.

Thankfully, the man in the suit laughs. "Glad to see it means so much to you," he says.

"Of course," I reply. "I'm very happy to do my part for the war effort."

"Is that so?" He comes over and looks me up and down. He has the kind of crinkly eyebrows that give his face a look of permanent amusement. I wonder if he has the temperament to match, or does his jovial exterior belie a cruel, hard interior? I'm not sure if it's an actor thing, but I'm always trying to figure out people's motivations and backstories. He glances down at a piece of paper in his hand. "Elena Garcia. Interesting name."

Hmm, I think to myself, *not when you're trying to land a meaty role in Hollywood.* "Thank you." I smile sweetly to mask my world-weary cynicism.

"Where's it from?"

I don't need to be a spy to crack that coded question. Whenever people ask me where my name's from, what they really mean is where are *you* from? "It's Spanish. My father's from Mexico."

Rather than act as a deterrent, this news seems to make him even more interested. "You speak Spanish?"

"*Sí,* and *oui.* I speak French also. My grandma's from France."

"Very interesting." He nods thoughtfully. "And you're happy to do your part for the war effort, you say?"

"Of course." I feel a fluttering in my stomach. I don't know who this guy is, but I'm guessing he must be a head honcho here at Hal Roach Studios—or "Fort Roach" as it's become known ever since the First Motion Picture Unit leased it to make recruitment and training films for the armed services. Could he be about to offer me another role?

"Perhaps we could meet sometime to discuss this further?" he says, tucking the piece of paper into his inside jacket pocket.

"That would be swell." I can't help grinning like a Cheshire cat.

"OK, I'll be in touch."

"Thank you." He starts walking away. "But how will you know how to contact me?" I call after him.

"Don't worry. I'll find you," he says over his shoulder, and with that he disappears into the darkened studio wings.

My darling Elena,

It is with a very heavy heart that I write this to you. This morning, our government fled Paris like rats flinging themselves from a sinking ship, and Hitler's occupation of France is now imminent. I know your mother will be wringing her hands, wishing I'd never left America, but no matter how bad things get, I'm glad I moved back here. The truth is, I'd been feeling the call to return home ever since your Grand-père Bob passed. My love of France runs so deep, I'm sure that if you cut me I would bleed blue and white as well as red. And now my beloved country is under attack like never before, I can't run and hide, I need to stay and fight for our liberty—although I'm not entirely sure what a sixty-six-year-old woman will be able to do!

Do you remember when you were about eight years old and you came home from school in tears because that bully in your class—I think he was named Raymond?— had picked on another kid for being Mexican? And you were crying not just for your friend but because you hadn't done anything to stop him. Do you remember the story I told you back then? About a bully of a wolf who lived in the forest and kept picking on the rabbits, growling at them and stealing their carrots. But then one day, the rabbits all got together and they burrowed and burrowed until they made a gigantic hole and they turned the hole into a trap for the wolf and they wouldn't let him out until he promised to be kind to them. I still believe in the moral of that story—that individually we might be no match for a bully, but together we can achieve miracles. Do you remember what you achieved when you went into school the following day and you got all the Latino kids to band together and you cornered Raymond in the school yard and told him if he messed with one of you he messed with all of you and that would mean SERIOUS CONSEQUENCES?! Oh Elena, how I miss your fiery spirit! And how I shall miss our letters.

It breaks my heart to have to say this, but I might not be able to contact you for a while, so I have condensed everything I need to say to you into nine words—which will hopefully be easy for you to remember!

> Love your fear
> Seek the wonder
> Embrace the mystery

I know that you find our correspondence a source of support—God knows I do too—and I tried so hard to come up with some words of wisdom that would work in every possible situation, especially in a world where there is so much fear. I know it sounds counterintuitive to love your fear; how and why should we love something that causes us so much discomfort? But, in my experience, love is the only way we can get our fear to subside. If it helps, try picturing your fear as an anxious child. I know how you love to create characters, so why not give your fear a name. Then the next time she starts taking over, imagine giving that part of yourself a hug and soothing her till she quiets down.

Another way to combat the trials and tribulations of the world today is to seek the wonder in any situation. And trust me, there is ALWAYS an opportunity to find wonder. Today, when I heard the terrible news of the French government's capitulation, I felt crushed. But *then I went into my garden and I looked at my beloved roses, I stroked their velvety soft petals, inhaled their rich perfume, and all at once I was filled with awe again.*

And something else I have learned in my almost seven decades on this planet is that life is a mystery. We humans crave explanations for everything, but some things are impossible to be explained—like why a mustachioed man from Austria named Adolf Hitler should want to cause so much suffering. Try to embrace the mystery that is life, Elena, the good and the bad. Accept that there will be some things you cannot explain, and that's OK. And when it doesn't feel OK, love your fear into submission and seek wonder.

Love, wonder, mystery. I pray that you will keep these words close to your heart until this hateful war is over and we are able to write again, or maybe even see each other. I shall be keeping you in my heart, my darling granddaughter, and praying for the day we will be together again. Every time I walk past my spare room —or darling granddaughter room, as I think of it—I picture you coming to visit me here in France. God willing, it will happen sooner rather than later.

All my love,

Grand-mère Rose

2

AMERICA, 1942

Two weeks pass with not a word from the man in the suit. I decide that his affable eyebrows mask the face of a cruel-hearted liar and that the only role I'm destined to play in this godforsaken town is that of a downtrodden waitress. As if on cue, a large man in an ill-fitting suit and crooked tie comes lumbering into the diner, positions himself on the stool at the counter, and belches loudly, emitting a sour waft of stale liquor.

"What can I getcha?" I say in the voice of my cheery-waitress-with-a-heart-of-gold persona. *A coupla Papoid tablets with an Alka-Seltzer chaser?* I silently add in my own, world-weary-actress-with-a-head-full-of-cynicism tone.

"I'll have a coffee," he growls like a bear and I see that half his bottom teeth are missing. The ones that remain stand crooked and crumbling, like a row of ancient gravestones.

"You betcha!" I cry gaily.

As I turn to fetch the coffee pot, I begin mentally composing the latest instalment of "Diner Woes"—a long-running saga that I perform for my kid sister, Maria, every time I come home from work. *Tonight's exciting episode is titled The Tale of the Belching Bear*, I rehearse in my mind.

I place a cup in front of the man and pour him a coffee. "Can I get you any breakfast?"

He looks at me like I'm the stupidest thing ever planted on God's green earth. "Obviously. Why would I be here if I didn't want breakfast?"

To make my life hell? I silently reply, while switching the beam of my smile to dazzle. "I'm sorry, sir, what can I getcha?" I take the pad from my apron pocket and the pencil from behind my ear.

"Hotcakes, syrup and bacon, and eggs."

"Sunny side up?" I reply, figuring he'll be too dumb to detect my sarcasm.

"Scrambled," he grunts.

"Sure thing."

As I go over to the kitchen hatch, I feel like crying. "Breakfast order," I mutter as I tear the page from my pad and pin it to the board. I catch a glimpse of one of the diner owner Rita's needlepoint mottos hanging on the wall and I fight the urge to smash it with my fist. It's titled *THE BEST RULE* and the jaunty stitching reads: *Just one rule you need to mind, and joy you'll never lack. First you have to love the world, and then it loves you back.*

I shoot a glance at the belching bear, who's now digging one of his fat hairy fingers into his nose like he's prospecting for gold. How is it possible to love a world like this? A world where fascism is spreading through Europe like a plague and I have to suck up to people who treat me like something they scraped from the bottom of their shoe?

Just then, the phone starts to ring, its shrill peal causing me to snap back into character.

"Good morning, Rita's Diner, this is Elena speaking, how may I help you?" I trill.

"Elena Garcia?" a man's voice asks, so softly I can barely hear him over the sizzle of bacon frying.

"Yes," I reply.

"We met at Fort Roach a couple weeks ago. Are you still interested in helping us?"

"Yes, yes, absolutely!" My skin prickles with excitement. His eyebrows didn't lie after all. He must have another part for me.

"Be at the Hollywood Hotel tomorrow evening at a quarter after six. A man will be there to meet you. He'll be holding a copy of the *LA Times*. Do not tell anyone about this."

"Sure. Whereabouts in the hotel should I meet him?" I ask, but all I hear in response is the click of the line going dead.

As soon as my shift ends at five, I board the bus home, my mind still abuzz from the mysterious phone call. While I'm thrilled at the prospect of another acting role, I don't understand why Mister Eyebrows had to be so cloak-and-dagger about it. And why do I need to go meet some mystery guy at a hotel instead of going to the studio? It doesn't make sense. If only I were able to call my friend, Mike, but ever since he—like so many others in the film industry—was conscripted into the First Motion Picture Unit and stationed at Fort Roach, he might as well be serving overseas. We're able to write each other, but that's no use when my meeting is tomorrow. And besides, I'm not allowed to tell anyone about it.

As the bus winds its way up the hill, I ring the bell for my stop. As soon as I set foot on the sidewalk, I can hear my father yelling something in Spanish. The only time he speaks in Spanish is when he's getting all lovey-dovey with Mom or something terrible's happened. From the shrill tone of his voice, it definitely sounds like the latter. I hurry up the path and find my kid sister, Maria, sitting on the front stoop in the twilight, carving one of her acorn people with a penknife. She just turned sixteen so these days she only carves little faces on acorns in secret and for comfort.

"What's up, buttercup?" I say in a comical high-pitched voice that's always guaranteed to make her giggle.

"Elena!" She leaps up and throws her skinny arms around me. "I'm so glad you're home. Papa's going crazy."

"Why?" Inside the house, Papa reaches a crescendo about the bitter injustices of this world.

"I dunno. Something to do with the bank."

"Uh-oh." My father owns an auto mechanics business and Mom is his personal assistant, taking care of the payments and bookings. Even though they work every hour God sends, there are times when they struggle to make ends meet and Papa has to go cap in hand to the bank manager. Seeing my parents work so hard to make a better life for Maria and me than they had as kids fuels my desire to make it as an actress. I dream of the day I'm able to take care of my folks as a way of saying thank you for all their love and support. "Come on, let's go inside. And remember—together we are stronger," I say dramatically as I link my fingers through Maria's.

We find our parents in the kitchen. The steamy air smells of a delicious mixture of tomatoes, onions and garlic. Mom's at the stove, her glossy raven hair piled on top of her head and her cheeks flushed from the heat of the pots bubbling away in front of her. Papa's pacing up and down, muttering to himself.

"You OK, Papa?"

"Oh, Elena, it has been a day from hell!" he exclaims, waving his hands in the air as if he's conducting an orchestra. Let's just say it's no great mystery where I got my theatrical gene from.

"What happened?" I ask, helping myself to a couple of grapes from the fruit bowl.

"I found out from the bank that someone has been investigating me."

"Investigating you? But why? You haven't been getting all Al Capone with the IRS, have you?" I quip.

Mom shakes her head. "Please don't joke about it, Elena, you'll make him even worse."

"I always pay my taxes. I'm just an honest Joe, trying to make a living," Papa wails. "Why do they have to hound me?"

"Well, if you're just an honest Joe, you've got nothing to worry about, have you?" I reply, planting a kiss on his cheek.

"It must be a case of mistaken identity," Mom says, putting some plates on the table.

"How?" Papa's dark eyes spark with indignation. "They asked the manager about me specifically."

I frown. What with my phone call and Papa's bank check, it's been a day of mysterious events. I long to tell my parents about my meeting tomorrow, but I mustn't do anything to blow it. This could be an important stepping stone in my Hollywood career—and toward the day when my parents never have to worry about money again.

Maria and I sit down at the table and Papa resumes his tirade in Spanish. *We can understand what you're saying,* I want to remind him as he unleashes a stream of colorful cuss words. *We are fluent in Spanish too!* He's finally silenced by an almighty crash as Mom drops the dish of enchiladas she was carrying to the table.

"No!" she exclaims, before bursting into tears.

I look across the table at Maria and raise my eyebrows, trying to lighten the mood. Poor Maria is like a timid mouse born into a family of passionate tigers and I know how she hates this kind of drama.

"It's OK, Mom," I say, leaping up to help her.

"No, no, it is not OK," she cries. "Nothing is OK."

Instantly, Papa springs to her side, his anger replaced by a look of concern. "What is it, Sylvia? What is wrong?"

Maria and I join the huddle, wrapping Mom in a tapestry of arms.

"Those Nazi pigs have now occupied all of France," she gasps. "I'm so worried about Maman, I feel my heart might actually break."

When Grand-mère Rose returned to France five years ago, just after I turned sixteen, I cried every day for two years, and for once, I'm not being melodramatic. Due to my parents having to work such long hours back when I was little, Grand-mère Rose practically brought me up. And she raised me in every sense of the word, teaching me to love my deep voice and gangly legs in spite of the schoolyard bullies; to stand tall and proudly take my place in the world.

It's been two years since I received a letter from her. Not being able to see her was hard, but not being able to communicate with her at all has felt like the cruelest punishment. Now I feel like crying all over again.

"But I-I thought the Nazis had agreed to leave half of the country to the French?" I stammer.

"Not anymore," Mom replies.

I sit back down, feeling stunned. At first, the war had felt so far away, with the vastness of the Atlantic Ocean between us and Hitler. But then, last year, the attack on Pearl Harbor happened and now all of France is infested with Nazis. It suddenly feels all too close and way too personal.

"Don't worry, the war will be over soon," Papa soothes as he strokes Mom's hair.

"How can you be sure?" Maria asks, kneeling to scrape the enchiladas from the floor.

"Because the Americans have finally joined," he replies. "There's no way Hitler's a match for Uncle Sam."

I nod, not wanting to upset Mom more, but inside I can't help feeling doubtful. So far, the Nazis seem to have destroyed every army in their wake; who's to say they won't do the same again? As I help clear up the food, I know one thing for certain —I'm going to go to that meeting tomorrow and I'm going to take any role they offer; I'm going to do anything I can to help beat the Germans and free Grand-mère Rose.

The following evening, I walk along Hollywood Boulevard feeling tense and unsettled. I've had another day of woe at the diner and the smell of cooking fat clings to my nostrils like a curse. I only hope it isn't clinging to my clothes. I smooth down my dress, which is crumpled from a day in my locker, and take a deep breath to try to calm myself.

The Hollywood Hotel is nestled amongst a cluster of lemon groves at the foot of the Hollywood Hills. As soon as the elegant wooden structure comes into view, I feel the tension begin to ebb from my body. So many stars of the silver screen have sat sipping drinks on those wide verandas and have danced up a storm in the ballroom. Treading in their hallowed footsteps reminds me that my escape from the diner could be just around the corner and I feel a renewed sense of hope as I hurry up the steps and into the lobby.

Jazz piano is playing softly in the background and the warm air is perfumed with the scent of the huge vases of pink lilies dotted around the place. I quickly case the joint for anyone carrying a copy of the *LA Times*. The lobby is bustling with guests checking in and soldiers in uniform heading to the bar, in search of some last-minute fun before heading off to fight, I guess. My skin erupts in goosebumps as I think of Grand-mère Rose. *Please help save her from the Germans.* I send my silent prayer after the soldiers like an invisible telegram.

I walk the length of the lobby, my kitten heels sinking into the plush green carpet. Finally, I spot a guy leaning against the wall by the telephone kiosk, reading a newspaper. It's not Mister Eyebrows, but he didn't say it would be him, he only said "a man" would be meeting me. He holds the paper up and a shiver runs down my spine as I see that it's the *LA Times*.

"Elena," he says quietly but with certainty, as if we're old acquaintances.

I nod.

"Come." He gestures at me to follow him into the bar and leads me to a table tucked out of sight behind a trellis partition covered with satin clambering roses. "I work for the War Department," he says as soon as we sit down. "I understand from my colleague that you're interested in doing your bit to help."

"Yes," I reply eagerly. "I recently acted in a training video at the Hal Roach Studios and I'd love the opportunity to play any similar roles." A thought occurs to me that's so exciting, I hardly dare think it; what if I've been summoned to this cloak-and-dagger meeting because he wants to offer me a part in a war effort movie like the James Stewart flick *Winning Your Wings*, which came out earlier this year and ended up persuading thousands of men to sign up to the Air Force.

"Very good." The man nods, taking off his hat and placing it neatly on the table beside his place setting. His short hair is graying at the temples and his cheeks sport the kind of ruddy glow gained from a lifetime outdoors. Perhaps he was a farmer before the war. A picture of him leaning against a tractor chewing a piece of straw begins forming in my mind.

A waiter comes over and takes our order. The man asks for a Scotch. I order a coffee. I need to keep my wits about me.

As soon as the waiter's gone, the man leans across the table. "We actually have some other work that might be of interest to you," he says, his voice so low he's practically whispering.

Could he mean a movie? I focus hard on containing my excitement. "Acting work?"

"In a manner of speaking, yes, but not on screen."

My heart sinks. "What do you mean?"

"I'm afraid I can't be more specific right now as you would need to pass some tests first. Would you be able to come to Washington in the next week?"

"Washington, DC?" I blurt out.

He frowns and puts his finger to his lips. "Yes," he whispers. "It would be for a couple of weeks at least, so you'd have to take some leave from your job in the diner."

The prospect of a break from that awful place and its sickly-sweet embroidered sayings is appealing for sure. "That would not be a problem."

"Great." He nods. "If it all works out, you wouldn't have to go back."

"That would be a blessing," I joke. He doesn't even crack a smile.

The waiter delivers our drinks and I watch as the man takes a small, well-thumbed appointment book from his jacket pocket and flicks through the pages. "How about next Wednesday?"

"Sure."

"I understand you live at home with your parents, and that your father has his own auto mechanics business."

"Yes—but how—?"

"Give this to them," he cuts in, taking a small card from inside the book. "Tell them you're being interviewed by the War Department for a job and if they need to contact you, they can do so here." He hands me the card. An address and telephone number are printed on it. "You won't actually be at that location, but they will be able to forward messages to you."

I stare at him blankly while my mind fills with questions. How does he know what Papa does for a living? Could he be behind the mysterious bank investigation? What the hell is this role he wants me to try out for?

"Bring a suitcase of clothes—" he eyes my fancy frock "—suitable for the outdoors. And you mustn't bring anything with your name or even your initials on." He takes another card from his pocket and passes it to me. "This is where you must go next week and when you get there, you are to go straight to the Q building. When you see the receptionist, you must give her a false name and address."

"What false name and address?" This is getting more mysterious by the minute.

"Whatever you like," he replies with a shrug.

"But how will she know that I'm supposed to be there?"

"You don't need to worry about that." He downs his drink and stands up, placing some money on the table. "Nice to meet you, Elena, and very best of luck." He extends his hand and shakes mine briskly.

Before I can even begin to process what just happened, he's heading for the door. All I can think as I watch him leave is, *Very best of luck with what?*

My dearest Elena,

Why am I writing this letter when I know that I'll never be able to send it and that I'll have to destroy it as soon as I've written it? Because I so desperately need an outlet.

It's three in the morning and I can't sleep. I have so much rage and despair building inside of me, and as I was lying here tossing and turning, I thought to myself, oh if only I could write to Elena (I hadn't realized quite how therapeutic our correspondence was until it ended). And then a thought dawned on me—what if I DID write to you and pretended that I had mailed the letter. Maybe it would have the same effect? So here goes...

My main news is that the Germans are here—in our country, in our town, and—my God, how it makes me sick to my stomach to have to write this—in my home. A company of their soldiers swept into town on the day of the occupation and they haven't left. We were all ordered to register at the town hall and those of us with spare rooms were told that we would be expected to house our German "guests."

As you know from my previous letters, I have a spare bedroom here in the cottage, my "darling granddaughter room," ready for whenever you and your sister might be able to visit. The day after the Germans arrived, one of them showed up at my door: a tall, thin streak of a man, with an intellectual air about him, which was rather at odds with his dreary gray uniform that has come to represent so much brutality.

"I shall be staying here for a while," he said to me in

flawless French. He at least had the good grace not to look me in the eye.

I said nothing in response, just led him up the stairs to the room that was supposed to be yours—that IS yours —and watched his lanky frame stoop as he entered. I hope he bangs his head on that sloped ceiling every day and that every time it is a reminder of the pain he and his beloved leader, Hitler, are causing.

I went back downstairs feeling numb to my core. Sat at the kitchen table willing myself not to cry. Thinking of your grandfather and how he'd tell me to stay strong and hold my head up high. If only he was still here. I don't think I've ever felt so alone, or so terrified. To have a strange man move himself into your home uninvited is bad enough, but when that man is a Nazi...

Oh Elena, I'm glad I won't be able to mail this to you, for I know it would send you into a frenzy, wanting to do something to help but not being able to. I'm so glad you have an entire ocean between you and Hitler. Knowing that you are all safe from him is the one shred of hope I have left to cling to.

All my love,

Grand-mère Rose

3

AMERICA, 1942

Prior to taking the train to Washington, the furthest I'd ever been from home was Nevada for a family vacation. As the locomotive chugs into Union Station after a three-day journey, my pulse quickens and fearful thoughts start clamoring for my attention. *What are you doing here? What if you can't find the address? What if it's all been some kind of ruse?* But why would anyone make a prank out of the war?

I take a deep breath, inhaling a lungful of the sickly-sweet perfume of the woman sitting opposite me. She looks so calm and composed in her fawn-colored coat and matching pillbox hat, gloves neatly folded on her lap. I give myself a quick inner pep talk in the style of my Grand-mère Rose. *Elena, ma chère, just imagine you are playing the part of a Very Confident and Supremely Accomplished Woman summoned to Washington to do her part for her country in their hour of need.* I stand up proud and tall, and fetch my case from the overhead shelf.

As the train judders to a halt, the air fills with the excited chatter of passengers disembarking. I adjust my hat, make sure my skirt is straight, and follow the hordes down onto the platform.

The main concourse, full of people weaving this way and that, reminds me of the ant colonies Maria and I used to discover at the end of our backyard. We'd watch those ants bustling about for hours, giving them all names and backstories and comedy voices. As I look around at my fellow passengers, I see that most of them share a common backstory—the war. There are so many young servicemen in uniform, kit bags slung over their shoulders, and young women fighting back tears as they wait to see them off. The walls of the station are plastered with posters about the war. *"AVENGE PEARL HARBOR! JOIN THE NAVY NOW!"* one of the captions yells. *"JOIN CAPTAIN AMERICA AND THE US ARMED FORCES! FIGHT FOR FREEDOM IN EUROPE AND THE PACIFIC!"* cries another.

As I weave through the masses to the nearest exit, I see a poster featuring a huge pair of red lips with a bold white cross plastered upon them. "CARELESS TALK COSTS LIVES," the caption reads. I think about my meeting in the Hollywood Hotel and how I've been sworn to secrecy about my trip to Washington. When I told my folks I'd be going away for a while to do some work for the War Department, I was greeted with an inquisition. In the end, I implied that I was going to be filming another training video. What if that's true and I've given away the secret? Will my indiscretion end up costing lives? *Don't be so ridiculous*, I scold myself. *We aren't living in an occupied country like Grand-mère Rose.*

I step outside and breathe in the crisp end-of-fall air. It's a beautiful day; the sky is cornflower blue, dotted with clouds wispy as cotton. It feels good to take a moment to appreciate the wonder in life's simple pleasures, and to remind myself that it still exists.

I head over to the queue for taxis. I've memorized the address on the card I was given, but as I get into the cab, I check it once more just to be sure.

"2430 East Street, please," I tell the driver, my mouth gritty as sandpaper from a mixture of nerves and thirst.

Thankfully, my driver isn't the chatty type and I settle back and gaze out of the window at the ornate granite buildings lining the street. I'm in Washington, DC, our nation's capital! But my excitement ebbs a little when we pass a sign for "Foggy Bottom" and the driver pulls up by a cluster of nondescript buildings set off the road.

I pay the driver and as the cab drives off, I run through my instructions like I'm running lines. *Go to the Q building. Give the receptionist a false name and address.*

It turns out that the Q building is the least impressive of all, dull and squat and prefabricated. It looks nothing like a Hollywood studio and again I'm flooded with feelings of apprehension. But I've come so far, I can't quit now.

The building is even more dreary on the inside. I head over to the reception desk, where a stout woman with wiry gray hair and a tight tweed suit peers at me over her half-moon spectacles.

"Hello, I was—uh—told to come here," I stammer like an incoherent fool.

She nods curtly. "Name?"

"Uh—Rose—Rose Stanwyck." *Quit stammering, act convincing!*

"Address?"

I take a breath and deliver my false address in a much calmer manner.

The woman jots down my name and address, then stands. "This way please."

She leads me down a sterile corridor. The walls have been painted the same pale gray as the linoleum floor. It kind of reminds me of a hospital and I half expect to see a patient being wheeled through one of the doors on a gurney. The only sounds I can hear are the faint ring of a telephone and the clickety-clack of typewriters. A terrible thought occurs to me—what if I've come all this way for a job in a typing pool? A knot forms in my stomach at the mere thought. No matter how hard I tried, I could never get the hang of typing in school. I was so slow, my forefingers laboriously picking out each letter like an elephant plodding through treacle, while the other girls gazed ahead serenely, their hands flying over the keys as deft and elegant as a pianist's.

We reach a door at the end of a corridor. The woman knocks and I hear a man's voice saying, "Come in." She opens the door and gestures at me to step inside.

"This is Rose," she announces.

I step inside and see the man with the amused eyebrows sitting behind a desk, smiling at me. I'm so relieved to see someone vaguely familiar, it takes all I've got not to throw my arms around him and greet him like a long-lost friend.

"Hello again," he says as the woman leaves.

"Hello."

"Please, take a seat."

I resist the nervous and completely inappropriate impulse to pull a Laurel and Hardy-style prank and walk out with one of the chairs. This always happens when I get nervous—I feel the inappropriate urge to kid around. I sit down and cross my legs. Then cross them the other way. Then uncross them altogether.

"You OK?" he asks.

"Sure thing," I reply breezily whilst inside my ribcage my heart starts beating a tattoo.

"I'm Jupiter," he says, taking a pipe from a wooden stand and tapping it on his desk.

And I'm Venus, I almost joke back, until I see from his somber expression that he definitely isn't kidding.

"I bet you must be wondering why I got you to come all the way out here." He takes a dented gold lighter from his breast pocket and lights his pipe.

"Uh-huh." Again, I feign nonchalance.

"Unfortunately, I'm still not in a position to be able to tell you very much, other than from this moment on you must endeavor not to say anything about your true identity to anyone." Wisps of smoke coil from his mouth as he speaks, adding to the overall air of intrigue.

"OK."

"You can't even tell people where you're from. For the next couple of weeks, you're going to be put through a series of tests."

"Screen tests?" I ask hopefully.

"No. We need to see how you adapt to different situations and how quickly you can learn new skills."

I think of typing and shudder. "It's not..."

"What?"

"I won't be required to type, will I? It's just that I'm not very fast and I always seem to get the m and the n confused."

He smiles and shakes his head. "The training you're about to receive is *very* different to typing."

I breathe a sigh of relief.

"The most important test is whether or not you're able to be discreet—*very* discreet."

I think of the huge lips on the careless talk poster. At least I didn't give anything away to my parents by implying to them that I was making a training video. "Don't worry, sir, I'm the model of discretion."

"That's good to know."

He opens his desk drawer and takes out a tiny slip of paper. "This is where you need to go now. I want you to memorize the address, then destroy this piece of paper. I figure you'll be good at memorizing things, given your background."

It takes a moment for me to realize that he must mean as an actor learning lines. I don't have the heart to tell him that all I've gotten so far are bit parts, with one or two mainly monosyllabic lines at most.

He stands up and I quickly follow suit. "You're to take a train to Lantz and wait outside the station for a blue Chevrolet, license TX96754. When the car pulls up, you're to ask the driver, 'Does this car belong to Mr. Samuel?'"

"Right." I start mentally rehearsing. Lantz, blue Chevrolet, Mr. Samuel, TX9... I can't remember the rest of the license number but don't want to tell him in case he thinks I'm not up to the role, whatever this mysterious role may be.

"And please be aware that from now on you may very well be followed and you are to trust no one." He extends his hand across the desk.

"Followed?" I shake his hand, feeling slightly dazed.

"Yes. And you must remain on guard at all times, even where you will be staying. There's every chance that one of your colleagues might go through your things looking for clues to your real identity."

Why? I long to ask, but think better of it, not wanting to appear stupid.

"Very best of luck," he says as he accompanies me to the door. And once again I'm left wondering, *Best of luck with what?*

My mind is so abuzz from these latest developments that I hurry from the building without even realizing that I have no idea where this Lantz place is. I'm grateful for the chance to take a walk in the fresh air though. I make my way back to the main street, my feet crunching on the crisp rust-colored leaves covering the ground. Obviously, I'm not wanted for any kind of acting role—all the talk of utmost secrecy and being followed have made that crystal clear.

I glance over my shoulder, but thankfully all I can see behind me is a row of trees, dark and skeletal against the sky. Whatever training I'm about to receive does not involve typing, so that's something. I'm not so sure about the prospect of my new colleagues riffling through my things, though. I do a mental roll call of the contents of my suitcase. Thankfully, I've done as instructed and removed all the labels from my clothes. The only thing I have that's in any way personal is one of Maria's little acorn people. She presented it to me when I was leaving. "Something for you to remember me by," she said solemnly as if she'd had some kind of premonition that I wouldn't be returning. But there's no way anyone snooping through my things would be able to glean anything from that—other than I must have once been in close proximity to an oak tree.

I shiver, and not just because it's quite a bit colder in Washington than it is in California. All this talk of being followed and snooped on has made me jittery.

I take a bus back to Union Station, where I head to a ticket booth and ask the clerk for a ticket to Lantz. Thankfully, he shows no surprise at my request so I figure it can't be far. "Next train's at a quarter after, platform five," he says, handing me the ticket and my change.

"Do you know how long it should take to get there?" I ask.

"About ninety minutes, I guess."

I breathe a sigh of relief.

The railroad station at Lantz is about as different from Union Street as two stations could be. When the train comes to a halt, I almost don't get off. All I can see is a white clapboard house with a couple of trucks parked outside. But then the guard yells, "Welcome to Lantz, Maryland!"

I quickly grab my things and fumble with the catch on the door. I jump down and look around. Twilight is falling, causing darkness to pool beneath the clusters of pine trees, and the air is filled with the cawing of crows. I pull my coat tighter around me.

The train pulls off with a long shriek of its whistle and a hiss of steam. As the noise fades, I scan the deserted landscape and a terrible thought occurs to me: what if no one shows up and I'm left to spend the night here all alone?

4

AMERICA, 1942

Thankfully, before my fears have time to take hold, I hear the crunch of tires on the narrow road. I blink in the dazzle of the headlights and try to make out the license number. What the hell was it supposed to be? For a terrible moment, my mind goes blank. I've had to retain so much information today, I'm unable to retrieve the full sequence, but I know it started with TX.

As the car draws closer, I see that it does indeed start with TX—the numbers seem familiar too. I pick up my case, walk over and tap on the driver's side window. A guy in a flat cap looks up and winds the window down an inch.

"Yup," he grunts.

"Is this Mister Samuel's car?" I ask, feeling slightly ridiculous.

He frowns for a second and looks me up and down before jumping from the car and taking my case.

"Get in," he says, putting my luggage in the trunk.

I do as I'm told, all the while trying to reassure myself that, contrary to all indicators, I'm not about to meet a grisly end in the outback of Maryland.

The driver gets back in and we pull out onto the road.

Given everything Mister Eyebrows told me about the need for secrecy, I decide against making conversation and sit huddled in the corner of the back seat. After a while, we pass a sign for somewhere named Clinton, Maryland, and I remember that it was in the address I was shown and relax a little. My relief is short-lived, however, as I notice that the driver looking in his mirror anxiously, as if he's worried we're being followed. Thankfully there's no sign of any other vehicle behind us.

He turns off the road onto a narrower track and I see the top of a large white house on a hill in the distance, just visible above a wall of trees. It's a complete contrast from the hustle and bustle of the city and I relax a little. It must be some kind of country club, the kind that Hollywood stars go to when they want to relax—or dry out, as my cynical papa would say. At the thought of my father, I feel a twinge of longing for home and I have to remind myself that I'm doing this to hopefully be able to help him and Mom and, of course, Grand-mère Rose.

We start driving up the hill through a tunnel of trees.

"It's beautiful," I can't help exclaiming, the first thing I've said all journey.

"Huh!" the driver grunts, instantly reminding me of my ruder diner customers. At least I won't have to wait on them for a while.

We pull up in front of the house and I get out and take a breath of the cool, fresh air, perfumed with the sweet scent of woodsmoke. But before I can get too relaxed, I hear a sharp crack ring out from somewhere at the back of the house.

"Was that... was that a gunshot?" I stammer.

Completely ignoring my question, the driver takes my suitcase from the trunk and leads me over to the grand entrance of the house—a set of white stone steps leading to a huge black door complete with brass knocker in the shape of a lion's head.

Before I can say or do anything, a guy in an army uniform comes bursting from the house and running down the steps.

"Welcome to The Farm," he says with a warm smile. His small round spectacles and curly brown hair remind me of my kind-hearted local bookstore owner and goes some way to ease my growing apprehension.

"Hello." I shake his hand, wondering if I should give him my pseudonym.

"Come inside," he says, taking my case from me and striding back up the steps.

I follow him into a large hallway with a brown and white checkered tiled floor. A huge staircase sweeps off to the right and an ornate chandelier bathes the place in soft gold light, but that's where any resemblance to a country club begins and ends. Model fighter planes hang from the ceiling as if engaged in a dogfight and the walls are lined with mannequins dressed in military uniforms, staring blankly through painted eyes. Unlike the soldier who came to greet me, none of the mannequins are in American uniforms and I can't help shuddering as I walk past one wearing a German uniform, complete with a red armband emblazoned with a swastika.

"Dinner's about to be served," the soldier tells me as he leads me upstairs. "I'll show you to your room and once you've got changed, you must come down to the mess to eat. There's a meeting for you new recruits after dinner."

"OK." As I follow him up the stairs, I try to make sense of what "new recruits" might mean. Clearly, we're not in a film studio, or a country club, or a farm for that matter. As we pass the dummy of a Japanese soldier lurking on a landing, it seems obvious that the house is some kind of military training facility. But why would they want me here? Women aren't allowed in the armed services.

We finally reach the top floor and the man leads me along a narrow corridor and into a room sparsely furnished with two small beds, a dresser and two chairs. A woman is sitting on one of the beds dressed in army fatigues. The soldier plonks my case on the other bed.

"You need to get changed," he says, pointing to a neatly folded uniform on the pillow.

"OK. Thank you," I reply, but he's already gone. I look back at the woman. She's a little on the plump side, with a square jaw, thick black shoulder-length hair and eyebrows so dark they look as if they've been painted on. "Hello, I'm—"

She raises her finger to her mouth, then points at the headboard of my bed. I spot a tiny microphone wired to the frame. What the hell is this place? Before I can respond, I hear a bell clanging away downstairs.

"It's time for dinner," the woman says softly. Her accent sounds similar to Papa's. "I'll wait for you to get changed."

"Thank you."

I quickly slip out of my clothes and into my fatigues. It's all so surreal, it feels as if I'm putting on a costume for a movie.

As soon as we get out of the room, the woman draws closer to me. "I've been here a couple of days already," she whispers. "The microphones above the beds are there to see if we talk in our sleep, but I wanted you to know right away so you didn't give anything away about your identity."

This instantly makes me warm to her. It's comforting that in this strange new world someone is looking out for me.

We go downstairs and through the hallway into a large dining room. A group of about ten men are sitting at a long table in the center. The chatter fades and all eyes look up as we walk in. *Pretend it's a futuristic movie,* I tell myself, *and you're playing the part of a female soldier.* My inner voice adopts the dramatic tone of a movie trailer voice-over: *"The kind of soldier that women look up to and grown men fear."*

Making sure to walk tall, I follow my new roommate over to a buffet set up on a trestle table by the window and help myself to a couple of scoops of mashed potato, a slice of indeterminable meat and some gravy. We take a seat at the end of the table.

The men continue making small talk, but it's stilted and awkward, giving me the impression that they're just as apprehensive as I am. The guy next to me turns and gives a curt nod of acknowledgment. With his slicked-back blond hair, arrogant stare and chiseled jaw, he looks like the type of guy who's stepped straight out of a gentlemen's club—or off a yacht. I try to suppress the feeling of inadequacy that always nibbles at my confidence when I'm around the wealthy. Something Grand-mère Rose once said after I returned from school crying because the rich kids had teased me about the holes in my shoes comes back to me. "Every time a person is mean to you, part of their soul becomes rusty from bitterness." She scooped me into her arms and kissed me on top of my head. "And part of your soul shines even brighter."

"Hey, Betty," the blond guy leans forward to address my roommate, "don't you think you ought to go easy on the potato given your performance in the run earlier."

"Teddy, you're such a gas!" another of the guys—clearly a prize-winning kiss-ass—exclaims.

"Or maybe I should say, on your *waddle* earlier?" Teddy continues. I picture his soul rusting and rotting away.

A couple of the other guys snort with laughter and my roommate, Betty, flushes angry red. Just as I instantly warmed to her, I take an instant dislike to the arrogant fathead, Teddy.

"My name's Rose," I say to her, shifting so my back's to Teddy. As I say my false name out loud, I feel a wave of warmth rush through me. It feels good to be connected to Grand-mère in this way.

"Betty," she mumbles, prodding listlessly at her potato with her fork. I long to make conversation with her, but I'm unsure what I'm allowed to say, so I shovel food into my mouth instead.

As soon as dinner is over, a soldier marches into the dining room and tells us that we're to come with him to the library. Now I have some food inside me, I feel better able to cope with whatever surprise twist will come next. We all file out of the room and into the hall in silence. Even loudmouth Teddy has gone quiet.

The library is at the back of the house, and the tall walls are lined from top to bottom with leather-bound books. A fire is crackling away in the huge hearth and a man of about fifty is standing beside it, watching us come in. Judging by the abundance of stripes on his uniform, he's clearly high-ranking.

"Good evening," he says as we sit down in the rows of chairs arranged in front of him. "I'm Captain Shaw. Welcome to The Farm. I guess you must have a lot of questions about why you're here."

"I think I've got it figured out," Teddy pipes up.

"And I'm sure you must be wondering about the cloak-and-dagger way in which we got you here," Captain Shaw continues, ignoring Teddy.

Murmurs of agreement ripple through the room. My pulse quickens; finally it seems as if I'm going to get some answers to the questions buzzing like gnats in my head.

"The Farm is in fact a school for espionage—the first of its kind here in America. And you..." He pauses as if for dramatic impact. "You are here to become spies."

Spies? My skin erupts in goosebumps.

I glance at Betty beside me. She's nodding in recognition as if she suspected this all along. Teddy is grinning smugly. Am I the only one who didn't have a clue? And does this instantly send me to the bottom of the class for not figuring it out?

"Over the next few weeks, you're going to be trained to potentially become members of the Office of Strategic Services, or OSS for short," Captain Shaw continues. "There are two main sections of the OSS—operations and intelligence." He looks around the room, taking the time to look each one of us in the eye. "I have to warn you now that some of you won't make it. This training is not for the faint-hearted. Some of you won't be able to complete the physical aspects of it." I notice Teddy shoot a sideways smirk at Betty. "Some of you won't have a sharp enough memory or responses. And some of you might struggle taking orders." Is it my imagination or does he look straight at Teddy when he says this? "You are all here because one of our recruiting officers saw the potential in you, but if any of you don't like the sound of what I've just said, you're free to say so now and we'll take you back to Washington right away. You just have to swear under oath not to repeat a word of what I've just said. Lives depend upon it."

I scan the room for any sign of movement, but everyone is staring at him steadfastly. Even though I never could have predicted this development, I don't feel the slightest inclination to leave. Being a spy sounds exciting, and so much better than a typist—or a waitress for that matter.

"OK, good." Captain Shaw smiles. "Now I suggest you turn in and get a good night's sleep. You'll be grateful for it in the morning."

That night, I sleep fitfully, terrified I might blab something incriminating into the microphone above my bed. Having shared a room for sixteen years, I'm pretty sure Maria would have let me know if I did talk in my sleep, but still—it would be just my luck to blow this opportunity when I'm not even awake.

We're woken early for a breakfast of sausage and hotcakes and as soon as I see the staff serving the food, any apprehension I've been feeling instantly vanishes as I'm reminded of the diner. If I play my cards right, I might never have to go back there—a prospect that floods me with relief, even if this hasn't turned out to be my big movie break.

After breakfast, we're called for a meeting in a room next to the library, backing onto the grounds at the rear of the house. Sunlight streams in shafts through the long windows, causing the dust motes in the air to glimmer. I guess it used to be a living room before the war, but now it's been transformed into a classroom, with rows of individual wooden desks facing a larger desk in front of the hearth. Captain Shaw is there to greet us and a man with an even more impressive array of stripes on his uniform stands beside him. There are no introductions and the man gets straight down to business.

"The OSS might officially stand for the Office of Strategic Services, but unofficially I want you to think of it as standing for *Of Supreme Secrecy*," he begins. "Once you're out in the field, you'll be gathering intelligence that will be top secret. So secret you could be killed just for knowing it."

I try not to think about getting killed and focus on "out in the field" instead. I have a flashback to the set of the training video and the sign saying WELCOME TO ENEMYAREA behind the bar. It had seemed kind of funny back then, but now... My body crackles with tension as I imagine being sent to a Nazi-occupied country. Am I really ready for this?

"What you will be doing will require grit, courage and great strength," the man continues, "but the reward is priceless. You will be saving countless lives with your work."

I imagine Grand-mère Rose sobbing at her kitchen table in her home in France and me bursting through the door, declaring that I'm there to save her and a shot of excitement dilutes my fear.

The man goes on to describe in more detail the kind of information we will be required to find and how to keep our cover secret. Again, I think of the training video and I can't help giving a wry smile. At least I know never to tuck a pistol into the back of my pants when in company.

Our next lesson is given by a tiny, pale-faced woman with auburn hair pulled into a tight bun.

"I'm here to teach you all about ciphers," she announces with the enthusiasm of someone about to declare the winner of the state lottery.

I look at her blankly, wondering if any of my fellow classmates also have no clue what she's talking about.

"Ciphers are of vital importance because they stop the enemy from intercepting our messages," she continues, pacing in front of the fireplace.

Aha, I think to myself, *ciphers must be another word for codes*.

"A cipher is not a code," the woman adds, and once again I feel embarrassed and out of my depth. "Codes have entire words replaced by other words, numbers, symbols or letters. Ciphers replace individual letters in messages with other letters."

The next couple of hours passes in a blur as we're shown examples of ciphers and then asked to create our own. I really struggle at first, and I feel even worse when I notice Betty, head down, scribbling away. I'm determined to figure it out though. The notion of being able to create my own secret form of communication really appeals to me. It reminds me of when Maria and I were younger and I came up with the harebrained scheme of creating our own language that our parents couldn't understand. It involved spelling words backwards, which I now know is a code rather than a cipher and pitifully easy to crack. Thankfully, I manage to create my first cipher before the end of class.

After a lunch of chunky baloney sandwiches and crisp red apples, we're told to assemble outside.

"Now the real fun begins," Teddy mutters as we file out into a field behind the house.

Halfway down the field, a white canvas screen has been erected. It's about eight-foot square, with the life-sized outline of a German soldier drawn upon it. Up at our end of the field, there's a table full of pistols, a sight that instantly causes me to gulp. The only time I've ever held a gun was on the set of a Western movie. I played the role of a woman of ill repute who lived in a brothel above a saloon bar. I had to try to wrestle a pistol from the bad guy, but got shot in the process. The only line I had was to "scream in agony." But it's one thing holding what I knew was an unloaded, fake gun and quite another being confronted with real, and presumably loaded, weapons.

"This is the Colt M1903," Captain Shaw declares, holding up a small, snub-nosed pistol. "They are standard issue for our SI agents because in your line of work you should only need a weapon in self-defense."

Hmm, that's something, I guess.

I glance at Betty. Chewing on her bottom lip, she looks as nervous as I feel.

"As you can see, they fit into your pocket." Captain Shaw tucks the gun into his trouser pocket. "Or for the ladies present, you can tuck it discreetly in your purse." He nods to Betty and me. "Who here has already used a pistol?"

Most of the men raise their hands.

"I've used a rifle many times," Teddy boasts. "My father and I often go duck shooting on our lake."

My hatred for him grows; not just because he appears to be the dictionary definition of braggadocious, but because I've always had an affection for ducks and their waddling, quacking ways.

"Great," Captain Shaw replies. "The point of this first class is to see how comfortable you are handling a weapon. Tomorrow, we'll move on to more detailed training."

We all line up to take a shot, with Betty and me hanging at the back of the queue. As I wait my turn, the bizarreness of the situation hits me. This isn't a movie set, this is a real-life situation—or training for a real-life situation at least. I think of the video I made, and how my character discovered the agent's pistol tucked into his waistband. I know from reading the rest of the script that things didn't end well for "Steve," that he was strip-searched and tortured by the enemy police. What if the same thing ends up happening to me?

Betty steps up to take her turn, and she misses the target completely. The men's laughter rings out around the field.

"Maybe we should all go take cover inside when Betty's holding a gun," Teddy quips and the laughter grows louder.

I shoot Betty a look of sympathy and she gives me a watery smile. I step up to take my turn and start to tremble as I feel all eyes upon me. Holding the pistol in both hands, with my arms fully extended, I take aim and shoot, managing to graze the German soldier on the ear.

"I don't understand why they've brought women here," I hear Teddy say.

I turn and glare at him, still holding the pistol extended.

"Lower your weapon!" Captain Shaw yells.

"Sorry." I place it back on the table, my face burning from a mixture of anger and embarrassment.

"Let's go round again," Captain Shaw calls.

I march past Teddy, my pride smarting as much as my face.

"When it comes to combat, you can't let your heart rule your head," Captain Shaw says as Teddy takes aim and hits the German right in the center of the chest.

"Take that, Adolf!" he cries triumphantly.

The other guys all cheer and clap him on the back. He turns and smirks at me.

"You have to do whatever it takes to keep your heart rate down and keep a cool head," the captain continues.

I feel a twinge of dread. If they were to ask my parents what my worst trait was, I know they'd say "hotheaded" without missing a beat. "Being as passionate as we are is both a blessing and a curse," Papa has said to me on numerous occasions. "And not only for us, but for those around us too." He always laughed when he said it, but now it feels anything but funny. What if my temper makes me a terrible spy? What if it winds up getting me killed? If only this were just a training video and there wasn't so much at stake. *Pretend it is,* an inner voice sounding uncannily like Grand-mère Rose instructs me. *Pretend you're playing a role.*

As I wait in the queue for my next turn, I start fleshing out my part. *My name is Rose Stanwyck and I am a deadly assassin. When I step up and take aim, I won't be shooting at the drawing of a Nazi, I'll be shooting at Hitler himself. I am calm and confident and my head always rules my heart.*

"Rose." As the captain calls me up to take my turn, I pretend he's a movie director telling me to go stand on my mark.

I pick up a pistol and this time I notice that my hands aren't trembling at all. *I am Rose Stanwyck, deadly assassin,* I remind myself as I take aim—and fire. My ears ring from the crack of the gunshot and then I hear a light ripple of applause. I look at the target and see that I hit the pretend soldier in the stomach. It's not exactly bullseye, but it's a whole lot better than my first attempt.

"Well done." Captain Shaw pats me on the back.

As I put the pistol back on the table, I notice Teddy frowning.

Our final class of the day is in map-reading, which goes a whole lot better than cipher training, then at dinner Captain Shaw announces that we will be having a talk from someone called William Fairbairn. I'd never heard of him before, but judging by the reaction from some of the men, he's something of a big deal.

"Apparently, he's known as Dangerous Dan," Teddy gushes. "Rumor has it, he knows one hundred ways to kill a man —with his bare hands!"

I'm more concerned about Betty, who's picking at her meat-loaf looking really subdued.

"You OK?" I ask her quietly as the men chat excitedly about a knife that this Dangerous Dan Fairbairn character apparently invented.

She nods, but I notice that her eyes are glassy as if she's fighting back tears.

"Everything's difficult at first," I say, trying to reassure her. "Give it another couple of days and I bet you'll be killing that paper Nazi no problem."

Unfortunately, Teddy overhears me. "If you ask me, you dames ought to stick to what you're good at," he says with a smirk. "Shame you don't need to know how to knit to be a good spy."

I stare daggers at him, wishing I could come up with some kind of scathingly witty retort, but the moment passes and the men return to their knife chat and poor Betty looks more despondent than ever.

"You were great in the cipher training," I whisper.

"Thank you," she murmurs, placing her fork down.

"Why don't we go eat over there?" I suggest, pointing to a small table in the corner by the window.

Betty agrees and as we take our seats at the other table, Teddy glances over. "What's up, ladies? Can't take a joke?" He looks back at the other guys. "How the hell are they going to cope against the Germans if they can't take a joke about knitting?"

"And how are you going to cope when you're up against something a whole lot bigger and tougher than Daffy Duck and you haven't got your daddy there to hold your hand?" I fire back.

The other guys chortle and raise their tin cups to me.

"Shut up!" Teddy slams his hand down on the table, causing the cutlery to clink on the plates.

"What's up, Teddy Bear? Can't take a joke?"

He gives me a murderous stare, but it's worth it to see the grin lighting up Betty's face.

"You are my hero," Betty says softly as the men resume their conversation. "I think I might like you even more than I like pork tamales."

"Well, that's praise indeed. I *love* pork tamales." We grin at each other and I feel awash with gratitude. Inadvertently, that fathead Teddy might have done me a huge favor and helped me find a true friend in this place. I sure hope so.

Once we've eaten, we go through to the library. Captain Shaw is standing in front of the fireplace and another man, also dressed in military uniform, is leaning against the oak desk. He's thin and wiry and his gray hair is cropped short. A pair of round spectacles perch on the bridge of his bulbous nose. If this is "Dangerous Dan," he doesn't look nearly as intimidating as I'd been expecting.

"Good evening," he says in a clipped British accent as we file into the room.

Once we're all seated, the captain introduces Fairbairn and they swap places, with Fairbairn taking center stage in front of the fireplace.

"Over the next few weeks, I'm going to be teaching you what I call gutter fighting," Fairbairn begins. My heart sinks. This sounds even worse than shooting! "There's no fair play in gutter fighting," he continues, "and no rules except one: kill or be killed."

I shoot a sideways glance at Betty. In spite of the warmth from the fire, all the color has drained from her face.

"In the arena of war, one is faced with an assailant that is of a different stamp entirely and it certainly isn't pretty, *but*"—I hold my breath, hoping he's going to offer some sliver of light amidst all this gloom—"once you have learned my scientific methods of self-defense, which require no great strength to perform"—he looks pointedly at Betty and me—"you will find yourself in a position of confidence and security against almost any form of attack."

OK, this is starting to sound a little more promising.

"I will also be teaching you methods for taking your enemy out—using just your bare hands."

Taking your enemy out... Is he saying he's going to teach us how to kill? What was it that Teddy said at dinner? Fairbairn knows one hundred ways to kill a man with his bare hands. I look down at my hands. Would I ever be able to bring myself to kill another human being?

Cold dread starts creeping through me. What the hell have I signed up for?

September 1940, France

My darling Elena,

The first "secret" letter I wrote you brought me some brief relief, so I'm hoping this one will do the same. I have so much grief inside of me, it feels like a boil that needs to be lanced, so lance it I shall, all over this page— before burning it, of course.

So many terrible things have been happening here, things I never thought I'd witness in my beloved home- land. As soon as the Germans hoisted their swastika on the Arc de Triomphe, Parisians began to flee the city. Many of them poured through here on their way south. I've never seen such scenes—people carting all of their worldly goods in teetering piles in a pram or a wheelbar- row, women wearing all of their winter clothes in the heat of summer because they had so much else to carry. Babies crying. Children wide-eyed with fear, begging for a rest. People defecating on the roadside.

But that wasn't the worst of it. The worst was when the German planes came. Some of them flew over the garden when I was out doing some weeding. I remember thinking, Where are they off to? Why are they flying so low? What more could they want? They've already stolen our country. *It didn't occur to me that they might still be lusting for blood, swooping like vultures, opening fire on women and children surrounded by fields with nowhere to hide.*

They mowed them down, Elena, innocent people fleeing. I can't stop crying every time I think of it. It makes no sense to me. Why, in a world where there is love, would anyone choose such hate?

5

AMERICA, 1942

I stand motionless, as my assailant points his gun at me.

Seize his right wrist with your left hand, I hear Fairbairn's voice calling in my head, as it has so many times since I've been at The Farm. I grab his wrist and twist rapidly to the right. *Seize his pistol and hand from underneath with your right hand.* I do as the Fairbairn in my head tells me and grab the weapon. *Now knee him in the testicles.* Oh if only! I bring my knee up to Teddy's crotch, stopping just before contact.

"Excellent job, Rose," Fairbairn says as he walks past our mat in the corner of the gymnasium.

"Obviously I let you get the gun," Teddy mutters in my ear. "In real life, it wouldn't be nearly so easy."

I sigh and let go. We've been training for over a week now and in spite of the fact that I can now shoot pretend Nazis in the heart from just about any position and throw a grown man to the ground, Teddy still won't give it a rest.

"What happened to make you hate women so?" I hiss in response. "Did Mommy drop you on your head when you were little?"

"If you don't shut up, I'll drop you on your head," he whispers back.

I roll my eyes. The other men might all be in awe of Teddy but I refuse to be scared of a spoiled daddy's boy. I turn away and search out Betty. She's been paired with a great hunk of a man called Hank and by the looks of things, she's not doing so well. As he blocks her attempts to disarm him, her face flushes. She clutches her stomach as if she's in pain and, quick as a flash, Hank flips her over and onto the mat. I instinctively wince. Betty and I have been room-mates for over a week now and even though we're not able to talk about anything remotely personal, we've managed to bond over our shared love of food and hatred of Teddy.

"What's that on her shorts?" Teddy says loudly.

I gasp with horror as I notice a dark red stain on her crotch.

"Eeew!" Teddy grimaces, causing the other guys to stop and stare at him. He nods toward Betty.

"Shut up!" I hiss before hurrying over to her.

All around the gym, I see the other men pulling faces of shock and disgust.

"Can we be excused to go to the bathroom?" I ask Captain Shaw.

"Of course," he replies. "Is everything OK?" He looks at Betty, concerned.

She nods, looking painfully close to tears.

I hand her my pullover. "Here, tie this around your waist."

She takes the pullover gratefully and gets to her feet. I position myself like a shield, trying to make sure no one else sees the bloodstain.

"Do you need a sanitary napkin?" I whisper as soon as we're out in the hall. "I have some up in the room."

"Yes please," she mutters, not making eye contact.

We hurry past the enemy mannequins lining the stairs and

into the room without exchanging another word. I give her a napkin and escort her to the bathroom.

"You mustn't let that idiot Teddy get to you," I say once she's come out of the stall. "We've just as much right to be here as he does."

Finally she meets my gaze. "Thank you," she says quietly, her voice cracking. "It's just... I'm so sick of having to deal with people like him. People thinking they're better than me because of where I come from. I'm so tired of it."

I'm not sure if there are microphones hidden in the bathroom so to be on the safe side, I turn on the faucet.

"I understand," I whisper, "I've experienced it too."

"You have?" She looks at me, surprised.

"For sure. If I had a dollar for every time someone's called me a spic, I'd be able to buy all of Mexico."

Betty nods.

"And the schoolyard bullies used to have a field day making fun of my gangly legs."

"Well, you've had the last laugh there," she says with a faint smile.

"What do you mean?"

"Most women would die for legs as long as yours."

"Hmm, I'm not so sure, they can be mighty clumsy, especially in heels."

Betty comes close and whispers in my ear. "I didn't expect it to happen here though. I thought we were all supposed to be on the same side." Her face flushes an angry red.

"I guess there are dimwits on every side," I sigh. "The important thing is to not let him win. You have to hold your head up high, be proud of who you are." I can picture Grandmère Rose smiling and nodding along. I know I'm not supposed to breathe a word of my real life, but Betty looks so hurt and upset I have to do something. I turn the faucet on full blast and gesture at her to join me sitting on the floor. "Can I tell you about my grandma?" I whisper. "She's the wisest woman I've ever known and she's really helped me all my life, so maybe she can help you too?"

Betty nods tearfully. I shift closer and link my arm through hers. For the next twenty minutes or so, I give her a potted account of Grand-mère Rose's wise quotes, sayings and stories on the theme of standing up to bullies and having confidence in yourself.

"You're not alone, OK?" I say in conclusion. "I've got your back."

"Thank you." She stands up and helps me to my feet. "Now I like you even more than I like *beef* tamales," she says with a smile. "And they're my absolute favorite."

"Attagirl!" I clap my hands together. "Let's go show those fatheads what we're made of."

"OK, folks, can I have your attention," Fairbairn calls as he marches into the dining room after lunch. "This afternoon, you will be taking part in our indoor mystery range—or as some like to call it, the House of Horrors."

"Yes!" Teddy gleefully exclaims. I'm starting to think that he might actually be a psychopath. Rumors about the House of Horrors have been buzzing around the mess for days—by all accounts, only the very toughest emerge unscathed. My heart sinks for Betty being faced with this challenge today of all days.

"Inside the range, you will experience varying degrees of light and dark," Fairbairn continues, "because, of course, once you're out in the field you will have no control over the conditions in which you'll be confronted by the enemy. To that end, there will also be sound effects, moving targets and various surprises designed to startle you. And there will be innocent bystanders present. The point of the indoor course is to see how you react under pressure. Or, as my fellow Brit Rudyard

Kipling once wrote: 'If you can keep your head while all around you are losing theirs...'" He smiles at us slightly menacingly over his spectacles. "Every time you are faced with an enemy target, your task is to fire two shots at them. Any questions?"

Betty raises her hand.

"Yes?"

"What will the targets look like?"

I inwardly groan. In any other setting, this might be a perfectly reasonable question, but I've been at The Farm long enough to know that this is bound to be deemed dumb—and seen by certain people as more proof that us women shouldn't be here.

Predictably, I hear a derisory snort coming from Teddy's direction.

"What will they look like?" Fairbairn frowns at Betty. "Do you think that when you're out in the field you're going to be given some kind of yearbook full of pictures of the enemy?" A couple of the men snigger.

"No, I—uh—I didn't mean that, I meant, will they be like the targets we've had in the outdoor firing range or something else." I can feel poor Betty's embarrassment seeping from her like hot lava.

"It's called the indoor *mystery* range," Fairbairn replies impatiently. "The clue is in the title."

"Yes, sir," Betty murmurs.

"Come on, let's go." He marches out the door and we all follow him like a line of ducklings.

To get to the indoor mystery range, we have to tramp through the woodland at the back of the property, finally emerging into a field containing what looks like a large barn. But I'm guessing there's a whole lot more than bales of hay waiting for us inside.

"All right, which of you wants to go first?" Fairbairn asks.

Teddy marches straight to the front of the queue. I feel Betty shifting nervously beside me.

"I'll go," I call, figuring that if I can get through it and come out the other side still in one piece it will help her feel more confident.

"Excellent," Fairbairn says and he hands me a .45 caliber pistol. "OK, Rose, why don't you show these boys how it's done."

It's just pretend, like a movie set, I try to reassure myself as he opens the door and I step inside. *Nothing in here can actually hurt you.*

The door creaks shut behind me like something out of a horror flick and I'm plunged into total darkness. Keeping my pistol arm raised, I use my other hand to feel about. It seems as if I'm in a narrow passageway; the darkness is so thick it feels choking. I start edging my way forwards. *It's just a movie set, it's just a movie set*, I chant silently. *Nothing can—*

I gasp as the floorboard beneath me almost gives way. Thankfully, I find a door at the end of the corridor and I open it slowly, allowing a dim shaft of light to spill out.

"Aaaaargh!" I can't help shrieking as there's a whirring sound and a figure looms before me. Forgetting all I'd been told about making sure not to kill any innocent bystanders, I squeeze the trigger, once, twice. The sound of the shots is deafening in such a confined space and the air is instantly filled with gunpowder fumes. As I keep moving forwards, I see to my relief that it was an enemy target, a canvas figure of a German soldier that must be on some kind of runners. Drawing closer, I note that there are two bullet-holes in his face. OK, that's good, but I have to make sure not to shriek next time.

I reach a door and fumble for the handle. It opens onto a room lit by a flickering lantern. Two mannequins dressed in ordinary clothes are sitting in a couple of armchairs facing each other. As

I'm quickly casing the joint, I hear a thudding sound coming from inside a cupboard. Remembering my training, I crouch behind a table in the corner, opposite the cupboard. The door swings open and I hear a gunshot, but I haven't fired yet. *Is someone firing at me?* My mouth goes dry and my heart thuds and I see not one but two signs of movement. Something is coming out of the cupboard, but someone else is opening the door I just came through. I take aim at the cupboard, then change my mind and swing my arm toward the door. The lamplight is so dim, it's hard to make out a thing. The rumors were right, this truly is a house of horrors.

I see a peaked cap emerge through the door, just like the cap on the mannequins dressed as Nazis back in the house. I squeeze the trigger—once, twice—aiming this time for the chest. Then I spin back to the cupboard and breathe a sigh of relief. The cardboard head and shoulders of a child is peering out. I check the rest of the room for any other would-be assailants, then head to another door.

After making my way through several rooms and corridors, and only missing one target, when I'd paused to reload my pistol, I go through a door leading to the indoor re-creation of a woodland scene, complete with pretend bushes and fake trees. *It's just a movie set,* I remind myself once more, as I step out onto the earthy floor and quickly position myself behind one of the trees.

Now I've gotten over my initial panic, I feel slightly more prepared. I take a deep breath and smell the sour scent of urine. *Fairbairn said there'd be odors; don't let that distract you. Remember to retain your square stance,* I tell myself, thinking back to my training.

I hear a sound from across the pretend clearing and prepare to aim. But within a second, there's a sound right behind me. I shorten my arm, bringing my pistol to the close hip position and leap around. A model of Adolf Hitler is lumbering toward me. I squeeze the trigger twice in quick succession, then once more for luck.

"Geez Louise!" I exclaim, suddenly short of breath. I take a step closer and see that I've shot him twice in the stomach and once in the balls.

Regaining my composure, I slowly make my way across the clearing. Spying a door behind one of the trees, I go over and open it very slowly, adopting a shooting stance, ready for the next assailant to greet me. But as soon as I open the door, I blink at the sight of broad daylight and breathe in fresh air.

"She made it!" I hear Fairbairn saying over the ringing in my ears.

I quickly lower my pistol and grin as I see the others all gathered around applauding me.

"Holy cow!" I exclaim, shaking my head.

"What was it like?" a guy named Chad asks nervously.

I'm about to say that House of Horrors is definitely an apt description, but then I see Betty looking at me anxiously.

"It was a piece of cake," I say nonchalantly.

A soldier emerges from the range behind me, causing me to almost jump from my skin. The men start laughing, but warmly this time, I notice.

"How did she do?" Fairbairn asks him.

"What, were you in there with me?" I ask the soldier.

"Uh-huh." He smiles, then turns to Fairbairn.

"She did good. Only missed one assailant and didn't kill any of the innocent civilians. Plus she shot the final surprise in the balls."

Fairbairn laughs and pats me on the back. "Good job, Rose. Right, boys, you'd better not blow it, you don't want to be shown up by a girl."

I feel the same sense of elation I always get when Papa praises me, and something else... The adrenalin still coursing through my body feels strangely pleasant. I know it was just a practice run, but it's the closest I've come so far to the real deal, and I'm surprised at the kick of excitement it's given me.

I glance over at Betty, who's hovering at the back of the group, scuffing the toe of her boot on the ground. I try to send some of my strength her way.

That night in the mess, it feels as if something's shifted. Following my success in the House of Horrors, the men are treating me as if I'm one of them, and even Teddy is surprisingly genial, for him anyways. Much as I hate to admit it, it feels good to have gotten the men's approval. If only the same could be said for poor Betty. She emerged from the mystery range looking like she'd seen a ghost. The soldier who'd tailed her took Fairbairn aside to deliver his verdict, and judging from their grave expressions, it didn't look good. She barely ate a thing at dinner and went straight back to our room afterwards.

Leaving the boys to their beers, I slip out of the mess and upstairs.

I find Betty packing her belongings into her case.

"What are you doing?" I ask, even though it's patently obvious.

She frowns at the microphone on her headboard.

I tug on her arm and gesture at her to come out onto the landing.

"Where are you going?" I whisper once we're out of the room.

"I'm leaving," she says quietly.

"But why?" Again, I'm pretty certain I know the answer.

"I can't take any more," she hisses. "I'm not cut out for this."

"The men are just being jack-asses, and besides, it's not all about the combat training," I say softly. "You're so good at ciphers, way better than the rest of us. And once we're out in the field, what do you think is going to be the most important?" I take hold of her hands; they're icy cold. "Do you really think we're going to be in a house of horrors every day? Of course not. But we will need to pass messages—and decipher messages. And that's where you excel."

"Yes, but I don't get any respect for excelling in ciphers. The only way you get respect in this place is if you can shoot paper soldiers."

"Are you angry?" I ask, thinking of yet another tip Grand-mère Rose once shared with me.

"Of course I'm angry," she spits, her dark eyes sparking. "I'm so angry I could..." She breaks off and I notice her hands have clenched into fists.

"Wait here." I hurry back into the room and grab the pillow from my bed.

"What's that for?" Betty says as I bring the pillow out onto the landing.

"You'll see. Follow me." I lead her into the ladies' restroom and shut the door behind her. I go stand in the middle of the room and hold the pillow up in front of me. "From now on, I am no longer your beloved friend Rose." I peer out from behind the pillow. "May I call myself your beloved friend? You did say you liked me more than beef tamales."

"You may," she replies and I'm relieved to see the ghost of a smile on her lips.

"Great. Well, as I was saying, I am no longer your beloved friend, I am the duck-massacring fathead better known as Teddy and now is your chance to wreak revenge."

I hear a giggle from the other side of the pillow. "What do you mean?"

"I mean, you are most welcome to punch the hell out of me —or out of this pillow at least."

"Are you sure?"

"Sure I'm sure." I clear my throat and prepare to deepen my

voice. "My name's Teddy Bear and I hate ducks and women. Go on, sock it to him," I add in my own voice.

Betty punches the pillow so faintly it feels like being tapped by a small child.

"I said sock it to him!"

"But I'm scared of hurting you."

"Ah, she's scared of hurting me," I say, mimicking Teddy. "Why don't you go back to your knitting, you timid little—"

Betty lands a hook on the pillow that would have made Joe Louis proud.

"Holy moly!" I exclaim as I career sideways into the sink.

"Are you OK?" she asks anxiously.

"Of course I'm OK. Do it again!" I hold up the pillow and brace myself and she unleashes a volley of punches.

"Go to hell! Go to hell!" she mutters in time with each blow. Finally, she stops and bends over to catch her breath, grinning up at me. "Was that another tip from your grandmother?" she asks.

"It sure was. And do you feel better for it?"

"Yes," she replies firmly. Then she grabs me in a hug. "Thank you."

"Of course." I hug her tightly. "You mustn't let the guys get to you—if you do, you prove them right."

She lets go and smiles.

"You have to take the anger they make you feel and use it to your advantage," I add.

"What do you mean?"

"See it as fuel. Let it fire you up."

She nods thoughtfully.

"Captain Shaw told me the other day that us women are vital out in the field because no one suspects that we're spies. It's so much easier for us to keep our cover."

She nods again.

"We're needed out there," I whisper, warming to my theme.

"OK," she murmurs.

"You'll stay?" I ask hopefully.

"Yes."

"That's great! Shall I help you unpack?"

"Sure."

I have to bite my lip to stifle a cheer. And once again I'm awash with gratitude for Grand-mère Rose and the words of wisdom she's embedded inside of me.

6

AMERICA, 1942

The next morning, just as I'm finishing breakfast, and once again giving thanks for not having to serve up greasy eggs in the diner, I feel a tap on my shoulder. I turn and see Captain Shaw smiling down at me.

"When you're finished, can you go and change into your civvies and report to the reception," he says.

Dread courses through me. Civvies are army slang for civilian clothes. Does he want me to leave? And here I was thinking that I'd been doing OK.

"You need to go back to Washington for a meeting," Shaw continues.

I look at him anxiously, still unsure if I'm in trouble. But before I have time to say, "Yes, sir," he's turned on his heel and gone.

"What do you think that's about?" Betty asks.

I shrug, hoping she'll be OK while I'm gone.

"What did Captain Shaw want?" Teddy calls across the table.

"None of your business," I reply.

"Has he set up a sewing circle for you girls?" Teddy mocks

—clearly my being in his good graces was short-lived. "Or maybe he's getting them fitted for diapers." He looks pointedly at Betty and a couple of the other men snigger.

I squeeze her hand under the table. "Remember what I said last night," I mutter through gritted teeth. "Use your anger as fuel."

She squeezes my hand in response, so tightly I almost yelp from her nails digging into my palm.

"Let's get out of here," I say, standing up.

When I reach Teddy, I stop.

"I find it strange that you have such a problem with women," I say loudly enough for everyone to hear. "Perhaps you prefer the company of men in *every* respect."

"I think you might be right," Betty sniggers.

"Shut up, you stupid bitches," Teddy snaps.

"I rest my case," I say, and Betty and I sweep from the room to the sound of the men's laughter, which for once isn't directed at us.

"Why do you think you have to go to Washington?" Betty asks as we make our way upstairs.

"I don't know."

"I hope you'll be coming back. It's going to suck here without you." She pauses and gives me an anxious smile. "My beloved, even better than a beef tamale, friend."

"Don't worry, I'll be back," I reply with a confidence that belies the fear bubbling away in my stomach.

After two weeks of wearing nothing but army fatigues, it feels weird as hell putting on a dress and stockings, and my heeled shoes feel like clamps on my feet. When I totter my way into the reception, I find Captain Shaw waiting for me.

"You've got a meeting with Duke back at the Q building," he tells me.

"Duke?"

He nods but doesn't elaborate. "Your car's waiting outside."

.   .   .

The drive to Washington is a blur as my mind hums with questions. Just when I'd been starting to get the lay of the land, it feels as if the earth has shifted beneath my feet again. I'm taking the fact that I wasn't asked to pack my case as a positive sign that I'll be returning to The Farm. I only hope Betty will do OK while I'm gone.

Once I've been deposited back at the Q building, I ask for the mysterious "Duke" at the reception.

The woman behind the desk nods as if she's been expecting me.

"Follow me," she says, leading me down a sterile corridor and knocking on a door with no number or sign.

"Come in," a man calls in a crisp, businesslike voice.

The woman shows me into a nondescript room, as blandly decorated as the corridor outside.

A stocky man with the broad, flat nose of a boxer is sitting behind a large desk. He greets me with a warm smile, his eyes crinkling like two half-moons. A faint waft of cigar smoke hangs in the air. "Pleasure to meet you, Flamingo!" his deep voice booms.

I stare at him, bemused. "Flamingo?"

"It's our code name for you," he explains, although it really doesn't make things any clearer. "It's the one we'll be using for you when you're out in the field."

When I'm out in the field, not *if*. So I'm not about to be kicked out. But why have I been named after a bird? I've learned by now not to ask any questions that could come across as dumb, so I nod knowingly, as if I get called bird names every day of the week.

"Please, take a seat." He nods at the chair across from him and I sit down.

"I've been hearing very good things about you," he continues, prompting a warm burst of relief to course through me.

"That's great to hear, thank you."

"Very good indeed." He smiles and nods, looking down at a file on his desk. "So we are going to be assigning you to Secret Intelligence and your first posting is going to be in Spain."

"I'm going to Spain?" This I was not expecting. As far as I'm aware, Spain aren't involved in the war. "Aren't Spain... aren't they neutral?"

"On the surface, yes, but scratch beneath and it's extremely volatile, and there's no doubt that Franco has done many things to appease Hitler to try to prevent him from invading."

I nod, while desperately trying to figure out what all this might have to do with me as a Secret Intelligence operative.

"Spain is of huge strategic importance to us," Duke continues. "Because it is neutral, it's full of undercover agents from both sides."

"Both? You mean the Allies *and* the Germans?" The hairs on my arms prickle.

"Uh-huh. And not just any old Germans." He looks at me gravely. "The head of their intelligence service, the Abwehr, is a close friend of Franco and visits there frequently. And Himmler is known to have agents working for him there."

A shiver runs through me. As the head of the SS, Himmler is second in command to Adolf Hitler.

"We need operatives on the ground to try to figure out what the Germans are doing and who is working for them. We also need to help provide escape routes from France for our downed pilots and other people fleeing the Germans. So, what do you say?" He looks at me hopefully.

I nod, dumbstruck.

"That's great. We're going to be posting you to Madrid as that's where the Abwehr are the most active." He opens his desk drawer and takes out some documents. "Your cover story will be that you are a Mexican actress."

Excitement pierces my shock. "An actress?"

"Yes, it felt like the natural choice given your background.

And as an actress in Madrid, you'll be able to infiltrate the society scene and gain access to some high-level Nazis."

I can't help gulping at this. I'm not sure what I'd imagined my training at The Farm resulting in, but hobnobbing with high-level Nazis as a Mexican actress in Spain definitely didn't factor in even my wildest of dreams. Then a terrible thought occurs to me.

"But what if I..." I break off, not wanting to appear negative.

Duke looks at me questioningly.

"What if I don't get any acting roles?"

He smiles. "No need to worry about that, we've got you covered."

"Oh, OK."

He takes a document from the file in front of him and slides it across the desk to me. "I just need you to sign this."

The document is headed OATH OF OFFICE. I've become so used to using a false alias it's strange to see my real name, ELENA GARCIA, printed on it. *I, ELENA GARCIA, do solemnly swear (or affirm) that I will support and defend the Constitution of the United States against all enemies, foreign and domestic...* I scan down to the bottom of the page, where it says, *POSITION TO WHICH APPOINTED* and someone has written, *Spanish Desk*. I'm going to Spain as a spy. My life has become even more fantastical than a movie.

Duke hands me a pen. My gaze is drawn back to the words *"all enemies, foreign and domestic,"* and the name Himmler rings in my ears, scarier than any House of Horrors Fairbairn could come up with. I take a deep breath and sign the oath.

October 1940, France

My darling Elena,

It's been two months since the German occupation began and my house "guest" arrived. Thankfully, my worst fears have not come true—yet at least—and he's doing his best not to be too much of an imposition. Most mornings, he's up and out of here with the dawn call of the cockerel and doesn't return home until well after dinner. I know I should feel grateful that he isn't like some of the others—my friend Antoinette has two soldiers staying with her and they treat the place as if it's a hotel and she's their personal skivvy—but in some ways his cordiality makes it harder. No matter how polite he might appear, the fact remains that he is fighting for Hitler. If I exchange pleasantries with him, I feel I would be betraying my country. So I've adopted a policy of nodding or shaking my head when necessary and answering any questions he might have in as few words possible. When you feel powerless in the face of an enemy, even the smallest things matter. It's as if my words have become a vital currency and just as the Germans have rationed our food, I shall ration them with him.

As I write this, I'm aware of the futility—why should the Germans care if I speak to them or not? But I have to do something. I have to refuse to comply in some way. It's like these secret letters to you. They began as an act of desperation, but now they're an act of defiance. And even though the Germans won't allow us to send mail over-seas, I'm no longer going to burn them after writing. I'm going to keep them hidden in the hope that one day

France will be free again, and you will come here on vacation and reclaim the darling grand-daughter room. I will show you these letters then, so you'll know exactly what happened here—exactly what can happen if one man's hatred and fear and craving for power is left to go unchecked.

Sometimes, in my darkest, most hopeless moments, I wonder if it will be this way forever. But if I keep writing to you and keep these letters for you to read, perhaps I will magically will it to happen. You never know! The human spirit is a remarkable thing.

All my love,

Grand-mère Rose

After my meeting with Duke, I'm whisked back to The Farm for another week of training. I've been told not to breathe a word of our meeting to the others, which is frustrating to say the least, as being able to talk it through with Betty might have helped soothe my jitters.

I arrive back after dinner and find Betty sitting on her bed, staring into her lap.

"How are you doing, beloved friend?" I ask cheerily.

"Great," she replies, but it's the most unenthusiastic "great" I've ever heard.

I sit down on the end of her bed.

"Are you sure?"

She looks at me and nods, but her expression is blank. I take hold of her hand and give it a squeeze and, instantly, her eyes fill with tears.

"Hey, what is it? What's wrong?" I whisper.

"Something—" she begins but stops at the sound of shoes clipping up the corridor toward our room.

"Oh, you're back."

I turn to see Teddy standing in the doorway.

"Yes, what are you doing up here?" I reply with a frown. His room is on the floor below. He has no business being up here, unless he's come to see one of us. I shoot Betty a questioning look, but her gaze is now locked on Teddy.

"I came to see Betty," he replies tersely. "We've been doing some cipher training together." He looks at Betty. "I just wanted to check you understood the last message I sent you."

"Loud and clear," she replies.

"Good. That's good." He shifts awkwardly from one foot to the other. Is it my imagination or is know-it-all Teddy looking slightly nervous? "OK, I'll leave you gals to it," he says before turning to go.

"I take it you whooped his ass in cipher training," I joke as soon as he's gone.

"What?" She looks at me, confused.

"Well, you're so much better at it than him."

"Oh. Yes. I need to use the bathroom." She gets up and hurries from the room.

Training has been stepped up a notch, but over the next few days I'm grateful for the constant whir of combat classes and lessons in map-reading and lock-picking and cipher coding and decoding. It's all a welcome distraction from the enormity of what lies ahead of me. But at night it's impossible to ignore the thoughts crowding my mind.

Before I left Washington, Duke instructed me to learn all I could about Spain by reading books from the library at The Farm. Mindful of the need for secrecy, I also brought a pile of books about France, Britain and Poland up to my room. I start forcing myself to think in Spanish and when I'm doing my physical exercises, I softly sing the Mexican lullabies Papa used to sing to us when we were kids, copying his accent.

Then, one day, after breakfast, I'm summoned to see Captain Shaw.

"We're sending you on a trial mission," he announces. "Go upstairs and get changed into civilian clothes, then a car will take you to Washington. You're to take the train to this address." He hands me a slip of paper containing the address of a business. "When you get there, you have to deliver this pack of cigarettes to the proprietor by no later than four o'clock. There's a coded message inside. Under no circumstances are you to be followed."

I nod, trying to memorize the address.

"Good luck." He stands up and shakes my hand.

As soon as I get to the station, I buy a ticket, all the time looking over my shoulder for any sign that I'm being followed. As I have some time to kill before my train is due to depart, I decide to go to the wrong platform, just in case I've acquired a tail. I walk to the end of the platform, then start walking slowly back up again, observing the other passengers standing there waiting. There's a woman with a small child. Three soldiers huddled together laughing and chatting. A man in a suit reading a paper. An elderly woman clutching a basket. As I walk past the man in the suit, I notice his paper shift slightly as if he's watching me. My throat tightens. Could he be following me? Completely forgetting the fact that if anyone is following me it will be a fellow American, I feel as wired as if it were Himmler himself.

I carry on breezily toward the main concourse, then pretend to drop my handkerchief. As I bend down to pick it up, I glance sideways and see that the man in the suit is walking toward me. I pick up my handkerchief and hurry up onto the concourse, trying to remember what we were taught in training about how to throw off a tail. *Don't take the linear path to your destination,* my trainer's words echo in my ears.

I look at my watch, see that I still have twenty minutes, and go out to the taxi rank and join the queue. Sure enough, the man emerges from the station and gets in the queue just a couple of people behind me. My heart thuds as I wait, then, finally, it's my turn and I get into the cab.

"Where to?" the driver barks.

"Capitol Hill," I reply, saying the first thing that comes into my mind.

As the driver pulls out into the traffic, I see the man hustling to the front of the line about to get into a cab.

"Oh no!" I exclaim. "I left my case back in the station." I stuff some money into the driver's hand. "I'm sorry, could you drop me just round the corner."

When he sees how much I've paid him to go round the corner, the driver doesn't complain. I hurry into a darkened doorway and watch as he pulls off, followed a few seconds later by the other cab, the man in the suit in the back leaning forwards. As soon as he's out of sight, I race back to the station and onto my train, sweat beading my top lip and heart thudding.

I complete my trial mission successfully, and at the end of the third week of training, I'm told to go home and wait while they do some final background checks. Although I'm not at all sorry to see the back of Teddy, one person I am sorry to say goodbye to is Betty. As soon as I've packed my case, I hug her tightly to me. I hate that I'm not able to tell her where I'm going.

"I hope our paths cross again, beloved friend," I whisper.

"I hope so too." She smiles weakly. Ever since I got back from Washington, she seems to have withdrawn completely, barely saying a word in the mess and leaving as soon as she's eaten. And she's shut down any attempts I've made at proper conversation.

"Good luck." As I stare into her wide, dark eyes, I don't think I've ever so fervently wished a person well. I hope that wherever they post her, Betty won't be coming into direct contact with the Nazis. I have a horrible feeling the "theater of war," as Captain Shaw calls it, might chew her up and spit her out.

I return home to another inquisition from my family after I tell them that I've been recruited to work as a typist for the War Department in Washington.

"But you hate typing!" Maria exclaims.

"You said it was as fun as jabbing your fingers onto the spikes of a cactus," Papa agrees.

"Not just any old cactus," Mom adds. "You said it was like jabbing your fingers onto the spikes of a San Pedro."

Clearly my anguished soliloquies following typing class are still vivid in their memories.

"Maybe that is what she's been doing while she was away," Papa jokes. "And she's high on the mescaline."

"What can I say? Desperate times call for desperate measures," I tell them. "And anyways, I hate Hitler a whole lot more than I hate typing."

At this, their smiles fade and Mom hugs me tightly.

"Your Grand-mère Rose would be so proud of you," she murmurs in my ear. Her words fortify my heart. It's been so tough not being able to communicate with Grand-mère Rose these past two years. Hopefully as a spy I'll be able to do something to help bring about the fall of Hitler.

"I'm so proud of you," says Papa, flinging his long thin arms around both of us.

"Me too," Maria cries, joining the embrace.

. . .

Christmas comes and goes and a couple of weeks into 1943, I receive a phone call telling me to go to New York. As before, I'm told not to bring anything that could give away my real identity. I memorize Grand-mère Rose's final letter to me like it's a script, determined to bring it with me in my mind at least. I've come to see her nine words of wisdom as some kind of lucky talisman and I chant them in my mind whenever anxiety starts getting the better of me: *Love your fear. Seek the wonder. Embrace the mystery.*

It takes everything I've got not to cry when it's time to say goodbye to my family. The enormity of the fact that I might never see them again is overwhelming, but I know I have to play it cool if I don't want to arouse their suspicions over the supposed typing pool.

"So you don't forget about me," Mom says as she bids me farewell, tucking a bottle of her favorite Chanel perfume into my hand. "Just spritz some and I shall magically appear, in your mind at least."

"I can't take your perfume," I exclaim. "You saved for months to buy it."

She clasps my hands tightly around the bottle. "I insist."

"You will be the sweetest-smelling typist in all of DC," Papa says, planting a kiss on top of my head.

"I made you this," Maria says quietly when our parents aren't looking, and she hands me one of her acorn people. It has big eyes and a smiley face and she's etched a tiny heart at the base. I hug her so tightly, she squeals that she cannot breathe.

When the cab arrives to take me to the station I watch my family through the rear window waving at me from the sidewalk until they disappear from view. *What if you never see them again?* fear whispers, and a chill runs right through me. *Of course I'll see them again,* I tell myself, clutching my acorn person tightly.

· · ·

After a three-day cross-country train journey, I arrive in New York and go to the Royal York Hotel, as instructed, to await further orders. I spend most of my time practicing my Spanish, and Mexican accent, and working on the backstory for my alter ego, who is called Carmen De La Fuente. The OSS have provided me with a new wardrobe of clothes and a very convincing fake passport which I use as inspiration for my story. Carmen, I decide, is an only child—as this is easier to lie about—and she was born to poor peasant parents who work on the cotton haciendas, like my own grandparents in Mexico. She has dreamed of acting her whole life, in part to help her poor parents. I figure I'll be able to tell this part of the story the most convincingly as it's so close to mine. She has acted on the stage in Mexico—as that's a lot harder to verify than acting on the screen. And she has had one serious relationship—with a lowdown dirty rat named Miguel who broke her heart by cheating on her with a woman of loose morals named Alejandra —so she's decided to come to Spain for a fresh start.

By the third night in my hotel room, I'm beginning to think and dream in Spanish and I'm thoroughly sick of Carmen and her backstory. I'm pacing up and down thinking that the OSS must have forgotten all about me and I'll be stuck staring at the hideous hotel wallpaper forever when the phone by my bed starts to ring.

"Be ready to leave in ten minutes," a man's voice says crisply, as soon as I pick up, then the line goes dead.

I've been so desperate to get out of that hotel room, I'm up and ready in less than five.

After ten minutes exactly, there's a sharp rap on the door. I open it to find a man with thick brown hair glossy with Brilliantine dressed in a smart gray suit.

"Carmen?" he says softly and I nod. Time to step into my new role. "Come with me."

He takes my case and we go downstairs and out into the

darkness, where a black sedan is waiting for us with the motor running. The man opens the back door for me, then he gets into the passenger seat up front.

I don't say a word as we set off, waiting for him or the driver to take the lead, but neither of them acknowledge me. Then I hear the driver say something about "the clipper" to the other man and I bite down on my lip to stop myself grinning with delight. I assumed I'd be taking a boat to Europe, but apparently not. My mind travels back to the summer's day in 1939 when Pan Am launched their very first passenger service across the Atlantic in their huge flying boats. Some guy who worked for the railways paid $600 for the first round trip. We pored over the photographs of the huge plane balanced on the water in Papa's paper. "Those things look way too big to be able to fly," Maria wailed. "How do they take off from the water? And how are they able to stay up in the air?" Could it be that I'm about to find out? I bubble like a gin fizz in anticipation.

After a while, we pull in off the road and past a sign saying Marine Air Terminal. Marine Air—so it's true, I'll be traveling by clipper all the way across the Atlantic! We drive up to a pier, where a man in military uniform is waiting for us.

"Good luck," the guy with the glossy hair mutters, staying put in the passenger seat.

"Oh, er, thank you," I murmur.

As I step from the car, the man in the military uniform shakes my hand, takes my case from the trunk and leads me along the quay and down some steep stone steps into a motor-boat. It's a cold January night and a pearly sliver of moon is the only light for miles around. Another man is already sitting in the boat, dressed in a civilian suit and hat. He looks up at me and smiles and nods in greeting.

"Good evening," I say, as if we're just casually meeting in a bar. The whole thing feels like a surreal dream, and becomes even more so as the boat roars into life and we start bouncing across the water toward the clipper. It looks like an enormous metal whale bobbing up and down on the waves. As the belly of the beast gets closer, and even bigger, all I can hear is Maria wailing in my ear. *"How do they take off from the water? And how are they able to stay up in the air?"*

The guy steering the motorboat pulls up by a gangplank leading into the plane. A combination of the waves and wind is causing it to sway violently. As I stand, a sudden gust of wind almost knocks me from my feet. The man in the suit and hat comes and stands right behind me.

"You go first," he says. "I've got you covered." His voice is deep and firm and instantly reassuring.

I step onto the stairway; the railings are slick with sea spray, but I somehow make it to the top. Inside, the clipper is like nothing I've ever seen before. Instead of having seats arranged in rows, like other airplanes, there are luxurious leather armchairs and a couple of sofas arranged around the edges of what looks like a salon-style room with burgundy carpets and creamy walls.

A couple of guys are already sitting on one of the sofas and I can hear the chatter of other men's voices coming from a room beyond.

"Come," the man in the suit says, taking off his hat and gesturing at me to sit in one of the chairs.

I sit down and he shows me how to secure my arms through straps on the armrests. Before I'm able to thank him, there's a huge roar and I feel the plane judder forward. The whole space reverberates with the forceful throb of the engine and as my spine rattles against the chair, my excitement builds. There's something about the combination of the noise and the vibrations that feels intoxicating; it's as if my old, dull life is literally being shaken away.

The plane begins to tilt and I realize that we must be taking off out of the water. Adrenalin courses through me. This is it, I'm finally on my way to take part in the war effort! I glance through a porthole to my right and see nothing but darkness due to the New York blackout, but then the moon briefly comes into view. Finally, we level out and the plane stops shuddering and the engines quieten. The men undo the straps on their armrests and I follow suit. I wonder if there are any other women present and think of Betty. It would be so great to see my beloved friend's familiar face.

A man's voice comes crackling over a speaker in the corner, informing us that we will be refueling in Bermuda, then traveling on to Lisbon, where we should arrive in around twenty-seven hours.

The man from the boat leans forward and extends a hand.

"I'm Oscar," he says. "And you must be Carmen."

"Yes, nice to meet you," I reply.

"I'll be accompanying you to Lisbon," he says. "You'll be staying there for one night, then traveling on to Madrid."

"Are you going to Spain too?" I ask hopefully. Maybe it's the fact that his broad shoulders and square jaw make it look like he's been chiseled from stone, but there's something sturdy and reassuring about him.

"No, I'll be staying on in Lisbon," he replies. "There's a lot of activity in Portugal that needs monitoring—it's the main intelligence hub between Europe and the rest of the world. There are around fifty agencies operating there right now."

I raise my eyebrows in surprise. "I had no idea so much was going on in the so-called neutral countries," I say, instantly hoping he won't think me stupid or naïve.

"That's exactly what I thought before I got into all this," he says with a warm smile, and I decide right there and then that I like him. Unlike some of the men I encountered in training, Oscar doesn't seem to get a kick from getting one up on a woman. "But actually countries like Portugal, Spain and

Switzerland are critical in the war effort. They're where so much vital intelligence gets passed," he explains.

I nod, but the adrenalin from the takeoff is starting to wear off, replaced by the fear that I might be getting way out of my depth.

"Don't worry," he says, as if sensing my apprehension. "The trick is to see what we're doing like a game of chess."

My spirits lift a little. Playing chess is one of my favorite pastimes with Papa. "What do you mean?"

"We always need to be thinking a few moves ahead—always anticipating the enemy's moves."

"Right." I can't help shivering at his use of the word "enemy" rather than "opponent." Then I remember how Papa used to make me practice playing against myself when I was younger. "This way you will feel the whole board," he told me. "You will see what it is like to be two players at once." Back then, I didn't really understand what he meant—it felt pointless and boring playing myself. But now I see that Papa's lesson could come in useful. If I'm to succeed in my new role, I need to anticipate what the other side will be doing. I need to see the whole board at all times. I only hope I've got what it takes to outsmart my enemies.

8

LISBON, 1943

After we've been in the air for about an hour, there's an announcement over the speakers that dinner is ready to be served. I follow Oscar up a spiral staircase into a large room on the upper deck, lined with polished wood-paneled walls and tables laid with dazzlingly white tablecloths. Again, I have to pinch myself to make sure I'm not dreaming. I glance around, hoping to see Betty, but I'm the only woman present; even the stewards are all men.

After dinner and our refueling stop, the sofas on the plane are transformed into beds and we retire for the night, although the sky through the porthole is already beginning to brighten. I snuggle under my covers, feeling physically exhausted but way too excited to sleep. I spend the next few hours drifting in and out of a strange semiconscious haze.

By the time we're approaching Portugal, the sky is dark again and the lights of Lisbon glitter and glimmer like a tray of jewels. It feels surreal knowing that I'm now so much closer to the war, and yet here at least, there's no need for blackout. The engines begin to roar again and we take our seats in preparation for landing. I try not to give too much thought to how this huge beast is going to come down in the sea. We hit the water with a bump and a huge wave sloshes up over the porthole. For a horrible moment, I think we've gone under, but after another couple of bumps, I see the glimmering lights again.

"We're going to a hotel in a place called Estoril," Oscar tells me, as we disembark into a motorboat. "It will be a good taster of what you have in store in Madrid."

"How so?"

"You will start to see how all that glitters is not gold," he replies mysteriously.

I nod knowingly, once again not wishing to appear stupid.

After a half-hour taxi ride along a coastal highway, we pull into the driveway of the Hotel Palacio. The name is no exaggeration —with its grand façade and palm trees neatly dotted around like sentries on duty, it really does seem like a palace.

The interior is even more palatial, with a sumptuous crimson carpet and beautiful antique furnishings. I half expect to see a member of royalty come sweeping down the marble staircase.

We make our way to the reception desk, where we're asked for our passports. My hear thuds as the woman leafs through the pages of mine. Will she be able to tell that it's a counterfeit? Oscar has already warned me that the Portuguese secret police are always on the lookout for spies. Even though Lisbon is riddled with agents, espionage is actually illegal here.

I focus my gaze on the clock on the wall behind the woman, repeating, *I am Carmen De La Fuente, Mexican actress*, over and over in my head. Thankfully, she returns the passport to me and we're issued with our room keys.

"Let's meet in the lobby in half an hour," Oscar says as we arrive at my room—his is a couple of doors down from mine. "There's something I want to show you in the casino."

"Sure," I reply casually, although my heart is now pounding so wildly it feels as if Charles "Honi" Coles is doing a tap dance in my ribcage. I've only ever seen casinos in the movies. I'm so excited, I'm barely able to take in the splendor of my room and set about freshening up and getting changed into my most glamorous dress—a fitted number in emerald green, which I pair with my highest heels. A spritz of Mom's Chanel helps me get into character. Somehow, now I smell expensive, it's a whole lot easier to act it.

Walking into the casino, I feel the same gravity-shifting sensation as I did when the clipper took off. The grandeur and scale are breathtaking. The ceilings are the highest I've ever seen and huge chandeliers cast everywhere in sparkles of gold. Beautifully dressed people looking every bit as polished as the surroundings glide around the plush red carpet and gather in clusters at the tables. The air is filled with murmured conversation and the purr of the roulette wheels. It takes a lot of focus for me to remain in character as Carmen—who I feel would be used to casinos—and not wave my hands excitedly like a kid in a candy store.

"Quite something, huh," Oscar comments with a sideways grin.

"Uh-huh," I reply, trying to take it all in.

"Teeming with enemy agents," he mutters.

"Really?" I look around and notice a group of Asian men at one of the tables. Could they be Japanese agents?

"As I said, all that glitters is not gold," Oscar continues. "In this place, no one is who they might appear or claim to be. Let's go watch that table." He nods to the table where the Asian men are playing. "The Japanese use roulette as a way of receiving messages about our troop movements. We need to see if we can break the code. Pay close attention to the numbers that get called. See if you can decipher anything."

My heart sinks a little as we approach the table. Coding was my least favorite subject in training. If only Betty was here, she'd probably crack any code in seconds flat. As we reach the table, the croupier is sliding a pile of chips over to a plump pale-faced man with a painfully obvious toupee. One of the Japanese men is sighing like he just lost, but there's something about the hammy way in which he's doing it that makes me think he's acting. The hairs on the back of my neck stand on end. Could he be an agent?

"Red, thirty-two," the plump man calls in English but with a distinctly German accent. My mouth goes dry.

"Black five," the Japanese guy replies.

Could it be that they're communicating with each other? I see a look pass between the two men, then the plump man looks at me.

"Perhaps the lady would like to play?" He raises his eyebrows questioningly.

"I lost most of my husband's money already," I quip in broken English with a thick Mexican accent. My first line as Carmen.

"She's going to bankrupt me," Oscar says, playing along.

The man nods and smiles and I breathe a sigh of relief.

Oscar and I watch them play for a while, but there appears to be no pattern to the numbers being called, other than the German always calls even numbers and the Japanese guy, odd. I mention this to Oscar later in the bar and he says that he had noticed the same. I'm relieved that he wasn't able to decipher what was going on either.

The following morning, I fly to Spain in a much smaller plane. As it bounces through the air on its approach to Madrid, I peer through the porthole at the palette of faded greens, brown and orange beneath. The landscape reminds me of a patchwork quilt whose colors have run in the wash. In the distance beyond the fields lies a rugged gray mountain range. The caps are white with snow as if they've been sprinkled with powdered sugar. I know from my research back at The Farm that these are the Sierra de Guadarrama.

I lean back in my seat and take a few deep breaths, mentally running through my instructions for when I land. Oscar told me that I'm to check in at the Ritz Hotel, then make my way to a tearoom called Embassy. A man named Mitchell—my handler in Madrid—is going to meet me there. I feel a wistful pang as I think of Oscar back in Lisbon. If only he'd been coming to Spain too. In just a couple of days together, I felt like we'd built a great rapport and that I could really trust him. Now I'm back to knowing and trusting no one.

The plane banks to one side and I peer out of the window in search of Madrid's bustling metropolis. But as we begin our descent, all I see are endless fields and the occasional cluster of tiny cottages. It's way more rural than I was expecting.

As we land with a bump on the runway, it sends a bolt of fear through me. I'm totally on my own and just one border away from the Nazis. What if I mess things up? What if my cover gets blown?

You are Carmen De La Fuente, Mexican actress, I tell myself. *Love your fear. Seek the wonder. Embrace the mystery.* I take my compact from my purse and reapply my lipstick and remind myself why I am doing this. I have to help the Allies win the war so that my beloved Grand-mère Rose will be free again.

As I go down the tiny flight of steps from the plane, I look around for the airport, but all I see is a building no bigger than a house. The air is crisp and cold and a biting wind is causing the dust to whirl on the ground. Once I've gotten my case, I hurry over to the building, where I'm greeted by three officials, all wearing peaked caps and long, olive green capes.

"*Buenos días!*" one of them calls in greeting.

"*Buenos días,*" I reply, paying close attention to my accent.

One of them checks my passport, while another has a quick rummage through my case. I'm hardly able to breathe, but after what feels like hours, my passport is stamped and my case is closed and both are handed back to me. I ask them where I can get a cab and one of them shows me out of a door to the front of the building where a battered old cab is waiting.

So far, so good, I think to myself as I settle into the back seat, my heart pounding.

As we set off along what is more a dirt track than a road, I peer out of the grimy window. The place looks just as barren as it did from the air and nothing like the glamorous Madrid I read about when I was studying Spain back at The Farm. The terrible thought occurs to me that maybe I got on the wrong plane. And my fears grow as we drive past a mangy horse pulling a wooden cart. It's being driven by a toothless old man hunched over the reins, his spine curved like the letter C.

The roads grow bumpier and we barely see another car. Most of the buildings we pass are crumbling and riddled with holes like they've been the victim of some kind of stone-eating infestation. A chill courses through me as I remember the recent civil war and realize that they must be bullet holes. Spain may be neutral for now, but it's only been a few years since it was torn apart by conflict, and now another war is snarling and snapping at its borders. How much longer will it be able to maintain its façade of neutrality? The safety of America suddenly feels worlds away. I reach in my pocket for the trusty acorn that Maria gifted me and pray that it gives me the strength of a mighty oak tree.

Finally, the roads become smoother and the landscape changes and we start driving along a wide boulevard intersected every few blocks by large squares—or plazas as they're known here, I remind myself. Each plaza appears to follow a similar design, framed with trees and with a huge statue pride of place in the middle. It might be a whole lot grander here, but there's still barely any traffic to be seen. We reach a plaza with a huge statue of a bearded man holding a pitchfork standing on a carriage being pulled by two horses.

"*Es la fuente de Neptuno*," the cab driver says, looking at me in his mirror.

"Ah, *sí*," I reply, nodding knowingly. The Fountain of Neptune. I find a strange comfort hearing the similarity with my new surname—De La Fuente, of the fountain—as if it's some kind of sign that I'm in the right place.

We drive around the plaza and through a set of wrought-iron gates, the tops of which have been painted gold and are gleaming in the weak winter sunshine. A sign welcomes us to the Ritz Hotel. I gaze across the neatly manicured gardens to the ornate entrance, where a couple of smartly dressed porters are standing on duty.

"It has only recently been restored," the driver tells me as he opens my door and helps me out. "It was used as a military hospital during the war."

I shiver as I look up at the building, picturing the wounded soldiers who would have been brought here. I guess the ghosts of war must haunt every corner of this city.

Almost as soon as I've alighted from the cab, a bellboy with olive skin and rich brown eyes is at my side, welcoming me to the Ritz. The cab driver hands him my case from the trunk and wishes me well. For a second, I feel like flinging myself into the back seat and telling him to keep on driving. Instead, I bring my wrist to my nose to smell the fading Chanel perfume and I think of my family back home. I want to keep them safe and make them proud.

I am Carmen De La Fuente, Mexican actress.

The bellboy leads me through the grandest of lobbies to a gleaming desk, where a receptionist with a dazzling smile welcomes me. My pulse races as I wait for her to check my passport, but all is well and she hands me the key to my room on the fourth floor. The bellboy accompanies me to the elevator and as we wait for it to arrive, I casually scan the lobby. It's milling with people, and thanks to Oscar's tutorial at the Palacio, I'm instantly aware of a couple of Japanese men standing talking by a large vase of flowers to the right.

A bell pings as the elevator doors slide open and a heavyset man wearing a suit and fedora steps out. As we make eye contact, he raises his hat in greeting and I smile in response.

"Good day," he says in Spanish but with what sounds like a German accent.

"Hello," I reply, praying there's no hint of an American accent to my Spanish.

As I step into the elevator, it feels as if all the blood in my body has rushed to my face. I lean against the rear wall and focus on appearing as calm and serene as a swan. I think of what both Duke and Oscar told me about Madrid teeming with German agents. Have I just encountered my first? And did I look suspicious to him? Could he tell I was faking my accent?

As the elevator doors begin sliding shut, the man stops and glances back over his shoulder at me.

Go, go, go! I silently urge the elevator and mercifully it heeds my prayer, juddering into action. As I wait for it to reach the fourth floor, I take a moment to calm myself. I have an entirely believable cover story; there's no need to panic.

The elevator comes to a halt and the doors slide open and the bellboy leads me along a wide corridor, with a carpet so soft it seems to swallow my feet. Every so often, dotted between the rooms, we pass elegant side tables containing huge vases of lilies. The scent is intoxicating, but in my tense state it's wasted on me.

When we reach my room, I tip the bellboy, shut and lock the door behind him and perch down on the huge bed. I think of what Oscar said about this job being like a game of chess. If the German man was an agent, and if he did suspect me, what would he do? I ask myself. He'd follow me. So what would I do in anticipation of that move? I'd make sure I'm not followed.

My heart rate begins to calm down and I take a look around the room. A chandelier hangs from the center of the ceiling—a baby version of the one in the lobby. The windows are dressed with long velvet drapes in dusky rose, matching the pattern on the carpet and the bed linen. A dark wooden carriage clock ticks away on the creamy marble mantelpiece. On the nightstand next to the bed, there's a leather-bound book with the word *menú* embossed in gold on the front. I open it and as my eyes scan the lists of food, I have a sudden flashback to the diner back home. How did I get from serving hotcakes to here? It feels like a dream.

Things feel even more surreal when I go into the bathroom and discover that it's as big as the living room back home. The bathtub is long and deep and shaped like a kidney bean, standing on four brass feet. It's way too inviting to resist and as I still have a couple of hours before my meeting with Mitchell, I decide to take a bath, hoping it will help me relax. I'm as jumpy as a convict in a convent, as Papa would say. At the thought of my twinkly-eyed father, I feel a lump forming in my throat. I turn on the bath tap and force thoughts of my family from my mind. The last thing I need right now is to let my emotions get the better of me.

Once I've bathed, I dust myself in the complimentary lily of the valley talcum powder and put on one of the dresses I was given in Washington—all of them with Mexican labels for authenticity. I stare at my reflection in the mirrored door of the huge closet and clasp my hands in front of me.

"I am Carmen De La Fuente," I whisper. "*Fearless* Mexican actress."

There's still a chill in the air when I go outside and I pull my fur stole tighter around me. Although there was no sign of the German man lurking in the lobby waiting to follow me, I decide against hailing a cab from the hotel and walk out into the square. Having consulted my map, I've figured it should take about an hour to walk to my destination—a straightforward route along a wide road called Paseo de la Castellana. As well as giving me a feel for Madrid, I'm hoping that walking will help settle my nerves.

As soon as I get out onto the sidewalk, an old yellow trolley car goes trundling past. Most of the women I see are wearing headscarves and clad in black and most of the men wear long dark capes slung over one shoulder so that they can pull the top across their faces like a scarf. It doesn't take long for me to figure out why—the wind is biting.

After I've walked for a few minutes, I stop outside a huge church and pretend to look in my purse for something to make sure I'm not being followed. It was one thing doing this on a trial mission in America but quite another now I'm in Spain and could potentially be being followed by a member of the Nazi secret service. Thankfully, the coast appears to be clear.

Three nuns come out of the church and I tuck in behind them as they walk down the street, marveling at the width of their white starched caps, floating like clouds above their sky-blue habits.

After an hour of walking past palatial stone buildings and glamorous boutiques along sidewalks lined with beautiful trees, I'm invigorated and my stomach feels hollow from hunger. I spy a sign with round fat letters spelling out "embassy" up ahead of me on the corner of a block. I've reached the tearoom.

I'm just about to step inside when I notice a sight that chills me to the core. Next to the tearoom, there's a small church and on the other side of that there's a building with flags bearing swastikas either side of the door. It's the first time I've ever seen the Nazi emblem for real rather than in a newspaper or on a newsreel at the movies and I go cold all over. Why would my handler ask me to meet him here, right under the nose of the enemy?

My darling Elena,

I'm writing this to you on Christmas Eve and trying with all my might to remember the true spirit of Christmas. But it's so hard to remember to love when surrounded by so much fear. Not to mention hunger. This evening, my "guest" arrived home with a chicken. He gave up trying to have a conversation with me long ago and we've fallen into an awkward dance of avoidance—with him going straight up to his room—YOUR room—as soon as he gets here. So when he came into the kitchen this evening and put the chicken on the table (I guess I should make it clear that the chicken was already dead and plucked!), it caught me off guard and the word "Oh!" burst from my mouth before I could stop it. "For you, for Christmas," he replied, before turning on his heel and going upstairs.

And now I'm faced with a real dilemma. It's so hard to get meat these days, some people have taken to breeding and eating rabbits. There's a lovely young woman named Anna who lives down the lane and has a young son to feed. Her husband was killed earlier this year trying to defend the Maginot Line. I could roast this chicken and invite them for Christmas lunch. But if I accept this gift from my "guest," is it even worse than talking to him? Is it admitting defeat? Or, worse still, being a traitor to France? It's so hard to think straight when your belly aches with hunger.

I wonder what I would advise you to do, Elena, if you came to me with a similar dilemma. I know I would want you to eat, that's for sure—just as I want Anna and her son, Caleb, to eat. What if I gave them the chicken without telling them where it came from? That way, Anna wouldn't have to endure any moral dilemma. But I won't let a scrap of that chicken pass my lips. Instead of resenting my hunger, I'm going to see it as a badge of honor, a measure of my loyalty to France. I don't need that Nazi pig's gift. The only gift I have and need this Christmas is knowing that you and the rest of my family are safe from harm's way on the other side of the Atlantic.

Sending all of my love and wishes for a wonderful Christmas,

Grand-mère Rose

9

MADRID, 1943

For a horrible moment, I think it's a trap, then I reassure myself that it can't be. The instruction to meet here came from Oscar, who I trust implicitly.

I take a breath and step through the door and it's like stepping into another world—a genteel and distinctly British world. Waitresses clad in a smart black and white uniforms weave through the tables holding trays laden with china teapots and cups and silver stands filled with cakes and sandwiches. The neatly laid tables are populated with elegantly dressed men and women, quite different to the Spaniards I've encountered on my walk here, and a delicate symphony of laughter and chatter, interspersed with the clink of cutlery, fills the air. A shiny, glass-fronted counter containing a selection of the most delicious-looking cakes I've ever seen faces the door.

A petite, middle aged woman with delicate features and neatly rolled hair comes out from behind the counter to greet me. *"Buenas tardes,"* she says with what sounds like a British accent.

"Good afternoon," I reply, also in Spanish. "I have a reservation for three o'clock in the name of Carmen De La Fuente."

This is what I've been instructed to say and my heart flutters as I wait for her to check the bookings, hoping that there is one for me.

"Of course, come this way." She smiles and gestures at me to follow her into the tearoom.

As she leads me through the maze of tables, I keep my ears pricked for any German accents, but all I hear are Spanish voices and the occasional British. I relax a little. Hopefully, in spite of the dubious neighbors, I am on friendly territory.

She takes me to a table tucked away in the far corner, practically out of sight of the rest of the room. I sit down, hoping that my contact will be able to find me here.

"Will anyone be joining you?" the woman asks.

"Yes, a friend. He should be here soon."

"Very good. Someone will be over to take your order." She places two menus on the table.

As soon as she's gone, I take a copy of a novel entitled *María Luisa* by Mexican writer Mariano Azuela from my purse and place it on the table where it's clearly visible. This is my sign to Mitchell. When he arrives, he's supposed to remark that he's just read Azuela's novel *The Underdogs*.

I pick up the book and try to read to distract myself from the growing butterflies in my stomach, but the words all blur into a jumble of random letters. After a minute or two, I hear someone clear his throat and look up to see a man with neatly cropped auburn hair standing by the table. He's wearing a belted raincoat over his suit and holding his hat to his chest. Although he has to be at least forty, his bright blue eyes and the scattering of freckles on his nose give him a boyish look.

"Aha, Mariano Azuela," he exclaims, speaking Spanish with an American accent. "I've just finished reading *The Underdogs*."

"Mitchell," I cry in recognition, as instructed.

"Carmen!" he replies. "It's so good to see you again."

He gives me a quick hug, for the benefit of anyone who might be watching, I guess, then sits down opposite me.

"Any problems so far?" he asks quietly, no longer playing to the crowd.

"No, so far, so good."

"Good." He smiles. "I have to say, I'm very pleased that you're joining us here."

"You are?"

He nods. "I've heard very good reports from your training officers. Plus, it's refreshing to have someone from a different background."

I look at him questioningly.

"Most of the recruits we've been sent so far have been from high-society families. Bankers and suchlike. It's gotten to the point where people are joking that OSS stands for Oh So Social."

I instantly think of Teddy. I clearly was right in my assessment that he came from money, and it's good to hear that my background could actually work in my favor here.

A pretty young waitress arrives at our table and Mitchell orders us something called afternoon tea. I'm a little disappointed that we won't be eating as the sight of the delicious cakes on display have sparked an even more ravenous hunger in me.

"Now, to get down to business," he says as soon as the waitress has gone. "We've recently received some key intelligence that Himmler has an agent here in Madrid."

"Himmler?" I whisper, my pulse quickening.

"Uh-huh. Your main mission for now is to try to identify who that person is."

"Oh," is all I'm able to reply. *Love your fear!* I imagine Grand-mère Rose whispering in my ear. But it does little to help when faced with the prospect of the head of the infamous Schutzstaffel and Hitler's former bodyguard.

"I've arranged for you to have an audition tomorrow for a show called *Sisters in Love* that will be starting soon at the Teatro de la Zarzuela. After your audition, you will meet the rest of the cast for a table read of the script." Mitchell takes a piece of paper from his jacket pocket and passes it to me. It's a ticket for a show happening tonight at the theater—a celebration of flamenco. "I thought you might like to go to this tonight, to help give you a feel for the place."

"Thank you, but... but what if I don't pass the audition?"

"Don't worry, that's all taken care of. The director, Antonio, is a friend. When you get back to the hotel you'll find a copy of the script in your room with your role highlighted."

"I see." I look back at the ticket and my anxiety grows. I've been so focused on my role as a spy, I haven't given much thought to the fact that I'm going be acting in Spanish musical theater as part of my cover story. What if I'm not good enough? I try my hardest not to show my concern. The last thing I want is Mitchell thinking that I'm lily-livered.

"You have a minor role," Mitchell continues, slightly easing my fears. "Playing the sister of the main character."

"OK."

"The main character is played by a Spanish actress named Conchita Aldana. She's one of the people we want you to keep tabs on." He leans forward and lowers his voice to a whisper. "We think she could be Himmler's agent in Madrid."

"An actress?" I was not expecting this, but it's a pretty exciting twist.

"It's not so unbelievable. An actress as popular as her has access to the cream of Spanish society, including the aristocracy and politicians. We're hoping that if you befriend her, you'll start to get a similar level of access."

"I see." I take a breath. The notion that Himmler's agent might be an actress makes my task slightly less intimidating. In fact, I kind of relish the opportunity to get one over on a woman who's working for Himmler. "What makes you think she might be his agent?"

"She's been seen having dinner in Horcher with another known German agent."

"Horcher?"

"It's a restaurant a couple of blocks away, one of the finest in Madrid. It's the sister restaurant to Horcher in Berlin and a great favorite with Abwehr and SS officers. You'll have to go there."

My appetite is killed stone dead at the prospect.

"Don't worry, as a Mexican no one will suspect you." Mitchell briefs me on life in Madrid, and the nocturnal routine of the inhabitants. "People never normally go out for dinner until at least ten o'clock," he tells me. "We want you to take full advantage of the social scene—as an actress, you'll be invited to lots of dinners and nightclubs, and after that, flamenco parties, which tend to go on until dawn. Accept as many invitations as you can. We don't know for sure that Conchita Aldana is working for Himmler. It could be anyone. You need to keep your eyes and ears open for anything suspicious."

"Sure thing."

"And you'll need to keep your wits about you at all times. No getting drunk..." He pauses. "Or falling in love."

"Falling in love?" I frown. He's got to be kidding. Surely I'll have way more important things on my mind than affairs of the heart—like not blowing my cover or getting killed!

"Uh-huh. You shouldn't do anything that might leave you compromised. Obviously, you are going to be propositioned by men and if you feel they might be of some use to you intelligence wise, then by all means go out with them. Just don't allow feelings to develop."

"You've got nothing to worry about on that score. Carmen is still reeling from a dirty love rat's cruel betrayal."

He looks at me blankly.

"It's from the backstory I've created for her," I explain in hushed tones. "There's no way she'll be falling in love with anyone, she's far too cynical and world-weary."

"Glad to hear it," Mitchell replies, raising his eyebrows. "Another thing we'd like you to do here is identify any locals who might be interested in working with the Allies—women in particular."

I nod. The need to create a network of locals sympathetic to the Allies' cause was something we covered quite extensively in our training.

"My tip is to go for the communists," Mitchell continues.

I stare at him, shocked. "Communists? Will they want to help us?"

"Yes, remember the Russians are our allies in this conflict, plus the communists in Spain are not supporters of Franco."

Once again, Oscar's chess analogy comes back to me. It sounds like I need to be a grand master to win here in Madrid!

Two waitresses arrive at the table, one holding a tray containing a bone china teapot and matching cups and saucers, the other a three-tiered silver stand. Each of the tiers is filled with delicate finger sandwiches and all manner of little cakes.

"*Dios mío!*" I exclaim, my eyes on stalks.

"Margarita's afternoon teas are one of the best things in this city," Mitchell says once the waitresses have gone, pouring some tea from the pot into my cup.

"Margarita?" I ask.

"The woman who owns this place. She's from Ireland originally."

I'm mighty relieved to discover that the tearoom is owned by an Irishwoman; it's starting to make more sense that we're meeting here.

"What's the building a couple of doors down? The one with the swastikas?" I ask.

"That's the German embassy. A lot of embassies are based around here."

"Ah, I see, hence the tearoom name."

"Exactly."

I take a cucumber sandwich from the stand. "Isn't it strange, living in such close proximity to the enemy?"

He nods. "We're really outnumbered too. Canaris, the head of the Abwehr, has about a thousand agents in the city, at our last estimate. We only have a handful."

"Whoa!"

"And to cap it all, espionage is a capital crime here in Spain. If your cover is blown, you will have no diplomatic immunity."

The mouthful of sandwich I am eating seems to turn to dust in my mouth. A capital crime means capital punishment, so it's not just the Germans who might kill me—my hosts might execute me too.

"I have something for you," Mitchell continues, taking an envelope from his pocket and passing it to me beneath the table.

"What is it?" I slide the envelope into my purse.

"22,000 pesetas—in case you get into trouble with the Spanish, or if the Germans invade. Keep it on you at all times, and use it for bribes or emergency transportation if you get into a tight spot."

The feeling that I'm now living in a movie grows with every bizarre revelation. I half expect a camera assistant to jump out from behind the plants with a clapperboard.

"You'll receive an income from the theater and one from the OSS. I'll arrange for you to meet our station chief soon. His code name is Argus. Yours, as you know, is Flamingo. Mine is Bruno and I'll be your handler."

"Is the Madrid station based at the American embassy?" I ask.

"No. The staff who work there don't have the same level of security clearance as we do, so they have no idea as to our identities. The station is in an office a few blocks away. We have a couple of secretaries and admin staff, and a couple of coders and a chief cipher clerk."

I wait for him to add more, but he falls silent. "Is that it?"

"Uh-huh. Our radio operator will be coming soon, and we're meant to be getting another coder."

I say a silent prayer that one of them will be Betty. It sounds like we could really use her skills.

"Because you're here under a fake persona, we'll be keeping you away from the other staff. All they'll know is that we have an agent in the field codenamed Flamingo. If you run into any serious trouble, you're to call the number on the piece of paper under your napkin and say the code word 'chestnut.' They will let me know that you need help."

I frown. "What piece of paper under my napkin?"

He nods at the starched white napkin beside my plate. I pick it up and, sure enough, there's card with a number on it.

"Geez, you could give The Great Blackstone a run for his money."

He smiles enigmatically. "Memorize the number."

I study the card and use the system I learned in training to commit the number to memory. The first two digits are 11, the month of Papa's birth; the remaining three run in the sequence 789. Seven is Maria's favorite number. "I've done it."

Mitchell takes the piece of paper and puts it in his jacket pocket. "When you get back to your hotel room, you'll find something for you in a hatbox beneath the spare blankets in your closet."

I find myself in the unfamiliar position of being lost for words. There's so much to take in, I feel my head might explode.

"Do you have any questions?" he asks.

I have so many questions I'm barely able to think straight

but I don't want to look incompetent so I ask the one that's most pressing. "How will I pass information to you?"

"If it's urgent, ring the number, otherwise I will be in regular contact, don't worry." He smiles and raises his tea, the porcelain cup looking even more delicate in his thick fingers. "Welcome to Madrid."

I take the trolley back to the hotel and I'm impressed by the number of men who jump up to offer me their seats. Franco might be buddying up with the Nazis, but the Spanish people I've encountered so far seem charming.

As soon as I get to my room, I see the script waiting for me on my pillow. Then I check the giant oak closet and, sure enough, I find a hatbox beneath the pile of blankets. I open it with bated breath—to discover a hat! It's a very nice hat—turban-style in caramel-colored velvet—but not at all what I was expecting. I take the hat out and give the box a shake. Something rattles beneath the lining. I carefully slide the base from the box to discover a pistol. I recognize it immediately as a Hi-Standard .22 caliber semi-automatic. This was the weapon I liked best in training as it has a built-in silencer and barely any recoil. Perfect for eliminating enemy personnel at close range virtually undetected, as we were taught at The Farm.

I turn the gun over in my hands. I wonder if I'll end up using it here in Spain—if my new role trying to identify Himmler's agent will involve killing another human being. An icy chill runs through me. It seems almost impossible to believe that this is my new reality.

10

MADRID, 1943

The Teatro de la Zarzuela where I'll apparently be performing soon is only a short walk from the Ritz, so I set off for the flamenco show at just before nine. Thankfully, the cold wind that was whipping through the city earlier has now dropped and the streets are humming with people. Figuring that Carmen De La Fuente would want to make a splash on her first night in Madrid, I'm wearing the most figure-hugging of the dresses I was given before coming here, a midnight-blue number with a sprinkling of silver stars shimmering across one of the shoulders. I've teamed it with a fur stole and a pair of silver Mary Janes.

Just like on the trolley before, almost every man I encounter on the way to the theater tips his hat to me, and offers some words of praise on my appearance. None of them seem sleazy, so I smile and nod rather than resort to the impressive range of withering putdowns I've created for creepy guys back home.

With its dusky pink and white stone and intricate curlicues, the theater is as elegant and pretty as a wedding cake. Like so many of the other buildings I've encountered today, it looks hundreds of years old and steeped in history. I think of all the people who must have passed through the ornate wood-framed glass doors over the decades and my skin tingles. Can it really be true that I'll be performing here soon?

For the briefest of moments, I forget about the war and feel awash with joy at the prospect of being able to act again. My excitement soon turns sour, however, when a couple speaking German go past me up the steps and into the theater.

OK, Carmen, don't lose your focus; it's time for you to make your entrance, I hear Grand-mère Rose encouraging me as I stride up the steps behind them.

The theater lobby is abuzz with chatter and the air is filled with a heady mixture of perfume and cologne. The walls are covered in velvety plum-colored paper, embossed with golden swirls. A sweeping staircase in the center leads up to the circles. I take a moment to breathe it all in before buying a program, then a smiling male usher shows me to my seat in the stalls— which turns out to be slap bang in the middle of the front row. Clearly, Mitchell wants Carmen to be noticed on her first night in town.

As the auditorium fills and the noise builds, I fan myself with my program and stare straight ahead, expressionless. Carmen would take a night at the theater in her stride, I tell myself, fighting the urge to grin like a kid on Christmas Eve. The only shows I've ever seen before were high school produc- tions; this is truly one of the most magical places I've ever set foot in. The orchestra begin warming up in the pit below and my heart thuds along with the crashing of cymbals. I know from the research I did at The Farm that Spaniards have two loves— bullfighting and flamenco—so I'm excited to see what all the fuss is about.

A quick glance through my program informs me that the star of tonight's show is the hottest new flamenco dancer in town—a guy called Santiago Lozano. I study the black and white photo of him on the inside page. He has curly, dark, shoulder-length hair and he's wearing tight-fitting, high-waisted pants and a polka dot shirt, unbuttoned almost to the waist. *How about leaving something to the imagination*, I think to myself, wondering if I'll be able to take flamenco seriously. I sure hope I can—sitting in the middle of the front row, I won't be able to hide it if I burst out laughing.

A girl who looks to be about eighteen and an older couple start making their way along the row toward me, sitting down in the empty seats beside mine.

"*Hola*," the young woman greets me warmly. With her glossy black hair and bright green eyes, she looks like a native Spaniard.

"*Hola*," I reply.

The older couple lean forward and smile warmly. There's a definite resemblance, so I'm guessing they're her parents.

"Oh, I am so nervous!" the woman exclaims, clasping the man's elbow.

"My brother's in the show," the younger woman explains.

"He's the star of the show," the man says proudly.

"Santiago Lozano?" I say, widening my eyes in admiration.

"The one and only." The girl grins. "I'm his sister, Josefa, and these are my parents." She offers her hand and I shake it firmly—figuring Carmen would be a firm handshake kind of gal.

"I'm Carmen. Nice to meet you."

"You are here alone?" Josefa asks, looking at the occupied seats the other side of me.

"Yes. I've just arrived in Madrid from Mexico. Ever since I was a child, I have dreamed of coming to Spain," I add, relishing the opportunity to bring Carmen's backstory to life. "And now, my dream has come true. I'm going to be performing in a show here myself soon." I mentally cross my fingers, hoping that I haven't just jinxed my rigged audition tomorrow.

"How exciting!" Her eyes widen. There's a sweetness about her that reminds me of Maria and I feel a sharp pang of homesickness. "Are you a dancer too?"

"No, an actress."

Josefa relays this information to her parents, who react in an equally delighted way.

"Are you a fan of flamenco?" the mother asks.

"Oh yes," I reply, marveling at how easily the lie flows from me. "Although I have to confess that I don't know all that much about Spanish flamenco, but I'm really looking forward to learning more."

"You should come to the party after the show as our guest," Josefa says. "I can introduce you to Santiago and the other dancers."

"That would be wonderful." I flash her my warmest smile. Playing the role of Carmen is proving easier than I thought, for now at least.

The house lights dim and a hush falls over the theater. I settle back in my seat, hardly able to believe my luck. This party will be my introduction into Spanish society. My role as an OSS agent has well and truly begun.

There's a sudden trumpet fanfare and the crimson velvet curtains sweep open and a single spotlight falls upon the stage. A man, whom I recognize instantly as Santiago, is standing there motionless. He's wearing tight blue pants, a matching short jacket trimmed with gold brocade and he's holding a red cape. As the music swells, he starts waving the cape, and the crowd roar their appreciation. It takes me a moment to realize that he's dressed as a matador, which I have to say is a stroke of genius, combining Spain's two loves in one performance. Santiago stares intently into the audience. His hair is rich chestnut brown and tumbles in wild curls to his shoulders. His eyes are piercing green and the tightness of his clothes reveals a body rippling with muscle. In the photo in the program, his flamboyance seemed too much, but in the flesh, well, let's just say both Carmen and I are impressed.

The music builds and he starts strutting toward us, waving

his cape as if taunting a bull. The audience love it and their excitement is infectious. He begins clicking his heels, dancing faster and faster, and he's so convincing, I can practically see the bull and hear it snorting and stamping its foot. At one point in the dance, Santiago staggers backwards, as if he's been gored. The entire audience, including me, gasp, but then he regains his balance and comes charging back to the front of the stage. He's so close now, I can see a bead of sweat trickle down the side of his olive-skinned face.

"Isn't he amazing," Josefa exclaims breathlessly in my ear. Her adoring gaze reminds me of the way Maria looks at me and again I feel a twinge of homesickness.

"Yes, he really is," I agree and this time I'm not acting.

With a final flurry of dance steps and a twirl of his cape, the bull is defeated and Santiago stands defiant, hands planted on his lithe hips. The crowd leap to their feet, cheering loudly. As I stand, I see him smile down at Josefa and his parents with a small nod of recognition, then, for a second, he turns his gaze upon me. The intensity of his stare jolts right through me. Then the moment is gone and he's radiating a beaming smile to the whole theater, one hand behind his back, the other on his stomach, as he gives a neat bow to the stalls and the circles.

There then follows an hour or so of the most wonderful dancing I've ever seen. Maybe it's the magnificence of the venue, or maybe it's the adrenalin coursing through my body, but by the time the show comes to a close, I'm completely sold on flamenco. The passion of the dancers and the drama of the music is intoxicating.

As we stand to leave, I hope Josefa hasn't forgotten about her invitation to the party, but to my relief, she turns to me and smiles.

"Santiago said we were to meet him by the stage door," she informs me.

"How fun!" I reply and my heart rate quickens in anticipation, not only at the opportunity to begin my mission for Mitchell, but also at the thought of meeting the fiery star of the show.

Outside, the air is cold and crisp and a sharp breeze nips at my warm cheeks. Once again, I hear German voices and turn to see two men in suits smoking brown Spanish cigarillos. Interestingly, now that I've begun playing my role as Carmen and I have company, I don't feel nearly as nervous as before.

"Come," Josefa says, leading me and her parents round the side of the building.

Compared to the grand entrance at the front, the stage door is a nondescript affair. A cluster of young women have already gathered there.

"Fans of Santiago," Josefa informs me with a weary sigh. "They hover around him like flies on horseshit."

"A fine way to talk about your brother." Her father chuckles and I can't help laughing too.

Josefa shrugs and raps on the stage door loudly. "We're here for Santiago," she announces as soon as the door opens. "I'm his sister."

The women look at us enviously as we're ushered inside.

A man sitting behind a small reception desk checks off Josefa and her parents' names, then frowns at me. "And you are?"

"A friend of the family," Josefa declares.

"Is she indeed?" a deep man's voice asks from behind us.

I turn and see Santiago standing in a doorway, still in costume, grinning inquisitively.

"She's a recent friend," Josefa explains before running over and giving him a hug.

"Very recent," I murmur as he continues grinning at me over her shoulder.

"How recent?" he enquires.

My true self squirms with embarrassment, but I somehow

manage to snap back into Carmen's character. There's no way she'd be fazed by Santiago; she'd see him as her equal.

"About an hour," I reply drily.

He throws back his head and gives one of the most raucous laughs I've ever heard. "Well, you must have made quite the impression for them to bring you back here."

"She's an actress," Josefa says excitedly. "She's going to be performing here soon."

"Is that so?" He raises his eyebrows.

"Yes, I have a role in the show *Sisters in Love*, beginning next month." Again, I silently pray that I haven't cursed my supposed audition.

"Ah, I know someone who is in that show also—Conchita Aldana. She is playing the lead, I believe."

Conchita Aldana, the woman Mitchell said could be working for Himmler. The plot thickens. "Yes, that's right," I reply, wondering how well Santiago knows her.

"Are you coming to the party at Chicote's?" he asks.

"Yes, she is," Josefa replies before I'm able, not that I have any objections. "Mama, Papa, will you come too?" she asks her parents.

"Ah, we're too old for that kind of thing," her mother replies with a smile.

"Says who?" Her father gives Josefa a playful nudge. "No, you youngsters go and enjoy yourselves."

Santiago's parents envelop him in a loving embrace, and seeing the obvious warmth between them again makes me pine for my own family. I force the thoughts of Papa, Mom and Maria from my mind and focus on being Carmen instead, looking about the place coolly, trying not to be intimidated by the framed posters from previous shows lining the walls.

Josefa and I wait in the green room while Santiago gets changed. The corridor outside is alive with the chatter of the dancers and musicians. The energy is infectious and fizzes like static in my veins. This is the life I always dreamed of. The life of a performer. But even in my wildest of dreams I couldn't have predicted that I'd end up performing the role of an actor—as a spy.

After a few minutes, Santiago reappears. Now free from stage makeup, his face is even more striking and his eyes even brighter green. He's wearing smart black pants and a black silk shirt with a floral print. "Come," he says, beckoning to Josefa and me. "We have a driver waiting."

Josefa and I get into the back of the cab and Santiago sits next to the driver. Within seconds, they're chatting away like old friends. While Josefa makes small talk about fashion, I keep one ear on the conversation up front, trying to glean all I can about Santiago. It turns out that both he and the driver are Romani and thankfully the driver is making my job a whole lot easier by peppering him with questions. By the time we pull up outside the bar, I've learned that Santiago discovered his love of dancing as a young child when he used to accompany his father to the bars and restaurants where he played guitar for tips. One day, the five-year-old Santiago started dancing to his father's music and they received way more money from the customers, so a new father-and-son double act was born. Hearing that Santiago comes from a similarly humble background to mine makes me feel a certain kinship with him but I quickly snap back to my senses. It doesn't matter where he's from or how charming he might seem—he knows someone who could be working for Himmler, and for all I know, he could be working for the enemy too.

Santiago springs from the cab and opens my door, offering me his hand to help me out. His grip is warm and strong and it feels so nice to have some physical contact for the first time in what feels like forever.

Calm yourself, I imagine my Carmen persona barking, and I

withdraw my hand, gazing up at the art deco sign running along the front of the bar.

"Chicote's is the first American bar in all of Spain," he tells me. "I take it you are a fan of all things American?"

The hairs on the back of my neck prickle. Has he detected my accent? Is my cover blown before it's even begun?

"What makes you say that?" I ask nonchalantly, while my stomach churns.

"Well, doesn't every actress dream of making it in Hollywood?"

I shrug as if I, personally, could not give a fig.

"Where did you say you were from?" he asks, again staring at me intently.

"Mexico City."

"Aha, I knew there was something different about you, that you weren't from Spain. Come..."

Santiago ushers Josefa and me toward a gilt framed revolving door. It deposits us at the top of some wide marble steps leading to a dimly lit, art deco-style interior. Green leather armchairs and sofas are arranged around low, polished wood tables. It's like stepping back into the roaring twenties. Jazz music is playing loudly and the place is full of guys in dapper suits, hair glossy with Brilliantine, and women with mouths as red and ripe as rosebuds, their hair perfectly set in victory rolls. An American-style bar runs along one side, glowing gold, manned by bartenders clad in white suits with black bow ties. Behind them, shelves glisten with row upon row of polished glasses and bottles of liquor. One of the bartenders is shaking a cocktail in time with the music, as if he's part of the show. Glamor oozes from every pore of the place and it's instantly intoxicating.

"You like it?" Santiago looks at me hopefully.

"It's amazing," I breathe, forgetting for a moment to be the cool, collected Carmen.

"Santiago!" A cheer goes up from a booth over to our right, where a group of young men and women have gathered, sipping cocktails. I recognize some of them as dancers from the chorus in Santiago's show.

"Grand performance!" a round-faced gentleman with receding hair greets Santiago, with what sounds like an Irish accent. Although he's wearing a suit, he strikes me as the kind of person who could never look neat and tidy. One of his shirt buttons is open and his tie is slightly askew. He starts talking to Santiago in a language I don't recognize. I get the impression that he must be praising him as he keeps patting him on the back.

"They're speaking Romani," Josefa explains. "That man's Walter Starkie. He's an author from Ireland, but he loves us Romanis."

"Did I hear my name being taken in vain?" Starkie says in Spanish with a twinkle in his eye.

"I was just telling my friend Carmen about you," Josefa replies.

"Carmen's a *very* recent friend of the family," Santiago says with a grin. "An actress from Mexico, no less."

"That's wonderful!" Starkie says, shaking my hand warmly. "How long have you been in Madrid?"

"Oh, all of a day," I reply drily.

"No way!" Santiago exclaims. "In that case, you must surely be in need of a tour guide."

My heart thuds at the prospect of spending more time with him, and the potential intelligence that might bring. "I guess I could be," I reply in what I hope is the crisp, Katharine Hepburn-esque manner that sends guys into a frenzy.

"I'd love to show you around," Josefa pipes up.

My heart sinks. Much as I like her, I very much doubt Josefa would be able to provide me with much information for Mitchell.

"I don't think Carmen wants to see the local playgrounds, little sis," Santiago teases affectionately. Josefa nudges him in the ribs.

"You've clearly made quite a first impression to have the siblings fighting over you already," Starkie says to me with a grin. "Anyway, must go, I have to get back to the institute. I just wanted to congratulate you, Santiago, you were magnificent."

I make a mental note to ask Mitchell if he knows anything about this Starkie character.

The two men hug and then, as Starkie disappears out of the revolving door, a woman comes sweeping in. I'm not sure if it's my imagination, but the entire bar seems to hush slightly at her entrance. It's impossible not to stare; with her waist-length raven hair, high cheekbones and hourglass figure, her beauty is breathtaking.

"Oh no," I hear Josefa mutter and I look at her questioningly.

"It's Conchita Aldana," she informs me.

My stomach clenches. This is the woman I'll be performing alongside in the zarzuela. The woman I'll be spying on for Mitchell. The woman who might be Himmler's rat.

She sweeps down the marble steps, casting a cool gaze about the place. When she sees Santiago, it's like a switch has been flicked and her tight bud of a mouth breaks into a smile, revealing two rows of perfect but slightly large teeth.

"When she smiles, she reminds me of an alligator," Josefa murmurs in my ear. I stifle a laugh.

"Santiago, darling," Conchita cries. From her appearance, I'd been expecting her voice to be softer, but it's surprisingly shrill. "How did it go?"

"It was good. Shame you couldn't make it," he replies, slightly flatly.

"I'm so sorry. Perhaps one of these days you could treat me

to a private performance." She gazes at him coquettishly through her long dark eyelashes.

"Perhaps," he replies before turning back to Josefa and me. "Let's get a drink. Carmen, in my first duty as your tour guide, I must buy you one of Chicote's gin and red vermouth cocktails—they're famous for them."

"That sounds divine," I reply, shooting a glance at Conchita. Her smile has wilted into a frown and the souring effect this has upon her face is quite astounding.

"Josefa!" One of the young male dancers from the show comes hurrying over, beaming widely.

Even in the dim lighting, I can see her face flush. "H-hello, Marco," she stammers.

Santiago looks at me and raises his eyebrows. "Remember what I said, Marco," he says, pulling a mock-menacing face.

"Of course." Marco nods respectfully.

"Santiago, stop being so annoying!" Josefa exclaims. She links arms with Marco and they go sit on a couple of the stools lining the bar.

"Young love," Santiago says with a grin. "At least now I get you to myself. Come..." He leads me a little further up the bar.

"Hmm, maybe I'll be the decider of that," I say.

He laughs. "I see I shall have to be at my most persuasive."

"I hope your persuasive skills are in the same league as your dancing."

"So you are a fan of my dancing?" His face lights up.

"I've only seen you perform once. It's far too early to make that kind of commitment." I fight to keep a straight face. It would appear that the spirit of my fictional creation, Carmen, has taken over and I have to say I'm enjoying my new role.

Santiago chuckles. "I love a challenge."

I glance over his shoulder and see Conchita glowering at me. Now would probably not be the best time to tell her that

I'm going to be auditioning for the part of her sister in the zarzuela tomorrow.

Once Santiago's ordered our drinks, we walk through the bar to an empty booth at the back. I have a flashback to the training video I made, what now feels like years ago, and I can't help shivering. I very much doubt that Santiago is carrying a concealed weapon like "Steve" from the video—his clothes are too tight for a start—but I need to stay on high alert. The warmth I've been feeling from our flirtation cools. I take the seat facing out into the bar, so I can keep an eye on Conchita. She has now positioned herself on a stool at the bar with three men gathered around her, all gazing at her adoringly, like seals waiting to be thrown a fish.

"Cheers," Santiago says, clinking his glass against mine. "Now, tell me everything about you."

"Everything?" I reply, raising an eyebrow, a move I've honed in front of the mirror when getting into Carmen's character.

"Yes, well, perhaps start with the best and the worst things," he replies with a grin.

"The worst?"

"Why not? Isn't that what forms people and makes them so interesting? The hardest times of their lives. Who wants to know the boring in-between bits? I want to know all about your joy and pain!" His eyes twinkle in the soft golden light.

I stare at him, temporarily dumbstruck. Up until this point in my life and my limited experience of dating, the man has done most of the talking—usually about himself. I've never had a guy appear this interested in me before. Once again, my skin prickles. What if he's working for the other side and suspicious of me? What if he's trying to find cracks in my cover story?

"OK, I shall help you out," he says. "What is your fondest childhood memory?"

"Playing chess with my father," I blurt out before I have

time to check that it's something Carmen would say, but I realize that it could fit just as well with her backstory. "He was so busy normally, working on the cotton hacienda. It was the only time I felt I had his undivided attention. He made it really fun too."

"How so?" Santiago looks genuinely interested.

"He would create characters for the pieces, and give them all voices. So, for example, the queen might be all haughty, like a real queen, and the pawns would have regional accents and talk like famers. He'd get me to do the same too. The only problem was sometimes I'd get so attached to the characters I'd create I'd start crying if he captured one of them!" I laugh at the memory.

Santiago smiles at me warmly and for a moment I feel as if I'm seeing beneath the flamboyant façade of Santiago the dancer. "Perhaps that is why you became an actress? He made you fall in love with playing different parts."

"Yes, I've never thought of that before. I surely inherited his tendency for melodrama." I smile at the thought.

"Is that so?"

"So how about you?" I ask quickly, keen to shift the spotlight. "What is your fondest childhood memory?"

"Mine is also with my father." He grins. "He and I were performing at a wedding back in Andalusia, where we are from, and the bride and groom were so delighted with our show that they let me have a piece of their wedding cake."

"That's it?" I ask when he falls silent.

"Yes. It was the most delicious cake I have ever tasted. The almond nougat, the custard filling that melted in my mouth, the toasted egg yolk..." He breaks off and laughs. "Do you think it's silly?"

"No," I reply, thinking of the first time I was treated to a milkshake and how it felt as if I was experiencing heaven on earth. When you are born poor, the simplest things can feel like a luxury.

"We never had money for things like cake, let alone a wedding cake," he continues.

"I understand. My beginnings were very humble too."

We look at each other and smile and again I feel a connection forming between us.

"I never dreamed I'd end up someplace like this," I say, looking over at the gleaming bar. A man wearing a trench coat has come over to Conchita. Josefa and Marco are still huddled tight in conversation, clasping each other's hands.

"When you come from nothing you are able to see things clearer, no?" Santiago replies.

"How do you mean?"

"You are able to see through the sheen. You know what really matters. What is truly beautiful."

I nod. The man in the trench coat whispers something in Conchita's ear, then walks past us and through a door at the back of the bar bearing a sign for the restrooms.

"It's great to see Madrid get its sparkle back after so many years of civil war," Santiago continues, "but some of the best places in this city are off the beaten track. Perhaps you will allow me to show you sometime?" He looks at me hopefully.

"I would really like that," I reply, and I mean it. I'm actually enjoying his company. Not that I'm going to lower my guard, but his openness and warmth are making me feel slightly more at ease.

I notice Conchita get up and she sashays past us, following in the footsteps of the man who just whispered in her ear. Could it be she's arranged to meet him out back? Instantly, my training kicks in. As soon as she's disappeared through the door, I stand up. "Will you excuse me? I just need to use the bathroom."

"Of course." Santiago stands as I leave. "I'll order us some food. Or do you need persuading on that front too?" He gives me another of his warm grins.

"When it comes to food, I need no persuading. Now, I must go powder my nose in preparation."

I head to the back of the bar and through the door. It opens onto a dimly lit corridor that smells of floor polish and stale cigarette smoke. I go past a couple of doors marked "Private" before reaching the ladies' powder room on the left and the gentlemen's restroom on the right. I take a breath and step inside the powder room.

One of the three cubicle doors is shut. Conchita must be inside. I feel a little foolish, but I guess it's better to be overly alert. I'm about to make my way into one of the cubicles myself when I hear the toilet flush and the door opens and a woman comes out. A plump woman with sandy-colored hair who is most definitely not Conchita. I glance back at the other cubicles to make sure they're empty—they are. If Conchita didn't come in here, she must be in one of the rooms marked "Private."

As the woman goes over to the sinks, I exclaim as if I've forgotten something and hurry back out. I press my ear to the door of one of the private rooms but hear nothing. I hurry to the other door and do the same. This time, I hear the low murmur of a man's voice. Now what do I do? I can hardly walk in on them—or can I?

I open my purse and pretend to be looking for something, then barge inside, gaze fixed firmly on the contents of my purse. I pull out my compact and look up, preparing to splutter that I'd meant to go into the ladies' room. But what I see leaves me speechless. The man's coat has been discarded on the floor and he's standing in front of Conchita, who's perched on a desk, her legs wrapped around his waist.

"What the hell?" Conchita snaps, pushing the man away and buttoning up the front of her dress.

The man has flushed as red as I feel and stares at the ground, not saying a word.

"I-I'm sorry," I splutter. "I thought it was the powder room. I was told it was on the left. I was looking for my compact."

"It's the next door on the left," the man replies, but he doesn't have a German accent—if anything, it sounds as if he's British.

"The next on the left?" I echo, hoping to get him to speak again so I can be sure.

"Yes! Are you deaf?" Conchita yells.

"No... I-I'm sorry to have bothered you." I back out of the room, my heart pounding. I might not know for certain that Conchita's working for the Germans, but one thing I do know is that I sure as hell don't like her. I make a mental note of the man's description for when I have to report back to Mitchell. My very first piece of potential intelligence.

11

MADRID, 1943

I return to the booth, trying not to appear flustered. Santiago is ordering some food from one of the staff.

"That was quick," he says, with a smile.

"Turns out my nose didn't need that much powdering," I reply, taking a large gulp of my cocktail. I glance over my shoulder and see the back door opening. "So, tell me something else about yourself?" I say quickly. "What has been... what has been your most frightening experience?"

"Most frightening?"

"Yes." I focus my gaze on him so that it will appear that we're deep in conversation and I'm not the slightest bit ruffled by what just happened. Conchita sweeps by on a cloud of perfume. Thankfully she doesn't look anywhere near my direction, but I notice Santiago glancing up at her. "You said we should talk about all of life, remember. The pain and the joy."

"Yes, of course." He looks thoughtful for a moment and I notice that his gaze remains on Conchita as she stalks her way through the bar. "It was when I saw a black widow spider," he eventually replies, but something tells me his heart is no longer really in the conversation. "How about you?"

I choose one of the anecdotes I created for Carmen's backstory. "It was when I had my first audition for an acting role." I don't know if it's because I'm not being genuine, but as I tell the fictional tale, the conversation seems to fall even flatter. The jazz music that was being piped through the speakers comes to an abrupt halt and someone starts playing a fiddle. I turn to see that some of the musicians from Santiago's show have formed an impromptu band at the end of the bar.

"Enough of this talk about fear, let's dance," Santiago cries, grabbing me by the hands and pulling me to my feet. "Come on!" he calls to his dancer friends. "It's time to party!"

When we finally emerge from the bar some hours later, the sky is still dark, but the first of the dawn chorus are starting to tweet. Josefa left with Marco a couple of hours ago and gradually the remaining dancers peeled off until it was just Santiago and me left. Although I tried my hardest not to drink too much, as we begin walking along the boulevard, I feel lightheaded from the liquor and dancing.

"Where are you staying?" he asks.

"At the Ritz."

"Very nice. If you like, I could try to find you a cab—or we could walk. It will only take around fifteen minutes from here."

"Walking would be good," I reply, eager for the chance to freshen up in the cool air.

I hear the click of hooves and see a cart trundling toward us along the deserted road. It's being pulled by an old donkey.

"The garbage men are beginning their shift," Santiago explains.

"This is a very strange city," I say as I watch the cart go by.

"How so?" Once again, he appears to be genuinely interested in what I have to say.

"There seem to be so many contrasts—rich and poor, glitzy and rundown..."

"Good and evil," he adds quietly.

I glance at him. "Yes," I agree, hoping it might make him say more. But the moment passes and the twinkle returns to his eye as he spots a single red rose lying in the gutter.

"And here, to prove your point, we have a rose in a gutter." He picks up the flower and twirls it in his fingers before presenting it to me with a flourish. "For you, my lady."

"Why, thank you, kind sir." I try to ignore the tingling in the pit of my stomach and focus instead on the far less appealing vision of Mitchell telling me that I mustn't fall in love. Not that I am falling in love, of course, but there's no denying the fact that I'm really starting to like what I've seen of Santiago.

"Perhaps you would do me the honor of coming to dinner with me tonight?" he asks tentatively.

"Seeing as you asked so nicely, I feel it would be awfully impolite to refuse," I reply like a frightfully well-to-do character from a British movie.

But instead of laughing, his face beams with happiness. "Really?"

I nod. That's if I live to tell the tale after my first table read with Conchita.

The table read is in a studio in the north of the city. I've been instructed by Mitchell to get there early to meet with the director for my pretend audition—so we can make sure to get our stories of how I landed the part straight, I guess.

After a couple hours' sleep and another run-through of the script, I take the trolley car from outside the hotel and once again several men offer me their seats, and once again I feel slightly comforted by their warmth. I need to soak it up before coming face to face with Conchita again, that's for sure.

The studio turns out to be on a bustling main street, above a bakery. I try not to drool at the array of delicious-looking pastries and cakes on display. I was too nervous to eat breakfast at the hotel, but now my stomach's growling like an angry bear. I press the bell by the door for the studio and wait.

After a few moments, the door opens a crack. I catch a glimpse of a pair of round spectacles perched lopsidedly on top of a long, thin nose.

"Yes?" the owner of the nose says.

"I'm Carmen De La Fuente," I reply, way more confidently than I feel. "I'm here to see Antonio Perez—for the rehearsal."

"I *am* Antonio Perez," he declares dramatically, flinging the door open wider. "Don't just stand there, come in. Come in."

I step into the gloomy entrance and follow him up a narrow flight of steep steps. It's only when we emerge into the light of the studio at the top that I'm able to get a good look at him. He's thin and wiry with wavy, graying hair and flamboyantly dressed in baggy purple corduroy pants and a pink shirt, topped off with a lime-green cravat. His high forehead creases into a frown as he looks me up and down.

"So, you're to play Alba," he says finally.

"Yes." I feel a hot flush of embarrassment at the fact that I haven't had to audition. I know Mitchell said that Antonio was a "friend," but I can't help wondering if he feels resentful at the fact that he had no say in my casting. His dubious expression brings back painful memories of previous failed auditions in Hollywood.

"You're a lot taller than I was imagining."

"Oh." I instinctively slouch my shoulders. "Sorry."

"No, no, that's OK, we could use if for comic effect." He starts nodding enthusiastically and his frown fades.

Seizing upon this glimmer of hope, I feel the desperate urge to prove that I've got what it takes and I'm not just a pair of comically long legs. "I've been rehearsing on my own; perhaps I could read one of the scenes for you?"

"Very well," he says, taking a chair from a table at the far side of the room and positioning it in front of one of the long windows looking out onto the street below. He sits down and crosses his legs and clasps his hands together under his chin, watching me expectantly, his dark eyes as beady and alert as a bird's.

I put down my purse and take off my coat and launch into my character's biggest scene, where she's bemoaning the fact that her beautiful sister has all the luck when it comes to love. When I rehearsed this scene on my own, I came up with the idea of adding in a few choked sobs for effect, hoping to inject the comedy with a little poignancy and give my character more depth. I think of my family and how much I miss them to summon a genuine feeling of sorrow and I feel myself slipping into the character's skin.

When I reach the end of my monologue and come back to myself—or the Carmen version of me, anyways—I see that Antonio is staring at me, completely expressionless. My heart sinks. I hope I haven't messed up by not sticking rigidly to the script.

"That was very interesting," he says finally, pursing his lips. "Very interesting indeed." He starts pacing up and down in front of the windows, hands clasped behind his back. "Yes, yes, I can see this working magnificently. With your intelligence and quirky charm, you will be the perfect foil to your sister's vacuousness and beauty."

"Er, thank you."

"No, thank *you*," he replies, coming over and staring at me intently. "Mitchell is a very good friend of mine so I was happy to do him a favor by casting you, but now I see that he has done me a favor also!"

"I'm so happy to hear that, truly!" I exclaim. "I've never

liked handouts, even as a kid. My grandma always said I was too proud for my own good. But it's better to be proud than to suffer the embarrassment of another's pity, surely?"

"Hmm." He gives me a bemused smile.

The relief I feel is short-lived, however, when I hear the sound of footsteps on the stairs and Conchita sweeps into the room, accompanied by two other women. *Perhaps she won't remember me*, I think to myself as I gaze out of the window at an old woman selling oranges from a stall on the other side of the street. Perhaps what happened last night will be no big deal.

"Good day, Antonio," she says. "What a terrible morning I've had, I—" As she breaks off, I glance at her and, sure enough, she's staring at me. "Who is this?"

"This is Carmen De La Fuente," Antonio replies. "She's playing Alba, your sister."

"Carmen?"

My skin prickles as she spits out my name.

"More like Peeping Tomasita." She scowls at me.

"I don't understand," Antonio looks at me, confused. "Have you met already?"

"I... We... bumped into each other last night, in a bar," I stammer. "I didn't realize who you were though."

She frowns and I instantly want to kick myself. Conchita is famous here in Spain. As a Mexican actress, my alter ego Carmen would surely recognize her. In fact, she would probably idolize her.

"It was so dark—I didn't realize it was you," I add hastily, internally cringing. This is the worst possible start to my undercover role. I'm supposed to be earning Conchita's trust and building a friendship, not making her want to have my guts for garters. "Which makes me feel all the more embarrassed," I continue, "as you are such a role model to me."

"I am?" To my huge relief, appealing to her vanity appears to have paid off and her frown fades. "Yes, well, accidents happen, I suppose." She turns back to Antonio. "Can we get going with the read-through; I have an important lunch date and I can't be late."

My skin erupts in goosebumps as I wonder if she's meeting with a German agent again. Or could it be with the Brit she was with last night? Looks like I'll soon be embarking upon my first proper tail.

Despite the shaky start, the table read goes smoothly and my confidence grows with every scene. I think it helps greatly that my character is the comedy stooge to Conchita's. Seeing her perform, even at a table read, is like watching a flower come into bloom. With every laugh she gets from the rest of the cast, with every word of praise from Antonio, her spine grows taller and the sheen on her skin appears to gleam brighter, until her glow lights up the room.

"Well, that didn't go nearly as badly as I was anticipating," she says once we're done, with a pointed stare in my direction.

"It's an honor to work with you," I murmur, hoping I'm not laying it on too thick. But it would appear that where Conchita's concerned, there's no such thing as too much praise.

She looks at me and smiles—the kind of patronizing smile you'd grant a young child.

"I have to go," she says, putting on her glossy fur coat. "Adios, everyone." And with a wave of her hand, she glides from the room.

I wait a few seconds before saying goodbye to the others and hurrying out after her. When I get out onto the street, I glance both ways, hoping she hasn't jumped into a cab, not that there appear to be many cabs in this town. Thankfully, I glimpse her striding off to my right. I cross the road and start following her. Most of my training at The Farm involved shaking off a tail, not being one, but, really, the same rules apply, simply in reverse. I make sure to hang back far enough so she won't be able to see me reflected behind her in a store window. I've also taken my map book from my purse just in case she turns round suddenly and I can pretend to be engrossed in it, looking for directions. After last night's debacle, I'm determined not to mess up again.

As we approach the Puerta de Alcalá monument, I realize that we're coming back toward the Ritz and I feel a wave of relief. If she does see me now, I can just say that I'm returning to my room at the hotel. Thankfully, there's a park coming up on my side of the road so the trees should provide me with the perfect cover. As I'm weaving my way through them, Conchita suddenly stops outside a building and grinds her cigarette beneath her shoe. I duck behind a tree and peer around the trunk. She glances this way and that, as if checking she isn't being followed, then disappears inside.

I hurry through the park until I'm parallel with the building and my heart thuds. Two huge stone pillars stand either side of the door and flower boxes bursting with life partially obscure windows made of tiny square panes. It would look like a perfectly sweet and harmless establishment if it weren't for the stark black, art deco-style sign on the gray stone above the door: HORCHER. The restaurant Mitchell told me about—the favorite restaurant of the German intelligence and high-ranking Nazis.

January 1941, France

My darling Elena,

I'm sorry to report that things are going from bad to worse here. The Vichy government have now abandoned the Republican slogan of "Liberté, égalité, fraternité" in favor of the distinctly uninspiring "Travail, famille, patrie." There's something so sickening about Pétain so willingly becoming Hitler's puppet, so willingly abandoning our hard-won liberty, equality and fraternity. He's like the kid in the schoolyard who sucks up to the bully. And again I'm reminded of a tale from your childhood. I wonder if you remember it too? You must have been about ten years old and I'd taken you to the beach for the day. We were on our way to get a soda and you saw a young man kicking his dog because it wouldn't stop barking. He was with his friends and none of them did anything to stop him, they just laughed. Before I knew it, you were over there shouting at all of them and calling them "turnip heads" of all things! When I asked you why you called them that, you said you'd been trying to stop yourself from cussing and it was the first thing that came into your mind! You made me so proud that day—even though I was worried you were going to get us into serious trouble! I need to channel some of your righteous indignant spirit now. I feel like I'll go mad if I don't do something, but what?

Ever since I gave Anna the chicken for Christmas, we've become firm friends and I've been taking care of her son, Caleb, when she goes into town to queue for their rations. He's seven years old and a real live wire just like you—you would love him, I'm sure. He already loves you. I've been telling him all about the things you and I used to get up to when you were younger, including the turnip head story, and it's been making me so nostalgic for those days. I don't think I ever told you this, but taking care of you when you were younger helped me just as much as it helped your parents, perhaps even more so. I'd always imagined that if your Grandpa Bob died before me, I'd go to pieces completely, but you gave my life purpose at a time when it felt as if all meaning had gone. Helping Anna with Caleb is doing the same thing now. Teaching him all about the flowers and plants in my garden and the stars in the sky helps me escape the insanity for a while. So I shall keep helping them and thinking of you and dreaming of the day when France will be free again and you shall all finally get to meet each other, God willing.

All my love,

Grand-mère Rose

12

MADRID, 1943

By the time Conchita emerges from the restaurant, the weak winter sun has begun its descent behind the trees and a bitter wind is racing along the boulevard. I've positioned myself on a bench in the park, partially obscured by trees, but giving me a clear line of sight to the restaurant entrance. At first, it seems that Conchita is leaving exactly as she arrived—on her own—and my heart sinks. But then I see a man stepping out behind her. Conchita turns and places her hand on the man's lapel, a sure sign of intimacy. Even from this distance, I can tell that he isn't the man I caught her with last night. He's much shorter for a start and has a thin moustache. They exchange a few words, then Conchita starts heading back the way she came and the man hails a passing cab. When both are safely out of sight, I hurry down the street, back to the welcoming warmth and light of the Ritz Hotel.

"Ah, I have a message for you, Señorita De La Fuente," the clerk on the reception desk informs me. I assume it will be from Mitchell, with instructions on where to meet him next, but it's a handwritten note from Santiago. *Tonight you are cordially invited to dine at the oldest restaurant in the world,* he has written in handwriting perfectly reflecting his personality, bold and full of flamboyant flourishes. *Your tour guide shall pick you up at ten.* I try to suppress the feelings of excitement this causes in me. He might be good company but I've just seen someone he seems to know well dining at Horcher; I definitely don't know if I can trust him.

I head up to my room for a long soak in a warm bath. It's only when I get out of the tub that I notice a small cream envelope tucked beneath the complimentary talcum powder on the dresser. *Usual place, usual time tomorrow, M,* the tiny writing says. Given that Mitchell and I have only been to one place at one time, it's not difficult to crack the code. I hope he'll be pleased with the information I've already gathered. And who knows what tonight with Santiago will bring. It would be good to get a clearer understanding on his connection to Conchita and try to sniff out any German sympathies—from her or from him.

At just after ten, I come down to the lobby to find Santiago standing in front of the elevators, dressed in sharply tailored black pants and a sapphire satin shirt, with a pink rose between his teeth. It's a sight that instantly makes me laugh. He takes the rose from his mouth and presents it to me with a deep bow.

"Señorita, I am honored that you accepted my invitation. I thought you might leave me standing like this all night."

"Now that would have been a sight." I chuckle. "But how could I resist such an invitation? The oldest restaurant in the world is a very intriguing prospect."

"I hope that you found the prospect of an evening with your tour guide a little intriguing too?" he replies, his emerald eyes sparkling.

"Hmm, the trouble with intrigue is that it's so easy to be disappointed."

He laughs. "You are a hard taskmaster, Carmen De La Fuente."

Hearing him say my false name feels slightly unsettling, and a pertinent reminder that I mustn't ever get too relaxed, no matter how entertaining he might be.

"So where is this mysterious place?" I ask as we walk through the lobby. All eyes appear to be magnetized our way, reminding me that Santiago is a pretty big deal here in Spain. The fact that, unlike Conchita, he appears to have remained humble endears him to me, or at least it would, in other circumstances.

"It is about a mile away. Would you like to take a cab there or would you prefer to walk?"

"Let's walk," I say, eager for the chance to explore a little more of Madrid on foot.

He grins. "I'm glad you said that; I like walking with you."

"I like walking with you too," I reply as we make our way out of the hotel. The night sky is pinpricked with stars, like tiny holes in a black velvet curtain.

"You do?" He looks at me hopefully.

"So far, but the night is young," I reply, quickly slipping back into Carmen's wisecracking persona.

"So far, so good, huh." He laughs. "As I told you last night, I like a challenge."

As we walk along the street, I notice that none of the men we pass tip their hat to me or compliment me on my outfit.

"The Spanish men aren't so friendly now I'm with you," I quip.

"What do you mean?"

"Well, every time I've been out on my own, they compliment me on my outfit. But tonight, nothing. Perhaps I shouldn't have worn this dress."

"Let me tell you, there is nothing wrong with that dress," he says firmly. "Over here, it is considered chivalrous to compliment a woman on how she looks. It is a Spanish custom, known as *piropos*. It's very good-natured and harmless, but obviously you don't do it when the woman is with her man."

"But you aren't my man," I reply.

"Not yet, but I can dream, can't I?" he replies, dancing around me as I walk, as light on his feet as a fairy—a very muscular, rugged fairy. It takes everything I've got to ignore the tingle running up my spine and not smile back at him.

"As far as I'm aware, dreaming hasn't been declared illegal," I reply drily.

"Hmm, not yet at least," he mutters.

"What do you mean?"

He glances over his shoulder. "I'm sure it would be, if the Nazis had their way."

Relief washes through me at this development. It would appear that Santiago isn't a fan of the Germans. Of course, it could be a façade and I know that I mustn't show my own hand, so I change the subject instead.

"Are we really going to the oldest restaurant in the world?"

"Yes. Apparently it was founded in 1725."

"What?" I stare at him in disbelief.

"It's true. And not only that, but they serve the most delicious suckling pig."

Suckling? I try to force the image of a sweet, curly-tailed piglet from my mind. "That sounds delicious."

Santiago is such entertaining company that our walk flies by and before I know it, we've arrived at a huge square framed by majestic red-brick buildings, all lined with row upon row of tall windows. At the center of the square, a huge statue of a man on a horse overlooks the people milling about and flickering gas lamps cast everywhere in a magical amber glow. It's so stunning, and so unlike anything I've ever seen in America, it takes my breath away.

"This is the Plaza Mayor," Santiago announces. "It dates

back to the sixteenth century, when it was the main market square for all of Madrid."

"These buildings don't date back that far though, surely," I say, slowly turning in a full circle to take it all in.

"Oh no, these were built after a fire in 1790."

"The height of modernity then." I laugh.

"Exactly. Come." He leads me to a corner of the square, up a set of stone steps worn smooth by centuries of footfall and through an archway onto a narrow street. In marked contrast to the formal splendor of the plaza, the buildings on this street are narrow, brightly painted and ooze a cozy, quirky charm. The air is filled with the sound of music, chatter and laughter and the delicious aroma of food drifting from the many restaurants.

"This is magical," I gasp. And for a moment I forget all about my alter ego Carmen and the damned Nazis and the war and I revel in the feeling of having stepped inside the pages of a fairy-tale.

"Aha!" Santiago exclaims, taking hold of my hands. "There she is!"

"There who is?" I instantly stiffen.

"The real Carmen."

"I don't know what you mean." I pull my hands away, embarrassed.

"I'm sorry, I didn't mean to cause offense." He looks crest-fallen. "I just mean, we all have a joyful child inside of us—the person we were before the world forced us to grow up—and I thought I just caught a glimpse of yours."

Yes, yes, yes! I want to exclaim, thinking back to my job in the diner, and how I felt my true, joyful self slip further from my grasp with every obnoxious customer I served. But I can't let Santiago see the real me. It's too risky. "Yes, well, some of us have had to grow up," I reply curtly, channeling Carmen.

The disappointment I see in his eyes makes me squirm and a sudden wave of exhaustion threatens to overwhelm me. The focus required to keep up the pretense of my new life combined with several nights of restless sleep have left me feeling annoyingly drained. "I'm sorry, I'm very tired. I had my first table read for the show today."

"I see," he replies, but his joyful inner child seems to have vanished without trace. "Well, here it is," he says flatly, pointing to a restaurant. The front has been paneled in golden varnished wood and the sign above the door says: RESTAURANTE SOBRINO DE BOTÍN. It looks warm and homely and very inviting.

"It's lovely," I say softly.

"Do you mean that?" Santiago looks at me intently.

"Yes. And I really appreciate you bringing me here."

"*Excelente!*" he exclaims. Clearly it's impossible to keep his indomitable spirit down for long. "Wait till you see the inside. It's so amazing, it's been featured in several novels."

He ushers me inside and a waiter leads us down some stairs and into a long, tunnel-shaped room with exposed brick walls and a low arched ceiling. The room is lined either side with neatly laid tables topped with gleaming white tablecloths. The waiter takes us to a table at the far end, where a large tapestry hangs on the wall. BOTÍN 1725 has been woven onto it, along with a couple of large pink and white flowers. I take the seat facing out into the restaurant and notice a tiny doorway to my left opening onto a set of steep stone steps descending into darkness.

"The infamous Botín wine cellar," Santiago informs me, following my gaze. "Their Rioja Alta is out of this world. Would you like to join me in sharing a bottle?"

I nod and the waiter heads off down the steps to fetch it.

"I can see exactly why novelists would write about this," I say, taking a moment to drink it all in. About half the tables are occupied, but it's still relatively early for dining in Madrid. "It's fascinating."

Santiago nods in agreement. "I believe Ernest Hemingway put it in two of his novels. He used to love coming here before the war."

I keep a completely deadpan expression—I'm not sure Hemingway would mean all that much to Carmen; I have no idea if he's that big of a deal in Mexico.

"Do you like to read?" Santiago asks.

"Not especially," I say, although the truth is, I love books—I just don't want to be caught out hardly knowing any Mexican authors. "How about you?"

"I am a great fan of Walter Starkie's books—the man you met in the bar last night," he adds when I look blank. Of course I remember Starkie very well, but I don't want Santiago to know that. "He wrote a wonderful book called *Don Gypsy*, all about his travels in Andalusia with his fiddle. That's where I met him for the first time. He was playing his fiddle one night in a bar owned by my uncle. I started dancing along and that was it—" Santiago laughs and his whole face lights up "—a lifelong friendship was formed. He convinced me to come to Madrid— he is the reason for my success."

The waiter reappears at our table with an earthenware jug painted white with pink flowers and I picture a cozy bar in rural Spain, Starkie playing the violin, Santiago dancing, people laughing and clapping. It all sounds so innocent, so much fun. I wonder if we will ever live to see such carefree days again, and my mind darkens.

"Tell me, what are you thinking?" Santiago asks once the waiter has poured us both a glass and taken our food order.

"I was feeling a little wistful, I guess." I smile as I remember a conversation I once had with Maria about how I had a perverse fondness for the feeling of wistfulness. I'm not sure if it's the warmth of the restaurant or the sweet aroma of the wine, but I feel the urge to open up to Santiago some more. "I've always loved feeling wistful."

He looks confused. "Why?"

"Because the longing you feel is caused by missing something beautiful."

I expect him to look even more puzzled at this, but to my delight he nods thoughtfully.

"I think I know what you mean. I feel that way when I think of the mountains back home." We look at each other and smile, and he raises his glass. "To feeling wistful."

I clink my glass to his.

"May I ask what you were feeling wistful for?"

"Happy, carefree times. My home and my family." I take a sip of wine; it's as delicious as it smells, rich and smooth with a hint of cherries. "Mmm," I murmur appreciatively.

"It is good, yes?" Santiago takes a drink. "Hopefully, I can help you feel less wistful while you're here, and we can share some happy times together."

"Thank you. I hope so too." I take another sip of Rioja, trying to ignore the butterflies I feel in my stomach whenever our eyes meet. I mustn't drink too much; I have to remain focused. I have a job to do here. "So, you were saying that Starkie helped you become successful..."

"Yes, he asked me to dance at the British Institute that he runs here in Madrid. Franco's brother-in-law, Serrano Suñer, was at the show and he asked me to dance at his wife's birthday celebrations. He was a government minister back then, so a lot of very important people were at the party—including Franco himself."

"What an opportunity!" I exclaim, but inside I feel sick. Spain might officially be neutral, but there's no denying Franco's sympathies lie with his fellow dictator Hitler. I know from my training that his brother-in-law, Serrano Suñer, supports the Third Reich—he even sent a unit of Spanish volunteers to fight alongside the Germans on the Russian front. I need to find out more. Could Starkie be an agent for the Nazis despite working for the Brits at their institute? Could he be Himmler's agent? Mitchell did warn that it could be anyone. I take another sip of wine. "I'm surprised Suñer would visit the British Institute—didn't he support the Germans against the Russians—or did I just imagine that?" I say, hoping to create the impression that Carmen is not all that well informed about politics.

"Ah yes, but Franco is a fan of Starkie's—in spite of his Romani spirit, they share the same religious and political leanings."

"I see. This wine is delicious," I gush, before taking another sip. I mustn't give away the impact his revelation has had upon me. If Starkie shares the same political leanings as Franco, could Santiago too?

"Wait until the food arrives." His eyes widen. "It is almost as good as..." He breaks off, looking sheepish.

"Almost as good as?" I raise an eyebrow.

"Dancing beneath the light of the moon in the Plaza Mayor," he says quickly.

"I can't say I've ever had that experience."

"Yet," he adds with a grin.

The waiter arrives at our table carrying a silver platter containing a roasted suckling pig surrounded by a bed of golden roast potatoes. He quickly sets to work carving the meat, placing a leg on my plate with some potatoes, over which he drizzles some of the roasting juices. Santiago watches, knife and fork poised, as I take my first mouthful of meat, trying to push the image of a dear, sweet curly-tailed piglet from my mind. It's tender and juicy, salty with a hint of woodsmoke.

"Oh!" I gasp in delight.

"What did I tell you?" He cuts a piece of his own. "Better than moonlight dancing in the Plaza—almost."

"Yes, well, I think I'll have to try that before I can pass judgment," I reply. I'm not sure if it's the wine or the atmosphere, or that I'm becoming increasingly possessed by the spirit of Carmen, but I've never been so boldly flirtatious with a man before. *I'm doing it for my country though,* I reassure myself. Now that I've learned that Santiago has danced for Franco and his Nazi-supporting brother-in-law, I need to find out more. Could he and his friend Starkie both have German sympathies? Could he have been trying to throw me off with his comment about the Nazis earlier?

"Yes, you will," he replies with a smile.

I'm not sure how long we're in the restaurant for; the conversation flows so freely, I lose all track of time. Thankfully, everything we talk about—music, dance, acting and the arts—is safe ground and requires little pretense on my part.

As we finally emerge into the crisp night air, I'm hit by another wistful pang. In ordinary times, this would have been the perfect night, but these are not ordinary times and I can't afford to let my guard slip.

"Look." Santiago points to a half moon hanging in the inky black sky. It has a beautiful pale pink glow. Next to it, a star glints like a diamond. Somewhere on the other side of the Plaza, someone is playing flamenco guitar and the notes dance around us on the air. "And now you must discover if what I told you was the truth."

I look at him questioningly.

"Is Botín's suckling pig better than dancing here beneath the moon," he explains, holding out his hand to me.

"Ah yes." I take his hand and he wraps his other arm around my waist. Although the music is upbeat, we dance slowly, swaying gently, our bodies pulling closer to each other until I feel his lithe hips against mine and our cheeks are gently brushing. His arms feel so strong and safe. If only I could relax fully.

If only the world hadn't gone crazy. Completely unexpectedly my eyes fill with tears.

"So, what do you think?" he asks, pulling away slightly to look at me. "Hey! Why are you crying?" He stops dancing and brings his hand to my face, gently wiping away my tears.

"I'm sorry, I'm being stupid," I say, wanting to kick myself for showing such vulnerability.

"It is never stupid to show your emotions; it is only to stupid hide them," he replies. "Why are you sad?"

"It's just all so... so beautiful," I stammer, unable to find anything witty and Carmen-esque to say.

Santiago nods, his expression grave. "I feel like this also, these days. It's as if any beauty you find comes tinged with sadness."

"Yes."

"But I think that the sadness makes me appreciate the beauty all the more," he continues. "These moments are so special now, to be cherished, no?"

I nod. There's an authenticity in his words, in his gaze, that reaches deep inside of me, beneath the façade of Carmen, beyond my fear, into a place of truth untouched by the war. A gravitational force pulls us closer and closer, until I feel his lips, soft and warm, upon mine.

My darling Elena,

One of the first things the Germans did when they got here was impose a curfew. We are no longer able to go out after nine o'clock at night. Of all their mean-spirited rules, this is the one that gets to me the most. I've always loved walking at night, ever since I was a young girl. There's something so magical about wandering the streets while the world is asleep, especially around here, where the sky is so huge and the moon and stars so bright.

Do you remember the walks you and I used to take at night, and how I'd teach you about the constellations? I remember you once gazing up at the sky and wondering if it was possible to pass a message via the moon if both people were looking at it at the same time. Do you remember that? I thought of it earlier tonight as I sat in the living room staring at the clock, its small hand brushing up against the nine, like a prison guard wagging his finger. My "guest" still hadn't returned. He has dinner at a hotel in town most nights. All of a sudden, the ridiculousness of the situation struck me. Here I was, a grown woman, a prisoner in my own home because of the hands on a clock. It was as if an alien force took over my body and I grabbed my coat and I marched out the front door and down the lane to the place where the town melts away into open fields.

As if in celebration of my act of defiance, a huge full moon lit up the sky and I thought of you, Elena, and I wondered if you were looking at it too. And I sent all of my love up into the moon, and I imagined it beaming back down upon you in America. Then I remembered that you're hours behind us and that by the time the moon is shining on you, I would be back home getting ready to greet another day of German occupation. And in that moment my newfound defiance shrank away to nothing and I scurried back home in the shadows.

All my love,

Grand-mère Rose

13

MADRID, 1943

I wake the next morning cocooned in a warm nest of crisp Ritz bed linen. Memories from the night before start slipping into my mind, like the daylight creeping under the drapes. When Santiago walked me back to the hotel, he was the perfect gentleman, seeing me to the elevator, then kissing me goodnight on the back of my hand. After our night together, I'm almost certain that he can't be working for the Nazis. Beneath his fiery flamenco persona, there's a sweet and sensitive soul, I'm sure of it.

But regardless, I haven't done anything wrong, I reassure myself. *We only shared one kiss.*

"I am not falling in love," I mutter as I get up to go to the bathroom.

The morning's rehearsal goes smoothly; Conchita is in particularly buoyant spirits, and I can't help wondering if this is down to her lunch date yesterday at Horcher. I go over to her before we leave to shower her with praise.

"I feel so honored to be working with you," I gush. "I just

know I'm going to learn so much from you as an actor."

"Yes," she replies crisply, but I notice a flicker of smug delight in her gaze. That's the good thing about vain people; they're always in need of minions to stroke their ego. It's not a role I'd normally consider, but if it helps me expose Conchita as Himmler's spy, it's one I'll gladly perform.

I'm eager to report back to Mitchell and arrive at the Embassy tearoom promptly for our meeting. There's no sign of the owner, Margarita, this time and a waitress shows me to the same table as before, tucked away in the back corner. Mitchell is there already and he greets me warmly.

As soon as we've placed our order for afternoon tea, I fill him in on my invitation to Santiago's party and my discovery of Conchita with the British man, giving as detailed a description of him as possible. Whenever I mention Santiago, I'm careful to be nonchalant and not give away my inner feelings. Then I tell Mitchell about following Conchita to Horcher and describe the man she left with.

"Hmm, sounds like it might have been Hans Lazar," he murmurs thoughtfully. "Horcher is his favorite restaurant."

"Lazar?" I echo, wracking my brains for the reason why the name sounds familiar. "He's the press attaché for the German embassy, right?"

"Oh, he's much more than that," Mitchell replies. "In fact, he could be the most powerful Nazi in all of Madrid."

My pulse quickens. "How so?"

"He's good buddies with Serrano Suñer, who controls the Spanish press."

"Franco's brother-in-law?"

Mitchell nods and I suppress a shudder as I think of Santiago dancing for his wife. Could he have done any more favors for Serrano Suñer, beyond dancing?

"Suñer has given Lazar free rein to plant pro-German propaganda in the press," Mitchell continues. "He has a huge budget for bribing Spanish journalists and employing informants. Our intelligence has shown that he has hundreds of spies working for him here in Madrid. If Conchita was lunching with him yesterday, she could well be one of them."

"So she could be working for Lazar instead of Himmler," I whisper.

"Or as well as," Mitchell replies, leaning in closer to me. "I have to warn you that one of Lazar's informants' main roles is to shadow suspected Allied agents."

Before I'm able to reply, a waitress arrives at our table with the food. In light of Mitchell's revelation, the sight of the silver stand filled with dainty cakes and sandwiches makes me feel queasy. Could Conchita be trained to look out for potential Allied spies—like me?

This way you will feel the whole board. Papa's words echo in my mind, instantly bringing some comfort. *You will see what it is like to be two players at once.* If she is working for Lazar, it's better to be forewarned, I guess.

"I think you should go eat at Horcher sometime soon," Mitchell says once the waitress leaves. "How well did you get on with that dancer, the one who knows Conchita?"

"Pretty well," I say casually, helping myself to one of the delicate, crustless sandwiches.

"Good. See if you can arrange a dinner date with him there. Tell him you've heard that Horcher is one of the finest dining experiences in Madrid and you'd like to try it."

"OK." I stare at my sandwich, feeling slightly sick.

"You will need to be on your guard at all times though—it's effectively the German embassy's unofficial staff canteen. There will be enemy eyes and ears everywhere and there's every chance the place could be bugged."

"What, even at the tables?" I stare at him, shocked.

"Yep."

I take a sip of tea to steady my nerves. "There's someone else who's come to my attention, who might be of interest."

"Oh yes?"

"A guy I met at the party—Walter Starkie. Apparently he runs the British Institute."

Mitchell gives a nod of recognition. "Ah yes, the Irish writer who plays the fiddle."

"That's right. I understand he might have connections to Franco and his brother-in-law."

"Hmm, that isn't always such a bad thing."

"What do you mean?"

"In the current climate, being friends with Franco can bring a certain level of protection."

I stare at him, confused.

"Margarita, the owner of this place, is friends with Serrano Suñer and several other high-ranking Germans."

"What?" I can't help exclaiming. "But why would we...?" I break off.

"Why would we meet here?"

I nod.

"The friendship acts as an insurance policy."

"I don't understand."

"Against the place getting raided. Keep your friends close, keep your enemies closer. You don't need to worry about Starkie —unless, of course, you find cause for concern."

I nod. Could Margarita and Starkie be the greatest chess players of them all? I feel a frisson of excitement as I picture them getting one over on the Germans by pretending to be their friends.

"You've got off to a great start, Flamingo, well done." Mitchell tops up my tea from the pot. "And we've just had a new radio operator arrive, so that should make things a little easier."

I feel a pang of yearning at this news, hoping that it's Betty —not only because she's so excellent on the wireless, but she'd be the closest thing I'd have to a true friend in this place, although I know we wouldn't be able to meet up or even acknowledge each other if our paths did cross. It would just make me feel better knowing there's a friend close by.

Mitchell leans forward again and lowers his voice. "Things are hotting up in France now, so we need to have a clear line of communication for the escape route."

"Escape route?" I whisper back.

"Yes, for any of our personnel who are on the run from the Germans and for Jewish refugees and POWs."

I shiver as I think of the OSS staff stationed in enemy territory. It's hairy enough being in Madrid with the place crawling with Germans; I can't begin to imagine what it must be like to be in the middle of the war zone. Although at least in France it's easier to identify the enemy. I shiver as I think of Grand-mère Rose.

"For now, I want you to focus on getting closer to Conchita Aldana and go to Horcher," Mitchell continues. "See if you can spot Lazar, or any other high-ranking officials. There's a private dining room out back—apparently Himmler's eaten there before."

"Here in Madrid?" I gulp at the thought of Hitler's second in command being here.

"Yes." He raises his teacup as if it's a wine glass. "Here's to catching Himmler's rat."

I clink my cup against his, hoping against hope that my rat-catching won't involve any unwelcome surprises.

I arrive back at the Ritz to another message from Santiago. *I can't stop thinking about you*, the sprawling handwriting reads. I feel a bittersweet mixture of relief and sorrow. The truth is, I haven't stopped thinking about him either, but every time my skin tingles at the memory of us dancing in the square, my stomach lurches at the thought that he could be working for the other side. *Perhaps you would do me the honor of accompanying me...?* the message ends. I look in the envelope and pull out a ticket for a gala screening of the movie *Gone with the Wind*. It's taking place on Friday night, hosted by the American embassy.

I have to fight the urge to skip to the elevators, I'm so darn excited. *Gone with the Wind* is one of my all-time favorite movies, and even though it's being hosted by the Americans, going as Santiago's guest gives me the perfect cover story. I wonder if Conchita will be going too.

Thankfully, our rehearsal ends promptly on Friday, giving me enough time to get back to the Ritz for an appointment at the hotel beauty salon. As I walk through the glass door of the salon, I'm hit by a powerful waft of floral perfume. A woman who looks beautiful enough to be a pin-up model is standing behind the reception desk, speaking on the telephone. Her auburn hair is immaculately styled into thick shiny victory rolls and she's wearing a beautifully fitted jade green dress. The gold bangles on her wrist jingle as she places one hand over the receiver and smiles at me.

I smile back, trying to remain calm and collected, like I'm the type of gal who regularly visits a salon, rather than gets her kid sister to trim her hair in the bathroom.

"Hello, my name's Carmen De La Fuente, I have an appointment."

"Welcome, señorita," she greets me warmly in Spanish but with an accent. "I'm Baroness von Podewils, owner of the salon. Please take a seat. One of my girls will be with you soon." She gestures to a row of gilt-framed chairs upholstered in claret velvet.

"Thank you." I sit down and fold my hands in my lap, concentrating on looking as poised and confident as Carmen surely would.

The baroness turns away and continues her phone call, her voice lowered. I try to tune out the noise from the salon and listen in. She appears to be making plans for a dinner date. Then I hear her slip from speaking in Spanish to another language. It sounds like German. Suddenly, I am on high alert. I strain to hear over the music playing and hear the word "*schatzi*."

Unfortunately, before I'm able to hear any more, one of the beauticians, a young woman with raven hair and thin dark eyebrows, comes over. Like the other beauticians, she's wearing an immaculately pressed white housecoat, with the Ritz insignia embroidered in gold on the breast pocket.

"Carmen?" she says.

"Yes, indeed." I flash her a confident smile, effortlessly slipping back into Carmen's shoes.

"I'm Elisa, I'm going to be doing your hair."

She takes me over to a seat facing away from the reception, but I'm still able to see the baroness in the mirror and I watch as she jots something down, keeping the receiver pressed to her ear.

"It must be quite something having a baroness as a boss," I say to Elisa once she's started work on my hair.

"Hmm," she replies through a mouthful of hairpins. Is it my imagination or does she look distinctly unimpressed?

"Where's she from?" I continue. "It doesn't sound like a Spanish name."

Elisa takes the pins from her mouth and starts putting them in my hair. "It's not—her family are German." Again, she seems noticeably underwhelmed. I make a mental note that Elisa could be a potential recruit to our network. I'll need to get to know her better first. Carmen will have to start making regular appointments at the salon.

"Are you going anywhere nice this evening?" Elisa asks. In the mirror, I see the baroness finish her call and put on a fur coat as black and glossy as ebony.

"Yes, I've been invited to a gala screening of *Gone with the Wind*."

"*Gone with the Wind*?" Elisa sighs. "You're so lucky!" She leans closer and lowers her voice. "I do hope Franco ignores the critics and allows it to go on general release here in Spain."

"What critics?"

"Haven't you seen in the papers? They're saying that it should be banned—that it shows life at its most decadent and immoral."

"I hadn't seen that, no."

As Elisa bends down to get some rollers from a drawer, I notice the baroness approaching in the mirror.

"They're just trying to appease the Germans," Elisa mutters, completely unaware that the baroness is now standing right behind her.

"Who's trying to appease the Germans?" Something about her smile reminds me of a shark about to devour its prey.

Elisa jumps, sending the rollers cascading onto the floor.

"Oh, I didn't see you there, I'm sorry, I-I was just getting some rollers," she stammers, her face flushing bright red.

"I don't think our clients come here to get a lecture in politics, Elisa," the baroness says, her tone now ice-cold.

"No, of course not. I was just talking about *Gone with the Wind*."

I study the baroness's reflection for her reaction. To my surprise, she breaks into what appears to be a genuine smile. "Ah, such a delightful movie!" she exclaims. She looks at me. "Have you seen it?"

"No, not yet," I reply, although the truth is, I saw it four times when it was released in 1939 and still have a framed lobby card of Leslie Howard and Vivien Leigh engaged in a passionate clinch above my bed back at home.

"She's going to see it tonight," Elisa chips in.

"Yes, and as an actress, I cannot wait to see what all the hullabaloo is about," I say with grin.

"You're an actress?" the baroness asks, keeping her gaze firmly upon mine in the mirror.

"I am indeed—all the way from Mexico City."

"That's why I said what I did about the press trying to stop it being shown here," Elisa says, looking at her boss anxiously.

"I see." The baroness keeps looking at me. "You are very lucky to get an invite. I understand the American embassy are hosting the screening. Do you have friends there?"

My skin prickles. Why would she ask me that? Is she making polite conversation, or is she trying to figure out if I have links with the Americans? Or am I simply overthinking things? Better to overthink than to reveal my hand.

"No, señora. I was invited there by a Spaniard, a flamenco dancer by the name of Santiago Lozano—perhaps you've heard of him?"

Again, I study her face for the slightest reaction and I notice a look of surprise, followed by a warm smile.

"I have heard of him, yes," she replies. "Well, you're a very lucky lady indeed." She lifts her hand and glances at the diamond-encrusted watch on her wrist. "I must go. I have an important date of my own. Enjoy your night, Carmen."

"Thank you. I certainly intend to." I flash her a grin.

As I watch her sweep out of the salon, I can't help wondering if she's yet another player in this game of chess. I'm starting to think that everyone in this city is, and that no one at all can be trusted.

14

MADRID, 1943

I decide to wear my most colorful dress to the gala screening, figuring that Carmen would definitely want to wow the crowd. As I look at myself in the wardrobe mirror, I barely recognize the woman gazing back at me. I run my hands over the sky-blue satin clinging to my hips like a second skin. I never would have worn something so revealing in my former life as Elena. But, strangely, this seems to work in my favor as it feels as if I'm wearing a costume and bolsters my confidence.

I spritz myself with Chanel and instantly feel a jab of pain. Mom was right. Every time I wear her perfume, it's as if I conjure her up like a ghostly presence in the scent, and it's as unsettling as it is comforting. I miss my family so much, I've taken to creating an elaborate system of distraction to stop myself from thinking about them by turning multiplication tables into songs.

I come down to the lobby mentally singing the five times table to the tune of "The Star-Spangled Banner" and find Santiago waiting in front of the elevators, his wavy hair gleaming and a white rose between his teeth. As soon as I step from the elevator, he gasps in delight, causing the rose to fall from his mouth. He catches it deftly and hands it to me. As our fingertips brush, I feel a tingling sensation in the pit of my stomach.

"You look even more delicious than a Botín suckling pig!" he declares, causing me to laugh so hard I snort. "And you snort like one too! You are the perfect woman."

I try to ignore the delight fizzing through me as he kisses me on the cheek. It's as if my head has been annexed from the rest of my body—telling me that I mustn't let my guard slip, that I don't know if I can trust him—while the rest of me feels effervescent as champagne in his mere presence. However hard I try to remain as cool as Carmen, his exuberance and enthusiasm for life is infectious.

"I have missed you with a passion!" he announces theatrically. "I cannot concentrate on anything. When I danced today, I made two mistakes. I never make mistakes!"

"Never?" I raise my eyebrows.

"Well, hardly ever." He gives me a bashful grin. "Are you excited for the movie?"

"I'm so excited, I almost made a mistake in rehearsals today."

"Very funny." He grins. "Did you get to see it before? Has it been shown in Mexico?"

This is the question I was dreading him asking as I don't know the answer. "I didn't, sadly," I reply, deliberately keeping my response vague. Thankfully, he doesn't press any further.

"Come, I have a car waiting outside."

The lobby is bustling with well-dressed guests on their way out or to the hotel bar. The women in gowns and pearls, the men in sharply pressed suits, the air filled with a heady mixture of perfume, cologne and cigarillo smoke. Once again, I'm aware of all eyes being drawn to Santiago and some of the women turning envious gazes upon me. A sudden wave of insecurity hits me. I'm only here, walking through this lobby arm-in-arm with this man, because of the war, because I'm playing a role. Santiago is only with me because he thinks I'm Carmen. Antonio only cast me because of Mitchell. Nothing about this existence is real.

"You chariot awaits, my lady," Santiago says, pointing to an old black sedan parked outside the hotel entrance. Like the other cars I've seen in Madrid, the paintwork is peeling and rusty. He opens the back door for me to get in.

A slightly older, thickset man with graying curly hair fills the driver's seat. "Good evening, señorita," he greets me.

"Good evening," I reply, shuffling along so that Santiago can get in beside me. Just like the bodywork, the leathers seats are peeling like sunburned skin.

"This is my driver, Javier," Santiago says as the car moves off.

The driver gives a sarcastic cough and says something in a language I don't understand. Santiago laughs and replies to him in the same language, and I realize that it must be Romani.

"He is actually my cousin," Santiago explains with a sheepish grin. "I asked him to pretend to be my chauffeur, but he always has to be difficult!"

I laugh. "Why did you ask him to pretend?"

"I wanted to impress you."

"Really?" I can't help the word bursting out, even though I know Carmen would never doubt a man trying to impress her.

"Of course. But Javier here can never resist the opportunity to make me look like a fool."

Javier makes eye contact with me in the rearview mirror and grins. I can see the family resemblance in the dimple on his chin. "Would sir like me to serenade you?" he asks before breaking into song.

"I'm so sorry," Santiago says as Javier's serenading grows louder and louder. "This is not how I imagined it to be."

"Don't apologize. I have a feeling this is going to be much more entertaining than whatever you had planned." I laugh.

As the car turns a corner, Santiago's leg slides into mine and I don't move away. The warmth from his body feels comforting and grounding.

The drive to the theater only takes a few minutes, which I'm kind of sad about as it feels so nice to be cocooned in the car next to Santiago, listening to Javier sing. As we pull up behind a line of vehicles, I see that a crowd of people have gathered by the theater entrance and assume they must be guests for the screening. But as soon as Santiago opens the door, I hear angry yells echoing up the street.

"Uh-oh," he says.

"What's wrong?"

"There's some kind of protest going on."

"What do you want me to do?" Javier asks, suddenly serious.

Santiago turns and looks at me. "I think they're protesting about the movie. Some people are saying that it shouldn't be shown. If you like, we could go somewhere else?"

"No," I reply firmly. And, for once, both of my personas are in agreement. The fact that Santiago has invited me to something the German sympathizers don't agree with is an encouraging sign that he can be trusted. Plus, I need to see who else is there. "We can't let a few protestors spoil our fun. It's only a movie," I add to make it clear that I'm not being political.

"That's the spirit!" Santiago gets out of the car and offers me his hand.

"Good luck," Javier says.

"Thank you," I reply. "And thank you for being the most entertaining chauffeur."

"Hmm, I need to be careful that cousin of mine doesn't steal my spotlight," Santiago jokes as I get out of the car.

"I don't think there's much chance of that," I say, linking my arm through his and I get a beaming smile in return.

As we get closer to the theater, the shouts from the crowd grow louder and easier to decipher. I hear a man yelling, "American scum!" and I have to suppress a burst of anger. The fact that these people sympathize with Hitler and call Americans scum beggars belief.

"You OK?" Santiago asks.

I nod and he pulls me closer.

"Don't worry, I will protect you," he says in my ear.

I smile, contemplating the fact that, thanks to William Fairbairn, I now know how to kill someone with my bare hands and could probably protect Santiago better than he could me.

As we reach the steps to the theater, I spot the very same lobby card I have in my bedroom back home, of Leslie Howard and Vivien Leigh embracing.

"It is like us, the other night." Santiago grins, pointing to the picture.

I laugh, then feel something sharp hit the back of my hand. "Ow!"

"What is it?" Santiago stops and looks at me, concerned. The roars of the crowd grow louder.

"Immoral! Corrupt! Ban American propaganda! Heil Hitler!"

I suppress a shudder at the sound of Hitler's name.

"They threw something." I look down and see a nail on the step by my foot. But before I can say any more, something hits me on the face just below my eye. "It's a nail, they're throwing nails!" I exclaim, putting my hand to my stinging cheek. I stare out into the crowd of young men all shouting and jeering. *Which of you did this?* I want to yell, before launching myself at them. But, of course, I can't because I very much doubt Carmen would be an expert in hand-to-hand combat.

Quick as lightning, Santiago switches to my other side, acting like a shield.

"You are the scum!" he yells at the crowd before bustling me inside. "Are you OK?" He cups my face in his hands. "Your cheek, it's bleeding!"

An elderly man in a suit comes hurrying in behind us, nursing the side of his head. "Bunch of assholes," he mutters with an American accent.

"Wait here," Santiago instructs before hurrying over to the ticket desk and talking to a member of staff. He comes back holding a first-aid box. "Come," he says, ushering me to a sofa in the corner. "I am so sorry," he says as he opens the box and takes out a cloth and a bottle of iodine.

"It's not your fault."

"I brought you here."

"Trust me, it takes a lot more than a little shouting to ruffle me." This time I'm not channeling Carmen; my anger is real. If the mob outside really knew what life was like under the Nazis would they still be throwing their nails?

Santiago tenderly dabs the gauze on my face. "It was more than a little shouting; you could have lost your eye."

"But I didn't." Our eyes meet and for a moment all of the background noise seems to fade away.

He clasps his hands around mine. "I'm so glad I met you, Carmen De La Fuente."

"I'm so glad I met you too," I reply softly. And I mean it. His reaction to the protestors was so spontaneous and heartfelt, and the biggest indication yet that he also hates the Nazis, a thought that fills me with relief.

Once we have all filed into the theater and taken our seats, the US ambassador to Spain, Carlton Hayes, goes up onto the stage in front of the screen.

"Good evening and welcome, everyone. We're so glad you could make it to this special screening of one of the greatest movies to come out of Hollywood in recent years." The familiar sound of another American accent warms me to my bones. I sink into my cushioned seat, the tension from earlier draining away.

"I would love to go to Hollywood," Santiago whispers.

"Me too," I reply, suppressing a grin. If only he knew the truth.

The ambassador welcomes the Bishop of Madrid and the Spanish foreign minister, Gómez-Jordana, who are sitting in the front row. "I'm so sorry about the protests outside. I'm afraid the local population has been whipped into a frenzy by certain elements in the press and media."

A rumble of disapproval ripples around the theater.

"But we will not be beaten, or censored." The rumble turns to cheers. "And we are very hopeful that due to its depiction of a country thrown into turmoil by a civil war, Franco will see that this is a movie that will resonate deeply with most Spaniards. So, without further ado, I present to you *Gone with the Wind!*"

The lights go down and the word OVERTURE over a crimson sky appears on the screen. I feel giddy with excitement as the sweeping orchestral music builds. I think back to the first time I saw the movie, and how I had wished it was my name instead of Vivien Leigh's in the list of players. Now as I see her name appear, I can't help smiling. I might not be performing on the silver screen alongside the likes of Clark Gable and Leslie Howard, but the role fate has cast me in is even more exciting. I glance at Santiago; he's staring at the screen, mesmerized.

Watching Scarlett, Melanie, Rhett and Ashley is like being reunited with old friends, but certain elements of the story affect me differently now that I'm personally involved in a war. The scene where the men all run off excitedly to enlist sends a shiver down my spine and when Leslie Howard utters his line about most of the miseries of the world being caused by wars, the silence in the theater thickens and my eyes become moist with tears. When Scarlett delivers her final rousing line before the intermission, it resonates deep within me.

"As God is my witness, they're not going to lick me!" Her determined cry rings around the theater. "I'm going to live through this."

It feels as if the words are etching themselves into my heart. *I'm going to live through this, goddammit! And I'm going to love my fear, seek the wonder and embrace the mystery!*

The houselights come up and the word INTERMISSION appears on the screen and the audience bursts into spontaneous applause. I look at Santiago and see that his eyes are also shiny with tears.

"I'm not crying," he whispers defiantly, wiping his eyes.

I smile. Maybe it's because I have such an emotional father, but I've never seen a man's tears as a sign of weakness, I see them as a sign of his humanity, and at this point in time, seeing Santiago moved to tears is a very reassuring thing.

We weave our way out of the auditorium, through the crowded corridor and into the bar. It's thronging with people, and judging by the animated nature of the chatter, they're clearly all enjoying the show.

"What do you think of it so far?" Santiago asks, once he's ordered us martinis.

"I love it! The acting is sublime, and the story is so powerful. Oh to play a role like Scarlett O'Hara!" I reply, reminding myself that as far as he's concerned this is the first time I've seen it. "How about you? Did you love it too?" I look at him hopefully. Even though I know I shouldn't care, it feels really important to me that he likes it, as if it's some kind of critical test of character.

"It's fantastic. The depiction of the civil war is very realistic." He sighs. "War can be so brutal."

"Of course, you've lived through a civil war here," I say, eager for a chance to find out more about his political leanings.

The sparkle leaves his eyes. "Yes, and I never want to see my country brought to its knees like that again. Although, if the rumors are true and the Germans invade Spain, it could all start up again."

My heart skips a beat. "Do you think they will invade?"

"It's what they're saying."

Before I can ask him more about the "they" he's referring to, I hear a familiar woman's voice calling his name and my heart sinks. I turn to see Conchita sashaying her way over, the crowd parting like the Red Sea to let her through, all eyes upon her. And it's not hard to see why. She's a vision in her coral satin dress and matching high-heeled shoes. Her long black hair hangs loose in waves down her back, a coral fabric flower pinned above one ear. The closer she gets, the smaller and plainer I feel. It's as if she's sucking all the light from the room to form a halo around her.

"I didn't know you were going to be here tonight," she says, looking straight at Santiago and completely ignoring me.

"Yes, well, life is full of surprises," he mutters.

"It is indeed." She turns to look pointedly at me. "Anyone would think you were following me, Carmen. Every time I turn around, there you are."

It takes everything I've got not to show my alarm at this. Surely she couldn't have seen me the other day when I followed her to Horcher. I smile at her coolly, not wanting to appear defensive by replying.

Thankfully, she turns back to Santiago, leaning in so close, I catch a waft of her cloying perfume. "You and I need to talk," she murmurs and all of the warmth I've been feeling toward him evaporates. I look around the bar, pretending not to be interested, my ears straining to pick up his response.

"I'm sure I'll see you around sometime soon," he mutters.

As I scan the room, I do a double take as I notice a man standing at the bar with his back to me. There's something strangely familiar about his broad shoulders and slicked-back blond hair. Could it be...? He takes his drink from the bartender and turns and for a moment our eyes meet and a bolt of shock passes through me. It's Teddy. I see the faintest flicker of recognition in his eyes before he turns away. So he must be the new radio operator. My heart sinks and I quickly turn back to Conchita and Santiago.

"You'll have to come and collect the watch you left in my apartment," she says to Santiago loudly and, I can't help thinking, for my benefit. My stomach clenches. Why would he have left his watch in her apartment?

Conchita turns on her heel and the sea of people parts once more for her to sweep through.

"I'm very sorry for that interruption," Santiago says, looking flustered.

"Don't mention it," I reply coolly.

"It... it isn't what it seems," he stammers, not realizing that this only makes matters worse. If he hasn't been romantically involved with Conchita, it means he could be working with her for the Germans. Either way, my trust in him has ebbed once again.

"Shall we go back to the auditorium?" I say. "It's a bit too crowded in here for my liking." I place my drink down and turn to go, slipping back into my Carmen persona like it's a suit of armor.

December 1941, France

My darling Elena,

I just heard that America have joined the war! Of course I'm heartbroken at the thought of all the souls who perished at Pearl Harbor, but maybe this will hasten the end of this terrible time. For the past few months, I'd become so despondent. I'd even stopped writing these secret letters to you. It's awful to admit, but I'd started giving up hope that you'd ever get to read them, and that we'd ever be free again. But now, with the might of the American forces joining the Allies, surely there's a chance. I'm just so relieved that you and your sister are girls and you won't be called up to fight. The fact that you're free to get on with your lives is my one shining light in the darkness of this occupation. I wonder if you've had any exciting acting roles lately. I pray that you're not still serving people bacon and eggs in that diner! I'm sure you must be making a living as an actress by now, you are so talented.

Women in France have been told that they can no longer wear trousers or smoke, or do anything that makes them in any way like a man. According to Pétain, a French woman's sole purpose now is to reproduce. I'm so glad my childbearing days are long behind me; these rules would have driven me mad and I dread to think what you would make of them!

I'm still minding Caleb for Anna and he now regularly asks me for an "Elena adventure" as he calls them. I've had to start making some up, the way I used to make up stories about you when you were little. Do you remember the adventures I'd send you on at bedtime?

They were all set in Paris if I remember correctly. I think I was trying to make you fall in love with my country before you'd even set foot here, so you'd want to visit when you were older. But the thought of you coming to France now makes me want to weep. It's as if the Germans marched in like a giant eraser and stripped it of all color. I pray for the day that freedom and joy return to our country. And now, thanks to today's news, I can dare to believe that my prayers might actually be answered.

All my love,

Grand-mère Rose

15

MADRID, 1943

"I need you to go to Barcelona for me," Mitchell says as we make our way through the sunlit park. It's late February and the wind sweeping down from the mountains has lost its bite, the trees are alive with orange blossom and the air is heady with their perfume.

"Barcelona?" I echo, feeling a mixture of nerves and excitement. This will be the first time I've left Madrid in the six weeks I've been here.

"Yes. I need you to courier some maps to one of our contacts there."

"OK." The words "HOLY COW!" imprint themselves on my mind, big and bold like "THE END" on a movie screen. My work here has just shifted up a gear and I'm glad of it. I'm longing to do something more useful than go to parties and rehearse the play. In spite of my nausea-inducing attempts at appealing to her vanity, my friendship with Conchita is not progressing nearly as fast as I would have liked.

"The maps show safe houses on the escape route through Spain. They're concealed in these playing cards." He glances up and down the path to make sure the coast is clear before taking a deck of cards from his jacket pocket and handing them to me. I slip them into my purse.

"How are the maps concealed?" I ask, hoping that they aren't simply tucked inside the deck and easy to find if I happen to be searched.

"They're inside the cards themselves. As soon as you submerge them in water, you can peel off the fronts to reveal the map beneath."

"Ingenious!"

"Indeed." He takes an envelope from his pocket and passes it to me. "You're to take the train to Barcelona—here are your tickets. Once you get there, you need to go to Basilica de Santa Maria del Mar—one of Barcelona's oldest churches—where your contact will meet you."

"How will I know it's them?" I ask, slipping the envelope into my coat pocket.

"You're to sit on the back pew and pretend to pray. Your contact will come sit beside you and drop their prayer book on the floor. You're to reach down to get it and return it to them with the cards, then leave straight away without saying a word."

"Got it." I give him what I hope is a smile beaming with confidence. "Don't worry, those maps will be safe with me."

"They'd better, or a hell of a lot of lives could be in danger," Mitchell replies tersely as we follow the path past a waterless fountain. A couple of little kids have jumped inside and are playing chase around the statue in the middle. My mouth goes dry as I think of the cards in my purse and all the brave lives they represent. My resolve hardens. There's no way I'm going to fail in this mission. "Are you still seeing the flamenco dancer?" Mitchell asks.

"I'm still in touch with him, yes," I reply. It's been almost four weeks since I last saw Santiago at the movie gala. Since then, I've been studiously ignoring the messages he's left for me at the Ritz reception. When he called my room yesterday, I told him I was too tired to go out due to the long rehearsals, which wasn't exactly a lie; Antonio has been working us like dogs to get us ready for next week's opening night.

"Excellent."

"I think he's connected to Conchita Aldana in some way," I say, trying to ignore the feelings of disappointment this still creates in me.

"Really? In what way?"

"I'm not sure. It could have been romantic. He's certainly been to her apartment."

Mitchell laughs drily. "By all accounts, so has half of Madrid—the male half anyways."

I'm not sure if this is any consolation. Even if they only had a fleeting affair, the fact that Santiago would choose to be with someone like Conchita is hardly a glowing reflection of his character. Perhaps he had me fooled and is just as vain and shallow as she is. Ever since the gala screening, I've been plagued with thoughts of him seducing her with the same lines he used on me and it's made me sick to my stomach.

"I want you to get closer to him," Mitchell continues. "See if you can find out more about her through him."

"OK." *Go away!* I silently yell as an image of Santiago dancing with Conchita in the moonlight, a rose between his teeth, pops into my head.

"Excellent. So, anything else to report?"

"Yes, I might have found a potential recruit for you in the beauty salon at the Ritz. A local named Elisa. She's shown definite anti-German sentiment several times when she's styled my hair."

"Elisa," Mitchell echoes. "Good. I'll send one of our other contacts into the salon to try to get to know her."

"You don't want me to do it?"

He shakes his head. "I don't want to risk blowing your cover."

"OK. I don't suppose you know anything about the woman who owns the salon?"

He shakes his head.

"She's a baroness apparently, German origin. I'm going to keep an eye on her."

"Good work." He stops walking and smiles at me. "And good luck in Barcelona. I'll be in touch the day after to find out how you get on."

"Thank you." As he leaves, I look after him wistfully. Mitchell's the closest thing I've got to a friend in this place, the only person I know I can trust. I wish our meetings didn't have to be so fleeting, especially now I've been given such a high-risk mission.

Love your fear. Grand-mère Rose's beautiful lilting voice rings through my mind, and I picture giving my fearful self a hug before turning and heading off.

I decide to call in at a boutique called Eisa to buy some new dresses on my way back to the Ritz. According to Elisa, the boutique is *the* place to go in Madrid for fashion—and not just because it has practically the same name as hers. The clothes in Eisa are made by a designer named Cristóbal Balenciaga, who has been causing quite a splash in Paris.

As the assistant helps me try on various beautiful creations in rich shades of brown and bright magenta, it's like I'm having a costume fitting for Carmen and I feel a renewed enthusiasm for the role. I'm even able to see a silver lining in what's happened with Santiago as my disappointment hardens into a determination to find out exactly who is working for Himmler.

I emerge from the store an hour later laden with bags containing beautiful Balenciaga creations—a fitted dress in coffee-colored velvet decorated with black brocade, and a bright pink affair with black satin leaves adorning the shoulders. Elisa was right, his dresses are like wearing works of art.

As I approach the entrance of the Ritz, a bellboy who had been standing sentry-like by the door springs into action, whisking my bags from my hands.

"Thank you," I say, looking in my purse for some money to tip him.

"You are welcome," he replies. There's something strangely familiar about his voice. I look up, but he's already marching ahead of me across the lobby.

Surely I must be mistaken. I hurry after him and tap him on the shoulder. He turns and looks at me and I see those familiar green eyes twinkling beneath the bellboy's cap.

"What are you doing?" I hiss, unable to stop myself from laughing in spite of my intentions to be as cold as the iceberg that did for the *Titanic*.

"Trying to get your attention," Santiago replies with a mischievous grin. He takes off his hat and his dark curls tumble free.

"Well, you certainly did that," I reply, shaking my head.

"How fortuitous," he says, glancing at my bags.

"What is?"

"That you should buy a new outfit on the day I'm taking you out."

Hmm, or that you should show up on the day I've been told to see more of you, I think to myself wryly. "And is that how you will be dressed to accompany me?" I reply, eyeing his burgundy bellboy's uniform. I guess when you're the most popular flamenco dancer in Madrid it's possible to acquire anything.

"I think it suits me." He studies his reflection in the mirrored wall between the elevators. "It really accentuates my eyes, don't you think?" He pouts and pulls a ridiculous pose.

The elevator door pings open and a man walks out catching Santiago mid-pout.

"Good afternoon, sir, have a wonderful day!" Santiago calls after him. Then he turns back to me, dropping down to one knee. "So, will you?"

"You look as if you're proposing marriage," I say, trying not to laugh. A couple of women in the lobby notice and gaze at us, open-mouthed.

"Please, I beg of you, say yes!" Santiago cries, playing to the crowd.

"*Madre mía!*" I exclaim. "If it means an end to this fiasco, yes!"

"She said yes!" Santiago cries before leaping to his feet and kissing my hand. "I shall meet you at this exact spot in an hour."

"OK, but only because I have absolutely nothing better to do."

"Of course you have nothing better to do than see me!" He throws his bellboy's hat in the air and dances off.

As I step into the elevator, I have to battle every muscle in my face to stop it from grinning. There's no way I'm going to be fooled by Santiago again. Why does my body have to be such a traitor?

"So, where are you taking me?" I ask as Santiago and I make our way out of the hotel and on to the Plaza de la Lealtad an hour later.

"I am taking you to see the oldest tree in Madrid, then we shall get something to eat."

"First the oldest restaurant in the world, now the oldest tree in Madrid—what is it with you and antiquities?" I quip.

"I am a great fan of history," he replies, his expression suddenly growing serious. "I like to be reminded that so much has happened before we were here. It reminds me to make the most of the present moment, for, one day, it will be history too."

"I like that." I nod. I wonder how history will remember the war. I wonder if, in years to come, people will know what went on here in Madrid—about the high-stakes chess game that was played out in its bars and restaurants and on these streets—or if it will only be a footnote.

Santiago stops walking. "Thank you," he says softly.

"What for?"

"For giving me another chance. I was starting to lose hope." He looks so genuine, but I know now that the best chess players can smile sweetly before delivering a deadly move.

"I'm sorry I didn't reply to your messages," I reply briskly, firmly in Carmen's character. "I've been very busy."

"As long as that's the real reason." He looks at me questioningly. "I thought I might have done something to upset you."

I shake my head. "Not at all."

He offers me his arm and I tuck mine through it. We continue walking on to Calle de Alfonso XII and the park where I now meet Mitchell comes into view.

"The Parque del Buen Retiro," he announces.

"It looks lovely," I say, as if I've never set foot in it before. Still, this is a promising development. If he's taking me to the park, I could suggest we go eat in Horcher as it's just across the street.

"It's been here since the seventeenth century." He smiles down at me. "Doesn't it make you wonder at the sights these trees must have seen?"

I think of myself hiding behind one of them just a few weeks ago, when I was spying on Conchita, and nod.

"Let's walk around the lake first," he says, leading me along one of the tree-lined paths.

The lake is a large rectangular affair. Every so often, we come across someone performing—singing, playing the fiddle, juggling—and every time, Santiago reaches into his pocket for some money to throw into their hat. *Don't be taken in by his generosity,* my inner voice of Carmen warns me. *It's probably just a cunning ploy to make you fall for him.*

Once we've walked around the lake, Santiago leads me through the trees until we reach one with a trunk as thick as four barrels. A few feet up, it splits into about eight other narrower trunks, all reaching for the sky, long thin leaves trailing down from the branches like ticker tape.

"Ta-da!" Santiago exclaims, presenting it to me with a flourish.

"It's beautiful," I gasp, too moved by the extraordinary structure of the tree to maintain my cool façade.

"According to legend, it's almost four hundred years old," he tells me. "Apparently the French troops chopped down all the other trees for wood during the Napoleonic invasion, but they spared this one as it was big enough to hide an artillery weapon."

"It's big enough to hide a tank!" I reach for one of the long thin leaves and allow it to caress my fingertips.

"And, of course, it is an ahuehuete." He looks at me expectantly and I shrug.

"An ahuehuete," he says again.

"I'm sorry, I don't know what you mean."

"The national tree of Mexico." He frowns.

Damn! I had no idea. "Of course. I'm sorry, I misheard you," I stammer. I feel my face flushing and quickly turn away to gaze at the gnarly trunk. "It's so nice to be reminded of home."

"I guess you must have a lot of them there," he says.

"Yes," I reply, hoping he isn't trying to catch me out.

"And you must know about the origin of the name?"

Why is he asking all these questions?

"The name?" I echo, praying that he'll answer it for me.

"Yes, what it means."

"I remember my father once telling me, but I'm afraid I've forgotten." I turn back and see that he's still frowning.

"Old man of the water," he says.

"Ah, of course," I say. "Well, this one really is an old man." I place my hand on the trunk to try to calm my pounding heart. "Thank you so much for bringing me to see it. Perhaps we could go for some lunch now? I'm really hungry."

"Of course." *Why is he still frowning?*

"There's a restaurant I've been hearing very good things about; I think it's near to here."

"Oh yes?"

"It's called Horcher. It's supposed to be one of the best in the city." I note that his frown has deepened.

"Horcher, oh, I'm not so sure—"

"Please," I cut in. Why does he look so unimpressed at the thought of dining at the Germans' favorite restaurant? Is it because he hates them? Or is it because he works for them and doesn't want me finding out?

"Well, if you insist." He offers me his arm and we walk on in silence. If only life were like a comic strip and I was able to read his thoughts in a bubble over his head.

As we walk into the restaurant and the maître d' comes over to greet us, I watch like a hawk, looking for any sign that Santiago is known here, but there appears to be no flicker of recognition on either part. As the maître d' leads us through to the restaurant, I can't help shivering as Mitchell's words come back to me: *It's effectively the German embassy's unofficial staff canteen.* With its high ceilings, fern-green velvet drapes and soft lighting, it's far more elegant than any staff canteen I've ever seen. I glance around at the men in suits populating the round tables, deep in conversation, and sure enough, all I can hear is German being spoken.

The maître d' shows us to a table in the corner and I quickly slip into the seat with the best view of the restaurant. I take off my coat and notice Santiago glance appraisingly at my new dress.

As soon as I sit down, a waiter appears at my side holding a cushion. "For your feet, señorita," he explains before crouching down and placing it on the floor by me as a footrest.

I look at Santiago and raise my eyebrows.

"The best service in all of Madrid," he says. Is it my imagination or is there a hint of sarcasm in his voice?

"Have you been here before? What would you recommend?" I ask casually as I look at the menu, wondering if he will give away the fact that he's a regular here by having a favorite. But he simply shrugs.

I order something called *Kartoffelpuffer*—potato pancakes with fermented herring in a cream sauce.

"I will have the same," Santiago says to the waiter. He definitely seems deflated since we arrived here.

"Somebody told me that eating here was as close to heaven as man can hope to get," I say, again waiting for his reaction.

"Hmm," is his only response.

The waiter returns with our drinks and I see the maître d' leading a much shorter man through the restaurant toward us. Could it be...? I lean slightly to the side to get a better look. He has the same thin moustache and slicked-back hair as the man I saw with Conchita the day I followed her. Could it be Hans Lazar? My stomach churns at the thought of being so close to the man Mitchell described as the most powerful Nazi in Spain with a direct line to Himmler.

As they draw closer, the man says something to the maître d' in German, and even though Santiago has his back to them, I notice that he tenses slightly. As they draw level with our table, the man glances down at me and for a moment our eyes meet and a chill runs right through me. I don't know if it's the coldness in his gaze or the dark shadows beneath his eyes, but I feel certain that I'm looking right at Spain's most powerful Nazi.

He tips his hat slightly in greeting, then glances down at Santiago and I see a flicker of recognition in his eyes. He doesn't say anything though and they pass by and through a door at the back. Could it be the private meeting room Mitchell told me about? The one Himmler dined in when he last visited Madrid in 1941.

I glance back at Santiago. He's fiddling with the edge of his napkin, all trace of his normal carefree self gone.

"Are you OK?" I ask softly.

"Yes, fine," he replies tersely.

I watch as a waiter glides past us carrying a tray with four drinks and through the door at the back. So there are already three other people in there. I wonder if I'll be able to get Santiago to stay here until they leave so I can get eyes on the others. Something tells me it will be quite a task, unless I can get him to relax.

"I'm so glad I met you," I say, leaning in closer.

I see a spark of happiness in his eyes. "You are?"

"Yes. It's tough being so far from home, in a city where I have no friends or family..." This part at least, is true. "Thank you for making me feel so welcome—and for taking me to see so many very old things."

He laughs and the old light returns to his face. "You are very welcome. You have also made my life a lot brighter."

His words seem so authentic and heartfelt, it's hard for me not to feel warm toward him in response, but I mustn't, I remind myself. Not with so many questions surrounding his connection to Conchita.

"I'm sure your life was full of brightness before I came along," I joke, hoping he might open up to me a little.

He shakes his head and sighs.

"What?" I ask softly.

One of the men at the table closest to us laughs and shouts something in German at his companion.

Santiago glances around the place uneasily. "Yes, I am very lucky. I have a very glamorous and exciting life," he says, but there's a despondency to his tone, as if he's delivering a line rather than speaking from the heart. I fight the instinct to reach across the table and take hold of his hand. "So, tell me more about yourself," he says. "Tell me more about Mexico."

I take a sip of my gin fizz and launch into Carmen's backstory, hoping it will make up for my faux pas over the tree.

Midway through our lunch, I see a waiter heading toward us carrying a tray laden with food. He must be taking it into the private dining room. I need to get a glimpse inside.

"I just need to visit the restroom," I mumble through a mouthful of food.

"Oh—OK." Santiago looks at me in surprise as I stand up, almost tripping on my footrest in my haste.

I follow the waiter to the back of the restaurant as he's knocking on the private door. As he waits, I stop behind him, take my compact from my purse and drop it on the floor. As I bend down to pick it up, the door opens and I glance over. A haze of cigarette smoke hangs over a table where three men are seated. The man I'm convinced is Lazar has opened the door and once again our eyes meet. I quickly pick up my compact and start walking toward the ladies' room.

"*Hola*," he says with a German accent.

I stop and turn, my heart thudding, hoping he's talking to the waiter, but his cold, dead eyes are looking straight at me.

"*Hola*," I reply with a calm smile that belies the adrenalin coursing through my body.

"I don't believe we've met before."

"I don't think so, no." *What would Carmen do?* I step forward and offer my hand. "I'm Carmen De La Fuente."

"What a beautiful name," he says, his tone as cold as his

gaze. Paranoia sweeps through me. He takes my hand and shakes it. His palm is clammy. "Hans Lazar. Nice to meet you."

My mouth goes dry. "And you. What a wonderful restaurant this is."

He smiles, but it doesn't reach his eyes. "Yes, the finest in all Madrid. I'd better get back to my meeting. Give my regards to Mr. Lozano."

My stomach lurches, but I manage to maintain my composure. "You know each other?" I force a delighted smile.

"We're acquaintances, yes."

"How lovely. Perhaps you could join us for a drink after your meeting?" I glance back into the room; the other men are talking in hushed tones as the waiter places their food on the table in front of them.

"I doubt I'll have time today. Maybe next time."

"Of course. Enjoy your lunch." I turn and head into the restroom, lock myself in one of the cubicles and press my face against the cool tiled wall. I've just met Hans Lazar. And he knows Santiago.

16

MADRID, 1943

I return to the table with a new steely resolve. While I was in the restroom, I took a moment to view the chessboard from every angle. Knowing that Santiago is in some way connected to Conchita was one thing, but his being acquainted with Lazar takes this game to a dangerous new level. My next moves are critical. I need to find out more.

"Is everything all right?" Santiago asks as I sit down. I notice that he's hardly touched his food.

"Yes, sorry, I ran into an acquaintance of yours." I smile gaily. "Hans something ... Lazar, I think he said." I keep my gaze fixed on Santiago and notice that he gulps.

"What did he say?" There's an urgency in his voice.

"Just that he sends his regards." I take a sip of my drink. "How do you know him?"

"How I know just about everyone in this city—through my dancing," he replies casually before knocking back half of his drink in one gulp. He starts tapping the edge of the table with his long fingers. "And speaking of which, I have to go soon. I need to take a siesta before my show tonight."

"Of course." I fight to hide my disappointment. It would

have been good to see the two men meet, although, by the sounds of things, Lazar isn't going to be out of his meeting anytime soon.

As soon as we finish eating, Santiago pays the bill and we leave.

"Are you OK?" I ask as he strides off along the street. "You seem a little subdued."

He stops walking and looks at the ground, scuffing the toe of his shoe on the dusty sidewalk. "I..." He breaks off and sighs. "Do you ever wish for a simpler life?"

"What do you mean?" I ask, wanting him to lead this conversation.

"When I was a child, I dreamed of escaping the poverty I grew up in. When Walter asked me to come to Madrid with him, I didn't think twice, but now..."

"Now?" I nudge gently.

He frowns. "Now I see that riches and fame, they come with a new set of complications."

I nod knowingly while trying to analyze what he's just said. Could one of the "complications" he's referring to be working with the Germans?

"What sort of complications?" I probe.

He looks at me searchingly and for a moment I think he's going to say something, but the moment passes and he grins instead. "Enough of this melancholy talk. Let's get you back to the hotel."

When we arrive back at the Ritz, Santiago walks me into the lobby.

"I have tickets for the bullfight this Sunday and I would very much like to take you, if you would like?" He looks at me hopefully.

"I would like that, thank you." The prospect of watching a bull and a human battle it out till the death isn't exactly appealing but now that I know Santiago is connected to Lazar, I have to try and find out more.

Santiago smiles, but his eyes are still tinged with sadness.

We say goodbye and I make my way over to the elevators where I see the baroness deep in conversation with a Japanese man in a business suit. I think of Pearl Harbor and all the lives lost there and shudder.

I'm here to help win a war, I mustn't allow my emotions to come into it, I remind myself. *If Santiago is working for the Germans, then he's no different to those Japanese bombers.*

The following morning I have no need for the six o'clock alarm I'd set on my travel clock for my trip to Barcelona. I woke in a cold sweat from a nightmare at three and I've lain staring at the ceiling ever since. In my dream, Santiago and I were dining at Horcher and I realized that our waiter was Adolf Hitler. When we tried to leave, the door was locked and I discovered that all of the diners around us were in fact Lazar's spies and we'd been lured into a trap. Then Hitler greeted Santiago like they were old buddies and I realized that my worst fears were correct and he was one of them.

I turn the alarm off and try to comfort myself with thoughts of my family back home in LA. But picturing Mom and Papa and Maria all together without me only makes me feel more anxious and sad, so I sing my seven times table to the tune of "Minnie the Moocher" and think of Grand-mère Rose instead. I wonder what she'd think if she knew I was in Europe. I hope she'd be comforted by the thought.

"Don't worry, Grand-mère Rose," I whisper into the early dawn light, "I'm going to help save you."

Feeling emboldened by my vow, I go through to the bathroom and start running a bath. While the tub is filling, I come back into the bedroom and take the hatbox from the wardrobe. I remove the pack of playing cards from the secret lining in the bottom and brush my fingers over the cold metal of the pistol. I know I shouldn't take it with me to Barcelona, but I'm sorely tempted. This is the first time I'll have acted as a courier and I know from my training that this puts me at a significant risk of capture.

In the end, I leave the pistol in its hiding place but I take one of the cyanide capsules from the glass bottle I was given upon completion of my training and tuck it into the hiding place in the heel of my shoe. I try not to think about why I might need it.

Once I'm ready, I decide to walk to the station to calm my nerves and mentally rehearse a cover story in case I get stopped and questioned by the Spanish authorities at any point. *I, Carmen De La Fuente, Mexican actress new to Spain, am taking advantage of a rare day off to do some sightseeing.* It's a straightforward and believable story so I've no real need to be nervous. Maybe it's meeting Lazar yesterday and my subsequent nightmare that's gotten me so jittery.

I stop and pretend to look for something in my purse to check I'm not being followed. A middle-aged couple walk past, smiling, and the man tips his hat in greeting. Their friendliness reassures me and I continue on my way.

I arrive at Atocha Station feeling slightly calmer, the rhythmic motion of walking having soothed my anxiety. As I stare up at the grand red-brick façade, I'm once again awestruck by the sense of history seeping from every crevice. The old-fashioned gas lamps flicker amber against a sky thick with cloud.

Inside the station, people are buzzing around like bees in a hive. It reminds me of Washington Union Station and I marvel at how much has happened since my introduction to the world of the OSS. I locate the platform for the Barcelona train and show my ticket to the conductor, breathing a sigh of relief as he waves me on board.

My compartment is empty and I settle back in my seat by the window. The journey to Barcelona takes over three hours. It will be nice to see some more of the Spanish countryside. I hear the sound of the train doors being slammed shut and a piercing whistle cuts through the air. I hope the compartment remains empty; I could do with a little space to mentally prepare for the drop. But just as the train starts juddering forwards, the door opens and the conductor appears, showing two men inside.

"*Danke*," one of the men says, causing a shiver to run up my spine.

The men sit down opposite me and nod in greeting.

"*Hola!*" I say cheerily, opening my purse and taking out a book.

They both say hello and then, once the train starts chugging out of the station, they start talking to each other in German. Still pretending to read, I listen intently, trying to pick up any recognizable words from the basic training I received at The Farm.

The train has just left the city and is carving its way through the muted browns and greens of the countryside when the door to the compartment opens once more and two Spanish policemen come in.

"Hello, we are conducting a search," one of them announces, looking straight at me. "Please can we check your bags?"

My heart beats so violently I can hear the blood pulsing in my ears.

There's nothing to worry about, I try to reassure myself. *The playing cards look completely innocent. Unless, of course, they know that cards are being used to pass messages.*

Calling upon all of my acting skills, I smile up at them and nonchalantly hand them my purse.

"Terrible weather," one of them says, looking out the window, while the other begins placing the contents of my bag on the seat beside me. I'm acutely aware of the Germans opposite watching. *Is this a set-up? Did they follow me onto the train?*

I focus on breathing deep and slow, trying not to think about the fact that in Spain espionage is a capital offense.

The policeman takes out the pack of playing cards and turns them over in his hand. The Germans are still watching his every move and my skin erupts in a clammy sweat. After what feels like forever, the policeman places the cards on top of the rest of the contents of my purse, then he gives me a warm smile.

"Thank you very much, señorita, sorry for the intrusion."

"No problem at all," I reply.

I wait for them to check the Germans' cases, but they just exchange a few pleasantries, then bid them good day and leave. Another reminder that although Spain might officially be neutral in the war, it's far from it.

I'm about to put the playing cards back in my purse when one of the men gestures at me.

"Excuse me, are those playing cards?" he says in perfect Spanish.

My heart practically stops beating. "Yes."

"I don't suppose we could borrow them, could we?" He smiles at me.

"Borrow them?" My mouth's so dry I'm barely able to speak.

"Yes." He turns to his companion. "What do you say, Johan, fancy a game of poker?"

Johan nods enthusiastically.

The man looks back at me. With his chiseled jaw and athletic frame, he could be classed as conventionally handsome, but his blue eyes are a little too pale and his lips a little too thin. There's an air of meanness about him that suggests he's not to be messed with. "It's a long journey; it would be good to kill some time."

"Of course." I pass the pack to him, willing my body not to betray me by trembling.

"I'm Horst," he says, extending his hand to me. His fingers are long and spindly, but his grip is strong.

"Carmen," I reply. "Nice to meet you."

"Would you care to join us? Perhaps you could be our dealer."

I swallow hard and nod, barely able to believe this turn of events.

Horst hands the cards back to me and I begin to shuffle, praying that in my nervousness, I don't drop them all over the floor.

The men begin talking to each other in German and fear rushes through me. Mitchell has warned me about the Ablege Kommandos, the German snatch squads operating in Spain, who regularly kill or kidnap Allied agents right under the noses of the Spanish authorities, who do nothing to stop them. Whoever these men are, the fact that they are Germans in Spain means it's practically guaranteed that they will be working for the Nazis in some capacity.

"We are just discussing how much to bet," Horst explains to me in Spanish.

"Ah, I see." I force myself to giggle. "Well, as long as you don't end up fighting over it."

Horst smiles at me again, but it's one of those smiles that doesn't quite make it to the eyes. "Johan is used to losing to me, aren't you?"

Johan raises his light blond eyebrows. "He likes to think so."

"Ha! Fighting talk, I love it," I say, warming to my role.

I deal them each five cards, face down. As they examine the hands they've been dealt, I take a deep breath. *It's OK, they don't suspect me.* What at first appeared to be a calamity could actually be a great opportunity, as long as I play my cards right.

· · ·

An hour passes and, true to his word, Horst wins almost every hand. Even though they're playing for matches rather than money, with every victory he cheers at the top of his voice. From examining the body language between them, I'd say that he is the higher ranking of the two and the one I should try getting closer to.

"Another round?" I say, shuffling the deck once again.

"No, I cannot do it to him," Horst says. "Look at the poor man; I fear I've crushed his spirit."

Johan sighs theatrically.

"Perhaps you would like to join us for a drink in the restaurant car?" Horst asks.

"That would be great." I put the cards back in their pack and into my purse. If Mitchell knew they'd been handled by two Germans, he'd have a kitten. It will make for a great story though—as long as I make it back from the drop in one piece.

We make our way along the narrow, swaying corridor of the train to the restaurant car. Frilly white curtains frame the windows, and the rows of tables have been laid with pristine white linen cloths. A steward shows us to a table and we sit down and order coffee and cake.

"So, what brings you to Barcelona?" Horst asks once the steward has gone.

"I fancied doing some sightseeing on my day off," I reply, mimicking the lines I practiced earlier. "I'm in Madrid to act in a show and I've been very busy with rehearsals."

Horst instantly looks impressed. "You're an actress?"

"Yes, at Teatro de la Zarzuela. The show starts next week. Perhaps you could come and see it. Or were you just visiting Madrid?"

"No," he replies quickly. "I will be back in Madrid soon. I'd love to come and see you. I'm a huge fan of the theater."

"How about you?" I ask Johan.

"Oh no, he's a philistine." Horst laughs.

"I'm afraid it's true." Johan shrugs.

"So, what do you guys do?" I ask casually.

"We are in the import-export business," Horst replies. I notice the flicker of a smile play upon Johan's lips.

"How interesting." And it is. Mitchell has briefed me that Spain is becoming a hub for Germans smuggling artwork and other treasure they've plundered from Europe. Could this be the "importing and exporting" Horst is referring to?

"In the wine trade," Johan adds.

"Yes, yes," Horst says quickly.

"Even more interesting." I laugh. "Wine is one of my favorite subjects."

"In that case, perhaps I could take you for a drink after seeing your show?" Horst suggests as a waiter brings our coffee over.

"That would be wonderful." I sit back in my seat and take a sip of my café con leche, its milkiness immediately soured by the bile rising in the back of my throat. Could it be that I've just made a date with a Nazi?

My darling Elena,

I'd stopped writing these letters as relations with our occupiers have become so hostile I hadn't wanted to take the risk, but today something so terrible happened I'm desperate for an outlet and I'm so angry, I don't care if they find this.

A statute has been passed in France forcing all Jewish people over the age of six to wear a yellow star on their clothes with the word Juif in the center. The fact that this law has been passed by the French government fills me with such horror and shame.

Today, all of the Jewish people in town had to go and get their stars—to add insult to injury, they had to use a month's worth of textile rations to buy them—and Anna was one of them.

I hadn't written in these letters to you that she was Jewish, in case they were found by the Germans, but now I guess it no longer matters. She was beside herself yesterday, not knowing what to do. I advised her not to get the stars, but she was terrified someone might denounce her for being Jewish. I told her if that happened they'd have me and my cast-iron frying pan to answer to! But she said she'd feel terrible if she pretended not to be Jewish, that it would be disloyal to all of the other Jewish people in France. I couldn't argue with that; I knew instantly that I would do the same. But to see Caleb having to wear that hideous thing, and to try to explain why to him when I don't understand myself, oh Elena, it was heartbreaking. He looked at me with tears in his eyes and he said, "Grand-mère Rose..." (he asked

me recently if I would become his honorary grandmother) "did Elena ever have to wear a star?" My countless tales of your exploits have made you a hero to him,
and I could tell that he wanted me to say yes, that you
had once been made to wear a star too and it all turned
out well in the end, but I was so sickened, I didn't have
the will to lie to him.

He looked crushed when I shook my head, but then I
remembered the time when your parents made you wear
that pink satin dress you hated to Maria's christening, so
I told him that story instead. I know it bears no comparison, but thankfully it seemed to comfort him, or distract
him at least, especially the part where you purposefully
tore it on the brambles!

Oh Elena, please keep us in your prayers. I am
beginning to despair for humanity. Do you remember the
time you got in a rage about that girl in your class
stealing your favorite pen? And how I told you to take
your anger out on your pillow? Well, tonight, I beat my
own pillow senseless, imagining it was Adolf Hitler, but
I'm sad to report it brought little relief.

All my love,

Grand-mère Rose

17

BARCELONA, 1943

By the time we arrive in Barcelona, I've given Horst full details of my show at Teatro de la Zarzuela, and instructions for him to message me via the stage door when he's back in Madrid. Boy, am I glad my family don't know what I'm up to. Papa would go crazy for sure. He gave my poor classmate Joey McGuire the third degree when he asked me to the high-school prom. Lord knows what he'd do to Horst if given the opportunity. The fact is, though, I'd rather kiss a blunt-snouted salamander than be wined and dined by a Nazi, but the prospect is sweetened by the potential intelligence I could gather if he is smuggling stolen artwork.

After bidding the men a cheery farewell, the first thing I do upon leaving the station is call in at the nearest café, ordering a café con leche and taking a table by the window. I need to be sure Horst and Johan—or anyone else for that matter—aren't following me and I still have over an hour before I need to be at the church. I gaze out onto the tree-lined street. There's no sign of the men or anyone else loitering about. Women bustle by in their long black skirts and headscarves, the men in pants and shirtsleeves. The weather is much warmer here than it was this morning in Madrid—the sky is bright blue and the sun is filtering through the trees, creating a mosaic-like pattern on the sidewalk.

Once I've finished my coffee, I go back outside and scan the street before heading back to the station to get a cab. As soon as I tell my driver to take me to the Basilica de Santa Maria del Mar, he throws up his hands in delight and launches into an impassioned speech about the church. Apparently it was built in 1324. I have to check that I heard this correctly as I can't believe something that old could still be in existence.

"She has survived so many things." The driver looks at me in the rearview mirror, where a string of rosary beads sways in rhythm with the car. "An earthquake in the fifteenth century destroyed the rose window, then, at the start of the civil war, she was on fire for eleven days!"

"*Dios mío*! And she's still standing?" I exclaim, liking the way he refers to the basilica as a female.

"Yes, she is a miracle." He turns onto a narrow side street, lined with six-story buildings painted cornflower blue, primrose yellow and warm terracotta. Washing hangs on lines strung across the windows above, and people sit on the tiny balconies, their faces tilted to the afternoon sun. "It is hard to get a good look at her from here," the driver says as he pulls up alongside the church. "The street is so narrow. But when you get to the square in front, you will see how beautiful she is."

"Thank you." I hand him some pesetas, including a generous tip. His history lesson was the perfect distraction from what I'm about to do and helped keep my nerves at bay.

"You are welcome. Enjoy," he says. If only he knew the truth—that I'm about to pass over the locations of countless brave souls willing to risk their lives helping others escape the Nazis. Brave souls whose lives will be in peril if I mess this up.

Before I get out, I glance at the tiny cross on the rosary

hanging from the mirror and say a quick prayer. *Please let this go smoothly.*

I stroll into the plaza with all the nonchalance of a sightseeing tourist, then turn and look up at the church. The driver was right—it's breathtaking—and for a moment I forget why I'm here as I gaze in awe at the huge rose window above the arched doorway, and the thin, sand-colored turrets reaching up into the sky. Two flickering gas lamps stand sentry-like either side of the steps leading to the door.

I take a breath and glance around the square. Could my contact be here already, watching and waiting for me to arrive? My stomach tightens and a sour taste fills my mouth as my earlier coffee repeats on me. This is it, the moment of truth. I stroll across the square and up the steps into the church.

The view inside is even more breathtaking. A vastness that you couldn't possibly imagine from outside, as if the church is some kind of optical illusion. Stone columns stretch up to high vaulted ceilings and the walls are lined with arched alcoves, brought to life by flickering candlelight. Rows of polished mahogany pews lead to an altar that's barely visible it's so far away. The cool air smells of incense, which is strangely comforting.

As I glance around, I see a couple of people dotted on the pews closer to the altar, heads bowed in prayer. I slip into the pew at the back, my hands clasped on top of my open purse on my lap. I bow my head and close my eyes, but instead of praying, I mentally rehearse my instructions from Mitchell. *"Your contact will come sit beside you and drop their prayer book on the floor. You're to reach down to get it and return it to them with the cards, then leave straight away without saying a word."*

I hear a clock somewhere outside start chiming four and my heart begins to thud. *What if my contact doesn't turn up? What if they've been intercepted and a member of the Abwehr turns up instead? What if I'm about to be kidnapped or killed?*

The door behind me creaks open and footsteps start padding across the stone floor. I open my eyes a fraction and see a figure pause for a moment, then slide into the pew beside me. A waft of lily of the valley perfume mingles with the incense and my spine tingles. Could my contact be a woman? Or has a random woman decided to pray beside me, despite there being acres of empty pews in front?

I risk taking a sideways glance and can't help gasping out loud. Despite her hat being pulled down low and her face being thinner, I instantly realize that it's Betty sitting beside me.

"It's you!" she gasps, even though I'm certain she will have been given the same instructions not to say a word.

I nod and smile. It's such a relief to see her, part of me wants to cry and another wants to laugh for joy. I notice that her eyes have filled with tears and I feel a stab of concern; I hope she's OK. She must have been posted to the Barcelona station, which, being closer to the border with France, must involve some dangerous missions helping people escape.

I bow my head again, waiting for her to drop her prayer book, but nothing happens. I glance at her and see that she's wiping her eyes with a handkerchief.

"Are you OK?" I whisper.

She nods and stuffs the handkerchief back in her pocket. "I think I might have been followed," she whispers, sending a chill right through me.

"What? Why did you come here then?" I hiss.

"I'm not certain I was and I-I didn't want to jeopardize the drop."

But coming to meet me jeopardizes things for both of us, I want to yell.

Somehow, I manage to keep my cool, mainly because she looks so distraught. "We can't be seen together. You need to go," I whisper. "And I need to get the hell out of here."

"OK." She looks at me anxiously, her face pale. "Do you... do you want to do the drop anyway?" she stammers.

"What? No! Just go." I instantly feel guilty for snapping and grab her hand and give it a squeeze. "And please be safe." Much as I'm annoyed at her for messing up, she's just as much at risk as I am right now. More so, if her tail hasn't seen her meet with me.

I glance over my shoulder. The back of the church is still deserted.

She squeezes my hand in response, then slides along the pew, mouthing, "I'm so sorry."

I bow my head, clasping my hands so tight, my nails cut into the backs of my hands. I wait until I hear the door creak shut after her, then I step out into the aisle. I need to find another exit. I cross myself, and make my way toward the altar. I hear a woman murmuring the rosary and see a man deep in prayer.

To my relief, I notice a door tucked away behind the altar. *Please, please, let it be unlocked,* I silently pray. I lift the old iron latch and push and, to my relief, it creaks open. I step out into one of the narrow streets surrounding the church. What seemed quaint before now seems claustrophobic.

What if the person who was tailing Betty is now tailing me? No one came into the church after her. They would be waiting for her at the main entrance at the front. As far as they're concerned, she might have just popped in to pray and at least she doesn't have the playing cards, so hopefully she'll be let off if she is stopped and searched.

Spotting a landmark from my cab journey, I start hurrying along the narrow street in the direction of the station. It was a good couple of miles away, so there's no way I'll remember it all. Hopefully at some point, I'll be able to flag down a taxi.

I turn down an even narrower street and what's left of the daylight rapidly fades. I hear the distant bark of a dog, and a woman shrieking at her children to come inside. Then I hear the sharp clip of footsteps on the sidewalk behind me. I take my compact from my purse and open it, whilst still walking briskly. I lift the mirror and pretend to check my lipstick and see the dark figure of a man walking behind me. In spite of the warmth, he's wearing a trench coat over his suit, collar up and hat pulled down so I'm unable to see his face. His footsteps get faster and louder—he's gaining on me.

I decide to cut down an alleyway to my right, figuring an innocent passer-by would carry on walking down the street. The alley smells of old trash and a raggedy-looking cat flits across my path like a shadow. I keep walking, praying that I'll hear the footsteps recede, but to my horror they grow louder. The man *is* following me.

From the backs of the apartments surrounding me, I can hear the sound of normal life going on—the chatter of kids, the sound of music, the clatter of plates and cutlery. It feels surreal to think of what might be about to happen to me in the middle of all this domesticity.

I bring my mirror up to shoulder height and see the man advancing on me. Then I see a brief glint from something in his hand. The blade of a knife. And now something else kicks in, slicing through my fear—some kind of primitive survival instinct. Adrenalin courses through my body, turning my nerves to steel. *I am not going to die here. I am not going to let the Germans discover the locations of the brave people on our escape route.*

Fairbairn's voice echoes through my mind: *There's no rules except one: kill or be killed.* And now all of those hours spent training in the makeshift gym at The Farm pay off. A series of moves automatically begins playing in my head. I slow my pace slightly, then stop and turn. The man keeps marching toward me and again I see the glint of a blade in his right hand. *Adopt a square stance,* I hear Fairbairn urge.

"Is everything all right?" I ask meekly, planting my feet about half a foot apart.

The man says nothing and as he bears down on me, he raises the knife above his shoulder.

Block the pathway, Fairbairn yells inside my head. I drop my purse and swing my body to the left, bringing both my arms up to block the inside of his, then I elbow him in the ear. *Testicles*! Fairbairn yells. I slam my right knee into his crotch and the man recoils in pain, yelling a stream of what I guess must be German cuss words. I clasp my hands together around his arm, forcing him to his knees. Some kind of superhuman strength seems to be pulsing through me. There's a crack as his arm breaks and the knife clatters to the floor. He wails in pain as I grab the knife and my purse. I could kill him right now, but I can't bring myself to deliver the fatal blow. Instead I deliver a sharp kick to his face and he collapses back onto the ground. I stuff the knife in my purse and start to run.

18

BARCELONA, 1943

I'm not sure how long I run for. It feels like hours. I run until my lungs are on fire and my legs feel like lead. Finally, I spot a cab parked outside a store.

"Can you take me to the station please?" I ask the driver and he looks at me like I'm crazy. For a horrible moment, I think he's going to refuse.

"Barcelona station?" he asks.

"Yes," I gasp.

"It is just round the corner." He gestures to the right.

"Oh thank God! Thank you!" I pant.

"You're welcome," he replies, clearly bemused.

As soon as I reach the station, I hurry to the restroom, lock myself in a cubicle and collapse onto the toilet, my legs quivering like jello. Panicked thoughts speed through my mind like the carriages of a runaway train. *Betty was tailed. Her tail must have seen us together and followed me. Or were there more than one of them? What if Betty was attacked too?* I think of her performance in combat training and shudder. But I can't afford to worry about her now. I need to get back to Madrid safely. More importantly, I need to get the pack of cards back safely. I take a few deep breaths before relieving my bursting bladder, then I take the knife from my purse and hide it in the cistern.

Once I've composed myself, I go back out onto the concourse, my eyes darting this way and that, searching for any sign that I might have been followed. When I'm as sure as I can be that I'm not being tailed, I make my way to the platform for Madrid.

It seems like a miracle that, in spite of everything, I'm back in time for my return train. When the conductor shows me to my carriage, I want to cry with relief that a Spanish couple with two young children are taking up the other seats.

"I hope they won't disturb you," the mother says to me with an apologetic smile as the kids bicker over a toy.

"Not at all!" I reply, wanting to hug her, I'm so grateful.

As the train chugs from the city and the lights of Barcelona fade into the dusk gathering over the fields, I gaze at my reflection in the window and it's like looking at a ghost. I can't believe I came so close to death. If it weren't for Fairbairn's training, I wouldn't be here now, staring at my reflection. *But you didn't die*, I feel him urging me on. *You beat the enemy.*

I settle back in my seat and close my eyes, my pulse pounding in time with the rattle of the train on the tracks.

As soon as I get back to Madrid, I call the number Mitchell gave me to ring in an emergency. A woman answers, saying, "*Hola.*"

"Chestnut." My voice comes out dry and raspy. "It's Flamingo."

There's a moment's silence before she speaks again, her voice lowered. "Are you able to meet with Bruno?"

"Yes."

"Be at the fountain in Plaza de Cibeles at eleven o'clock."

"OK," I say, and the line goes dead.

. . .

The Plaza de Cibeles is only a five-minute walk from the Ritz and, as a major intersection in the heart of the city, it's bustling with people on their way out for the night when I get there. I'm not sure whether to be comforted or alarmed by the fact that it's so busy. On the one hand, it's reassuring to not be alone, but on the other, every person I see could be a potential enemy and paranoia gnaws at me.

I spot Mitchell standing by the large circular fountain at the center of the square smoking a cigarillo and the relief I feel at seeing a friendly face almost floors me. When he spots me, he gives an almost imperceptible nod, then starts walking off. I follow a few yards behind, every so often glancing over my shoulder to make sure I'm not being followed. After a few minutes, he disappears round a corner and I find him waiting for me in a doorway beside a butcher's shop.

"Come," he whispers, ushering me inside.

I follow him up a flight of steps and into an apartment. The door opens straight onto a living room and the air inside is cool and musty, as if it hasn't been lived in for quite some time. As he closes and locks the door behind me, my knees buckle. I lean on the wall to keep from collapsing to the floor.

"What's happened?" he asks, his face creased with concern.

"My contact in Barcelona was followed," I blurt out.

His jaw drops open. "How do you know?"

"She told me." I feel a stab of disloyalty to Betty at sharing this but I have no choice.

"You met with her?"

"Yes, in the church."

"Sit." He gestures at a small straight-backed sofa perched on four spindly legs. As I sit down, he goes over to a table in the corner and picks up a half-drunk bottle of Scotch. "Drink?"

"Please."

Mitchell fetches a couple of tin cups from another room and pours us each a generous measure.

"So, she told you she was being followed?" he asks, handing me my drink.

"Yes." I take a slug of Scotch and cough as it burns the back of my throat.

"But why did she meet with you if she knew she was being tailed?"

I take a moment before responding. I've never been a snitch, but in this line of work it's too dangerous not to tell the whole truth—Betty's error breaking protocol almost got me killed. "She was panicking. I—uh—I trained with her back in Virginia and she wasn't the best under pressure. She's a great radio operator though," I add, not wanting to completely defame her character.

"What happened to the cards?" He looks at me anxiously.

"I still have them." I take the deck from my purse and hand them to him. I feel terrible. My first courier mission and I've failed spectacularly.

"Thank God!" he exclaims, plonking himself down on the sofa beside me. "We thought they must have got them from her."

"What do you mean, got them from her?"

"The agent you met hasn't reported back to her station."

"Oh no!" I think of Betty trying to fend off an attacker. She was already so jittery, she wouldn't have stood a chance. A lump grows in the back of my throat. But I can't show any emotion in front of Mitchell; I can't show any vulnerability. I don't want him to lose confidence in me.

"We thought they might have got you too. Until you checked in, of course."

"They nearly did."

He looks at me, horrified.

I tell him about the man who followed me and how I fought him off.

"They must have had someone in the church watching

you," Mitchell says after a moment's silence. "They probably slipped in through the door at the back, the one you left by."

"Of course." I shiver as I think of the man I saw on my way out; the one I thought was deep in prayer was probably my assailant.

"So Magnolia spoke to you in the church?"

"Magnolia?"

"The code name for your contact."

"Yes. We'd gotten pretty close during our training, so I guess she couldn't help herself. And she wanted to warn me about the tail."

"Right. So the guy in the church would have known for sure that you were working with her." He frowns.

I nod. Walking into the basilica had been walking straight into a trap. But at least I escaped, unlike Betty.

"What do you think they've done to her?" I say quietly.

"Well, if it's the same as the other cases, the Germans will spirit her out of the country—to France probably—where they'll interrogate her," he adds grimly.

I shiver. We both know that, where the Germans are concerned, "interrogate" is code for torture.

"Did you tell her anything about your cover story here in Madrid?"

"No."

"OK, that's good. She didn't know anything about who she was meeting or where you were coming from, so no matter what they do to her, you should be safe."

Any relief I feel at this is instantly soured at the thought of Betty being tortured. "I'm so sorry I didn't get the maps to the Barcelona station."

"Don't be silly. You kept them from falling into the wrong hands. You saved countless lives today—including your own."

But not Betty's, I can't help thinking. "Would you like me to try again?" I offer, desperate to prove that I've got what it takes to courier vital information.

"No, it's OK. I'll find another way to get the cards there. For now, just focus on being Carmen and keeping eyes on Conchita."

And Santiago, I mentally add, my heart sinking.

"I did have an unexpected success today," I say, suddenly remembering the German men on the train.

"Oh yes?"

I tell him about Horst and our potential date, omitting the part about the poker game for fear that his blood pressure might not be able to take it. "I think the import-export wine business could be a cover for something else. There was something shifty about them."

Mitchell nods. "We know that the Germans are starting to export artworks and gold that they've looted from the countries they're occupying, in preparation for an Allied invasion. Bringing their stolen loot from France into Spain is a natural route. If these guys are involved, there could be the opportunity for you to get some very useful intelligence." He clinks his cup against mine. "Great work, Flamingo. You're shaping up to be an excellent agent."

My face flushes from the Scotch and his praise, but once again any relief I feel soon fades. All I'm able to think about is my last sighting of Betty, pale and terrified, as she slid from the pew to meet God knows what fate.

Oh Elena, I can barely write for crying. Today, the very worst thing imaginable has happened. Anna dropped Caleb here before going into town to get some bread. She asked me if I could have him all day as she had some other chores she needed to do. I happily obliged and took Caleb out into the fields for the day to try to burn off some of his seemingly inexhaustible energy. He chattered away ten to the dozen about how he used to want to be a doctor when he grows up but now he wants to be a veterinary surgeon. When I asked him why, he said that he feels safer with animals than with people—with the exception of his mother and me. I joked that he might not want to test this theory with a bear or a tiger, but inside I wanted to wail. What is this war doing to our children?

We got back home and waited, but there was no sign of Anna. It got later and later and then the town busybody, Madame Blanchet, knocked on the door. When she saw Caleb sitting at the kitchen table, she gasped and gestured at me to come outside. "They've taken the Jews," she whispered. I asked her what on earth she meant and she told me that while Caleb and I had been off on our expedition, the Jewish residents of the town had been rounded up into a truck and taken off to God knows where. "Was Anna amongst them?" I asked and she nodded.

Oh Elena, I can't begin to describe what I felt in that moment. The sorrow for Anna, the absolute terror for Caleb. And the enormity of the fact that I was now responsible for his safety. And to top it all—my German "guest" could be arriving home at any minute. "You need to hide him," Madame Blanchet hissed before hurrying off on her way. So I've hidden him in my bedroom and told him that his mother had said he could spend the night with me, but we had to play a game of tricking the German. I told him it was a game I used to play with you, getting you to hide from your grandpa so that he wouldn't know you were in the house.

Now he's fast asleep in my bed beside me and I don't know what to do. My "guest" knows that he's Anna's son. He knows that they're Jewish; he's seen the hideous stars on their clothes. What will he do if he finds him here? What will I do if he finds him? I'd die for that boy, as surely as I'd die protecting you or your sister. I wonder, did Anna intend to leave him behind? Was she trying to save him? Did she want me to take care of him? I have so many questions but no answers.

Oh Elena, what shall I do?

19

MADRID, 1943

I spend all of Sunday in my hotel room, manically practicing my combat training, using the hat stand and the bolster from the bed as dummy assailants. In spite of Mitchell's assurances that I'm safe, yesterday's attack has me seriously rattled.

Once I've finished fending off countless phantom knife and gun attacks, I drop to my knees in front of the fireplace and say a prayer of thanks to William Fairbairn for his training, then I pray for a miracle and that Betty will somehow escape her captors. That's if she's still alive.

A memory comes back to me of the two of us talking on our morning run about what we'd do in the event of capture. Betty said she'd take her cyanide capsule as soon as she could. The thought is so sobering, I contemplate canceling my date with Santiago to the bullfight, but I know I can't afford such an indulgence. Now more than ever, I need to identify who is working for the enemy.

I come down to the lobby at half past four to find Santiago waiting by the elevators. This time there's no rose between his teeth, but there are two scarlet velvet cushions tucked beneath his arms. His twinkly-eyed smile, which I used to find so attractive, now makes my stomach churn as I think of him possibly being on the same side as the man who tried to stab me.

I take a breath, switch on a smile and slip into Carmen.

"What are they for?" I ask, gesturing at the cushions. "To protect your knees the next time you beg for my company?"

"You'll see," he replies enigmatically. "How are you?"

"Very well, thank you, and you?"

"I have been pining for you like a wolf pines for the moon," he declares, clutching his hands to his chest and dropping the cushions in the process.

"I thought a wolf *howls* at the moon," I play along.

"Yes, because it's pining," he says, crouching down to pick up the cushions. "I can howl at you if you like?"

"No!"

But it's too late. He throws back his head and howls at the top of his voice. All eyes in the lobby turn to stare at us.

"You're crazy." I laugh, shaking my head.

"Yes, crazy about you." He hands me one of the cushions.

And I'd be crazy too, to fall for your fake charm, my inner voice retorts. "Well, no one's ever given me a cushion before," I say wryly. "But it's good to see you back to your old self."

His smile fades. "I'm sorry I wasn't at my best the last time we met. I was very tired. I hope to make it up to you this evening."

"Ever the optimist," I say drily, growing into Carmen's character.

We leave the hotel and I see Javier waiting for us in his car, the engine idling.

"Hello again," he greets me warmly as I get into the back.

"Aha, it's the singing chauffeur," I joke.

"He's under strict instructions not to steal my limelight tonight," Santiago says.

"Huh," Javier grunts and immediately starts singing.

"We are having a party this evening, after the bullfight, at the British Institute," Santiago says as we pull out onto the plaza. "I hope you will come?"

"Sounds great," I say, my ears pricking up at the mention of the Institute. Hopefully, Franco's buddy Walter Starkie will be there. It would be good to get to know him a little better.

According to Santiago, the Plaza de Toros de Las Ventas is the third largest bullring in the world.

"Of course, the largest is in your homeland," he says and for a moment I'm about to say, but we don't have bullfighting in America, when I realize he must mean Mexico.

"But of course," I reply knowingly, my heart skipping a beat at nearly committing such a blunder.

"Maybe one day you will take me there." He smiles at me.

"Maybe." *The only place I'll be taking you is down if you're working for the Germans, buddy.* I gaze out of the window at the huge round red-brick structure. With its towers and arched windows, it looks like something from a bygone age. "How old is it?"

"It was opened in 1931." He laughs when he sees my look of surprise. "It looks much older, right? The architect copied the style the Moors used back in the twelfth century. Their buildings are magnificent. When I take you to my home in Andalusia, I shall show you."

"*When?*" I look at him and raise my eyebrows.

"Yes," he replies firmly. He leans closer so he can whisper in my ear. "I think life is too short and fragile to fight the kind of connection we have."

Once again, my traitorous body lets me down and I feel a fluttering of excitement deep inside. But now my head is firmly in control and I ignore the feeling, smiling out of the window at the hordes of people streaming into the various entrances of the bullring like ants into an anthill.

"How many people does the bullring hold?" I ask, eager to change the subject.

"Twenty-four thousand," Javier replies from the driver's seat.

"I know you feel it too," Santiago whispers in my ear, causing my treacherous skin to erupt in goosebumps.

Javier drops us off outside the fort-like tower of the main entrance.

"Enjoy! I shall hopefully see you later," he says as I get out of the car. He seems so warm and genuine. *Could his cousin really be a Nazi informant, or connected to one?* my heart wheedles. *Shut up!* my head replies.

As we enter the arena, I can't help gasping in awe. Huge tiers of seats ripple out high above the ring, the ground of which is lined with sand. A band is playing over to one side of the stadium and the excited chatter of the growing crowd mingles with the melody, like a concerto building to its climax. On every stone column we pass there are posters advertising the fight. A matador named Juanito Belmonte has the top billing, beneath a picture of a fighter swirling his cape at a charging bull.

"How does this compare with the bullrings in Mexico?" Santiago asks.

"I would say it is definitely on a par," I call back over the noise.

"Excellent!" He gently places his hand in the small of my back and guides me into one of the rows of stone benches at the front of the ring. "Now you see why I brought the cushions," he says, pointing at the stone seat.

I notice a ripple of interest as the people around us recognize Santiago and a man calls his name. Santiago returns his cheery greeting.

"I hope you don't mind," he says to me. "We could have

gone up there in one of the boxes—" he points to a ring of boxes higher up, full of beautifully dolled-up women and suited men "—but I prefer to be down here in the grit and the dirt and the drama. It is how the bullfight was meant to be experienced. To us Spanish, bullfighting is so much more than a mere sport. It is an art. The only dance where your partner can kill you."

I nod, although I feel a little apprehensive. After yesterday's events, I'm not sure my nerves could stomach much blood and gore.

"You'll see," Santiago says, moving closer to me on the bench so that our legs are just touching. I don't move my leg away, telling myself that this is what Carmen would do.

The band stop playing and the noise of the crowd instantly dies down.

"Now for the parade," Santiago says, looking excited.

A trumpet fanfare rings out and a gate at the other side of the ring opens. Two men dressed in old-fashioned costume emerge, followed by three matadors dressed in their satin suits and stockings. When I was researching Spain back at The Farm, I read that their outfit is known as "*traje de luces*," or a "suit of lights," and now I see why. The colors are so beautiful and vibrant, the satin gleaming in the honey glow of the early-evening sun.

After the bullfighters comes a procession of six horses, their bridles decorated with flowers. The men riding them are dressed in pale yellow suits decorated with a pink brocade, carrying lances and wearing wide-brimmed hats.

"Aha, the picadors," I say, remembering from my research and wanting Santiago to think I'm an old hand at this bullfighting business.

At the rear of the procession come a half-dozen mules. The procession parades around the ring, coming to a halt in front of the largest box above us. All of the men remove their hats and bow to the box. I strain my eyes to try to see who they're bowing to. I spot a couple of suited men.

"Who are they bowing to?" I ask Santiago.

"Franco," he says with a shrug.

My heart thuds as I stare up at the Spanish dictator and Nazi appeaser. "Who's the other guy?"

"Hans-Adolf von Moltke, the German ambassador," he replies flatly.

I feel a twinge of unease. Moltke has only been the German ambassador to Spain since the start of January. How does Santiago recognize him so easily already?

"Why do you ask?" Now Santiago appears to be studying my face for a reaction.

"Just curious at who would have friends in such high places," I quip.

"I see." He glances back at the box, but before I can analyze our interaction any further, there's a clap of a drum as loud as thunder, followed by another trumpet fanfare and an enormous black bull comes storming into the ring. The crowd goes wild as it stops in the center and stomps its foot, snorting and looking around as if searching for something to gore.

"Let the dance begin!" Santiago cries as one of the matadors enters the ring.

Any apprehension I was feeling about watching a bullfight dissolves within minutes. The whole experience is so gripping, I find it strangely soothing. Watching each of the matadors take their turn dancing with death makes me reflect on my experience in Barcelona, fighting off my attacker. The bullfights seem strangely symbolic of the fact that all over Europe, people are fighting against a wild beast for their right to exist. I'm proud to be a part of that fight.

The matador with the top billing, Juanito Belmonte, is

particularly inspiring and I'm unable to contain my excitement when he comes back from what looks like certain death, and I leap to my feet, screaming my relief. Even when Santiago grabs me in a celebratory hug, I'm unable to stop smiling.

"So, how does Belmonte measure up to your Mexican fighters back home?" Santiago asks as we prepare to leave.

"Hmm, he's almost as good," I reply.

Santiago grins. "Well, before this night is over, I hope to have won a victory for Madrid. Let's go to El British."

"El British?"

"The British Institute. My friend Walter has organized a night of flamenco and Romani guitars. Something you don't get back at home in Mexico."

I smile at him and nod. It's only when we're back in Javier's car that I remember my father telling me about the flamenco dancers he liked to watch as a kid. Does Santiago really not know that they love flamenco in Mexico or is he trying to trap me? I shoot him a sideways glance and catch him smiling at me. Hopefully, my cover story remains intact, but I need to be more careful.

The British Institute is a square building painted primrose yellow, with pale gray surrounds framing the windows. It's set off the road behind a black metal fence. Entering the building with Santiago must be a bit like entering the Plaza de Toros de Las Ventas with Belmonte—everyone we pass greets him effusively.

"Carmen!" I hear a woman cry and turn to see his sister, Josefa. "It's so good to see you again. I hope my brother has been taking good care of you." She looks at me expectantly.

"Very good," I reply as we embrace.

"Can I leave you together while I go and get ready to dance?" Santiago asks.

"Of course." I nod.

"Yes, I'm eager to hear all about you two." Josefa chuckles and Santiago groans good-naturedly. Once again, their sibling jesting reminds me of me and Maria and I feel a stab of longing for home so sharp it almost winds me.

Seven times seven is forty-nine! I sing in my head to distract myself.

"Come with me," Josefa says, linking her arm through mine. We walk down the corridor and into a large hall. There's a stage at one end and round tables line each side, leaving a dance floor in the middle. A heavily set man in a red and white polka dot shirt open almost to the waist is playing the fiddle right in front of the stage. His bow is moving so fast, it's blurring. "Are you hungry?" Josefa asks.

"Yes, starving," I reply without hesitation. My appetite, which had completely vanished after Barcelona, appears to have returned with a vengeance.

We go over to a long trestle table laden with platters of cheese and cold meats and bread. At the end of the table, there are rows of brightly painted earthenware jugs full of red wine. Once we've filled our plates and glasses, we take them over to a table by the stage. The fiddle player nods at us as we sit down. His hair is dark and wavy like Santiago's but it's graying at the temples and his ears are adorned with gold hoops.

"So, do you like him?" Josefa asks eagerly as soon as we sit down.

"Yes, he's wonderful," I reply, assuming she means the fiddle player. "I've never seen anyone so fast with a bow."

"No, not him, Santiago!" Josefa grins. "Please tell me you like him."

I laugh, feeling slightly unnerved by the question. "Why is it so important to you?"

"Because I know he really likes you." Her smile fades as she spears a piece of chorizo with her fork. "And I don't want to see him get hurt again."

"What do you mean?" My mind starts whirring into action at this revelation. Could she be referring to Conchita?

But before Josefa can reply, a woman of about forty appears at our table. Her raven hair is swept back from her face with a peacock-blue headscarf. She's wearing a matching floor-length blue skirt, with a laced black bodice over a white blouse with baggy sleeves. She greets Josefa warmly with a kiss on each cheek, then turns to look at me.

"This is my aunt, Esmerelda," Josefa says to me. "Esmerelda, this is Carmen, the woman I was telling you about."

"Aha, Santiago's friend," she says. Her voice is deep and raspy, like she smokes an entire pack of Lucky Strikes for breakfast. "Welcome to Spain." She takes my hand in both of hers.

"Thank you." There's something about her piercing green eyes that puts me on edge and I look down at the table. Instead of letting go of my hand, her grip tightens.

"My dear, is everything all right?"

"Yes." I look back at her and see her face is full of concern. Still, she keeps hold of my hand.

"Esmerelda, you've only just met her!" Josefa exclaims. "My aunt tells fortunes," she says to me. "She's only supposed to do it upon request, but sometimes she just can't help herself."

"I can't help it if I pick something up, especially when it's of a serious nature." She looks back at me. "You need to be careful."

My mouth goes dry. "What do you mean?"

She closes her eyes, still holding my hand. "I see a man following you. He wants to hurt you."

"Esmerelda!" Rose exclaims. She gives me an apologetic smile. "I'm so sorry."

"Would you rather I didn't warn her?" Esmerelda retorts.

"I'd rather you didn't terrify her!"

"It's OK," I say, pulling my hand from her grasp and taking a sip of wine.

"You need to be careful," Esmerelda says quietly, fixing me with her stare. "Someone close to you is going to betray you."

"Enough!" Josefa says and, tutting, Esmerelda turns on her heel and heads off along the hall.

In spite of the warmth in the room, I feel suddenly cold. I've always believed that fortune telling was a load of hogwash, but the fact that she saw a man following me so soon after my experience in Barcelona has unnerved me. If she was right about that, could she be right that someone close to me is going to betray me too. And if so, who?

The music stops and the house lights dim. A spotlight falls upon the stage and Santiago comes running out.

20

MADRID, 1943

The entire hall watches, mesmerized, as Santiago dances, and once again, my body begins its internal battle. My head warning me in no uncertain terms that he can't be trusted, my heart melting with every flick of the wrist and twist of his lithe hips. At the end of his routine, he looks straight at me and blows me a kiss.

"I told you!" Josefa cries. "He likes you so much."

"What did you mean earlier when you said he'd been hurt?" I ask, taking advantage of the fact that Santiago has been deluged by people wanting to congratulate him on his performance to try and find out more.

"He suffered a terrible personal loss a while ago," she says. "I was worried he might never recover."

I feel sick at the thought that Conchita could have potentially meant so much to him. Although on the positive side, if it is Conchita who broke his heart it could mean that he's not connected to her because of the Germans.

"Jolly good show, old chap!" I hear a British man congratulate Santiago and pat him on the back, and I feel another surge of hope. The fact that Santiago is so popular here at the British

Institute is encouraging. But it doesn't explain how he knows Lazar. I still need to be very careful.

Needing to use the restroom, I excuse myself and make my way to the back of the hall. As I'm passing a table, I hear a familiar man's voice and glance down to see Teddy deep in conversation with a dark-haired woman.

"I work in the oil trade," he's saying, leaning right into her. I can't help grimacing, there's something so slimy and arrogant about him.

When I get back to my table, I find Santiago standing there looking about eagerly. When he sees me, his face lights up.

"Well?" he says. "Did I make you fall in love with me?"

Josefa giggles and I can't help laughing in spite of myself.

"Not even the smallest bit?" he asks hopefully. "Not even your little finger?"

What would Carmen say? "My little finger might be slightly smitten."

"Yes!" He grabs my hand and kisses my little finger. "And it will be you next," he says, addressing my ring finger. There's a moment of embarrassment as we both realize the significance.

"Hmm, I don't think so," I say crisply.

"Perhaps not yet," he says, taking my hand and leading me to the dance floor. A flamenco band have started playing an upbeat melody, but he holds me close as if they're playing a ballad. "Thank you so much for coming out with me this evening. You've made me—and my sister—very happy."

I glance over to our table, where Josefa is smiling and waving enthusiastically.

"I met your aunt earlier," I say. "Esmerelda."

"Oh, I hope she didn't try to tell your fortune."

"She did. She said I need to be very careful. Apparently someone close to me is going to betray me."

He stops dancing and stares at me, deadly serious. "I would never, ever betray you." His expression is so open, his tone so heartfelt, it's almost impossible not to believe what he's saying. He wraps his arms around me. "You are the best thing that has happened to me in a very long time."

We're so close, I can feel his heart beating. I close my eyes, momentarily overcome with longing. It feels so good to be held like this: the perfect antidote to the constant pulse of tension and fear thrumming through my body. But I can't allow myself to relax and let go. To do so could be the equivalent of signing my own death warrant.

Our show at Teatro de la Zarzuela opens in the beginning of March to a rapturous reception from the audience and critics alike. It soon becomes apparent that I'm getting almost as many mentions as Conchita in the reviews. The general consensus seems to be that I am the more interesting and complex sister. One critic even bemoaned the fact that I didn't have more lines. I'm tickled pink at receiving such a warm response to my first substantial acting role—I only wish it could have been under happier circumstances. Antonio is also delighted and I'm hugely relieved to have rewarded him for being forced to cast me. Conchita, however, is far from pleased. At the start of the second week, I turn up at the theater to hear her berating Antonio in her dressing room.

"Why the hell has she added in the bit where she cries?" she shrieks. "That wasn't in the script. She's trying to steal my thunder."

My heart sinks. I'm supposed to be befriending Conchita and earning her trust, not making her angry.

"She isn't trying to steal anything," Antonio soothes. "It was my idea to add in the crying."

I take a deep breath and knock on her dressing-room door.

"Yes?" she barks.

"I couldn't help overhearing," I say, stepping inside.

Conchita is sitting in front of her mirror clad in a crimson satin robe. The counter either side of the mirror is full to the brim with vases of roses, their rich scent perfuming the air. Antonio is hovering anxiously by a rack of costumes. "And I just wanted to say that I'm happy to revert to the original script if that would make things easier," I continue.

Antonio frowns at me.

Conchita stares at him defiantly. "There, see, even Carmen doesn't want your changes."

I nod, trying to ignore Antonio's glowering expression.

"Fine!" he exclaims, flouncing past me from the room.

I smile at Conchita. "As I said before, I only want to learn from you, not upset you."

"Very well," she replies with a tight little smile.

"Perhaps one day we could go for lunch. My treat of course. I'd love to ask your advice on acting. I mean, I know I'll never be as gifted as you, but I'd love to improve." I have to fight the urge to retch on my sickly-sweet words, but they seem to do the trick and Conchita nods briskly.

"OK, we'll see." She turns back to her mirror and starts applying her stage makeup. Her way of telling me I'm dismissed, I guess.

I go into my dressing room to find an envelope stuck into the frame of my mirror. It's thick and creamy and my name has been written in elegant black script. I sit down and pull out the card inside and start to read.

Dear Carmen,

I don't know if you remember me, but we met on the Barcelona train a few weeks ago. I am back in Madrid for a couple of days and I was wondering if you'd do me the honor of spending some time with me? I have a ticket for your show tonight and would love to take you out for dinner afterwards if

*you are free. I shall wait by the stage door after the perfor-
mance on the off-chance. Break a leg!*

Horst

As I read the note, I feel a strange mixture of excitement
and dread. On the one hand, going to dinner with a German
and potential Nazi kills any appetite I might have stone dead,
but the prospect of the intelligence it might uncover is thrilling.

When it comes time to perform, I'm faced with the awkward
task of keeping Conchita happy by downplaying my role, yet
still wanting to impress Horst. It's an unnerving feeling, looking
into the darkened auditorium knowing he's out there somewhere, watching, but as soon as I become immersed in the part
I'm able to forget for a while.

As soon as the show is over, I get changed and apply a spritz
of perfume. Once again, the scent of Chanel makes an appari-
tion of Mom appear before me like a genie from a lamp. I
imagine her giving me one of her gentle hugs and hurry down to
the stage door.

At first, I think he hasn't shown up, but then I see the
silhouette of a man standing a few yards away with his back to
me, smoking a cigarette beneath one of the flickering gaslights.
He's wearing a trench coat over his suit, just like the man who
tailed me in Barcelona—a sight that sends fear coursing
through me.

Love your fear, I urge myself, picturing Mom hugging me
again, and he turns and his face breaks into a smile.

"You came!" Horst says, striding over and tipping his hat.

"I was just about to say exactly the same." I smile. "Thank
you so much for coming to the show. I hope you enjoyed it."

"I loved it. You were wonderful," he gushes. "So funny. And

it was so good to be back in a theater. It's been a long time since I've seen a show."

I wonder why this would be. Surely if he's just a humble wine importer, he would have plenty of time to go to the theater.

"Are you able to come to dinner with me?" he asks hopefully.

"I would love that, thank you," I reply.

"My favorite restaurant is just down the road from here." He gestures along Calle de Jovellanos.

"How convenient." I smile, ignoring the dread growing heavy as a stone in the pit of my stomach. The German restaurant Edelweiss is down there, another known favorite with the Nazis.

Sure enough, as we walk down the street he comes to a halt outside Restaurante Edelweiss and Horst ushers me inside. The bottom half of the walls are paneled in highly polished wood, the top half painted cream and lined with framed photographs of people and places. It's not as plush as Horcher, but smart nonetheless.

Horst greets the maître d' in German as if they are old friends and we're taken to a table at the back, for which I'm grateful as the last thing I want is to be spotted here and for it to get back to Santiago. I try to push Santiago from my mind and focus on Horst. I wanted to take the seat facing into the restaurant, but he beats me to it.

"You have to try their pork knuckle," he says, "it's exquisite."

"Sounds delicious," I gush.

"And have you ever had German beer before?"

I shake my head. "No, but I'm the kind of gal who's game for anything."

"Are you indeed?"

I suppress a shudder at his knowing grin.

He orders us both beer and takes off his hat. His hair has

been cropped shorter than when I last saw him and shimmers silver against his tanned skin. When he smiles at me, his face appears younger, but the smile doesn't quite reach his cool blue eyes.

"I thought you would have ordered wine," I say casually.

He looks at me blankly. "Why?"

"Given the nature of your job."

Again he looks blank before a look of realization dawns. "Ah, yes. No, I have enough wine tastings in my job. Drinking beer is like being on holiday."

"I can imagine." I grin, but I make a mental note that for a moment it appeared he had forgotten what he did for a living— or at least what he told me he did. I knew the wine story was a pile of horseshit.

I have Carmen's backstory all prepared, but it turns out Horst isn't one for showing much interest in his dinner companion; he's the type of man more prone to monologue than dialogue. So I settle back in my chair and laugh and gasp and nod in all the right places as he tells me about his childhood in Berlin, the terrible poverty the Germans endured after the Great War, and how he worked so hard to overcome it, starting his own business. Although he doesn't overtly say anything pro-Hitler, he says enough for me to be able to fill in the gaps. Hitler gained support by playing on the fact that Germany was in financial dire straits after the war. He played on people's fear, and he used that fear to blame others. From what Horst has told me, it would be easy to imagine him being prime fodder for Hitler's propaganda. The question is, how far, and to what extent, has his devotion to Hitler gone?

The pork knuckle arrives, accompanied by a portion of sauerkraut and a bed of mashed potato.

"This is divine!" I trill, trying not to wince in shock at the sour taste of the fermented cabbage.

I can't help thinking back to the warmth of my first dinner

with Santiago and how our conversation flowed back and forth. This meal couldn't be more different. Once again, I push him from my mind and focus on the food.

"Yes, German cuisine is the best," Horst mumbles through a mouthful.

"I dined at a German restaurant called Horcher recently," I say.

"Oh really?" For once, he looks genuinely interested in what I have to say. "That's another of my favorites. We seem to have a lot in common."

I'm really not sure how he's come to this conclusion given that he hasn't asked me a single question about myself, but I nod nonetheless. I get the sense that Carmen needs to be a lot less sparky with Horst, and much more meek and adoring. This will be quite the challenge.

"Perhaps I could take you there the next time I'm in Madrid," he adds.

"I would like that a lot."

"Excellent." He tops up his beer from the earthenware jug —without enquiring if I would like any, I note. I add "potential alcoholic" to the list of character traits I'm compiling in my head.

"So, where are you off to next on your travels?" I ask casually.

"I have to go up north," he replies vaguely.

"Nice," I reply casually as if this means nothing, while inside my heart is pounding as I wonder how far north and could he mean France? "I can't wait until I next travel; I've hardly seen anything of Spain since I've been here."

"Is that so?" He looks at me. "Where is it you're from again?"

"Mexico."

"Ah yes. I love South America."

"You've been?" I say, ignoring the fact that Mexico is actually classed as being in North America. Something tells me Horst isn't the kind of guy who likes being corrected.

"Yes, to Argentina. Great wine country," he adds quickly.

"How nice." I gaze at him as if this is the most impressive thing I've ever heard. Meanwhile, it feels as if a klaxon is sounding in my head, alerting me to the fact that the Argentinian leader Perón, supposedly neutral in the war, has made no secret of his sympathy for Hitler.

"Have you been there often? I do love a man who's well-traveled," I quickly add to try and soften my probing.

"Often enough," he replies enigmatically. "Perhaps one day you and I could go on a trip somewhere?"

"I would like that very much."

He smiles smugly, as if my agreement was never really up for debate.

A waitress comes to clear away our plates and I notice that Horst isn't nearly as friendly to her as he was to the maître d'. When she asks if we would like dessert, he brusquely replies, "Of course!" then looks at me and raises his eyebrows as if to say, *What a fool*.

I instantly bristle, thinking back to the countless customers like him I had to deal with in the diner. Still, at least if I hate him, it will make it a whole lot easier to spy on him, I reason.

"We will have the apple strudel," he says, without consulting me.

I bite my lip, reminding myself that this iteration of Carmen must be submissive.

He leans forward and takes hold of my hand. His long fingers are icy cold. "Thank you for agreeing to meet me."

"You're very welcome. Thank you for the lovely dinner."

"Well, the night isn't over yet—I hope." He smiles suggestively.

Every muscle in my body tenses, as if morphing into a suit of armor to protect me from this creep.

"I'm afraid I have to get back to my hotel. I have a very long day ahead of me tomorrow—we have a matinee performance, as well as in the evening."

He frowns at me and for a moment I think I might have blown it.

"Next time, we must go out on my day off," I add quickly. "Then I'll be able to spend way more time with you."

His frown fades. "That sounds like an excellent plan."

"I'm really craving an adventure," I add, hoping I'm not overegging things.

"Is that so?"

I nod and hold his gaze across the table, in what I hope is a provocative manner, although inside I feel like vomiting.

"I shall have to think of a suitable adventure for us then."

"I imagine you're capable of the most exciting adventures." *Geez, who knew I was capable of the most excruciating lines?*

Finally, he thaws and a smile spreads across his face. "This is very true, yes."

I shudder at the thought of what he might be imagining.

Once we've finished our apple strudel, Horst walks me back to the Ritz, even though it's only a couple of minutes away and I assured him I'd be fine on my own. Unlike the fun conversations I have on my walks with Santiago, I'm treated to yet another monologue by Horst about Horst. There's a shrillness to his voice that sets my nerves on edge and makes my head hurt.

We're just approaching the safety of the hotel entrance when he stops walking and grabs hold of my hand.

"I'm very glad our paths crossed," he says. "I think we were supposed to meet."

"Really?" I gaze at him coquettishly, while inside I curse fate for orchestrating our meeting.

He nods and pulls me closer. Over his shoulder, I can see

the golden glow of light spilling out from the Ritz, so near and yet so far. "Don't you feel it too?" he asks with an urgency to his tone.

"I do," I say, glancing longingly at the hotel entrance.

"I wish I didn't have to go."

I try my hardest not to grimace at the thought of what he might be hinting at.

"Me too, but think how great it will be the next time we meet."

He smiles. "That's very true." He leans in so close I smell the sour beer on his breath, and for a horrible moment I think he's going to kiss me on the mouth, but he kisses me forcefully on the cheek instead. "I'll be back in Madrid next month hopefully. Don't forget about me."

"How would that even be possible?" I gush, relieved that the end of this torture appears to be in sight.

"Goodnight, Carmen," he says, tipping his hat.

"Goodnight, Horst." I turn and stroll away, fighting the instinct to run for my life.

As I hurry across the hotel lobby, I see a bright flash of auburn hair and notice the baroness deep in conversation with a man, huddled together in the armchairs in the corner. My evening with Horst has left me jittery and tense and seeing her only makes it worse. The German infestation of Spain seems to be growing worse by the day—or they're getting closer to me by the day. I'll have to brief Mitchell about my dinner with Horst when we meet tomorrow and I know what he'll say—he'll encourage me to see more of him, but where will that end?

I think of Horst's pale eyes and cold hands and my stomach churns, the sour reminder of pickled cabbage burning in the back of my throat. At least the man who followed me in Barcelona was trying to attack me. Deciding what to do in response was straightforward—I had no option but to fight back. But with Horst it's a whole other ball game. I'm meant to be getting closer to him, not fighting with him, but how far would Mitchell expect me to go? And, more importantly, how far would I be willing to go?

A mixture of anger and fear combines inside of me as I think of Teddy sweet-talking the Spanish woman at the British Institute. Oh to be a male agent, and not have to worry about whoever you're trying to seduce in the name of intelligence-gathering because you physically have the upper hand.

I turn the corner for the elevators and see a familiar figure sitting in one of the chairs, head slumped to one side and eyes closed.

"Santiago!"

His eyes spring open and he breaks into a smile. "Carmen."

"I almost didn't recognize you without a rose or a cushion," I quip, and even though I don't know if I can trust him, it feels so good to be able to joke after my time with Horst.

"I hope you don't mind me coming by like this," he says. "I just..." He breaks off, looking dejected.

"Are you OK?"

He nods but still looks really sad. "I know you've been busy with your play, and I've tried so hard to stay away and give you your space but I so badly wanted to see you."

There's something about the plaintive way in which he says this that makes the tension within me begin to ease.

You don't know if you can trust him, my head warns.

Yes, but he seems so genuine and kind, my heart responds. *And he has never, ever made you feel unsafe, the way Horst does.*

As I look at Santiago a wave of longing rushes through me.

"I'm very happy to see you," I murmur, taking a step closer to him.

The elevator door pings open and I glance over my shoulder. There's no one in sight. And in that moment, my heart takes full control. I take his hand and pull him inside the elevator.

"Are you sure?" he whispers as I press the button for my floor.

"Yes," I reply softly. And after an evening of lying through my teeth, it feels so darn good to be able to tell the truth.

The doors slide shut behind us and he takes me in his arms.

21

MADRID, 1943

"I have a confession to make," Santiago says as soon as we go into my room.

I instantly freeze, and the longing building inside me starts to subside. What is he about to tell me?

"What is it?" I ask. I'd left the drapes open when I went out earlier and a pearly shaft of moonlight is spilling in through the window.

"I'm terrified."

"Of what?"

"You," he whispers. We're standing so close, I can feel his breath warm and soft on my face.

"Me? But why?" Fears crowd my mind. *Does he know or suspect that I'm not who I claim to be?* "I'm not that scary surely," I joke.

"I'm scared of how you make me feel," he replies softly.

"How do I make you feel?" Excitement mingles with my fear.

"Like I'm standing on the edge of a cliff."

I frown. "I don't understand."

"I want to leap off and into this with you, but what if..." He breaks off and looks down at the floor.

"I understand," I whisper, and I truly do, for more reasons than he can ever know.

"You do?"

"Yes."

"Perhaps we could take the leap together?" he says, looking back at me, his gaze so heartfelt. And once again I feel that I'm looking straight into the truth of who Santiago is and that I can completely and utterly trust what he's saying.

You mustn't fall in love! As I remember Mitchell's instruction, my head wrests back control.

"Yes," I reply, "but would it be possible to leap slowly?" I look down at the floor, grateful that the darkness will hide my blushes. "Physically, I mean," I mutter. I know that Carmen would probably have had lots of experience with men but this is one area where I can't bring myself to lie—it feels too important —and hopefully it will help to deflect Santiago's advances.

"Of course." He takes my hands in his. "Would you like me to go?"

The contrast between Santiago's tenderness and Horst's forcefulness is so sharp, it warms my heart.

"No." The word leaves my lips before my head has time to censor it. "Please stay."

He pulls me close and wraps his arms around me.

"I—I've never been with a man before," I whisper.

"And I've never felt this way before," he whispers back.

I fight the urge to tell him that I know that someone before me—quite possibly Conchita—broke his heart.

What if he's feeding you a line? my head cautions.

I just want to be held, my body pleads.

"I want to hold you all night long," he says, as if he can sense my body's longing. "Shall we?" He gestures at the bed and I nod. He kicks off his shoes and reclines against the bolster, opening his arms, inviting me to join him. I nestle into the crook of his shoulder and he pulls me close. The tension of the past couple of weeks starts to drain from my body.

As he strokes my hair, I close my eyes and a memory of Grand-mère Rose comes drifting back to me. It was just after my Grandpa Bob had died and I found her sobbing at the kitchen sink. "I'm so sorry," I said, hugging her tightly. "Don't be," she replied. I asked her what she meant and she explained that the sorrow you feel in response to someone's death is in direct proportion to the joy they brought you while they were alive. "The sorrow I'm feeling now is all part of the blessing." She sniffed. "Your grandpa gave me the greatest gift a human can give another; he really saw me, he really heard me, he really, truly loved me." I remember wondering wistfully if I'd ever get to experience a love like theirs. In my limited romantic experience, I've always felt kind of disconnected from the men I've dated. The conversation has felt stilted and whenever they've tried to get physical, I've felt pawed at. Until now.

I nestle closer to Santiago and slow my breathing to the soft thud of his heartbeat, and finally I sink into a deep, peaceful sleep.

The next morning, I wake to the sound of birds tweeting in the trees outside. Santiago is lying on his side facing me, his dark curls tumbling over his face. I resist the urge to brush them aside and plant a kiss on his cheek. He looks so sweet and innocent asleep. If only I could freeze time, stay like this forever, but I can't. Tears build in my eyes as the reality of my situation returns to me. Even if my instincts are right and I can trust Santiago and he isn't working for the Germans, I can't get too close to him if I'm to get closer to Horst too. A tear spills onto my cheek and I wipe it away, cursing myself for my stupidity. I shouldn't have invited Santiago to stay last night; I shouldn't have given in to my longing.

Santiago opens his eyes and beams with delight.

"Our first night together," he murmurs, pulling my close.

My despair grows. *What have I done? How can I get out of this?*

"I'm so happy I feel like a goat with a carrot," he declares, kissing me on the tip of my nose.

I can't help laughing. "I've never heard that one before."

"Well, I've never felt this happy before," he replies. "And I have just woken up. You cannot expect me to come up with my most poetic phrases so early in the morning."

"I'm afraid I'm going to have to get up," I say and he groans, clutching his heart as if I just stabbed him.

"I have to go to a rehearsal," I lie.

"A rehearsal?" He frowns. "But your show has already started."

"I know, but Conchita wants Antonio to make some changes."

At my mention of Conchita, his frown deepens. I see an opportunity to ruin the moment and, much as it pains me, I take it.

"How long were you and she an item?" I ask casually, removing myself from his arms and sitting up.

"What?"

"Josefa told me that you'd had your heart broken."

"By Conchita?" He stares at me, incredulous.

"Well, she didn't actually say it was Conchita, but I assumed."

"And why would you assume that?"

I feel so awkward now, I'm unable to face him, so I get up and go over to light the fire. "After Conchita said you'd left your watch in her apartment, I assumed you must have had an intimate relationship with her. And I've noticed that you get quite tense around her. So when Josefa said you'd had your heart broken, I put two and two together."

"And came up with seven hundred and twenty-five," he exclaims.

I hear the rustle of sheets as he gets up. Part of me wants to run to him and tell him I'm sorry, but another more steely part can't allow it.

"Josefa should learn to mind her own business," he says and I hear him come up behind me. I prod at the fire with the poker. "Conchita means nothing to me and she did not break my heart."

"So it was just a casual fling," I say, spotting another opportunity to distance myself from him.

"No—I mean..." he stammers.

Now my disgust is genuine and I'm able to turn and look at him. "I need to get ready."

"Carmen." He puts his hand on my arm. "Please."

I shake his hand off. "I really have to. I'm sorry."

He stares at me for a moment and I long for him to come up with an innocent explanation, something that isn't that he had a one-night stand with Conchita, or that he's involved with her in some other more nefarious way, but he remains silent.

"It was before I even met you—it meant nothing," he eventually says.

So he has slept with her then. Disappointment descends upon me, dull and heavy. Perhaps if it had been under other circumstances, I could have accepted this. But we are at war. Conchita isn't just a love rival, she's the enemy. She could be Himmler's agent. I think of her lunching with Lazar at Horcher. Santiago must know that she fraternizes with the Germans and yet that wasn't enough to put him off being intimate with her.

"I'm sorry," I say again.

"But I don't understand. What has changed since last night?

Would you rather she *had* broken my heart? Would you rather she meant that much to me?"

Tension builds inside me. "I need to get ready," I say again coolly.

"Fine." It's horrible hearing him sound so exasperated, but I know it's necessary if I'm to do my job to the best of my ability.

I turn back to the fire as he puts his shoes on and I don't move until I hear the door close. Then, and only then, a tear spills from my eye and rolls down my cheek.

"Excellent work, Flamingo," Mitchell says as I finish telling him about my dinner with Horst. "You must accept any further invitation you receive from him."

I feel a strange mixture of pride at his praise and dread at the prospect of developing things further with Horst.

"I'm certain he must have something to do with the loot the Nazis have plundered," he continues. "Now that an Allied invasion is just a matter of time, the pressure is on them to get their stolen artworks and other treasure out of Europe."

"Where to?"

"My guess is South America."

"He said he'd been to Argentina," I reply excitedly. "He told me it was for wine, but with Perón being about as neutral as Franco in this war, do you think he could have been there on Nazi business?"

Mitchell nods. "There's a huge German immigrant population in Argentina, so it could be the perfect place to stash their loot." He stops to light a smoke. "How about your co-star, Conchita? Have you found out anything more? What about the dancer you thought might be involved with her?"

I feel sick as I think of Santiago. "Apparently it was just a casual fling."

"OK, good, but keep him close just in case you can find out more about her from him."

My heart sinks at the thought of having to keep Santiago close when I've just gone to such lengths to push him away. "Will do. Any word on Magnolia?" I ask casually, although Betty has been in my prayers every day since Barcelona.

"No. Which means the Germans must have her. The Barcelona station have taken all the necessary steps to protect their sources, so hopefully her capture won't do too much collateral damage."

There's something about the clinical way in which he refers to Betty's capture that sends a chill right through me. Would he be just as detached if I end up getting tortured or killed by the Germans?

Mitchell stops walking and smiles at me. "Right, I need to get back to the office. Keep me posted if you hear from Horst, and if you do, don't be afraid to use anything you can to get some intelligence." He looks at me knowingly and the icy dread inside of me increases.

"Of course," I reply.

"You women have certain advantages over us fellows," he jokes.

Try telling that to Betty, I feel like saying, but he's already turned and walked away.

For the next few weeks, a gloom descends upon me, in spite of spring arriving in all of her giddy floral glory. I find the scent of the blossom too sickly and the sun too bright and I keep the drapes in my room shut at all times. I miss my family with an ache that hollows out a pit inside of me and I fall asleep every night clutching my acorn person so tightly I've made the etched face fade. What I wouldn't give now to be sitting on the stoop with Maria, listening to one of our parents' melodramas. It's so funny how the prism of war is making me see everything back home so differently. The things that used to niggle the hell out of me now make me dewy-eyed with nostalgia, even the rudest customers at the diner. The only thing that motivates me to keep going is the thought of my Grand-mère Rose. I have to help defeat Hitler so that this nightmare will end and I'll finally be able to write to her again, or, better yet, see her.

One night after the show I have a brainwave. I might not be able to mail a letter to Grand-mère Rose anymore, but I could still write to her. I find an old poster for a play rolled up in the corner of my dressing room and tear it into writing-paper-sized quarters. I've already decided to destroy the letter as soon as I've written it and this gives me the freedom to pour my heart onto the page. I write and write and write, all about what's happened since I got to Spain and all about Santiago. I write about my hopes and my fears and how I long for her safety. As I write, tears plop down onto the page, darkening the ink. But it feels cathartic.

It's only when I finally run out of words to say that I realize how late it's gotten. I quickly tear the letter into tiny pieces and stuff it into my purse. I'll dispose of it on the walk back to the hotel, that's if I haven't been locked inside the theater!

I'm just about to leave my dressing room when I hear a voice in the corridor outside. Conchita's voice. Then she laughs flirtatiously and I hear the sound of a man clearing his throat. My heart pounds. Who is she with? I press my ear to the door.

"Come with me," she says, and I hear a door opening.

I wait a few seconds, then slowly open my dressing-room door. The corridor is deserted and steeped in darkness. The only light is coming from under Conchita's dressing-room door.

Clenching my hands into fists, I tiptoe along the corridor. I hear her laugh again, then the baritone hum of the man's voice. I stop just outside her door. Whatever happens, I can't make a noise; I can't have her discover me. But, equally, I need to know who she's with. It could be vital intelligence. I stoop down to peer through the keyhole.

"I've missed you," I hear her say, and I see a flicker of movement inside the room.

"How much?" the man replies and a shiver runs up my spine. He's speaking Spanish but with a German accent.

"This much," she says with a giggle.

The man gives a moan of pleasure and mutters something in German. Then he clears his throat. "Do you have something to tell me first?" he asks in Spanish.

"Yes," Conchita replies. "The Brit says the Allies are preparing to invade the west coast of France in two months' time. They are amassing troops in preparation."

I shiver with excitement at this revelation. Could it be true?

"Well, we shall be there to send them packing," the German replies and my excitement wanes. "Good work."

"My work here has only just begun," Conchita purrs and I hear fumbling and another moan from the man. My stomach churns and I straighten up, trying to decide what to do.

"Oh Ernst," Conchita sighs.

Ernst. I've gotten a name and some tangible evidence that she's working for the Germans; now it's time to leave. It's too risky to stay here any longer, and judging by all the moaning and gasping, I'm not going to hear anything else of any use. I tiptoe off along the corridor, repeating the name Ernst in my head to commit it to my memory.

My darling Elena,

It has almost been a month now since Anna and the others were taken. The town is rife with rumors about what has happened to them. Apparently thousands of Jews have been rounded up in Paris too and taken to internment camps just outside of the city. Again, I want to wail—how is this happening in my country? I told Caleb that his maman is playing the hiding game too, and she's hiding in another town. I'm certain he doesn't believe me, but I think he's decided that he'd rather believe my lie than know the truth—a bit like you when you refused to believe that Santa wasn't real after that kid in your class let the cat out of the bag.

We have fallen into a strange new routine—my "guest" is out of the house for such long hours, Caleb is always fast asleep by the time he returns. The only time I have to get him to be quiet is first thing in the morning. We snuggle in bed together and I whisper him stories until my "guest" has gone and then I make Caleb some breakfast and we play together. Thankfully, the cottage is at the end of the lane and the garden is secluded enough to be able to allow him outside to get some fresh air and sun on his skin. I try so hard to be an entertaining playmate but even when he smiles there's a sadness clouding his eyes that no amount of my clowning around can lift. Whenever I have to pop out to fetch my rations, I leave him in my room, under strict instructions not to come out. Thankfully, he's become obsessed with drawing pictures of animals so that keeps him amused. But how long are we going to be able to keep this up? How long before Caleb becomes frantic for his mother?

Oh Elena, I'm sure you're busy with your life and your acting but I hope that every so often you think of me in your prayers. God knows Caleb and I need all the prayers we can get.

All my love,

Grand-mère Rose

22

MADRID, 1943

I meet with Mitchell the following morning in the park by the lake to inform him of the latest developments.

"Ernst," he repeats thoughtfully when I tell him the German's name. "Could be a buddy of Himmler's. I'll check and get back to you."

I shiver, thinking of how close I'd been to him the night before. "And what about the Brit who leaked the information about the Allied invasion?"

"Hmm, could be a case of chicken feed," he replies.

I learned all about "chicken feed," or feeding false information to people suspected of being traitors or enemy agents, in training and my heart sinks. "So the invasion isn't happening on the west coast in a couple of months?"

Mitchell shakes his head. "The question is, who's being fed the false information? Conchita or her British lover."

"You mean the Brits might already suspect he's a traitor," I say, my head starting to spin from all the various possible permutations.

"Uh-huh. Do you see now why I told you not to fall in love?" He grins. "Pillow talk costs lives."

I nod, feeling guilty as I remember my night with Santiago. But at least I haven't given away any secrets, and I never would.

On Friday I go for my weekly appointment at the Ritz salon. Every week I keep my eyes and ear peeled for any sign of suspicious behavior from the baroness but so far there's been nothing. Today I notice a man talking with her at the counter so I take a seat in the waiting area and pick up a magazine, pretending to read as I tune in to their conversation.

"From Black Fox," I hear him say and I peep over the magazine to see him pass an envelope over the counter to her.

"Thank you," she replies, slipping the envelope into her purse.

Black Fox sounds like a definite code name and my skin prickles. Has she just received a message from her handler?

The man leaves and the baroness slips into the backroom, reappearing a moment later without her purse.

"Hello, Carmen," she says as she comes out from behind the counter. "Elisa will be with you shortly."

"Thank you," I reply, still holding the magazine.

"Can you tell her that I've just popped to the reception desk to see where our flower delivery has got to?"

"Of course."

As soon as she leaves, I stand up and glance into the salon. The beauticians are all busy buzzing around their clients. Elisa is taking the final rollers from a woman's hair. Do I have time to slip into the backroom and look in the baroness's purse? What would I say if I was caught?

Not wanting to waste a second, I slip behind the counter, my heart racing.

"Carmen!"

I practically jump out of my skin at the sound of Elisa's voice calling to me.

"Hello!" I turn to greet her, my cheeks burning as she comes hurrying over. *What the hell am I going to say?*

"What are you doing back there? Are you OK?" She looks at me curiously.

"Yes, no—oh, this is so embarrassing," I stutter.

"What's the matter?" Thankfully we've struck up a warm rapport over the past few weeks and her look of concern fuels my confidence in my performance.

I beckon her close and lower my voice. "I've just started my monthly and I'm worried about staining my clothes. Is there a bathroom I can use back here to clean myself up?" I nod to the backroom.

"Oh, you poor thing, yes of course." Elisa gives me a sympathetic smile. "It really is a curse to be a woman."

"I know!" I agree, although privately, in this moment, I feel hugely relieved to be a woman and to have this excuse.

Elisa takes me through to the backroom. A cluster of armchairs are grouped around a coffee table in the center and there's a small kitchen area with a kettle and some snacks in the corner. I quickly scan the room and spy the baroness's purse on top of a fur coat on one of the chairs.

"The bathroom is just through there," Elisa says, pointing to a door at the back. "I'll wait here for you."

My heart sinks. How can I get a look in the purse with her standing there?

Just at that moment, the phone on reception starts to ring.

"Oh, sorry, please excuse me," Elisa says, hurrying out.

No problem at all! I feel like exclaiming.

I move quickly over to the purse and look inside. The envelope is tucked in between a wallet and a pearl-framed compact mirror. My spirits lift as I see that it's already been opened, but when I look inside, it's empty. *Damn!*

I have a quick riffle through the purse, but there's no sign of any message of any kind. I put the purse back and go through to the bathroom to pretend to use the toilet. The baroness must have disposed of it already, which would be even more of an indication that it was something underhand, which makes it even worse that I wasn't able to find it.

I lock the door behind me and stare at my reflection in the mirror, momentarily startled by the dark rings beneath my eyes from lack of sleep. I'm about to flush the toilet in case Elisa has come back into the room when I notice a couple of scraps of paper floating in the water. I peer closer and see there's writing on them. Without a moment's thought I fish them out and place them on the sink. If the baroness felt the need to dispose of the message in a toilet rather than a trash can, I need to decipher it. But to my crushing disappointment, the letters are too blurred to read.

"Carmen are you OK?" I hear Elisa call, and then I hear the deeper tone of the baroness saying something.

Shit!

"Yes, just a moment," I call back. I stare at the scraps of paper once more, trying desperately to make something out, but it's impossible. I fling them back in the toilet and pull the chain. I watch as they swirl around the bowl and disappear.

I look back in the mirror and quickly practice a pained expression before opening the door. Elisa and the baroness are standing there staring at me.

"Thank you so much," I say, clutching my stomach.

"She has her monthly," Elisa says to the baroness conspiratorially.

"Really?" She stares at me up and down, her immaculately made-up face as expressionless as a mask.

"Would you still like to go ahead with your appointment?" Elisa asks.

"Yes, absolutely," I reply, figuring it would look way more suspicious if I did a flit. "I had a sanitary napkin in my purse, so the crisis has been averted." I give the baroness a grateful smile. "Thank you so much for the use of your facilities."

As I follow Elisa out of the room, I glance over my shoulder and see the baroness heading for the bathroom, perhaps wanting to make sure she'd gotten rid of any incriminating evidence. If only I'd been able to read it. Once again, my skin crawls at the sensation of the Nazi net closing in on me.

I feel on edge for the rest of the day and even end up fluffing a couple of my lines in the show. On the plus side, my ineptitude seems to make Conchita warm toward me and she throws me a smug smile during the curtain call.

When I finally make it to the refuge of my dressing room, I find a small, gift-wrapped package by my mirror. My first thought is that it is a peace offering from Santiago and, in spite of my better judgment, my spirits soar. I undo the scarlet bow and remove the gold paper to find what looks like a jewelry box. I open the box and see a beautiful gold bangle inside, nestled on a midnight-blue cushion. I take it out and hold it to the light. Some words have been engraved inside, but to my surprise, I see that they're in French not Spanish. Thanks to my Grand-mère Rose, I'm able to translate: *"There is nothing so whole as a broken heart."*

Is it from Santiago? Is he telling me that his heart is broken after what happened when we last met? I'm not sure whether this would make me feel better or worse.

I notice a small card inside the wrapping paper and turn it over to find a written message. My heart sinks as I read the words: *"A gift from Paris. I am very much looking forward to seeing you again and our next adventure. Yours, Horst."*

I drop the bangle as if it's contaminated.

The door opens and Conchita sweeps in, still in full stage

makeup and costume. I try not to think about what I heard her doing last night.

"Bad luck on your performance," she coos, smug grin still firmly in place. "Some of the cast are going for drinks at Pasapoga. I'm guessing you must need one after tonight." Her haughty gaze falls upon the bangle. "Oh, do you have an admirer?"

I force myself to smile back. "Something like that."

"How exciting," she says tersely. "We're meeting down in the lobby in fifteen minutes."

"Wonderful. Thank you."

As she sweeps back out, my skin prickles with excitement. This invitation is the warmest Conchita's been to me. I guess she figures my mistakes made her own performance seem virtuoso in comparison. If only I'd known, I'd have fluffed my lines way sooner.

I stuff the bracelet and card in my purse and hurriedly get changed. Hopefully, this drink will help me get some more intelligence for Mitchell.

Pasapoga is one of Madrid's liveliest music halls, situated on the ground floor of the Avenida cinema in Gran Vía. Normally, it has an American-style big band playing, but tonight as we walk through the grand entrance, past the stone columns and imitation ancient frescos on the walls, I hear the sound of flamenco guitars. The tables are laid out in a horseshoe shape around the dance floor. Conchita leads us to a group of tables that have been reserved at the front of the hall, closest to the band. Out of the corner of my eye, I see two flamenco dancers performing in the center of the dance floor.

"It's Santiago Lozano," one of the chorus girls calls excitedly, confirming my fears.

I'd been banking on getting into Conchita's good graces

tonight. The last thing I need is Santiago throwing me off my performance. I glance at Conchita and see that, once again, she's smiling smugly at me.

"Did Santiago give you that bracelet?" she asks, coming over to sit beside me.

I shake my head. Then I spot an opportunity. "Actually it's from a German gentleman."

She raises her eyebrows, looking genuinely surprised. "German?"

"Yes." I give a girlish giggle. "I met him on a train."

"Well, you must have made quite the impression." She smiles, but this time there's no smugness; in fact, I think I spy something close to admiration in her expression.

"I don't know about that." I make doe eyes at her. "The thing is I-I'm not very experienced with men and I've never been courted by a European man before." I refrain from saying German for fear of making it look too obvious. "I get the sense they're very different to Mexican men."

Conchita nods. "German men especially."

I work hard to maintain a deadpan expression. "Perhaps when I buy you lunch, you can give me some advice about men as well as acting." I add a giggle at the end to make sure it sounds lighthearted.

She purses her lips and I assume she hasn't taken the bait, but then she nods. "Yes, we never did get round to that lunch. Why don't we do it tomorrow?"

"That would be great!" I clasp my hands together like an awestruck fan but for once my enthusiasm is genuine. This is the opportunity I've been working towards since arriving in Madrid. "Where would you like to go?"

"I'll make us a reservation at Horcher. Do you know it?" She stares at me intently and I remember Mitchell's warning about her possibly being one of Lazar's agents. Could this be some kind of test?

"Oh yes," I reply casually. "I had lunch there once. That would be lovely."

"Great. I'll make a reservation for one o'clock."

"Are you sure you'll be able to get a table at such short notice?"

She frowns like I'm crazy for even suggesting such a thing. "Of course I'll be able to get one."

I give another foolish giggle. "Ah yes, the perks of being such a famous actress."

Yet again, my flattery works and her frown melts into an arrogant smile.

A waiter arrives at our table to take our drinks order and once I've ordered a gin fizz, I risk looking over to the dance floor. Santiago is dancing with a woman, and I could be imagining things, but his usual joie de vivre appears to be missing and his expression is grim. The music comes to an end and as Santiago and his dance partner turn to take their bows, our eyes meet. I quickly look into my lap, hoping he'll want to avoid me, but as the applause dies down, he comes running over.

"Carmen," he exclaims, "it is so good to see you."

"I didn't realize you'd be here," I say, and his face falls. Thankfully, Conchita has gone to mingle at another table, but for my story about my German beau to work, I can't have her thinking there's anything going on between me and Santiago. "I was just leaving," I say, standing up and putting on my coat.

"So soon?" He sounds really disappointed but I can't let that get to me. I can't let anything jeopardize my mission with Carmen.

"Yes, I'm really tired from tonight's show. Goodnight."

"But—"

Before he can say any more, I go over to Conchita and make my excuses, then weave my way through the crowded music hall.

As soon as I step out into the warm night air, my Carmen

persona falls to the ground like a shed skin and I'm left feeling raw and exposed. It was horrible being so cold to Santiago, but I had no choice. I'm so close to finding out the truth about Conchita now, I can feel it. And I mustn't do anything to blow it.

I march off along the sidewalk, scolding myself for letting my emotions get the better of me. Then I hear footsteps running up behind me and I'm instantly cast back to that alleyway in Barcelona and my skin erupts in a clammy sweat. *Prepare to counter-attack*, Fairbairn yells in my head.

"Carmen!" I hear Santiago call and my fear turns to relief and then anger that he made me so damn nervous.

"What?" I stop.

"Why did you run away?" He comes and stands in front of me, gazing at me imploringly. "I have been so sad since we last saw each other, I feel like a goat that lost his carrot."

"Perhaps you need to see a veterinarian for your ailment," I quip, but I can't stop my voice from wavering.

He gently places his hands on my arms. "There's something you need to know."

I stare at the ground, not wanting to make eye contact for fear that my will might crack.

"The reason for my heartbreak—the thing that Josefa was talking about. It wasn't to do with a woman. It was... I lost... I lost my best friend."

Hearing this, I can't help but look up at him and I see that his eyes are shiny with tears.

"His name was Pedro and he was the bravest, kindest man I've ever known. We were friends since we were babies and I... I saw him die right in front of me."

"What? How?" His pain is so apparent it makes my heart contract. I fight the urge to grab hold of his hand.

"During the war, the previous war, here in Spain. He was shot by the Nationalist army."

"The Nationalists?" My mind whirs at this latest development. The Nationalists were Franco's army and supported by Nazi Germany.

"Was he... were you fighting them?" I whisper, praying he says yes. If Santiago was a Republican during the civil war, then surely he wouldn't now support the Nazis, especially if his best friend was killed by the Nationalists.

"Yes," he mutters, wiping the tears from his eyes. "I know I've disappointed you, but please, I'm begging you, can we at least still be friends? I don't want to lose you from my life."

"And I don't want to lose you from mine," I reply softly. And I don't. The prospect of having one true friend in this city is too appealing.

"Oh thank God!" he exclaims.

"But just friends," I add quickly, knowing that I can't allow my emotions to overrule my head again. I need to speak to Josefa for confirmation that he isn't lying to me. Although if he is lying it would make his performance tonight worthy of an Academy Award.

"Of course! As long as I still have you in my life, I don't care. Are you hungry?"

His question takes me by surprise. "Oh! Yes, I guess."

"Good. Let's go and get some tapas like old friends do. There's a great little taverna just around the corner."

"Don't tell me—it's the oldest taverna in Spain?"

He laughs and shakes his head. "No, but their paella is the best in Madrid."

Santiago is true to his word and is the perfect gentleman all through dinner.

"I shall no longer kiss you goodnight with a fervor strong enough to cause a landslide," he announces as we arrive back at the Ritz. "I shall give you the kind of passionless kiss I would give a maiden aunt."

An image of his aunt, Esmerelda, pops into my head, her raspy voice informing me that someone close is going to betray me.

"Very good, I agree. It would probably be better if your lips don't even touch my skin."

"If you insist." He gives a pained sigh, before kissing the air either side of my face. "I'm sorry things went so wrong," he says quietly.

"Me too," I murmur.

"Perhaps you would do me the honor of coming to the Semana Santa parade next Thursday?" he asks. "It's quite a sight to behold."

"Well then, I would love to behold it." I learned all about the Spanish Holy Week celebrations back when I was doing my research at The Farm—they sound incredible.

"Excellent." He smiles and touches me gently on my cheek. "Goodnight, my friend."

I wonder if he remembers our conversation about the word "wistful." As I turn to walk away, I'm filled with a bone-deep yearning that takes my breath away.

I'm brought back to my senses as soon as I open my hotel-room door. The shaft of light spilling in from the hall behind me illuminates the outline of a man sitting at the end of my bed.

"What the hell!" I gasp.

"Come in," he says without turning round and I realize, to my relief, that it's Mitchell.

"You made me jump." I shut the door behind me, saying a silent prayer of thanks that he didn't pull this stunt the night I brought Santiago up here.

"Sorry. I needed to see you."

"Why? What is it?" I turn on the lamp and perch on the edge of one of the armchairs facing him.

Mitchell is sitting with his hat in his lap, his expression deadly serious. "I think the German guy you heard Conchita Aldana with was Ernst Schmidt, a very close personal friend of Himmler's. I received information this afternoon that he's here in Madrid."

"I see." My heart thuds as I think of what might have happened if they'd caught me eavesdropping at the door. "I had a bit of a breakthrough with her tonight."

"How?"

"Well, first of all, I fluffed my lines, which she took great delight in, and then I told her that I was being wooed by a German and it proved to be quite a bonding moment. We're going to lunch together tomorrow—at Horcher—her suggestion."

"Horcher?" Mitchell frowns. "OK, but be careful. Remember what I told you about the hidden microphones. And don't forget that she could be trained to sniff out Allied agents. The closer you get to blowing her cover, the more you risk blowing your own."

"Don't worry, there's no way that dame's getting one over on me," I respond with slightly more bravado than I feel. "I don't have the right anatomy for her to pay me much mind."

He chuckles. "Well, don't say I didn't warn you."

I tell him about my toilet-fishing fiasco in the beauty salon, which raises another laugh.

"The glamorous life of an undercover agent, eh," he chortles as he stands up and puts on his hat. "I'll be seeing you then, Flamingo."

"Yes, see you."

After he leaves, I double-lock the door. The hairs on the back of my neck prickle as I contemplate my lunch tomorrow. Dining at Horcher with a suspected agent of Himmler's feels like entering the lion's den. I wonder why Conchita suggested it. Could it be that she simply loves the place, or could it be that she's suspicious of me too? I try to convince myself that it has to be the former, but the feeling that a net is closing in around me keeps growing stronger. One thing's for certain—if I want to get a wink of sleep tonight, I need some company. I go over to the wardrobe and take my pistol from its hiding place and tuck it beneath my pillow.

23

MADRID, 1943

In spite of my .22 caliber companion, I barely sleep a wink for fear of what might happen at my lunch with Conchita, and as I make my way along the bustling Calle de Alfonso XII the next day, I feel lightheaded with fatigue.

You are Carmen De La Fuente, Mexican actress, I reassure myself. *Your cover story is watertight; there's no reason Conchita should doubt you. She's far too preoccupied thinking about herself to be suspicious of you.*

I arrive at the restaurant and say a quick prayer for fortification before going inside.

"Hello, I'm meeting my friend Conchita Aldana," I tell the maître d'. "She should have made a reservation."

"She has indeed," he replies, without even checking the bookings. This instantly triggers my paranoia that I'm walking into a trap. Perhaps the entire staff are in on it. What if Conchita's buddy from the other night, "Ernst," is here, waiting in the backroom to interrogate me? "Come this way." The maître d' leads me to a table in the middle of the restaurant. I quickly scan the other patrons. As before they are mostly suited men speaking in German. "Señorita Aldana is not here yet," the maître d' says, pulling a chair out for me. "Can I get you a drink while you're waiting?"

I ask for some water and force a smile as a waiter comes hurrying over with a cushion for my feet. Given the circumstances, the attention to detail feels claustrophobic rather than comforting. I stare at the plant in the center of the table and wonder if it could be concealing a microphone. Attempting to get any worthwhile intelligence from Conchita in this place without blowing my own cover is going to be tricky, to say the least.

I notice a slight lull in the chatter from the other diners and look up to see Conchita sweeping into the room. She's clad in a figure-hugging lime-green dress and her hair is pulled up into an intricate braided arrangement on top of her head, making her cheekbones appear even more pronounced. She nods in greeting to various people and my stomach clenches. Clearly she's pally with a lot of Germans. The maître d' is padding along behind her like a loyal puppy dog.

"Carmen," she says, fixing me with one of her fake smiles.

"Hello!" I exclaim, widening my eyes adoringly.

"I can't believe you left so early last night," she says, sitting down.

"I was so tired after the show. I don't know where you get your stamina."

She laughs. "Years of experience, darling. We'll have the goulash de ternera," she announces as a waiter crouches to place a cushion beneath her feet. Then she looks back at me. "That's my first piece of advice for you—the goulash here is divine."

"I bet it's delicious," I gush. I don't even care that she has ordered for me, not now I could be moments away from uncovering her identity as Himmler's spy. "I really appreciate you meeting me like this. As I said before, I feel there is so much I can learn from you—in many different areas."

"Yes indeed." She nods condescendingly. "So, tell me more

about your suitor." She glances at the bangle on my wrist, which I forced myself to wear for this exact purpose.

I give a coy smile. "He's wonderful—so successful and charismatic." I inwardly cringe as I think of Horst talking at me until I lost the will to live.

"Really. What does he do?"

"He works in the import-export business."

She raises her perfectly sculpted eyebrows. "Is that so?"

I grin naïvely as if it hasn't occurred to me what this might mean.

"And what is his name?" she presses.

"Hans," I reply. There's no way I can risk her identifying Horst.

I picked the name Hans to see if there was any reaction from Conchita. Sure enough, I see a flicker of surprise on her face.

"Oh, that's funny," she says.

"What is?" I ask innocently.

"I have a gentleman friend named Hans too."

"You don't say!" I exclaim.

"Yes. He's a press attaché though. You might have heard of him? Hans Lazar."

"You know Hans Lazar!" I gasp as if she's just told me she knows President Roosevelt.

Once more, she takes the bait. "I do indeed," she replies smugly.

I relax a fraction. If Conchita suspected I was an Allied agent, surely she wouldn't be boasting about knowing the most powerful Nazi in Madrid.

"Wowee!" I exclaim. Completely inconveniently, an image of Maria pops into my mind, sniggering behind her hand at my overacting.

"He's a very interesting man," Conchita continues, clearly feeding off my awe.

"How so?"

She leans forward, conspiratorially. "His bedroom is like a chapel," she whispers. "And he sleeps on the altar."

This I was not expecting, and it takes everything I've got not to burst out laughing. If Maria was here, she'd be howling.

"You've seen his bedroom," I whisper, then give a wistful sigh. "I wish I could be as confident with men as you." It's time for me to open up to her some more. "The truth is, I'm really anxious I'm going to blow it with Hans—my Hans. If you have any tips on how to play it cool, I'd be really grateful."

"Oh, my dear, you have come to the right person." Having been watered to the brim with my fawning adoration, Conchita is a like a peony bursting into bloom. I sit back in my chair, gazing with admiration as she embarks upon a colorful speech about her various sexual conquests. On and on, she drones. I picture locking her in a room with Horst to see who would win the battle of the monologues. "The war has definitely changed things for the better," she says, and my ears prick up.

"How do you mean?"

"Well, Madrid is awash with men from other countries."

I continue to look at her blankly.

"Germans, British, and more recently Americans."

I hardly dare breathe, but to my relief she continues.

"It is as if the menu suddenly got a whole lot more interesting." She laughs loudly and some of the men dining nearby turn to smile at her.

I giggle along. "May I ask what, or rather who, is your favorite dish?"

"Hmm." She thinks for a moment. "Well, the British are a challenge at first—all of that stiff upper lip business."

"I'm not so sure I'd like to be with a British man," I say. "They seem kind of cold."

She nods. "Yes, for sure, but as soon as you've won them over, they're soft as putty."

I think of the Brit she's been molding like putty in order to gain intelligence for the Germans and I have to fight the urge to slap the smug smile from her face. "I don't think I'd like to be with an American either," I say. "They seem a little too full of themselves."

"I have to admit I haven't been with an American man," she says quietly. "Yet at least." She chuckles and I have to suppress a shudder.

I take a sip of my drink. "So, do you have any tips when it comes to German men?"

She nods. "They are my favorite, for sure. So masterful."

"Yes!" I exclaim, fighting the urge to vomit. "So masterful. But how do you keep your cool when you're with someone as powerful as Hans Lazar?"

"A better question would be, how does he keep his cool when he's with me," she retorts.

I laugh. "Yes, of course."

She leans forward again and lowers her voice. "Trust me, he's small fry compared to some of the German men I know. I have been wined and dined by one of Hitler's closest confidantes."

My pulse quickens. This is it, the moment I've been working toward. She's practically admitting to me that she's Himmler's snitch. Whatever I do, I mustn't blow my cover. "I don't doubt it."

Cue another adoring smile in her direction.

"You need to understand that as women, we have a lot more power than men give us credit for," Conchita remarks.

"What do you mean?"

She looks down at her hourglass figure. "It's amazing what a woman can get a man to do using just her physical charms."

I give another wistful sigh. "If only I had a body as physically charming as yours." I picture an imaginary script editor grimacing and deleting my line for being so over the top. But once again Conchita laps it up, nodding as if in full agreement.

"You are attractive, Carmen," she says, her haughty gaze sweeping over my body. "You just don't know how to use it to your advantage."

"Hopefully one day I'll learn." My imaginary editor flings my script in the bin and pours himself a stiff drink.

The waiter arrives at our table with our food and I decide to shift the subject on to acting. I don't want to push my luck and risk blowing my cover and I feel certain I've gathered enough information to confirm that Conchita is indeed working for the Germans and for someone much higher-ranking than Lazar, which must surely mean Himmler.

"So, in summary, I think she's using her feminine wiles to compromise men," I tell Mitchell the following day when we meet for a debrief in the park. "And I think she's Himmler's rat, for sure."

"Yes, good work, Flamingo." He nods. "She certainly doesn't seem to be at all suspicious of you, so carry on building that friendship and we'll see what else she discloses. I want you to keep on seeing the dancer too."

I want to tell Mitchell that I really don't think there's any need to worry about Santiago, but equally I don't want to give away the fact that I've developed feelings for him, as much as I'm determined to keep him at arm's length. "I'm seeing him this week," I say instead and Mitchell nods approvingly.

On Holy Thursday, Santiago meets me in the lobby of the hotel rather than by the elevators, and I try to ignore the flatness I feel at the fact that there's no rose between his teeth.

"Hello, friend," he says, extending his hand.

"Good evening, friend," I reply, shaking it in a most business-like manner.

His face lights up in a grin. "Shall we walk? It's such a lovely evening."

As we set off along the street, I can't help sighing at the way the setting sun is painting the sky brilliant shades of tangerine and pink. It baffles me that humans are capable of creating so much horror when the world we live in is so beautiful. Surely we should be walking around permanently awestruck.

"What's wrong?" Santiago asks, looking concerned.

"Nothing. It's just the sky is so beautiful."

"So why is it making you sad?"

"Not sad," I say quickly. "More awestruck." I think of Grand-mère Rose's last letter and how she urged me to seek the wonder in every situation. If only I could remember to do it more often.

"Awestruck is the best way to be." Santiago nods in agreement. "It's a shame it can be so easy to forget."

"Yes!" I exclaim, once again feeling a deep sense of connection with him.

Santiago stops walking and clears his throat, as if he's preparing to say something important. But as he stops, I notice a man a way behind us also come to a halt and light a cigarette. Instantly my training kicks in. Is he following us or is it just coincidence?

"I'm so glad we can be friends," Santiago says.

"Me too." I link my arm through his. "Come, let's keep walking. I'm so excited to see the procession."

We carry on walking, but I'm barely able to concentrate as Santiago starts talking about the procession. Could the Germans be on to me? Did I say something at my lunch with Conchita that aroused her suspicions? And could Santiago now be at risk from being seen with me? When we reach an intersection, I look over my shoulder and I'm relieved to see that the man has gone. But then I glance at the other side of the street and I notice him waiting to cross in the same direction. He appears to be staring right at us, but his hat is tilted down over his eyes so I can't be sure. *Damn.* The worst thing is, I can hardly try to shake him off with Santiago in tow. Or can I?

As we cross the road, I notice a bar up ahead. Perhaps it has a rear exit we could slip out of.

"Do you fancy a quick drink?" I ask as we draw level with it.

"What, now?" Santiago raises his eyebrows in surprise.

"Yes, why not?" I notice the man slow down as we stop. "Come." I pull Santiago inside before he can put up a fight.

The bar looks more like something I'd expect to find in the Spanish countryside, with low, oak-beamed ceilings and brightly colored jugs and tankards hanging from pegs on the walls. I scan the back and see a door leading to the restrooms.

"Rioja?" Santiago asks as we head inside.

"Yes please. I just need to visit the bathroom."

"Of course." As he makes his way to the bar, I hurry through the door at the back and into a narrow corridor. There are doors to the restrooms, a door marked "Private" and what looks like an exit at the very end. I hurry over to check if it's locked. To my relief, it opens onto a small backyard and an alleyway, leading, I guess, to the street behind. We have our escape route! But how am I going to come up with a plausible excuse for leaving via the back?

I return to the bar and peer out of the front window. In the gathering twilight, I can just make out the man standing on the other side of the street and the red glow of his cigarette as he takes a drag.

Santiago calls me over to a small table tucked in a nook by the bar. A jug and two wine glasses are on the table.

As I sit down, he pours us both glasses of wine. "I love that you are so spontaneous." He grins. "I mean, I love to have spontaneous friends," he quickly adds.

"Excellent," I reply, downing almost half of my glass in one go.

"And I love hard-drinking friends too." He chuckles.

"Drink up then, I have another spontaneous suggestion." I gulp down the rest of my wine. It isn't ideal to drink so quickly when I need to have my wits about me, but all I can think of is the man who followed me in Barcelona. I got lucky that time, but this time I have Santiago to worry about too.

"Oh really?" He raises his eyebrows, then downs the rest of his drink. "What is this suggestion?"

"Come with me." I take his hand and lead him into the passageway at the back.

"You want us to spontaneously go to the bathroom? he chuckles.

"No." I lead him to the exit and into the back yard.

"I don't understand. Why—"

I take his face in both hands and kiss him on the lips.

"But I thought..." he whispers.

"I'm sorry," I murmur. "I know I've been acting strangely, but there's a very good reason. I, too, have had my heart broken."

"Oh, Carmen." He pulls me close and kisses me passionately. I think of the man outside the bar, watching and waiting, and my heart begins to race. "I am so happy to hear this," Santiago says, "because you make me more awestruck than even the most brilliant sunset."

I feel a twinge of guilt that what should be such a romantic moment has been orchestrated purely to help us escape.

Don't be emotional! I hear a voice very like William Fairbairn's bark inside my head. *It's kill or be killed!*

"Shall we go to the procession?" I say.

"Of course." Santiago turns to go back inside the bar, but I grab his arm to stop him.

"Why don't we go this way? Surely this alleyway leads onto the parallel street."

"OK." I'm so relieved that he agrees, it's hard not to kiss him again. "I'm so glad you have opened up to me," he says as we make our way along the passageway and again I wince with guilt.

As we get closer to the street where the procession is due to start, I'm relieved to see more and more people flocking the same way. By the time my tail realizes that I've given him the slip, he'll never be able to find us amongst the crowds.

A cheer goes up and Santiago gently guides me to the front of the sidewalk.

"Here come the penitents," he says excitedly.

I peer up the street and see a sight that sends a chill right through me. A parade of men wearing floor-length black gowns and long, pointy conical hats, with just a slit for their eyes, are making their way toward us. They look almost identical to the Ku Klux Klan, but instead of carrying burning crosses they're holding golden staffs with orange candles flickering in the glass compartments at the top.

"Why are they wearing those gowns?" I ask, trying to keep the fear from my voice. I remember my father telling me all about the Klan when I was a young girl, and how they lynched black people down in the south and hated Latinos too.

"So that no one will know their identity," Santiago explains.

"But why?"

"They are showing penance for their sins so publicly, I guess they don't want everyone to know. Here comes Jesus," says Santiago and I see a golden float with a scarlet velvet cape slowly coming toward us. A statue of Jesus hunched beneath the weight of a huge cross stands on top of the float. As it gets nearer, I see that a tear has been painted onto his face. "There are people beneath the float carrying it," Santiago explains as the float draws level and, sure enough, I spot some feet shuffling forward beneath the cape.

"But how? It's so low," I gasp.

"They want to be bowed down beneath the weight, like Jesus beneath his cross."

People in the crowd start calling "Macarena!" and I see another float coming toward us. This one is even more spectacular, like a huge golden four-poster bed, with a statue of the Virgin Mary upon it, clad in a gold and red cape. As the float goes past, I see that her cape is so long it trails right down to the floor.

"It's quite something, no?" Santiago says, his eyes wide with wonder.

I'm about to reply when I notice a man staring at us from the sidewalk opposite. Just like the man from before, his hat is pulled down low so his face is obscured. Is it the same guy? Has he found us? Dread begins growing in the pit of my stomach. A marching band is bringing up the rear of the procession, and the drumming reverberates right through me. More people push forward to try to take a look. As a family with three kids jostle in between Santiago and me, I seize the opportunity and slip back into the crowd. With so many people now cramming the streets, it's surely plausible that we could become separated and if the man sees me leave at least it will keep Santiago safe.

I start weaving through the crowd in the same direction as the procession. I know from Santiago that they are heading to Plaza Mayor. I push my way past the two floats until I'm level with the penitents in their black capes and ominous pointy hats. I glance over my shoulder and see a sight that makes my blood freeze. The man is pushing his way through the crowd behind me. *Damn!*

One of the penitents glances down at me through the slit in his hood. If only I, too, could be hidden like this. I glance either side of me, searching for some way to escape, and I spy a small church up ahead. Without thinking, I race over to it and dive inside. A cluster of candles flickering away by the altar provides the only light. I hurry over to a door at the back, but it's locked.

Damn! If I can't escape, I'll have to do the next best thing—wait behind the door so I can jump my tail if he comes in.

The cries of the crowd take on a sinister feel as they echo around the church. The music from the band gets louder as they grow closer—the drums pounding in time with my heart. More time elapses. Perhaps my tail didn't see me come in here. Or perhaps he's waiting outside to jump me, and we've reached a stalemate. But then I hear a low creak as the door opens and a blast of music rushes in. It fades as the door closes and the man walks into the church right in front of me. Once again, my training comes to the rescue and an almost animalistic need for survival kicks in. *Ball of the foot to the pressure point at the back of knee!* I hear Fairbairn calling in my head. *Then, as he drops down, grab him from behind in a chokehold.*

I press myself into the wall behind the door, hardly daring to breathe as the man stops a few yards in front of me. Up this close, I can see that he's about a foot taller than me. I creep forward, my mouth dry as dust and my hands clammy. *Kick to the back of the knee! Grab him in a chokehold!* I tiptoe another step forward, then kick his leg with the full force of the ball of my foot.

"Ow!" he yelps, and as his legs buckle, he comes down to my height. I throw my arms around his neck, and pull them in tight, preparing to choke. "Fla-min-go!" he splutters.

What the hell? I let go and he staggers forward, his hat falling off to reveal slicked-back blond hair.

"Teddy! What the hell are you doing? Why are you following me?" I hiss, as he leans against the back of a pew, rubbing his neck.

"I wasn't following you!"

"Of course you were. What are you doing here then?"

"I came to warn you."

"About what?"

"That dancer you're so pally with. He's the one I was following."

My skin prickles. "What do you mean?"

"I've been tailing him since yesterday, when I saw him having a meeting with Wilhelm Canaris."

"Canaris—the... the head of the Abwehr?" I feel sick to my stomach.

"Yes."

"Are you sure?"

"Yes, and I have the photographs to prove it." He takes a tiny spy camera from his jacket pocket and waves it in front of me.

The fact that my nemesis Teddy is the one to deliver such terrible news makes it even harder to swallow. I think of everything I said to Santiago tonight and our kiss, and my disgust grows. He must have been lying about his friend who was killed. What if Himmler has two rats here in Madrid? Santiago and Conchita. How could I have been so stupid?

"I know what I'm doing," I hiss, not wanting Teddy to think he's got one over on me.

"Yeah, well, don't say I didn't warn you." He puts his hat back on and limps over to the door, where he stops and turns. "I'd appreciate it if you didn't tell Mitchell what happened here tonight."

"What? How I nearly choked you to death?" I can't resist getting a jab in.

"I'll only deny it anyway." He turns on his heel and leaves, the door slamming behind him.

I drop down onto a pew and try to gather my thoughts. As the impact of Teddy's revelation sinks in, my disappointment and embarrassment harden into anger. Santiago has played me like a Romani fiddle but... I stand up and take a breath of the cool, incense-scented air. Now, after months of confusion, I've finally seen the board from his point of view. And now that I know for sure that he's my adversary, I have the upper hand. My anger morphs into a bitter determination. He and his ilk are not going to win this war. I'll outsmart them if it's the last thing I do.

I look at a statue of the Virgin Mary standing in an alcove, smiling serenely. As a child, I always secretly thought of her as quite an insipid Bible character. I always longed for there to be a more powerful woman doing swashbuckling things like walking on water. But for the first time ever, it dawns on me that Mary's strength ran far deeper than mere physical feats. Didn't she find the inner strength to witness her own son's execution when his friends and apostles had fled? I think of how Teddy taunted Betty and me relentlessly throughout our training for being women, and yet tonight I outsmarted him, and I'll outsmart Horst and Santiago too.

My eyes fill with tears as I smile back at Mother Mary and it feels as if a shield is slipping into place around my heart. From now on, I trust no one. From now on, my sole focus is beating the Germans and exposing as many of their rats as I can—and that includes the sneakiest rat of them all, Santiago.

I open the door and peer out into the street. The end of the procession is snaking its way round the corner. I slip off in the opposite direction, keeping to the shadows.

October 1942, France

My darling Elena,

I'm so confused, I don't know what to do. I'd thought that Caleb and I had been doing so well at our game of hiding, I'd actually dared entertain the notion that we could trick my "guest" forever. But this evening when Caleb was sleeping, my "guest" returned with a large lump of cheese wrapped in greaseproof paper. He placed it on the kitchen table in front of me and said, "For the child." My heart almost seized up I was so afraid, but somehow I managed to maintain my composure, staring at him blankly. "It is OK," he said, "just keep him hidden."

I sat there numbly as he went upstairs to his room, trying to make sense of this latest development. Does the fact that he knows my secret make Caleb safer or more at risk? I don't know what to make of it. In all the time the German has been here, I've studiously ignored him. Why would he want to help us? It doesn't make sense. But if he wanted to harm Caleb he'd have taken him, surely.

Oh Elena, what should I do?

24

MADRID, 1943

The next time I meet Mitchell, on Easter Sunday, the first thing I do is verify Teddy's story. I need to be absolutely certain that Santiago is working for the Germans. I'd returned to the Ritz on Thursday night to find him anxiously pacing the lobby. "I was so worried about you!" he cried as soon as he laid eyes on me. After assuring him all was well and I'd simply got lost in the crowds, I feigned a headache and went to bed, making vague promises to meet up with him next week.

"Would you like me to keep seeing the dancer, Santiago Lozano?" I ask nonchalantly as Mitchell and I meander our way through the park. The place is deserted and the sound of the crowds in the Easter parade drift through the trees from the heart of the city.

"I was just about to mention him," Mitchell replies. "He was spotted meeting with the head of the Abwehr this week, so your initial hunch about him was correct. Well done, Flamingo."

His praise feels more like a curse. Even though I've had a couple of days to process the news from Teddy, hearing it confirmed by Mitchell is still a bitter blow.

"I see," I reply. Above us, a bird chirps gaily from the branch of a tree. *Oh to be a bird, blissfully oblivious to the betrayals of this world.* "I assume you want me to get closer to him then."

"Yes, but be careful. He could have been told to get close to you."

My throat tightens. "What makes you think so?"

"The guy who followed you in Barcelona will have got a good look at you. He could have passed your description to German operatives here in Madrid and the dancer could have put two and two together."

I have to fight the urge to retch at the thought of Santiago betraying me in this way. He's seemed so genuine in his affection for me. Surely he can't suspect me. Then I remember the faux pas I made over the Mexican tree he took me to see. Could that have aroused his suspicions?

"But the guy in Barcelona had no idea I'd come from Madrid."

"No, but Magnolia could have figured it out—or guessed at least."

I shudder as I consider the implication of his statement: that Betty had cracked under torture and told her captors that I could have been stationed in Madrid.

"Keep seeing the dancer, see if you can find out any more about his connections to the Germans, but be very careful," Mitchell says, stopping to light a cigarillo. "How about Horst? Have you heard from him again?"

"Yes. He left me a message at the hotel saying he can't wait for us to have an adventure together."

Mitchell frowns at me through a cloud of exhaled smoke. "What kind of adventure?"

"I don't know. I told him I was craving some excitement. I thought it might persuade him to take me with him on his travels and give me a chance to figure out what he's really doing over here. But if the Germans are on to me..." The rest of the sentence floats unsaid between us... could my going away with Horst mean walking into a deadly trap?

"Perhaps it would be better to stay put for a while," Mitchell says. "Only see him in Madrid."

"But then I might not find out what he does."

Mitchell sighs. "Listen, Flamingo, you're a damned good agent. I want to keep you alive if at all possible."

"OK." I agree, and I know I should take comfort from the fact that he wants to protect me, but I can't help feeling disappointed. I feel so stupid falling for Santiago's spiel—falling for Santiago, period—I desperately want to do something to redeem myself. And then a thought occurs to me: Santiago might have his suspicions about me, but he doesn't know that I'm on to him. Maybe I could use this to my advantage—convince him that I'm perfectly innocent, then use him to try to gather counter-intelligence.

Mitchell stops walking, the signal that our meeting is drawing to a close.

"Don't worry," I say, firmly. "I'll get you something."

As if in answer to my prayer, I return to the Ritz to find another message from Horst waiting for me at the desk. Inside the creamy envelope are a bunch of peseta bills and a note. *To buy some new clothes for our adventure. They'll be expecting you...* he's written, above the address for what I assume must be a boutique, along with a time and date. Ten o'clock tomorrow morning.

How has he delivered these handwritten messages to me? Is he here in Madrid? I look around the lobby anxiously, half expecting to find him hiding behind one of the pillars, but there's no sign of him. I tuck the envelope into my purse and make my way over to the elevators. Much as it makes my skin crawl to think of accepting Horst's money, my desire to provide Mitchell with some quality intelligence overrules my pride.

After another terrible night's sleep with my pistol tucked beneath my pillow, I wake the next morning and take a moment to get into character. Even though the Carmen I've created would feel furious at Horst's desire to dress her like a doll, I know I must play demure Carmen today. I put on my plainest dress, a brown tweed affair, and apply the subtlest makeup. As I blot my pink lipstick with a tissue, I think of Grand-mère Rose.

"I'm sorry I got distracted," I whisper. "I'm sorry I let my heart rule my head. But not anymore. I'm going to help save you if it's the last thing I do."

As I gaze at my reflection, another memory of Grand-mère Rose comes rushing back to me, from when I was about twelve. She was brushing my hair in front of the mirror on my mother's dresser. I was distraught over some petty childhood drama or another and I thought my world was coming to an end. As Grand-mère Rose brushed my hair, she began speaking softly in French, reciting a quote from one of her favorite writers, Colette, from memory. "*So now, whenever I despair, I no longer expect my end, but some bit of luck, some commonplace little miracle, which, like a glittering link, will mend again the neck-lace of my days.*" I loved the notion of life's events being like a string of pearls, able to be fixed when all felt broken.

Going to a boutique on Horst's bidding might seem like a hideous prospect, but perhaps it will be the link that leads to me discovering some vital piece of intelligence that helps repay the love that Grand-mère Rose has poured into me over the years. I stand up feeling newly emboldened.

. . .

The store turns out to be a fifteen-minute walk from the hotel, situated on Calle de Serrano, a street lined with fashionable boutiques, restaurants and cafés. A lazy spring breeze is drifting down from the mountains and the sky above is cornflower blue. All around me, Spaniards are chatting, laughing, drinking coffee outside, as if blissfully unaware of the pestilence that has infested their beautiful city.

Horst has left strict instructions with the store regarding what I'm to buy and I return about an hour later laden with bags containing the kind of gaudy, revealing dresses and gowns I'd never normally be seen dead in.

I'm trudging through the Ritz lobby when I hear a man call my name. My skin prickles with goosebumps as I see Santiago sitting in one of the armchairs.

"Why haven't you returned my calls?" He comes hurrying over and looks at my bags of clothes. "I hope you bought yourself something nice because you're not going to believe where I'm taking you." His bright green eyes gleam with excitement.

Let me guess, I think to myself angrily. *Afternoon tea with Himmler? Or another cozy meeting with Canaris?*

"Is everything OK?" His smile fades.

Damn, I must have let my mask slip. "Yes, of course. So what is this surprise?"

He glances around as if to check no one's listening. "Guess who is coming to Madrid?" he whispers.

Your buddy Hitler? "I have no idea."

"Leslie Howard."

"What—*the* Leslie Howard?" I stare at him open-mouthed.

"The one and only."

"From *Gone with the Wind*?"

"Uh-huh. He is coming as Walter's guest, and he's staying here, at the Ritz." His eyes widen.

I'm so stunned by this revelation that for a moment I forget all about Santiago being a snake. All I can think of is one of my

Hollywood heroes coming here, to Spain, and to this very hotel. "Are you being serious?"

"Yes." He grins. "I knew it would make you happy. I was so excited to tell you. Walter has a whole program of events planned: drinks and talks and cocktail parties. You will have to come to them as my guest."

I'm cast back in time to my bedroom at home and all the hours I spent gazing at Leslie Howard and Vivien Leigh on the lobby card for *Gone with the Wind*, longing to be a part of their world. Never in my wildest dreams would I have imagined it happening in this way and under these circumstances. I don't know whether to laugh or cry.

Santiago takes hold of my hands in his. I try to ignore how warm and strong they feel. "Walter is meeting him from the station next Tuesday. He's having a flamenco welcome party for him at El British in the evening. I'm going to be dancing. Will you come?"

He looks so genuinely excited. *But Leslie Howard is British,* I feel like hissing at him. *The enemy of your beloved Germans. You don't deserve to breathe the same air as him, let alone dance for him.*

Get a grip, I urge myself, *don't let him see you're angry.*

I force my mouth into a smile. "This is so exciting! I'd love to come, thank you."

"Hurrah!" Santiago picks me up and twirls me round. "It will be so nice to spend an evening with you. I've been pining for you."

Liar! "It's only been a few days," I retort, then quickly force a laugh as I notice his face fall. "I can't wait."

"Excellent! Now, I must run, I have rehearsals to get to." He grabs my hand and kisses it passionately. "I've missed you."

"And I, you," I reply stiffly. Darn it! I need to work on my acting skills before I see him again, to keep my rage and disgust from seeping through.

. . .

The following Tuesday I go through the motions of my role in the zarzuela while the enormity of what is to come plays on a loop in my head. Tonight I shall be in the same room as Leslie Howard. I might even get the chance to speak to him. My true self is as excited as a kid, and thankfully I figure my alter ego, Carmen, would be just as impressed, although she'd definitely play it cooler. While I'm waiting in the wings to go on stage, I practice various greetings as if I'm running lines. "Good evening, Mr. Howard, it's a pleasure to make your acquaintance." Too formal. "Leslie! It's such an honor to meet you!" Too informal perhaps. I almost miss my cue I'm in such a tizzy.

Thankfully, Conchita, as always, brings me down to earth with a bump.

"Can we just do one curtain call tonight?" she calls to the stagehand at the end of the show as the cast lines up to take our bows. "I'm going to meet the famous actor Leslie Howard."

As the chorus girls gasp in delight, my heart sinks. The thought of having to spend the evening with two treacherous rats almost strips the sheen from the prospect of meeting Leslie Howard. Almost, but not quite.

As soon as the curtain call is over, I hurry to my dressing room to get changed. There's no way I'm wearing one of the showy dresses Horst picked for me, deciding on one of my Balenciaga dresses instead, a sleek, coffee-colored number with a black lace overlay. I apply a coat of dark red lipstick and a spritz of Chanel and my transition from one character to the next is complete. "Wish me luck, Mom," I whisper into the mist of perfume.

I arrive at the British Institute to find the lobby buzzing with people dressed to impress. Is Howard one of them? Has he arrived?

You are Carmen De La Fuente, Mexican actress and woman

of the world, I remind myself as a wave of near hysterical excitement rushes through me.

I scan the room for Santiago, or anyone else I know.

"Carmen!" I hear Josefa's voice from across the room and I feel a mixture of disappointment and relief. Much as I love Santiago's sweet-natured kid sister, knowing what I now do about him has tainted my feelings. What if she is in cahoots with the Germans too? One thing this experience has taught me is that I can't trust anyone. I feel a pang of longing for my own kid sister—who would never, ever betray me, or side with the Germans.

"Hello!" I cry, feigning delight as Josefa pulls me into an embrace.

"Isn't it exciting?" she exclaims. "I can't believe we're going to get to meet such a big Hollywood star!"

"I know, I'm thrilled."

"Let's go through to the hall." Josefa links her arm through mine. "Santiago is getting ready to dance, but he's reserved us a table right at the front. Who knows, we might be next to Señor Howard himself."

After the bright lights in the lobby, it takes a moment for my eyes to adjust as we walk into the hall. Round tables laid for dinner have been arranged around the dance floor and the only light is coming from the candles flickering in the center-pieces. Each table is numbered. Josefa leads me to table number two, which is right at the end of the dance floor by the stage. As we sit down, I notice a long table running parallel to the stage with an ornate floral centerpiece. This must be the head table, where Howard will be sitting. My breath catches in my throat. He will only be a few yards away from me.

The stage behind the table is bare apart from the British and Spanish flags displayed together on poles. It occurs to me that bringing Howard to Spain could be a genius move on the part of the British—a charm offensive designed to win favor with Franco and keep him from siding with the Germans.

Sure enough, as more people file in and take their seats at the tables around us, I notice a predominance of Spanish present and, judging by the amount of diamonds and pearls and finely tailored suits on display, I'd guess that some of Spain's most powerful people are here tonight.

I feel someone brush behind me and a woman sits down next to Josefa. I recognize her instantly. Esmerelda. A shiver runs up my spine. I sure hope she doesn't have any premonitions for me tonight, not when I'm already feeling so damn jittery.

"Hello again," she greets me.

"Hello." Thankfully, at that moment, some men come and sit at the table. Josefa introduces me to them: a selection of Spanish writers and artists.

The chatter in the hall grows louder and louder and I see Conchita sweep in, a vision in sapphire blue satin. I wonder if she's seated at the head table. Sure enough, the man with her leads her to a seat at the end of the table. It makes sense, as she's such a high-profile actress here in Spain, but I can't help feeling a bitter sting of jealousy. As she gazes around the room, our eyes meet and she frowns for a moment before waving, the way a member of royalty might wave to a peasant, with a casual flick of the wrist. A couple other people take their seats at the head table.

"That's the Duke of Alba," Josefa whispers in my ear, as a man with slicked-back black hair and pencil-thin moustache sits down next to Conchita. "He's Franco's official representative in London."

As I watch Conchita say something to the duke, my head starts to hurt. I understand why the Brits would invite someone close to Franco if they're trying to win his favor, but still... how can they know he can be trusted?

All of a sudden, the chatter fades.

"He's here!" Josefa gasps.

I turn and see Walter Starkie and a couple of other men, one of them instantly recognizable. The slim body, the high forehead, the wavy strawberry blond hair. It's Leslie Howard. They walk right past us and I catch a waft of cologne and for the briefest of moments he looks our way and smiles.

"Did you see that?" Josefa gasps. "He smiled at us!"

Esmerelda mutters something under her breath and reaches for a crucifix around her neck. Maybe she was one of the Spaniards who believed *Gone with the Wind* was a celebration of sin.

I grimace as I remember that night, and the men throwing nails at us. Although at least they were wearing their poisoned hearts on their sleeves, unlike that traitor Santiago, who faked his outrage so convincingly. The men take their seats at the head table, facing out into the hall, then Walter Starkie gets to his feet and clears his throat.

"Good evening, ladies and gentlemen," he cries. "Thank you so much for coming. I am delighted to welcome our guest of honor, the star of stage and screen, Mr. Leslie Howard!"

The place erupts in applause and Howard smiles broadly.

"Leslie will be very busy while he's here in Spain..." Starkie continues. "I have a program of events lined up for him and he's going to be heading up a conference on *Hamlet* here at the British Institute, delivering a lecture on the great play, which, of course, he starred in on Broadway." There's another ripple of applause. "And he is also here to discuss plans for a wonderful movie collaboration between Spain and Britain—a feature film about the life of Christopher Columbus!"

The Spaniards in the audience love this, whooping excitedly. Esmerelda is the only person to look distinctly unimpressed, still muttering and clutching her crucifix.

"And now, before our dinner, let the flamenco party begin!"

Starkie announces. "We are honored to have one of the greatest new talents in flamenco in all of Spain—Santiago Lozano!"

As the hall falls silent, a flamenco guitarist strolls out onto the dance floor playing softly. I notice that Esmerelda is still staring at the top table muttering something.

"Is your aunt OK?" I whisper to Josefa.

She turns to Esmerelda. "What's wrong?"

The guitar music grows louder and Santiago comes rushing out to a wave of applause.

"That man," Esmerelda calls over the clapping, pointing to Leslie Howard. "That man has death engraved upon his face." She shudders. "When I look at it, all I see is a skull."

November 1942, France

My darling Elena,

Germany are now occupying all of France and the company of soldiers who were stationed here have been moved out—including my "guest." Before he left last night, he came to see me. "Thank you very much for your hospitality," he said from the living-room doorway. I was in my chair by the fireplace, darning some socks. Ordinarily, I wouldn't have looked up, but as he was leaving and as he had turned a blind eye to Caleb's presence, I decided to acknowledge him for once. "Thank you for keeping my secret," I said. It was the first thing I've said to him of my own volition in the two years he's been here.

He nodded and gave a sad smile. "You remind me of my mother," he said quietly, and I'm not sure, but I think I saw a tear spill from his eye. And then he was gone.

Oh Elena, what a strange day it has been. I know I can't afford to relax—a new company of soldiers could move in at any time—but for tonight at least, I feel better able to breathe.

All my love,

Grand-mère Rose

25

MADRID, 1943

All through Santiago's set I'm unable to concentrate as Esmerelda's words keep echoing around my mind. She's just a crazy old woman, I try telling myself. It's all a lot of mumbo jumbo.

But she wasn't wrong about you, was she? another voice chides. *She saw you being followed. She saw that you'd be betrayed by someone close. What if she's right about Howard? What if he's going to die here in Spain? What if the Nazis get to him?*

I take a large swig of sangria to try to stop my fear. I'm over-tired and stressed. I mustn't think irrationally. Besides, there's no way the Brits would let anything bad happen to their star guest. I'm sure they'll keep him safe. Plus he's staying at the Ritz, so I can keep a lookout for him. The bizarre nature of the situation hits me. How have I gone from starstruck fan, gazing at Howard adoringly on a lobby card in my bedroom, to being in a position to protect him?

Santiago finishes his final dance with a flourish, looking right at me. I'm so lost in my thoughts, I forget to smile and instead stare at him blankly. He turns away and bows to the top table. Damn, I mustn't let my guard slip. I clap loudly and cheer with the others.

"I hope Esmerelda didn't give you the heebie-jeebies," Josefa jokes once the dancing is over and Santiago and the musicians have left the floor.

"Not at all," I lie. "But does she ever predict anything good happening?"

"Believe it or not, yes." Josefa's smile fades. "I guess there's not as much good in the world as there once was."

Before I have time to press her any further, a waiter arrives at our table and I notice Santiago coming over.

"Carmen, are you OK?" he asks, looking concerned.

"Yes!" I smile broadly. "That was a wonderful performance."

He crouches down beside me. "It was wonderful to dance for you again. Sometimes I find it easier to say what I want to you through my body."

"Really?"

Don't buy it, Carmen retorts inside my mind, *he's a smooth-talking snake.*

"Yes. My feet they never get tongue-tied."

"No, I don't suppose they would," I reply wryly.

"Walter is insisting that I sit up there." He points to the top table. "But as soon as the meal is over, I'm going to be glued to your side." He takes my hand and squeezes it gently. I imagine turning my body to stone so it doesn't betray me. "Are you sure you're OK?" he asks softly. Once again, he seems so genuine it unnerves me. He's an even better actor than Leslie Howard.

"Yes, yes, I'm fine," I reply, forcing a smile.

As Santiago takes his place at the table, I see Leslie Howard greet him effusively and it makes me feel sick. I wish I could warn Starkie that his new pal is cozying up to the Germans, but how can I without blowing my own cover? I'll have to ask Mitchell if he can send word via the British secret service.

Howard suddenly stands, looking concerned as he glances up and down the table. He says something to Starkie and I see Santiago say something, then point in my direction. Once again, Howard meets my gaze and I feel my face flush.

Santiago bounds over and grabs my hand.

"Come, you've been invited to sit at the top table," he says excitedly.

"What? Why?" I reply, hardly able to believe my ears.

"Leslie Howard doesn't like the fact that there are thirteen people sitting there. He says it's a bad omen." He gives a shrug as if to say, *Crazy, right?* "But I saw the opportunity and I seized it. They would love it if you would make it a lucky fourteen."

"Go, go," Josefa urges. "But I want a full report of everything he says."

"Of course." I get to my feet, almost knocking my chair over in my excitement. But then I notice Esmerelda staring at Howard, grim-faced, and my excitement wanes.

I end up sitting one seat away from Howard across the table, and far closer than Conchita, who scowls as soon as I arrive.

"This is Carmen De La Fuente," Santiago announces to Howard in English. I have to stop myself from looking shocked. I had no idea he could speak English—but then that's not the only thing he's been hiding from me. "She is a Mexican actress new to Madrid, a—how do you say?—rising star."

"How exciting," Howard replies. "I'm sorry, do you speak English?"

"A little, yes," I reply, with a Mexican accent.

"Perhaps I will have time to come and see you in your show —if Mr. Starkie allows." He shoots Starkie a stern look. "The itinerary he has planned for me is chock-full. He's working me like a dog!"

He winks at me and I give a high-pitched laugh. This is so surreal. It's well known in Hollywood that Howard is a ladies' man. He had an affair with his secretary and even lived with her while he was filming *Gone with the Wind*.

"We had a wonderful time at the gala screening of your movie *Gone with the Wind*," Santiago says to Howard, placing his hand on my arm.

"Oh God!" Howard rolls his eyes. "I hated that damn role."

"What? Why?" I can't help blurting out.

"I wasn't nearly young or pretty enough to play Ashley. They made me look like a sissy doorman at the Beverly Wiltshire."

I bite on my lip to try to hide my shock. I've always been so desperate for a decent part, it never occurred to me that a famous actor like Howard might actually end up hating a lead role.

"Have you never hated a role you've been given?" he asks.

I think of my current role alongside Conchita and how much I've hated playing it since she had me strip all the depth from the character. "Yes, once or twice," I say, figuring that's something the more experienced Carmen would say.

A Spanish man sitting beside Howard starts talking to him about the potential Christopher Columbus movies and I take a moment to compose myself.

"That's Ricardo Giménez-Arnau," Santiago says quietly in my ear. "He's a Spanish diplomat. He used to be head of Franco's Foreign Service."

I feign a look of mild interest, but inside, my mind is whirring. What with Giménez-Arnau and Franco's ambassador to London at the table, it's clear that the Brits are on a major charm offensive. But is Howard merely their puppet, or a willing participant? I glance across at him. Could it be that he, like me, is playing the role of his life right here in Madrid, directed by the British secret service, or even Churchill himself, to try to win Spain over and stop them from joining forces with the Nazis? If only I were able to talk candidly with him.

"Would you like to come out with me tomorrow?" Santiago asks, while the men continue chatting.

"Where to?" I say absently, trying to stay tuned in to Howard's conversation.

"I want to take you to see the oldest house in Madrid." Santiago grins. "The house of Don Álvaro de Luján. It dates back to 1494."

"That is old," I mutter, as Conchita leans forward across the table.

"How long are you in Spain for, Leslie?" she asks as if they're old buddies.

"Almost three weeks," he replies. "Then I'm off to Lisbon for a film screening."

"Lisbon, how interesting," Conchita replies. Then the duke cuts in and Conchita sits back in her seat, clearly fuming.

"So what do you say?" Santiago asks.

"About what?"

"About going out tomorrow, so I can show you another old building."

"I don't know," I reply offhandedly. "It's my only day off. I think I might need to rest instead."

"I see." Santiago glances from me to Howard and back again and he frowns. Clearly he thinks that I'm starstruck and only have eyes for Howard. Well, let him, the traitor. A churlish part of me wants him to hurt the way he's hurt me.

The next morning, I take breakfast in the hotel restaurant, hoping to see Howard, but there's no sign of him. I guess he must be sleeping off all the traveling of the day before. After eating, I fetch a newspaper from the stand by the desk and set up camp in an armchair in the corner of the lobby. I've read the damned paper front to back and back to front before he finally appears at just before midday. I hold the paper up and peer over the top, watching as he makes his way over to the desk and talks to one of the clerks.

Howard's just heading across to a cluster of armchairs by the door when the baroness comes sweeping in. What happens next is like watching a movie as they both catch each other's gaze, look away, then do a double take. The baroness halts in her tracks and greets him effusively. Although I can't hear what they're saying, it's clear from their body language that they're meeting for the first time and they both clearly like what they see. The baroness keeps touching her hair and giggling and Howard has puffed up his chest like a peacock. My heart sinks. *Don't talk to her; she can't be trusted,* I feel like yelling across the lobby.

The baroness opens her pocketbook and takes out a card, which she hands to Howard. He puts it in his inside jacket pocket and nods as if bowing to her. She turns and walks away, a smug smile plastered upon her face. The eggs I had for breakfast threaten to make a reappearance. My suspicions better have been unfounded. I hope to God she isn't working for the Nazis.

26

MADRID, 1943

"Do you think Howard could be working for the British secret service?" I ask Mitchell as we walk around the lake the following day.

"It's certainly possible," Mitchell replies. "I've heard on the grapevine that he's going to be meeting with Franco to discuss the potential Christopher Columbus movie."

"Franco?" I gasp.

"Uh-huh. It could be purely to do with the movie, but if Churchill wanted to get a message to him then..."

"What better way than to pass it via Howard." My skin tingles at the thought.

"Exactly. It's the perfect cover when you think about it," Mitchell says. "The English can pretend that it's about a movie and Franco doesn't piss off Hitler for openly having talks with the Allies."

My excitement grows. If Spain did join the Allies, it would be another bitter blow to the Nazis, whose grip on North Africa is on the brink of collapse. To think that a fellow actor could play a role in that makes my heart lift a little.

"But the Germans aren't going to go down without a fight,"

Mitchell continues. "It's going to get a whole lot worse before it gets better."

I think of Grand-mère Rose in France and shudder.

"Chin up," Mitchell says, clearly detecting my despondency. "Even the finest sword plunged into salt water will eventually rust."

"Who said that? Roosevelt?"

He laughs. "No, an ancient Chinese warrior named Sun Tzu. He wrote a book called *The Art of War*."

"Huh, I've never really thought of war as an art form."

"You should, it definitely helps." He lights a cigarillo. "Any word from the German, Horst?"

"No. Have you had any more intelligence on the dancer?" I hold my breath, hating that a tiny part of me still hopes we might have gotten it wrong about Santiago.

Mitchell shakes his head.

"Do you think we should warn the Brits about him, given his links to Starkie? He danced for Howard at his welcome party and I know he's going to see him a lot on his trip."

"I already have, don't worry."

"OK, good."

"All right, Flamingo." He stops walking and my heart sinks. Time with my one true confidante in Madrid is always so fleeting and the loneliness I've been trying to stave off is gnawing at me from the inside. "Until next time, keep up the good work."

"Thank you." I quickly turn and walk away so he won't see the completely inappropriate tears filling my eyes.

You need to keep focused on why you're doing this, I tell myself as I march back through the park. I recall how I said those same words to Betty at the end of last year, when Teddy's mocking had once again brought her to tears. *Oh Betty, if you're still alive, I hope you're somehow able to feel me thinking of you.*

.   .   .

I put off meeting with Santiago until he invites me to accompany him to Howard's lecture on *Hamlet* at the British Institute. This is an invitation I simply cannot refuse. In preparation, I make an appointment in the hotel salon to have my hair styled. Mitchell informed me a couple of weeks ago that Elisa has now been recruited to our network here in Madrid. If only I were able to confide in her and let her know that we're on the same side.

When I tell Elisa where I'm going that evening, she glances about the place before leaning in and looking at me in the mirror. "My boss went to dinner with him the other night."

"Leslie Howard?"

"Yes, she was full of it the next day. He's the one who had all the roses delivered." She nods to a huge vase of pink roses on the reception desk.

It's OK, Howard's only here for a couple more days before he leaves for his film screening in Portugal, I try to reassure myself as Elisa puts my hair in rollers. *He wouldn't be stupid enough to get emotionally involved while he's here.* My face flushes as I think of my own stupidity getting involved with Santiago.

Any doubts I might have had about Howard working for the British government are dispelled that night. His talk about *Hamlet* is clearly a thinly veiled attack on Hitler. As I watch him speak passionately, alluding to the dark forces of Nazism and comparing it to the courage of the Allies, I think back to the hours I spent watching him in *Gone with the Wind*. It might not get him nearly as much attention, but what he is doing here in Madrid to help the Allies must surely go down as his greatest role.

Once his speech is over, I'd been hoping that he'd hang around so I'd have a chance to talk to him, but he says a few words to Starkie, then promptly disappears.

Starkie appears visibly exasperated and marches over to Santiago and me.

"Howard's demanded some time off," he says to Santiago.

"Why?" Santiago replies.

"Apparently I'm working him too hard—I forgot to account for the fact that he needs to woo half of Madrid."

Santiago laughs. "Say no more."

But I'm unable to even pretend to smile. Has Howard asked for time off to spend with the baroness?

Starkie strides off muttering to himself crossly and Santiago takes my hands in his. "Carmen, is something wrong? You seem very distant."

I have a sudden flashback to Esmerelda seeing death written all over Howard's face and my stomach churns. "I'm fine. I'm just tired," I mutter.

"You're always tired these days."

"Yes, yes I am," I snap.

Santiago recoils as if I just slapped him. I know I should apologize, but I can't bring myself to.

"I think I understand what's going on here," he says.

"What?" My heart starts to pound. I've been so concerned with the truth about Santiago, what if he's uncovered the truth about me?

"You prefer Mr. Hollywood Howard over me."

Yes, actually, I do, I want to respond, *but not for the reasons you think.*

"Well, I wish you luck," he says, clearly taking my silence as an affirmation. "You heard what Walter said; by all accounts he's spending his spare time here seducing half the women in Madrid."

"I'm going back to the hotel," I say with a sigh.

"Fine," he replies. "Would you like me to get you a cab?"

"No, it's OK, I'll find my own way back."

There would have been a time when Santiago wouldn't

have heard of me leaving unaccompanied, but now he simply nods.

All the way to the Ritz, I berate myself. I shouldn't have made my disdain for Santiago so obvious. Still, at least he thinks it's because I've had my head turned by Howard and not that I'm on to him.

I get back to find an envelope waiting for me at the reception desk. I recognize the thick creamy paper instantly and feel sick. I take it up to my room and open it to find a train ticket and a card from Horst. *Let the adventure begin...* he's written. I study the train ticket. It's a return to a place called Canfranc, leaving next Wednesday. Why does that name sound familiar? As I remember, my skin prickles.

Canfranc is a village right by the French border. It's the only municipality in Spain under German control. They took it over last year so they could take charge of the railroad station there and police the border. Before then, thousands of Jewish refugees had fled to safety from France and spies had used it to travel back and forth. Why would Horst invite me there? Could it be just an innocent work trip? If he is involved in the import-export business, it would make sense that he'd have business to attend to there. But, on the other hand, it could be a ploy to get me into enemy-controlled territory so he can smuggle me into France to be interrogated and tortured, or worse. Once again, I think of Betty and wince.

I go over to the dresser and stare at my reflection in the mirror. The whole point of me being here is to try to uncover intelligence about the Germans. I'm sure as hell not going to find it hiding away in my room. Inspired by Leslie Howard and his work for the British, I'm going to go to Canfranc to see what I can find and Mitchell better not try to stop me.

27

MADRID, 1943

My next meeting with Mitchell is the day before I'm due to go to Canfranc. It's a beautiful warm afternoon and I'm hoping that the bright blue skies will predispose him to allow me to go. I find him waiting beneath the assigned tree, grim-faced and puffing away on a cigarillo.

"Have you heard the news?" he says by way of greeting. Just from his expression, I can tell it isn't good news and my heart sinks. *Has he heard about Betty? Has she been killed by the Germans?*

I shake my head.

"Leslie Howard," he says.

I look at him, surprised. "What about him?"

"He's dead."

"What?" I reach out blindly for the tree trunk to steady me. "Dead?" I gasp. "How?"

"His flight was shot down this morning."

"What flight?"

"His flight back to Britain from Portugal. It was shot down over the Bay of Biscay."

"But..." *No! No! No!* I press so hard on the tree, the bark cuts into my palm. "Who shot it down?"

"The Luftwaffe. It's the first time they've shot down a commercial airliner on that route. What did I tell you about it getting worse before it gets better?"

All I can see are images of Howard playing on a loop in my head—his first night in Madrid at dinner, his impassioned speech about *Hamlet*, playing Ashley in *Gone with the Wind*. "Why would the Luftwaffe have done that?"

"I don't know, but it was a German news agency who broke the story and they named Howard and his manager as being on board so..."

"So they must have been targeting him." I feel sick to my stomach.

"It looks that way, yes."

"Goddamn it!" I turn away, tears stinging my eyes. "How did they know he was going to be on that flight?" I feel sick as I think of Howard the night he arrived in Madrid, announcing to the table that he was going to Lisbon for a film screening. Any number of people at that table could have been reporting his movements back to the Germans, including Conchita—and Santiago.

"You OK, Flamingo?" Mitchell puts his hand on my arm, but I'm beyond calming.

"Yes, I just... He was an acting hero of mine. I can't believe he's gone. I should have done something."

"What could you have done?"

"I could have warned him that this godforsaken place is crawling with Germans—and to not trust anyone." Then I think of what Elisa told me about him going out to dinner with the baroness the day before he left Madrid. Could it have been that dinner that sealed his fate?

"He would have been warned by the Brits. There was nothing you could have done, Flamingo."

I smile at him through teary eyes. "I don't suppose you've got one of those *Art of War* quotes for what to do when war is testing your very last nerve?"

Mitchell laughs. "How about, 'It is only the enlightened ruler and wise general who will use the highest intelligence of the army for the purposes of spying and thereby they achieve great results.'"

"Hmm, I sure hope so." I blink away my tears, going into a strange numb daze as I tell him about Horst's invitation. All the while the same questions play on a loop in my head: *How did the Germans know Howard would be on that plane? Did I miss something? Could I have done something to save him?* "Do you think it's strange that he's invited me to Canfranc?" I ask Mitchell, once I've updated him.

He shakes his head. "By all accounts, Canfranc station is quite something. The Nazis like to do a lot of entertaining there."

"In the station?" I frown.

"Uh-huh. There's a really grand hotel there, full of bars and restaurants. The Spanish call it the *Titanic* of the mountains."

"I'm not sure that's such a great omen."

He grins. "Maybe not, but it makes sense that he'd have business there if he is involved in smuggling. And if he wants to impress you."

"OK." I'm not sure whether to feel reassured or repulsed by this.

"Are you sure you're up to it though? This will be your most dangerous mission to date."

"Of course." My shock over Howard's death is starting to solidify into a cold hard rage and desire for revenge.

Mitchell looks at me and nods. "All righty then. Good luck, Flamingo."

. . .

In some ways, it's a blessing that I have to leave for Canfranc the very next day. The need to focus stops me from falling into a pit of despair. After much deliberation, I decide to take my pistol with me—hidden inside the hatbox along with my miniature camera—and I tuck one of my cyanide capsules in the sole of my shoe. *Better safe than sorry*, I tell myself cheerily, to try to stop the fear gnawing at me.

But as soon as I reach Atocha Station, I become plagued by doubt. *What if Horst discovers my pistol? How would I explain it?* I think back to what happened to poor old "Steve" in the training video I performed in—the role that led to all of this. How ironic would it be if I end up blowing my cover in exactly the same way as him?

Well, it's too late to do anything about it now, I tell myself as I walk across the crowded concourse to the platform for the first leg of my journey. I need to take a train to a place named Zaragoza–Delicias where I'll change trains for Canfranc.

I've received no further word from Horst since the delivery of the tickets, so I have no idea if he'll be here to meet me. As the conductor shows me to my carriage, I half expect to see him already waiting in the compartment, but there's no sign of him. Instead, two nuns are sitting in the seats opposite mine—a sight that instantly reassures me.

Every time a passenger walks past the compartment, I expect to see Horst's icy blue eyes peering in at me. But then a whistle cuts through the noise outside and the train judders into life. Perhaps he's meeting me in Delicias or maybe he's meeting me in Canfranc. Part of me is relieved to have more time on my own, but another part is apprehensive at what to expect when we do meet.

About an hour and a half after leaving Madrid, we arrive at Delicias. I'd been hoping for the soothing presence of the nuns on the second leg of the journey, but sadly they disappear off toward the station exit.

Thankfully, there's only a forty-minute wait for the Canfranc train, which I board with a growing feeling of anxiety. Could this train be leading to my capture or even death? It's a sobering thought and I'm grateful to find a bickering young couple in my compartment. Their melodrama—over whether he was paying too much of the wrong kind of attention to the waitress who served them in a restaurant last night—is a welcome distraction. It's strangely reassuring to realize that there are still lives where this kind of drama is deemed important.

The second leg of the journey is almost six hours long, meaning I get into Canfranc at just before five in the evening. As the train begins cutting through a valley, I see the craggy outline of the Pyrenees in the distance and my pulse quickens. On the other side of those mountains is Occupied France. This is the closest I've been to Grand-mère Rose since leaving America. It's a realization that fills me with both hope and dread. Who knows how her life has changed under the occupation—or even if she's still alive? Mitchell has been briefing me about the atrocities going on in France—the thousands of people rounded up and sent to internment camps, the people executed in the streets. I push the thought away. Grand-mère Rose *has* to be alive.

Then I think of Betty. Could she have been brought on this exact same route to France, to be tortured or worse? The thought that the man I'm about to meet may very well be tangled up in Hitler's evil regime makes my blood boil. *All the more reason to keep your cool and be on your guard,* I remind myself.

As the train puffs its way into the station, I can't help gasping—it's the largest, most ornate structure I've ever seen, more like a castle. The mountains looming behind it provide the perfect dramatic backdrop, their tops draped in smoky wisps of cloud. As I step down onto the platform and take a breath of the cool, crisp air, I notice the stark red, white and black of a flag bearing a swastika fluttering from the building. It's a sharp reminder that I'm in German territory and no amount of grandeur can disguise the fact that this "*Titanic* of the mountains" is now rotten to the core.

As a porter helps me with my hatbox and case, I scan the platform for any sign of Horst. Suddenly he appears, striding through the cloud of smoke billowing from the train. I can't help being struck by the cinematic feel of the scene.

But this isn't a movie and he's part of the same organization who murdered one of my Hollywood idols and has very likely murdered my friend Betty, I remind myself, my jaw clenched.

"Carmen!" he cries as he reaches me. "I'm so happy that you accepted my invitation for an adventure."

"Of course—how could I refuse?" I trill, vowing to do Leslie Howard proud with my performance. "This place is incredible."

"Ah, trust me, the best is yet to come." He takes my case and hatbox from the porter and I say a silent prayer that he doesn't drop the box, revealing my pistol.

We walk to the end of the platform and into a ticket hall—although with its elegant high ceilings, white stone pillars and polished tiled floor, it could easily double as a ballroom. The hall is milling with people and I hear snatches of conversations —some in Spanish but most in German. A group of German soldiers march across the hall toward us and my throat tightens.

"Wait till you see the hotel upstairs," Horst says. "It is out of this world."

The soldiers march past us and out onto the platform and I'm able to breathe again.

"Thank you so much for this," I say, trying to ignore my growing dread at what Horst might be anticipating by way of repayment.

"You are very welcome. And tell me, did you enjoy your shopping trip?"

"Very much, but it was too generous of you."

"Nonsense." He leads me into a pristine white-tiled corridor and over to an elevator. "What use is having wealth if you can't share it with those you care about?" He looks me up and down appraisingly. "I knew you'd look fantastic in that dress."

I'm not your plaything, I want to snap, but I bite my tongue and smile sweetly.

The elevator up to the hotel feels uncomfortably small and Horst feels uncomfortably close. He appears to have doused himself in pine-scented cologne. It's so cloying, it makes my stomach churn. I wonder what the sleeping arrangements will be and if he has booked me a room of my own. We emerge into the plush lobby and I follow Horst to the reception desk, where a woman is giving us the kind of rictus grin that wouldn't look out of place in a toothpowder commercial. Her plum lipstick is a couple shades too dark and, combined with the smile, the overall effect is slightly unnerving.

"This is my guest, Carmen De La Fuente," Horst says to her.

She nods at me and, to my huge relief, fetches me a room key from the rack behind her on the wall.

"I asked for you to be in the room next door to mine," Horst says as we make our way along a corridor with a carpet so plush it feels like walking on a feather bed.

"Wonderful," I reply, trying to focus on the positive—being in such close proximity will make it far easier to keep tabs on him; I just hope he isn't imagining us having any late-night trysts.

When we reach my room, he deposits my case and hatbox just inside the door, then steps back into the corridor. "I have a quick business matter to attend to," he says. "So why don't you take some time to relax and freshen up and I'll come and get you for dinner at eight."

"That sounds great," I reply, instantly wondering what kind of business meeting he might be having and with whom.

"My room is just here," he says, pointing to the door to the left of mine.

"Excellent," I reply.

"Oh, and please wear one of the new dresses I bought you—the pink one tonight, I think."

I'm barely able to disguise my horror at the fact that he's lined up which outfits he wants me to wear and when, like some power-crazed wardrobe manager. "Of course," I mumble, and as I close the door, I feel cold with dread. He might not suspect me of working for the Allies, but he clearly sees me as some kind of puppet, here to do his bidding. "Yes, well, we'll see who's pulling whose strings," I mutter as I take a look around my room. There's a door to the bathroom to my left and a double bed to my right, with a huge wardrobe directly opposite and a matching oak dresser next to the window. A chaise longue runs along the far wall and a couple of stiff-backed armchairs are positioned in front of the fire.

I go straight over to the arched window and open the red velvet drapes. The room looks out onto the rear of the station, which I'm initially disappointed about, but then I notice a siding to the right leading to what looks like some kind of goods yard. A couple of men in overalls are busy carrying a pile of crates into one of two huge sheds. I know from Mitchell that any goods, or indeed passengers, passing between France and Spain have to disembark at Canfranc because the Spanish refused to use the same kind of rail lines as the French. This might cause huge inconvenience to passengers, but it will hopefully give me the perfect opportunity to snoop around and uncover something.

. . .

About half an hour later, I've just gotten out of a bath and into my robe when I hear men's voices in the corridor outside speaking in German. I hurry over to my door. Thankfully, it has one of those new-fangled peepholes fitted. I peer out and see two men, their heads horribly distorted by the concave lens. But one thing I can tell for certain—they're both wearing German military uniforms complete with swastikas on their armbands. They walk past, out of view, and I hear a knock—could it be on Horst's door? It has to be; I hear him greeting them. The voices fade, as they go inside his room.

I hurry over to the adjoining wall and press my ear to it. All I can hear is a low deep murmur. Damn. I glance around my room, searching for some kind of inspiration. Then I have a brainwave. I rummage in my case for the pink dress. By instructing me to wear it, Horst has inadvertently done me a huge favor. I put it on and do up the bottom buttons at the back, leaving the top few undone. Then I go out into the corridor in my stockinged feet, leaving my door open. Checking the coast is clear, I tiptoe over to Horst's room and, making sure to stand out of view of the peephole, I press my ear to the door. The men's voices are much clearer now.

I listen for a moment, trying to make out any key words and wishing I knew more German. "*Lieferung*" and "*Mitternacht*" are said a couple times, so I recite them over and over to commit them to my memory. I'm about to creep back to my room when Horst's door suddenly flies open and I have to bite my tongue to stop from crying out in shock. Instantly, I switch into my cover story, holding my hand up, pretending to be about to knock.

"Oh!" I exclaim as I see one of the soldiers standing there. "I'm so sorry to interrupt."

He looks me up and down coldly.

"Carmen, is that you?" I hear Horst call in Spanish from behind him in the room.

"Yes, I'm sorry. I need your help with something, but it can wait."

The soldier's scowl turns to a smirk and my head fills with cuss words as I bow my head and pretend to look bashful.

"What is it?" Horst appears at the door. He gasps in delight when he sees me. "Oh, I knew that dress would look divine on you!"

"Thank you." I gaze up at him through my eyelashes. "It's very embarrassing, but I was struggling doing up the top buttons." I turn to reveal my back. "But I don't want to interrupt anything. I can come back later."

"Not at all." Horst beams at me, clearly over the moon that a semi-naked woman has shown up at his door in front of the soldiers.

I feel his cool fingers brush the skin on my back, which instantly makes me shiver with dread.

"You have goosebumps," he says, his fingers lingering at the nape of my neck.

"Oh, do I?" I reply, horrified that he might think they're from excitement at being touched by him.

Finally, he does up the buttons.

"Thank you so much." I turn and smile at the men and back away toward my room. "Sorry again for the interruption."

"An interruption like that is welcome any time," Horst says, making me want to scrub the skin he's touched until it's red raw.

As I go back into my room, I hear one of the soldiers say something in German and the others laugh. Although I can't understand what he said, I can tell from the tone that it's salacious and my skin crawls even more.

I storm over to the window and look up at the wall of mountains. Now it's getting dark outside, their craggy outline appears ominous rather than breathtaking. I think of all the brave souls who have risked everything to come through this place, trying to escape. Now the Germans control Canfranc, those fleeing them are unable to escape via train—or it's a lot more perilous anyways—so they make the journey over the mountains on foot. I can't even begin to imagine how arduous and terrifying that must be.

I take my Spanish–German phrasebook from my case. I figured I was safe to bring it because if Horst sees it, I can just say that it's because I want to learn his mother tongue. He's conceited enough to believe this instantly. I look up the words I've memorized. "*Lieferung*" means delivery and "*Mitternacht*" means midnight. Once again, my skin erupts in goosebumps, but this time it *is* from excitement. Horst must be expecting some kind of delivery—but the question is, what?

28

CANFRANC, 1943

At just before eight, there's a knock on my door. I open it to find Horst standing there, smartly dressed in a black dinner suit and crisp white shirt.

"You look so smart!" I cry.

"Yes," he agrees. "I was going to ask for your help buttoning my shirt." He gives one of his high-pitched laughs, instantly setting my teeth on edge.

"Oh don't!" I put my hands to my face, feigning embarrassment. "I'm so embarrassed. I didn't realize you'd have guests. I'm sorry for interrupting your meeting."

"It was nothing. They'd just popped by to check some papers. I'm expecting a wine shipment tonight."

"How exciting, where from?"

"France."

"I hear their wine is very good."

"Oh yes, it's wonderful." He smiles smugly.

As we make our way to the elevator, I ponder what he's just told me. Would the Germans really be exporting the French wine to Spain? Wouldn't it be more likely that they'd send it back home to Germany?

We take the elevator down to the second floor and as the door slides open, I hear the sound of music and chatter. Horst takes me through to one of the most sumptuous restaurants I've ever seen—and I've seen more than a few lately. Enormous chandeliers cast beams of soft shimmering light upon the beautifully laid tables. The maître d' greets Horst like an old friend—clearly he's a regular diner here—and takes us over to a table by a huge arched window with a view of the station.

"Oh, how lovely," I say, gesturing at the view. "We can watch the trains come and go. That's if there are any more trains at this time of night?" I look at him questioningly.

"Yes, there will be a couple arriving from France," he says, picking up the menu. "You have to have the steak here. It's wonderful." The firmness of his tone indicates that this is an order rather than a recommendation.

"Of course," I happily agree, although inside I'm cussing his arrogance again.

A waiter appears at our table and Horst orders for us both, with me nodding along meekly.

"I knew that color would suit you," he says once the waiter's gone, staring appraisingly at the hideous pink dress, his gaze lingering a little too long on my chest.

"It's always been my most favorite color," I lie through gritted teeth.

"I told the shop assistant to make sure you bought it in that color."

"Oh, I see." Again, I feel a mixture of loathing and dread at his apparent need to control every last detail.

"So, tell me, were you excited to get my invitation to come and see me here?"

"Oh yes. It's so lovely to see you again, and to see some more of Spain—although I guess Canfranc could now be called part of Germany." I smile sweetly.

He laughs. "Yes. Well, we had to do something to stop the vermin from escaping."

"The vermin?"

He leans forward slightly. "The Jews."

"Oh, I see. Yes of course." *Nazi scum!* I think to myself. *You're the ones who are the vermin.* This is promising though. The fact that he's being so open about his poisonous views tells me that he doesn't suspect me at all and that hopefully I'll be able to worm some useful information out of him.

"I see you're wearing my bracelet." He nods at the bangle on my wrist.

"Yes, I love it. But you need to help me solve the mystery."

"What mystery?" He instantly looks defensive. Interesting.

"What does the inscription say?" I ask. "I assume it's in French."

"Oh... I—uh—I don't know."

"Didn't the jeweler you bought it from tell you?"

"No." His gaze flits about, as if he's searching for the perfect explanation at one of the other tables. "To be honest with you, I was in a hurry that day, and I thought it looked so nice, you would be happy with it."

"I am, I am!" I cry. "It's beautiful. You are such a kind and thoughtful man." I reach out and place my hand on his arm. Thankfully, my appeal to his vanity works and the smug smile returns to his face.

"It looks very nice on your arm. Just as you look nice upon my arm," he says and I fight the urge to retch. Did he get the bangle in a hurry because he stole it? Does he not know what the inscription means because there was no jeweler? My skin beneath the bangle begins to itch and burn as the horrible truth dawns upon me. Could the bracelet have belonged to a Jewish woman?

Just then, the whistle of a train echoes through the valley. I look out the window and see a locomotive chugging in from

France. As it comes to a halt, I hear the sharp clip of what sounds like hundreds of soldiers' jackboots marching along the platform. Barked instructions in German drift up through the air.

"It sounds like quite a commotion," I say with a laugh.

Horst seems completely unperturbed. "They're just checking for any unwanted visitors."

I raise my eyebrows questioningly.

"Escapees and enemy agents," he says, adjusting his gold knife and fork so that they're in perfect alignment. "You can't be too sure."

I suppress a shudder. What would he do, I wonder, if he knew an enemy agent was sitting right opposite him?

All through dinner, Horst drones on about tales from his youth in Germany. All through dessert—apple strudel, ordered by Horst, naturally—I hear about his supreme abilities as an archer and a horseman. Frustratingly, for someone who could talk the hind leg off a donkey, Horst hasn't said a thing that could be of potential interest to the OSS. By the time we're having our after-dinner coffee, I am bored out of my mind and hate him with even more of a passion. But while I've been nodding and cooing and laughing and gasping at all the appropriate moments, I've also been coming up with a plan for how I can give him the slip after dinner and sneak down to the goods yard out back.

A cheer goes up at a large round table close to ours, where a group of German officers have been dining and I look up to see a balding man in a smart suit approaching them. The soldiers all stand to greet him with hearty handshakes and pats on the back.

"Who's that?" I ask casually.

"Albert Le Lay. He's the head of French customs here and the hotel proprietor." Horst smiles. "He's a wonderful man."

As I watch Le Lay join the soldiers' table and light up a

cigar, I feel sick. What a traitor to his people, sucking up to the Germans like this.

"Would you like to go for a drink, or dancing?" Horst asks as he downs the last of his coffee. "There are several bars here."

"I hate to be a terrible killjoy, but I'm feeling very tired from the journey. Would it be all right if we called it a night? That way, I can be full of energy for whatever adventures you have planned tomorrow." I smile at him suggestively. I'm fully prepared for him to put up some resistance, but to my surprise and relief, he nods.

"Of course. I could do with an early night myself."

Hmm, does he really mean this or does he need to check on his mysterious wine delivery? I ponder. As we make our way back up to the bedrooms, I feel a wave of dread as another prospect dawns on me: what if he's eager for an early night because he thinks he'll be spending it with me?

As we reach my room, I look at him and smile. "Thank you so much for a lovely evening. I hope you sleep well."

"You are very welcome. Would it be all right if...?"

I prepare myself for the worst.

"If I gave you a goodnight kiss?"

I'm taken aback that he's polite enough to ask but also filled with dread that he might see a goodnight kiss as some kind of ticket straight to my bed.

"That would be lovely," I reply tersely.

He grips me by my shoulders and plants a kiss that feels more like a punch upon my lips. "Goodnight, Carmen. I very much look forward to more adventures with you tomorrow."

"Likewise," I reply, fighting the urge to wipe all trace of him from my mouth.

"I shall call for you for breakfast at nine."

"I look forward to it," I say as I unlock my door. "Sleep well."

"And you too."

I lock my door behind me and lean against it for a moment, waiting to hear the sound of his own door closing. When I don't, I turn and peer through the peephole and see that he's still standing there, hand raised as if he's about to knock. My heart plummets; of course it was too good to be true that he would meekly go off to bed. Of course he wants more from me. But then his hand drops and he turns to go. My body floods with relief as I hear his door close.

I hurry over to my bed and take the hatbox out from under it. Then I get changed into a far more comfortable dress of my own. I go over to the window and look out. All is quiet in the yard below. I can just make out the outline of some crates in the moonlight. I look at the clock by my bed. It's just after eleven. I decide to wait and watch to see if there's any sign of a delivery at midnight. And then, much later, at around three, when hopefully Horst should be fast asleep and dreaming of himself no doubt, I shall slip down to the yard to see what I can find. I take the pistol from its hiding place and tuck it into the pocket of my coat.

I spend the next few hours alternating between watching from the window and listening by my door for any sight or sound of Horst, but there's nothing. Every so often, I hear the drunken laughter and chatter of guests returning to their rooms from the bars, but other than that all is relatively quiet.

Finally, at just after three, I slip from my room. I've had plenty of time to work on a cover story for if I happen to bump into Horst, or I'm apprehended by a member of the station staff or, even worse, a German soldier: I'll tell them that I saw what I thought was an animal in distress down in the yard so I've slipped out to investigate.

Taking the elevator downstairs is far too risky, so I head in the opposite direction to a door marked "Fire exit" at the end of the corridor. It opens onto a flight of stone steps. Exposed pipes line the stark white walls and the air here is cold and drafty. It's a marked contrast to the warmth and elegance of the rest of the hotel and station and I can't help feeling it's somehow symbolic of the evil lurking beneath the splendor. I follow the stairs down to the bottom and very slowly open the door, wincing at the loud creak of the hinges. I wait a moment to see if anyone is out there and has heard me, but there's no sound or sign of movement.

I take a step out and shiver as the icy air hits me. The moon appears to have gone behind a cloud and it takes a moment for my eyes to adjust to the dark. Then I realize to my delight that I've come out right at the end of the station by the goods yard. The mountains loom above me like a great black fortress wall, pressing down on me and making me feel as tiny and vulnerable as a mouse. I search on the ground for something to stop the door from locking shut behind me. Finding a stone, I wedge it between the door and the frame and creep over to the pile of crates in the yard. Somewhere high above, there's the piercing shriek of a bird.

"Damn!" I whisper to stop myself from yelping in fright.

I thought I saw an animal in distress. I came down to check it was all right, I mentally rehearse as I slip behind the crates so that I won't be visible from any of the hotel rooms. Horst's room will have the same view as mine after all. As soon as I'm up close to the crates, my heart sinks. Made of wood, the lids have all been nailed shut. There's no way I'd be able to get inside one of them without a crowbar and making a hell of a noise. *Goddammit, there's no way I've risked everything to come down here to go back empty-handed.*

I glance over at the shed. It's highly unlikely that it will have been left unlocked, but thanks to the lock-picking training I was given at The Farm, that might not be too much of an obstacle. I take two of the pins from my hair in preparation. The only problem is that the shed is visible to the hotel, and to Horst's room. I creep closer and just as I'm about to make my move, the moon comes out from behind its cloud and shines a slivery spotlight right on the shed door. *You've got to be kidding me!*

I crouch down and look up at the sky. Another cloud, disturbingly shaped like a bomb, is scudding its way toward the moon. It isn't very big, so I reckon it will only give me a minute's cover at most. I wait until it creeps across the moon's face and make a break for the door, hairpins at the ready. But, to my surprise, when I try the door, it opens straight away. I frown. *Why would it be unlocked? What if it's Horst, checking on his midnight delivery?*

Thankfully, the shed door doesn't creak, so I'm able to slip inside in silence. The place is steeped in darkness, instantly reassuring me that I must be alone. I take a moment to look around the place. There are piles of open empty crates scattered on the floor to my left and towers of shut crates to my right. *What is inside them?*

I creep further into the shed. I might not be able to prise any of the crates open, but there might be some kind of paperwork giving a clue to the crates' contents. I spy a desk in the far corner and my pulse quickens. But when I reach it, all I find is a dirty cup and plate and a pot full of stubby pencils. There's no sign of any paperwork. I slip behind the desk and see three drawers on the left-hand side. I quickly try them to discover that they're all locked. I take my hairpins from my pocket and get to work.

It takes a couple of attempts, but I manage to get the first drawer open and I feel like cheering. I picture sharing any intelligence I uncover with Mitchell, and absolving myself for my stupidity over Santiago. This is my chance to prove my true worth as an agent and avenge Howard's murder.

I peer inside the drawer. The first thing I see is a picture of a scantily clad woman. I put it back and carefully remove a sheaf of papers from underneath. They're clearly some kind of customs documents with columns for cargo and quantity and weight. As I leaf through, I see something that makes my heart almost stop beating—*Original location: Switzerland, goods: gold bars, quantity: three tons*. I continue looking through the papers and see a document where the original location is listed as Spain. It's for something called tungsten. Final destination: Germany. *Tungsten, tungsten, tungsten*. It's too dark to use my camera and as I stand there trying to memorize the word, I hear a sound that makes my blood freeze. A slight shuffling from behind the pile of crates to my left. It's probably just a rat, I tell myself, quickly putting the papers back in the drawer. Then I hear another sound, like a footstep and far too loud to be a rat.

I crouch down behind the desk. Had someone been working in here and heard me coming and lain in wait? Could it be Horst? Or even worse, one of the soldiers? *Damn! Damn! Damn!* My cover story is of no use whatsoever now. I can hardly say I saw an animal in distress inside the desk drawer.

A thin finger of moonlight pokes through the grimy window above the desk and I see a shadowy figure flit between the crates. I fumble in my pocket for my pistol, keeping it there ready to use. But, to my surprise, no one appears.

I peer around the desk, watching and waiting, but whoever it is seems to be staying put, as if they might be hiding from me. But why? I quickly run through possible explanations. Whoever it is can't be German; they would have apprehended me already. So who else might be snooping around in here? Someone who wouldn't want to be discovered by the German authorities.

I hear the first of the dawn chorus begin to chirp outside. I can't stay here much longer. I'm going to have to risk moving. But do I make a break for the door, or try to apprehend whoever it is hiding behind the crates? I decide on the latter option. If I head for the door, I'll be leaving myself wide open to being attacked.

Crouching down low, I creep toward the pile of crates and peer behind them. There, at the other end, I see a figure hunched down facing the door. Are they getting ready to make a break for it too? I take a moment to figure out my next move. They clearly haven't heard me come behind the crates, so right now I have the upper hand. I take my pistol from my pocket and, holding it in front of me, I take one... two... three steps toward them. I'm so close now, I can hear their breathing and smell the sour scent of stale sweat. Could this person be a vagrant, sheltering here for the night? It hardly seems likely, in such a remote place. It seems far more likely that they're on the run. Could it be that we are on the same side?

Keeping my gun at the ready, I whisper, "*Hola.*"

The figure in front of me springs up and spins around.

"Holy cow!" he exclaims with a broad American accent. "Please don't shoot!"

I'm so shocked and relieved to hear a voice from home, I'm momentarily stunned. "Please!" he implores. "I-I'm only nineteen."

"It's OK," I whisper back in English but with a Mexican accent. I can't afford to give too much away. "We're on the same side—I think."

"What the hell?" His mouth falls open in shock.

"What are you doing here?" I ask, lowering my pistol but keeping it ready just in case.

"I was shot down over France. I'm a pilot. I'm trying to make my way back to Britain. I snuck onto a train that got in earlier tonight. I was hoping to make it out of here on another train tomorrow."

"Geez!" I shake my head.

"What are *you* doing here?" he asks.

"Long story. All I can say is we're definitely on the same

side and hopefully I'll be able to help you. This place is crawling with Germans."

"No kidding! I saw their reception committee when I got in. I thought I was done for, but I managed to slip into this yard when they weren't looking."

I take a moment to get a good look at him. He's wearing civilian clothes, but even in the dark, I can see that he's dirty and unshaven. He'd stick out like a sore thumb amongst the glamorous guests at the hotel. "How exactly were you planning on getting on a train tomorrow? No offense, but you sure as hell don't blend in."

"There's someone working for the French Resistance here at the station. I was hoping to get a message to him."

"And how exactly were you hoping to do that?"

He shrugs. "I don't know, I guess I thought I'd wing it."

"Hmm. Well, you can't stay here, it's way too risky."

His eyes widen with fear. "Where should I go then?"

"I have a room in the hotel here. I think you should hide out there while I try to get a message to the Resistance contact."

He gives a huge sigh of relief. "That would be awesome, thank you."

"There's only one small problem."

"What?"

"I'm staying here as a guest of a German."

He instantly stiffens.

"Don't worry, it's part of my job. You have to trust me, we're on the same side and we have to be real careful."

"Of course."

"OK, let's get out of here," I say, way more bravely than I feel.

We creep over to the door and I peer outside. Thankfully, the moon is obscured again, although the sky to the east is now lightening.

"Follow me," I whisper before skulking behind the crates

until I reach the closest point to the fire exit. I glance up at the hotel. The windows stare back at me like vacant black eyes. *Could anyone be watching from them? Could Horst be watching?* I have no choice but to take the risk. "Now," I whisper, hunching as low as I can and running on tiptoes to the door. Thankfully, the stone is still wedging it open and we both slip inside the stairwell.

I'm about to lead the pilot up the stairs when I hear the clang of a door somewhere above us and the sound of feet on steps. My stomach appears to do some kind of backflip as we both stand, frozen to the spot. The footsteps get louder as whoever it is gets closer. I frantically search my mind for some kind of plausible cover story as to why I might be pressed against a wall in the fire exit with an American man who bears all the telltale signs of being on the run. But the only thing my mind unhelpfully comes up with is, *Looks like you're both done for.* Left with no other option, I close my eyes and pray. And then I hear a sound as sweet as any birdsong—another door opening on the floor just above us and the footsteps disappearing.

"Whoa!" the pilot exclaims.

"Quick," I say, not wanting to linger there a moment longer. We run up the stairs all the way to the top floor. "OK, I need to check the coast is clear," I whisper, opening the door a crack. I instantly close it again as I see the back of a member of the hotel staff making their way along the corridor, thankfully in the opposite direction. I get my room key at the ready. "My room is just along the corridor," I whisper. "I'll go ahead and unlock the door, then when I give you the signal, make a run for it."

"Yes, ma'am."

I take a breath, then stride from the stairwell toward my room, praying Horst isn't looking out of his peephole as I pass his door. I unlock my own door with trembling fingers, then quickly look and listen for any sign of life before beckoning at the pilot. Quick as a flash, he sprints along the corridor and into my room. I quietly shut the door and lock it before bending forwards to catch my breath, hands on my knees to support me.

"Holy cow!" the pilot gasps.

"Yup." I take a couple of breaths, then head over to the window, pull the drapes tightly shut and light the lamp. The first thing that strikes me about the pilot is how young he looks beneath the dirt and patches of stubble. His eyes are wide and forget-me-not blue, made larger by the long lashes framing them, and there's a sprinkling of freckles across his nose.

"Thank you," he whispers.

"No problem. OK, you and I need to come up with a plan." I gesture at him to take a seat on the chaise longue. "My German host will be calling for me at nine to go for breakfast. I'll try to smuggle you some food from the restaurant. I take it you must be hungry?"

"Starving." He nods.

"Right, then you can hide out here while I'm out with the German." I look around the room, my gaze coming to a rest on the cavernous closet. "There will do," I say, pointing to it.

"Sure thing."

"We still have a few hours. Would you like to use the bathroom, freshen up?"

He grins and looks even more boyish as dimples appear either side of his mouth. "I guess I must stink a bit."

"Hmm, just a bit."

We both laugh quietly and it feels so sweet to have this precious moment of release.

"Go have a bath," I whisper, gesturing at the bathroom door. "But before you do that you must tell me, who is the Resistance contact, here at the station?"

He stops and turns by the bathroom door. "It's a guy named Albert Le Lay—the hotel proprietor."

29

CANFRANC, 1943

As I listen to the gush of the water in the bathroom, my mind spins. Albert Le Lay seemed so pally with the Germans in the restaurant. Horst described him as "wonderful." Could it be that the jovial hotel proprietor isn't a traitor to his people but a hero? The thought that Le Lay could be capable of hoodwinking the Germans in such a way is thrilling.

When the pilot reappears from the bathroom on a cloud of lavender-scented steam, I give him a couple of blankets and a pillow and tell him to get a couple of hours' sleep on the chaise.

I lie on my bed staring up at the ceiling, way too wired to sleep. My discovery of the documents about the gold has paled into insignificance compared to my other find. I have to get him out of here safely. The thought of what the Germans would do to the pilot if they found him doesn't bear thinking about.

I finally slip into a hazy sleep at about six, waking suddenly at the sound of someone talking in the corridor. I look at the clock and see that it's almost eight. I can hear the soft purr of the pilot's breathing and I wonder when he last had the chance to properly sleep. After slipping into the bathroom to freshen up and get changed, I put a couple of pillows and blanket inside the wardrobe to try to make it as comfortable as possible. Once I've got his hiding place ready, I go over to the pilot and tap him gently on the shoulder. He wakes with a start, his eyes wide with fright.

"It's OK," I whisper. "It's time for you to go hide."

"Sure." He rubs his eyes sleepily.

Once the pilot's used the bathroom, I help him get settled in the wardrobe with a glass of water.

"I'll knock three times on the wardrobe door when I get back so you know it's me," I tell him. "And I think you should have this too." I take my pistol from my coat pocket and hand it to him. "Just in case."

"Are you sure?" He cradles the gun to his chest.

"Yep."

He smiles up at me gratefully before I shut the closet door.

I sit on the edge of the bed anxiously waiting for Horst. At five before nine, there's a sharp knock on the door. I take a moment to get back into character, then open the door with a cheery grin plastered on my face.

"Good morning!" I cry, slipping back into Spanish.

"Hello. How are you?" He looks me up and down as if appraising a piece of meat in a market.

"Very good thanks, and you?" I quickly shut and lock the door behind me.

"I'm very well. I take it you had trouble sleeping?"

I freeze. *Did he see me in the yard? Did he see me with the pilot?* "What do you mean?" I hope he can't detect the slight waver in my voice.

"I heard you running a bath at four o'clock."

"Ah, yes." I give him a shy smile. "I was so excited about today I couldn't sleep, so I thought I'd get ready for you."

"Is that so?" A slimy smile slides onto his face, repulsing me and bringing relief in equal measure. "Well, let the adventures begin." He links his arm through mine and we walk toward the elevator.

The hotel restaurant is bustling with people, but unfortunately there's no sign of Albert Le Lay.

When the waiter arrives at our table, I don't give Horst the chance to order for me.

"Please could I have a café con leche and some churros and magdalenas?" I say quickly, figuring that the cakes will be the easiest things to slip into my purse for the pilot.

"Hungry?" Horst asks, raising his eyebrows.

"Very," I reply firmly.

He shakes his head. "You want to be careful you don't ruin that wonderful figure of yours."

And you want to go to hell, you arrogant pig! I yell inside my head, whilst smiling sweetly. "I don't think there's any danger of that, given the physical nature of my job."

"Hmm." The creepy smile returns to his face. "We'll have to think of something physical for you to do today then, as you won't be performing."

Oh, I'll be performing, I think to myself. *And it'll be the performance of my lifetime pretending to be smitten with you.* "Yes, indeed. Perhaps we could go for a walk in the mountains."

"Yes, or maybe we could do something a little closer to home." He reaches under the table and I feel his horrible thin fingers clutching at my knee.

Thankfully, it's not long before our breakfast arrives and I nibble on one of my churros, waiting for the opportunity to sneak some food into my purse. Horst wolfs down his tortilla, his gaze sliding up and down from my face to my chest. I'm about to give up hope, but then a man approaches the table, greeting Horst warmly in German. I sit there, patiently, nibbling away like a mouse, then finally Horst breaks away from their conversation to address me.

"Carmen, this is my good friend and colleague Fritz. Would

you excuse me for a moment while I go and say hello to some other colleagues at his table?"

"Of course!" I practically shriek, my relief is so immense.

As soon as they've gone, I open my purse on my lap and swipe two churros and a couple of magdalenas inside. Then I shut my purse, put it back on the floor and take a sip of coffee.

Horst returns to the table a couple of minutes later.

"You finished quickly," he remarks, examining my now empty plate.

"Yes, well, I'll be working it off later, shan't I?"

He smirks and I fantasize about grabbing him in a front stranglehold and throwing him over the table.

"How were your colleagues?" I ask nonchalantly.

"Very well. You'll be meeting them later at a special dinner."

"Excellent." My skin crawls at the prospect, even though dining with a group of potential Nazis could be a wonderful intelligence opportunity. It's hard to focus on anything other than saving the American pilot now.

"I have a couple of business matters to attend to, so shall we meet again at midday?" Horst says as we make our way out of the restaurant.

"Absolutely." Relief courses through me. This should give me enough time to feed the pilot and try to track down Le Lay.

We go our separate ways at the elevators, with Horst heading down to the station.

I return to my room and give the coded knock before opening the wardrobe door. The pilot grins from ear to ear at the sight of the cakes. He looks even happier when I tell him I'm about to try to locate Le Lay.

"Are you absolutely certain he can be trusted?" I ask.

"Yes. The members of the French Resistance who got me onto the train told me about him. Apparently he's helped smuggle many Jewish refugees and other fugitives to safety.

When you see him, you need to say that you understand from the kitchen that *pommes Anna* is on the menu tonight. That way, he'll know the Resistance have sent you."

"Great. I'll be back soon. Hopefully with good news."

But as soon as I step from the room, my heart sinks. Horst is striding up the corridor toward me.

"Where are you off to?" he calls as soon as he sees me.

"I was just going to see if there was anywhere I could buy a newspaper."

"No need for that, there's been a change of plan." He grins, causing my spirits to plummet. "My work matter was over much quicker than I anticipated, so we can take a trip into the village, do some sightseeing."

"That's great!" I cry, once again calling upon all of my acting skills.

"Come, let's go." He holds his arm out to me.

As we head off toward the elevator, I think of the pilot hiding and waiting. How am I ever going to give Horst the slip long enough to get to Le Lay so he can escape?

After a day filled with "sightseeing" in the local bars and cafés, featuring another serving of speeches from Horst about Horst, with a side order of sleazy innuendo, we arrive back at the station just as dusk is falling.

"Time to freshen up for tonight's party," Horst says as we reach our rooms. "I cannot wait to see you in your special dress. You're to wear the red one tonight," he adds.

"I do hope you like it," I reply demurely.

"Oh, I feel certain I will." He takes my hand in his icy fingers and kisses the back of it, instantly giving me a flashback to Santiago doing the exact same thing. Although when Santiago had done it, it didn't make my stomach churn. *Yes, well, he still turned out to be a snake, didn't he,* my inner voice chides. "I shall call for you in a couple of hours," Horst says, fetching his room key from his pocket.

"I can't wait."

I let myself into my room, feeling sick to my stomach that I've made the pilot wait all day and I still have no good news for him. I knock three times and open the wardrobe door. He stares up at me like a startled rabbit.

"What happened?" he hisses.

"I'm so sorry. I was intercepted by my German host and he insisted on taking me out for the day. I didn't want to arouse suspicion, so I had to go along with it."

His face falls. "So you weren't able to get a message to Le Lay?"

"No. But I'm going to a party tonight in the restaurant. He was there last night, so I'm confident I'll be able to get the message to him."

"OK," he replies glumly, and begins chewing on his thumbnail.

"Why don't you come out, stretch your legs. I got you some more food." I open my purse and the aroma of the Spanish sausage I managed to smuggle when Horst went to the bathroom during lunch wafts out.

The pilot instantly perks up a bit. I leave him tucking into the sausage and go through to the bathroom to draw a bath and mentally regroup. I only have one night left in Canfranc. My train to Madrid leaves tomorrow morning. Tonight will be my last chance to try to help the pilot. I have to get the message to Le Lay if it kills me.

"So, what's this dinner in aid of?" I ask casually as Horst and I make our way to the elevator.

"Huh?" he replies, his gaze fixed to my breasts, spilling over the top of the corset-tight dress.

"The dinner tonight, what's it in aid of?" I ask, trying as hard as I can to keep the exasperation from my voice.

"I'm sorry, it is very hard to concentrate when you are looking so delicious." He licks his thin lips.

Oh please! I force myself to giggle like a moron.

"It is in honor of a very special guest."

"Really? Do tell me more."

The elevator door slides open. I get in and Horst stands in front of me, way too close. Once again, he is drenched in pine-scented cologne. I curse him for probably giving me a lifelong loathing of forests.

"Karl Bömelburg," he replies.

I wrack my brains. I know this name.

"He is the head of the Gestapo in France."

My mouth goes dry as sandpaper. I've heard all about the Gestapo and their torturous methods of interrogation from Mitchell. I crowbar my mouth into a delighted smile. "How exciting."

"Yes, it is going to be an exciting evening all right." Again, he looks at my breasts.

For the briefest of moments, I feel completely over-whelmed. I have a teenage American pilot in my hotel room—in the same building as the head of the Gestapo in France. How the hell am I going to get him out of here?

I take a couple deep breaths. The elevator pings and we step out.

Please, please, please, let Le Lay be here, I silently plead, as we make our way into the crowded room. It's way busier than last night, noisy and hot. The maître d' takes us over to a table and my stomach clenches. There's no intimate table for two tonight. We've been seated on a large round table instead. I glance at our fellow diners. They're all men and judging from their florid complexions they've been drinking for some time.

Horst says something in German to the men and I catch my

name—or rather Carmen's name. They all look up at me and smile.

"I told them you are a famous Mexican actress," Horst informs me in Spanish.

"I see." So Horst is showing off his new doll.

As he fills our glasses with wine from the table and chats to the men, I glance around the restaurant for any sign of Le Lay. I'm about to give up hope when I notice a man who looks like him talking to the maître d' at the restaurant entrance.

"I just need to use the restroom," I say to Horst.

"Already?" he laughs.

I give another moronic giggle and slip from the table.

By the time I get to the door, the man has gone. Damn! I hurry out and see him disappearing off around a corner. What if the pilot is wrong? What if Le Lay really is in cahoots with the Germans? It's a risk I'm going to have to take.

"Excuse me?" I call after him.

He stops and turns. "Yes?" He smiles curiously.

"Are you Albert Le Lay?"

"I am. And who are you?" He's still smiling warmly.

"I need your help," I whisper, coming closer.

His smile fades. "If there's a problem with your room, you can see housekeeping."

"No, it's a more urgent problem." I lean closer to whisper in his ear, praying that the coded message the pilot gave me will mean something. "I understand from the kitchen that *pommes Anna* is on the menu tonight."

He steps back, visibly shocked, before composing himself. "I'm sorry, I don't know what—"

"Please—you have to help me!"

He glances up and down the corridor, then gestures at me to follow him into a cupboard full of mops and cleaning supplies.

"Who are you?" he hisses.

"There's someone here, in the hotel, who needs your help.

He was told to seek you out, to give you that message about the potatoes."

"Who told him?"

Could this be checkmate? I have no choice but to make my move, even though it leaves me wide open to instant defeat.

"The French Resistance," I whisper back. "We're on the same side. I'm here working undercover."

"Who for?"

"That doesn't matter. All you need to know is it isn't for the Germans."

He looks relieved.

"Last night I was down in the yard and I found someone hiding. Someone who's escaped from France. He needs to be got out of here. He was told you'd be able to arrange it."

Le Lay nods slowly. "Where is he now?"

"Hiding in my room."

"OK. Which room?"

I pause, unsure if my next move will be deadly for me and the pilot. But again I realize that I have no choice. I tell him the room number.

"There's a food delivery here at the hotel at just before dawn," Le Lay whispers. "He can escape in their truck when they leave. I shall come to your room to collect him. I'll bring a bellboy's uniform for him, so he won't arouse suspicion. Be ready. Four o'clock."

"Thank you."

He opens the door a fraction and peers out. "OK, go now."

I return to the table my heart pounding. Just as I sit down, the chatter quietens, all eyes turning to look at a handful of men and a couple of women entering the restaurant.

"That's him, that's Bömelburg," Horst tells me with the same excitement I felt the first time I saw Leslie Howard. I feel a sharp pang of sorrow at the thought of what happened to him.

As the group grows closer, heading I guess for the one

remaining empty table at the top of the room, my sorrow turns to fear. Bömelburg is fairly nondescript, with a small flat line of a mouth. The man behind him is far more terrifying, way over six feet tall, his neck almost as wide as his shaven head. Behind him is his companion, a woman with vivid red hair cut into a sharp bob. What kind of woman would be romantically involved with a Nazi? I wonder to myself as they sit down.

All through dinner, my mind buzzes with unanswered questions: will Le Lay really save the pilot? Will he make it out of the hotel safely? How will *I* make it out of this place safely?

As soon as dessert is over, Bömelburg gets to his feet to make a speech in German. Every so often, the audience bursts into applause, Horst among the most enthusiastic. There's no doubting his Nazi allegiances now and the contempt I feel for him grows. I've gotten some intelligence about the deliveries to and from France, but I want to bring back more for Mitchell. I need to get inside his room. I shudder as I realize the only sure-fire way to do this.

A plan starts forming in my head. I shall play along with Horst's excruciating attempts at seduction, make him believe that I'm also on the menu tonight, then en route to his room, I'll pop back to mine, telling Horst I need to freshen up but really to pass on the message to the pilot. Then I'll spend the night with Horst, leaving the pilot free to escape with the help of Le Ley. There's only one small fly in the ointment—the fact that I'll have to spend an entire night with Horst. As if reading my mind, he grabs my hand and gazes at me so lecherously I half expect to see drool frothing at the corners of his mouth. Over at the head table, Bömelburg reaches the climax of his speech.

"Heil Hitler!" he cries and, to my horror, the men in the room, including Horst, leap to their feet and fling their arms up in that chilling salute.

"Heil Hitler!" Horst cries, his voice shrill in my ear.

My resolve deepens. I'll do anything—*anything*—to get one over that Nazi pig.

I glance down at the bangle on my wrist and for the first time since I realized he must have stolen it, I feel inspired rather than horrified by it. Inspired to seek justice for the true owner of this bracelet.

Horst sits back down and clutches at my thigh, his eyes sparking with a horrible mixture of excitement and lust.

"Do you know Bömelburg?" I ask casually.

"Not quite, but I am friends with Wilhelm Schmidt." He nods to the man with the shaven head. "He's one of Bömelburg's most effective interrogators."

People start getting up from their tables and milling about.

I gaze at Horst adoringly, all the while thinking, *Who the hell are you? And how do you know these people?* I notice the woman with the red hair stand up and leave their table. All through the meal, she was sitting with her back to me, but now as she weaves her way through the restaurant, I get a good look at her face for the first time. There's something strangely familiar about it...

I have to stop myself from spluttering in shock. Her hair might be a totally different color, but the dark eyebrows and square jaw undeniably belong to Betty.

30

CANFRANC, 1943

"Do you want to go and meet him?" Horst asks, taking his napkin from his lap and dabbing at his mouth.

What the...? I sit speechless for a moment, my head whirring. How has Betty gone from being abducted by the Germans to sitting at their head table? Was she turned by them during her interrogation? Or has she pulled off the ultimate move? Did she use her capture as a way of infiltrating the vipers' nest? Has she become the greatest, bravest spy of the lot of us? But wouldn't Mitchell know if this was the case? Wouldn't he have told me? I realize immediately that he wouldn't. If Betty is now deep undercover with the Nazis in Paris, her identity would need to be protected at all costs. I feel a flush of admiration and pride. If only Teddy were able to see what us pathetic women are doing now, how much we're risking.

"Carmen?" Horst's voice snaps me back to the present. "Are you all right?"

"Yes."

"Would you like to meet Schmidt?"

I can't let Betty see me. Any flicker of recognition on her face might blow our cover.

"Actually, it's so hot in here, I was wondering if we could go somewhere a little cooler."

Horst frowns, so I place my hand on his leg and stroke his inner thigh. His eyes glaze over and he lets out a hideous moan. "Where were you thinking?" he asks, his voice cracking.

"I don't know, your room maybe?"

He practically pants with excitement. "But what about meeting Schmidt?"

"Why don't you tell me all about him—in bed."

He gets to his feet so abruptly, he almost knocks over his chair. "Let's go."

As I stand to leave, I feel his hand groping my butt. *Oh God, please help me get through this.*

We make our way through the restaurant to the elevator.

"So how do you know Schmidt?" I ask as we wait for it to arrive.

"We occasionally do some business together. He lets me stay in his apartment on the Avenue Foch when I'm in Paris."

"How lovely. Perhaps one day we could go to Paris and stay with him and his wife."

Horst frowns. "His wife is back in Berlin."

"Oh I'm sorry, I thought the woman he was with tonight was his..."

Horst laughs. "No, Erika is his latest mistress."

Erika. I don't know how Betty found the cojones to insert herself right into the heart of the Gestapo, but I'm blown away by her courage.

The elevator arrives and as soon we're inside, Horst presses himself against me.

"You've been driving me crazy all night in this dress," he gasps as his hands paw at my chest. What have I unleashed? I think of Betty with the equally unsavory Schmidt. If she can bring herself to be intimate with a Nazi, then so can I —can't I?

"You only have to be patient another couple of minutes," I say gaily.

"You're going to pay for making me wait all this time," he says.

What the hell does that mean?

We arrive at our floor and Horst adjusts himself before grabbing my hand and pulling me into the corridor. There's an animal-like urgency about him that I really don't like.

"I just need to go and freshen up," I say as we reach my room.

"OK." He makes no move toward his own room as I take my key from my purse.

"I'll meet you in your room in just a minute."

"That's all right, we can go to your room," he says.

My heart starts to race. "What, but... wouldn't you prefer to—"

"Open the door," he cuts in.

Shit! I open the door, my fingers trembling, praying the pilot is still in his hiding place.

"Are you sure you wouldn't rather go to your room?" I say loudly, to let him know I've got company.

"I told you no," Horst replies brusquely.

I turn the lamp on. Thankfully, there's no sign of the pilot.

Horst marches over to the bed and kicks off his shoes.

"Aren't you going to freshen up?" he asks.

"Yes, of course. Make yourself comfortable." I go into the bathroom and shut the door behind me, my heart pounding so loud I can hear the blood pulsing in my ears. *What am I going to do?* The notion of having to get intimate with Horst was horrific enough without the thought of the pilot crouched in the closet hearing everything. How can I get out of this? Could I feign illness?

"You'd better not be taking off that dress," Horst calls. "I'm going to be the one doing that."

"Of course not," I reply, feeling sick. No training at The Farm prepared me for this.

I stare at myself in the mirror. *You can do this. You're doing it to defeat the Nazis. You're doing it to save Grand-mère Rose.*

I have a flashback to the night Santiago stayed in my room at the Ritz. How he held me, never forced himself upon me. *Stop thinking about him; he's just as bad,* I berate myself.

I take a deep breath, then go back into the room. I find Horst beneath the covers, his pale naked shoulders just visible above the eiderdown.

"Stand there for a moment," he commands. "I want to look at you."

I stand in the bathroom doorway, framed by the light.

"Pull the dress up so I can see your legs."

Swallowing hard, I do as I'm told, pulling the dress up to reveal a stocking top.

Horst gasps. "Come here."

I make my way over to the bed, feeling like a condemned man on his way to the gallows.

Horst pulls back the quilt and I'm relieved to see that he still has his white saggy underwear on. "Get in."

I sidle into the bed feeling numb.

Horst hoists himself up so that he's kneeling above me. His pale flabby paunch hangs over the waistband of his shorts. I don't think I've ever felt so sick.

You're doing this for your country, for the war, to beat Hitler, to avenge Howard. But none of my trusty affirmations are working; all I feel is anger building inside of me at this man pawing away at me. This man who gave me a stolen bracelet, who was like a giddy child over members of the Gestapo. *You're scum!* I think as I look up at him. Exercises from Fairbairn's class start coming back to me. I could end him right now with a well-placed knee to the groin, and a pointed punch to the throat.

"Did you enjoy teasing me all night in that dress?" Horst rasps. "Spilling out of it like a common hooker."

What? You're the one who bought it for me.

He grabs at my dress, pulling at it until it tears and reveals my breast. He gives another lustful moan before grabbing at my breasts and squeezing so hard my eyes fill with tears.

"Ow!" I cry, but my pain only seems to make him more excited.

You're doing this to beat Hitler, I tell myself again, but all of a sudden the truth hits me like a jug of cold water to my face, bringing me back to my senses. Much as I am determined to beat Hitler, there's a limit to what I'm willing to endure.

"Get off me," I yell, pushing at his chest.

"What?" He looks momentarily stunned.

"Get your hands off me."

His shock fades and I see rage in his eyes. "You don't speak to me like that." He presses his hands on my shoulders and pins me to the bed. He's surprisingly strong and a bolt of fear goes through me. I try to wriggle out from his grasp, but he presses down harder. "I can see I'm going to have to teach you a lesson," he hisses, forcing his legs between mine. "After everything I've done for you, everything I've bought you," he pants. "I can't believe you would be this insolent and ungrateful."

I try to wriggle free, but it's no good. My arms are trapped and my legs are useless. The only weapon I have left is my head. I swallow hard, then jolt my head up with all I've got and my forehead cracks into his nose.

"Bitch!" he gasps as my vision becomes blurry with stars.

I feel something warm and wet dripping onto my face. Blood. His. I blink. It's coming from his nose.

He pulls one arm back and I close my eyes and brace myself

for the punch, but I hear a soft click instead and he drops down on me, his weight crushing the air from my lungs.

"What the—?" I open my eyes and see Horst staring blankly, a pool of blood spreading across the pillow. I shove him off me. The pilot is standing by the wardrobe, holding my pistol in his trembling hand.

31

CANFRANC, 1943

"You shot him!" I gasp, stumbling from the bed.

"I couldn't... He was going to... I had to stop him," the pilot stammers.

My teeth start chattering from a cocktail of fear and adrenalin. "It's OK." I grab a blanket to wrap around me and cover my exposed chest.

"He was hurting you."

I gently peel the pistol from his trembling fingers, trying not to choke on the smell of gunpowder hanging heavy in the air. "Thank you. Really. We just need to figure out what to do."

I look back at the body. Is it a body, or is Horst still alive? I go over and put my fingers on Horst's pale neck. There's no pulse. And then I see the bullet hole in the back of his head.

"Is he...?" The pilot trails off.

"Yes." Gratitude washes over me. Horst is dead; he's not going to hurt me. The pilot saved my skin; now I have to save his. "Here, give me a hand, let's wrap him in the quilt."

As we wrap him up, it feels surreal that someone who was living and breathing and groping at me just moments before is now utterly lifeless. *At least there's one less monster in the world now,* I try to reassure myself. *At least he'll never be able to hurt anyone ever again.* We take the body into the bathroom and put it in the bath.

"What are we going to do?" The pilot looks at me, terrified, and once again, all I see is a young freckle-faced boy standing in front of me.

"It's OK. I got the message to Le Ley. He's coming to get you just before dawn. He can smuggle you out on a food truck from the kitchen."

"But what about...?" He looks at the bathroom door.

"We'll ask Le Ley when he gets here. Hopefully, he'll be able to think of a way to smuggle it out of here."

"But won't anyone notice that he's missing?"

"Not at first. I know he wasn't due to leave here till tomorrow afternoon. My train leaves in the morning. So hopefully we should both be able to get out of here before people realize."

"OK." The pilot slumps to the floor, leaning against the wardrobe with his head in his hands. "I've never killed anyone before. Not like that anyways."

I look at him questioningly.

"When you drop bombs, you don't get to see the bodies," he murmurs.

"It's OK. He was a very bad man about to do a very bad thing, and you stopped that, just like your bombs will one day stop Hitler."

Thankfully, he looks heartened by this.

"And I'll be grateful to you for the rest of my life—even though I don't even know your name!"

"Really?" Now he's smiling.

"Of course."

"I'll never forget you either." His eyes become shiny with tears.

"Why don't you try to get some rest." I nod to the chaise longue.

He goes and lies down and I think of his folks somewhere back home in America, praying for his safety. I have to keep it together to give him the best chance of making it back to them. Then I think of my own family and pain squeezes my chest. I have to keep it together for there to be any hope of seeing them again. The thought is instantly focusing.

I pick up Horst's clothes from the floor and feel in his pockets for his room key. Then I get changed into my own dress, instantly feeling comforted that he didn't buy it. "I'm just going next door, to see what I can find," I tell the pilot before slipping out into the corridor.

What if Horst's Nazi friends come calling for him tonight? They'll assume he's otherwise engaged with his Mexican plaything. No one will be suspicious of his absence, I reassure myself.

I slip into his room and turn on the light. The scent of that damned pine cologne hangs in the air like a specter. I glance around. Everything is immaculately arranged. All of his clothes hanging in a neatly pressed row in the wardrobe, his shoes all lined up like soldiers on parade by the door. I picture Horst walking round with a slide rule, checking everything's just so. Then I get a flashback of him groping me. My breasts still sting and it makes me want to take a sledgehammer to the place.

Keep your cool, I imagine Grand-mère Rose urging. I wonder if, when she wrote me that I should embrace the mystery, she ever imagined me getting into this kind of a fix.

I head over to the desk and turn on the lamp. Three folders are neatly arranged side by side. I open one and see that it contains a couple of goods dockets similar to the ones I found in the yard. The next folder contains some letters. Using my miniature camera, I take photos of as many as I can, then head back to my room.

. . .

The next couple of hours pass torturously slowly. I use the time to take my pistol apart to clean and reload it. The pilot keeps his eyes closed, but I can tell from the tossing and turning and sighing that no sleep is being had over on the chaise. I wonder if he's having the same thought as me: could we be waiting for our executioner to arrive?

Finally, at a half after four, there's a soft knock on the door. I peer through the peephole and almost cry out in relief when I see Le Ley standing there on his own. I let him in. The pilot sits up rubbing his eyes.

"Put this on." Le Ley throws him a bellboy's uniform.

"There's—er—something else you need to see," I say and gesture at him to follow me into the bathroom.

"What happened?" Le Ley looks at Horst's body, horrified.

"He was attacking me and—"

"*Mon Dieu*." Le Ley scratches his head. "OK. I need to get a laundry trolley. I'll be right back."

He returns a couple minutes later with a trolley full of used white towels. He empties it onto the bathroom floor, then I help him put the body inside and cover it with the towels. We come out to find the pilot standing in the middle of the room in his bellboy's uniform. The trousers are a little on the small side, flapping above his ankles, but at least now he won't stand out like a sore thumb.

"You will have to push the trolley," Le Ley says to him. "It will look too suspicious if I'm seen pushing it."

"Yes, sir. Thank you." The pilot looks at him gratefully.

"And what about you?" Le Ley looks at me, concerned.

"I have a ticket for Madrid leaving in a few hours. As long as the Germans don't find it in the meantime—" I nod at the trolley "—I should be OK."

"All right."

The three of us stand there for a moment and I fight the urge to hug them both.

"Good luck," I whisper.

"And you," the pilot whispers back.

Once they've gone, I stand by the door for an age listening for any sign of commotion, but they appear to have made it safely from this floor at least.

I sink down onto the chaise, unable to go anywhere near the bed. The events of tonight are too huge to process. Horst is dead. Betty is here. The pilot is hopefully safe. If I make it out of this hellish place in one piece, it will be a miracle.

I put my camera in the hiding place in my hatbox and sit on the chaise, pistol in hand, listening to the seconds tick by on the clock on the mantel.

By the time I need to leave for my train, I feel nauseous from nerves and exhaustion. "Just one more performance," I tell my reflection in the dresser mirror. "One more performance to get out of this hellhole."

I give myself a quick spritz of Chanel so that I might feel some of Mom's love and protection—I need it now more than ever.

Mercifully, the corridor is deserted when I leave my room. I make my way to the elevator, singing stupid songs in my head to try to calm my hysterical thoughts. As I stand waiting for it to come, I hear someone behind me.

"Good morning," a man says. A man with a German accent.

I turn and my stomach drops. It's one of the men from our table last night—one of Horst's buddies.

"Good morning!" I trill, wincing at how shrill my voice sounds.

"Leaving already?" he asks, looking at my case.

"'Fraid so."

"Is Horst not coming to see you off?"

I laugh. "No, he was too tired from the celebrations last

night."

"But you left early."

"I mean our own private celebrations," I say, inwardly squirming.

"Aha, say no more!" He laughs. The elevator arrives and we make our way down in silence. "Are you not checking out?" he asks.

"No, Horst said he'd take care of that for me."

"Yes, he's quite enamored of you." He smirks.

"And I him." We emerge into the station ticket hall. I scan the place for any sign of trouble, but all seems calm. Could I dare dream that the pilot has been whisked to safety and that Le Ley has been able to dispose of the body? But what about Betty? I glance around the crowd for any sign of bright red hair, but to no avail.

"Well, it was very nice to meet you." He shakes my hand.

"And you. Hopefully see you again soon," I lie, cringing at the thought.

I go over to the entrance to the platform and show my ticket to the guard, my heart in my mouth. He waves me through with a smile and my knees almost buckle in relief as I see the train waiting. The conductor directs me to my compartment and again I have to endure a nail-biting wait. When the whistle finally blows, I'm so nervous I jump out of my skin. I take my book from my purse and hold it in front of my face, my eyes staring blindly at the page as the train slowly starts making its way from the station.

The long journey home gives me plenty of time to examine the chessboard from all angles. Too many of Horst's friends know my name and cover story. I won't be safe going back to the Ritz.

As soon as I reach Madrid, I call the emergency number for Mitchell and say the code word and tell the woman my life is in danger. It feels surreal saying the words out loud. After months and months of using Carmen's identity like a protective cloak, it could now be the thing to get me killed. I feel completely vulnerable and exposed, and so alone.

There's a beat of silence before the woman responds. "Go to the Embassy tearooms—wait in the bathrooms downstairs by the kitchen."

"The Embassy?" But before I'm able to question her further, the line goes dead.

I walk from the station with my head down, trying not to trip in my haste. When I get to the Embassy, I do as instructed, heading down the stairs by the entrance. The air is filled with clattering kitchen sounds. It all feels so normal, so carefree compared to what I've just been through, and I'm acutely aware that I no longer belong in this world of quaint teapots and delicate finger sandwiches.

I go into the restroom and lock myself in a cubicle, pressing my face against the cool wall. After about fifteen minutes, I hear the outer door open and a woman's voice.

"Carmen?"

I open the door and peer out. It's Margarita, the owner of the tearoom. "Yes." My voice comes out dry and raspy.

"Come, quick." She ushers me through the kitchen and out a back door, where a young man is waiting in a truck. "This is Mateo. He's going to take you somewhere safe," she whispers.

"Thank you." I smile at her gratefully.

Margarita helps me into the back of the truck and we drive off. About ten minutes later, we pull up somewhere. Mateo opens the door and I see that we're parked next to an apartment block.

"Go in there," he says, pointing to the building's entrance, "and up the stairs to number seven. They're expecting you."

"Thank you," I whisper, praying this isn't a trap.

I climb the stairs feeling weak from exhaustion. I finally

reach apartment seven and knock on the door, my hand trembling. *Please God, don't let this be a trap. Please don't let me have been delivered straight to the Nazis.*

The door opens, and I gasp in shock. Standing there is Walter Starkie.

My darling Elena,

Why am I writing this? I know I will have to destroy it, I daren't hide this one with the others, but I need somewhere to process my thoughts. I need someone to talk to, so I'm yet again turning to you, my darling granddaughter.

In the five months since I last wrote to you, a new company of soldiers have taken over the town and the mood has reached rock bottom—on both sides. These new soldiers don't even try to hide their disdain for us; it oozes from their every pore. Thankfully, I don't have a "guest" this time.

In the brief respite before they arrived, I decided that I could no longer keep Caleb hidden. I spoke to my good friend Jacqueline about it and she said that I should pretend he's my grandson. He already calls me Grand-mère Rose so that made things slightly easier, but I've had to change his name so he can't be traced. I decided upon Robert, after your grandfather. Hopefully, it will act as a lucky charm.

Once again, I had to rely upon a tale about you to persuade Caleb to play along. Do you remember the time you became fascinated with dinosaurs and you demanded to be renamed Stegosaurus? You drove your parents mad refusing to answer to anything else. Caleb thought it was hilarious, so I told him he'd be just like you if he changed his name and refused to answer to Caleb. The only problem was, he then wanted to be renamed Sabertooth Tiger after his favorite animal! Thankfully, I've persuaded him that Robert is just as exciting. I told him that your grandpa was a famous zookeeper to try to inspire him. I hope God will forgive me for all the lies I've had to tell to keep this child safe!

I took him into town for the first time in months just before the new company of soldiers arrived and I introduced him to people as my grandson Robert. He's certainly taller and thinner than when they last saw him and I've cut his hair a lot shorter, but I could tell from some people's reactions that they recognized him immediately. Thankfully, they all figured out what had happened and played along, but the fear that someone will denounce us is overwhelming at times.

Last night, I couldn't sleep a wink. I kept imagining the sound of boots marching down the lane and the pummeling of fists on the door. In the end, I crept out of bed and into the back garden. It was a beautiful spring night. An owl was hooting somewhere in the distance and I could smell the soil on the warm breeze. I'm ashamed to say that I've been neglecting my beloved garden and haven't tended to it in months. As I sat down on the back step, I was suddenly reminded of a quote from Martin Luther: "Even if I knew that tomorrow the world would go to pieces, I would still plant my apple tree." It was as if God Himself had plucked the exact quote I needed to hear from my memory. No matter how terrifying or dire the prospect of tomorrow might seem, we have to keep planting and growing hope today.

So today I took Caleb into the garden and we tended to the flower beds, which had become as overwhelmed with weeds as my mind had with fear. A ladybug landed on Caleb's arm and he became completely transfixed. "Why do ladybugs have spots?" he asked. The truth is, I don't know the answer, but I immediately saw it as an opportunity to spark his imagination. "Every time they do something really brave, a spot magically appears," I told him. His eyes grew wide as saucers as he counted the number of spots on her back. "She's been really brave seven times!" he exclaimed. "If you were a ladybug, you'd have so many spots I wouldn't be able to count them," I replied.

The ladybug flew away and Caleb chattered on about the kind of brave things she might have done and with every weed we pulled and every cutting I took, I felt his sense of wonder infuse me. Perhaps the greatest tragedy of becoming an adult is the way in which we lose our childlike sense of awe. We become so cynical, so jaded to life's mysteries, especially during times of hardship, but isn't that when we need a sense of awe the most?

Oh Elena, I am so, so glad that you and your sister will never have to endure the kind of hardship and fear we're living through. And I hope that wherever you are, you are planting metaphorical apple trees of your own.

All my love,

Grand-mère Rose

32

MADRID, 1943

"What are you doing here?" I gasp as Walter pulls me through the door into a darkened hallway.

"I live here." He looks at me for a second, then laughs and shakes his head. "You're working for the Americans?"

I freeze, all of my training telling me to say nothing. But I rang the OSS, who sent me to the tearoom, who sent me here. What does this mean?

"It's OK." He takes a step closer. "I work for the British secret service. That's why you're here."

"You work for the British?" I'm completely blindsided by this development.

He nods.

"And Margarita?"

"Yes. We're part of the network that manages the escape route from France. You're not the first to end up here."

I instantly think of his friendship with Santiago. Mitchell told the Brits about Santiago working for the Germans, so Starkie must know the truth about him.

"There's someone here who'll be very relieved to see you," he says with a smile.

I follow him into a living room, expecting to see Mitchell, but to my horror, Santiago is standing in front of the fireplace.

"Carmen!" he exclaims.

My stomach lurches. Starkie can't know the truth about him after all. I start backing out of the room. "I have to go."

"What? No!" Starkie exclaims.

"I can't be here."

"What's wrong?" Santiago comes out into the hallway.

"You!" I say, my voice wavering. "I can't be near you." Images of Horst come back to haunt me—groping at my breasts, bearing down on me, his blood spreading across the pillow. Santiago works for the same people. And now he knows that I'm working for the Allies.

"I don't understand," Starkie says, looking from me to Santiago and back again. "I thought you two were..."

"We are nothing," I spit out and Santiago flinches. "Your good buddy here is working for the Germans."

"What?" Starkie stares at me, horrified.

"Carmen, no," Santiago exclaims.

"Don't try to deny it; we have proof." I look at Starkie. "I thought you'd have known. We passed photos of him meeting with Canaris to the British." I stare at Santiago defiantly. What can he do, right here in front of Starkie? I want to see him squirm. After months of his deception, it feels so damned good to finally be able to speak the truth.

Santiago barges past Starkie toward me and I feel a bolt of fear. "You think that I would work for them," he hisses. "After what those bastards have been doing to my people."

Don't let him fool you again, my inner voice warns. "What do you mean your people?"

"The Romani people." His eyes spark with anger. "It's not just the Jews the Germans want to wipe off the face of the earth. The Nazis in Germany sent the Romanis to live in the ghettos too. At first, Himmler gave the order for us to be sterilized, but now..." His voice cracks. "Now we are being sent to the death camps."

"It's true," Starkie says, and I'm not sure whether he means the persecution of the Romani people or that Santiago isn't working for the Germans. Either way, my mind feels tangled up in knots over this new information. "Please, Carmen, come back inside. We need to talk."

I look at the front door. If I leave, I'll have nowhere to go. Mitchell must know I'm here. He'll be here soon. I nod and follow them back into the room.

"How could you?" Santiago looks at me, his expression a mixture of hurt and furious.

"But—but I know you've met with Canaris. Are you going to deny that?"

"No!" he exclaims. "No, I am not going to deny that."

"Then why were you meeting with him? Please don't tell me it was to arrange a dance party," I scoff.

"Of course it wasn't."

"Santiago also works for the British," Starkie says softly. "He's a double agent."

"A double agent?" I stare at Santiago, stunned.

Santiago nods, still looking really angry.

"The Germans think he's working for them but really..." Starkie breaks off. "What he's doing is incredibly brave. But I'm sure you know all about that."

"What do you mean?" Santiago asks him.

Starkie and I exchange glances. "It's OK," he tells me softly. "I guarantee it's safe."

I look at Santiago, trying to fit this new identity of double agent to him. All of the discrepancies I've found about him suddenly make sense—the way he was so uncomfortable in Horcher, the times he let his anti-Nazi sentiment show, outside the cinema and talking about the Spanish Civil War. Even his relationship with Conchita now makes sense. Has he been spying on her too? The adrenalin that has been keeping me upright drains from my body and my knees go weak. I sink down onto one of the chairs.

"What did he mean, you'd know all about that?" Santiago asks. "And how did you know I've had meetings with Canaris?"

"Because I-I'm working for the Americans."

Starkie chuckles.

Santiago looks speechless. "But—how?"

"I can't say any more. But that's why I'm here now. A mission I was on went badly wrong." I can barely hear myself speak over my clamoring thoughts as they try to process these latest developments. After months of not knowing, have Santiago and I been working for the same side all along?

"You were on a mission?" He stares at me like I just announced I'd been to the moon.

"Yes."

We're interrupted by a loud knock at the door.

"That'll be your handler," Starkie says.

As he goes to answer the door, Santiago takes hold of my hands. "I feel as if I don't know you at all," he whispers.

Yes, well, that makes two of us, I want to say but refrain. I've spent so long convinced Santiago's a Nazi, I still can't relax fully.

Starkie comes back into the room with Mitchell. I watch his face for any flicker of shock as he sees Santiago, but he remains expressionless.

"Is there someplace we can talk alone?" he asks Starkie.

"Of course. We'll go to the kitchen."

Starkie and Santiago leave, closing the door behind them.

"Starkie says that the dancer's a double agent, working for the British," I blurt out. "Do you think it's true? I don't know what to believe anymore, everything's so—"

"Hey." He places his hand on my shoulder and the strength of his grip is instantly grounding. "Take a breath."

I do as he says and feel some of my tension ease.

"What happened in Canfranc?" he asks. "Why are you in danger?"

I whisper him the story and take my camera from my pocket. "I got some snaps of the paperwork I found in Horst's room."

"What happened to the body?" Mitchell asks, taking the camera from me.

"I don't know. Le Ley said he'd take care of it, but there's only so long before someone notices Horst's missing. He had a bunch of colleagues there with him. But that's not all..."

"It's not?" Mitchell raises his eyebrows.

"I saw Bet—Magnolia—while I was there."

"Magnolia. At Canfranc?" He looks genuinely stunned, which immediately troubles me.

"Uh-huh. She was with one of Horst's Gestapo pals."

"What do you mean, *with* him?"

"I mean as his mistress. According to Horst, she's shacked up with him in his Parisian apartment, someplace called Avenue Foch."

"Avenue Foch, that's where the Gestapo have their head-quarters." He looks horrified. "What the hell?"

I stare at him imploringly. "Please be honest with me. Is she still working for us, deep undercover?"

He shakes his head. "If she is, the Barcelona station sure as hell don't know about it."

The disappointment I feel at this is crushing. "Is there any way you could find out for sure? Ask higher up? We need to know because if she isn't still working for us..." My unsaid words echo in the silence: *she'll be working for the Germans*. It's a prospect that hits me like a punch to the gut.

"I'll check. Did she see you?"

"No."

"OK." Mitchell sighs and shakes his head. "Geez, Flamingo."

"I'm sorry."

"What are you sorry for?" He stares at me. "You saved a pilot's life and you got some great intelligence on the deals the Germans are doing with Spain for tungsten."

"What *is* tungsten?"

"It's a metal used for building tanks and bombs. The Germans don't have any, so they have to import it."

I feel sick. So much for Franco's neutrality. Thanks to his greed, the Nazi killing machine is being kept in tanks and bombs.

"Will you be OK staying here tonight?" Mitchell looks at me, concerned. "I need to check on Magnolia and decide where to send you. Obviously, you can't stay in Madrid. I'm afraid Carmen De La Fuente's days are over. Too many people would have seen you and Horst together."

I nod, feeling strangely bereft. Carmen's wisecracking, hard-nosed persona has gotten me through this so far. "As long you don't send me back home." If I was sent back to America now I'm not sure I'd be able to deal with the bitter disappointment. I've come so far, I can't quit now. I've got to help win freedom for France and Grand-mère Rose.

"Trust me, you're way too good an agent to send back home. Leave it with me." He stands up and puts on his hat. "Try to get some rest, and about the dancer..."

"Yes?" I look at him, my heart thudding.

"He is a double agent. I found out when I told the Brits we'd seen him with Canaris. I didn't let you know because I didn't want to do anything to jeopardize his cover. You think you've got problems with the Germans; I hate to think what they'd do to him if they found out the truth."

I nod, too numb and exhausted to speak. Nothing is what it seems in this crazy war. The one person I thought I could trust,

Betty, could be the world's biggest traitor, and the one person I felt the most betrayed by never betrayed me at all.

"I'll see you tomorrow, Flamingo," Mitchell says before leaving the room.

I sit there breathing slowly to try to calm my racing pulse.

"Carmen," I hear Santiago whisper and look up to see him standing in the doorway.

Carmen's dead, I want to say, *my real name's Elena.* Tears fill my eyes. We still aren't able to be completely honest with each other. But am I really Elena anymore? So much has happened. I feel so changed. I long for my family, for someone or something familiar to cling onto.

I try to stand but my legs feel too feeble. Santiago comes and crouches before me, and gently wipes away my tears. I can trust him. I can really trust him. For once, Carmen doesn't pipe up with one of her warnings. Carmen is dead.

I lean forward into his arms.

33

MADRID, 1943

Slowly, my shock fades. Starkie brings me a tumbler half full of whiskey and the first mouthful blazes a welcome trail of warmth through my body. Somewhere in another room, I hear the murmur of a woman's voice and the sweet tinkle of a girl's laughter—his family, I guess. The notion that this home is also a safe haven for people fleeing the Germans fills me with both joy and fear. Who knows what would happen to them if the Germans found out.

Starkie leaves the room to fetch some food and Santiago sits on the arm of my chair stroking my hair. With every touch, I feel my tension easing and my trust in him growing. I tentatively reach out and place my hand on his.

"Oh Carmen. I've been so sad, thinking that I'd lost you," he says softly. "When you were so cold to me, was it because you thought I was working for them?"

"Yes." My voice wavers.

"You must have hated me."

"Uh-huh. I even thought you might have been spying on me."

"What?" His green eyes widen. "Why would I be spying on you? I was madly in love with you!" His words make my heart sing. "Carmen De La Fuente, you are the most incredible woman I've ever met—and not just because you snort like a pig when you laugh. No one has ever taken up so many of my thoughts as you."

But Carmen wasn't real, I think to myself glumly.

"Don't look so sad. I don't need you to love me too—not yet, at least. Just please say that you like me."

"I like you," I say instantly. "It's just that..."

"What?"

"You don't know the real me."

"Oh really?" He frowns. "I beg to disagree!"

I can't help smiling at his melodramatic tone.

"That's better." He grins. "I like making you smile. It makes me happy. And anyway, I have seen the real you. I saw her that night in Plaza Mayor. I saw her when she told me one of her favorite words in the world was 'wistful.' Are you telling me that was a lie?"

I shake my head. I love that he remembers this detail about me.

"And now I want to make a solemn pledge to you." He slips from the arm of the chair and kneels in front of me. "When all this is over and we have beaten the Germans and sanity has returned to this beautiful world of ours, I am going to take you to Andalusia and I am going to make passionate love to you for seven whole days!"

"What?"

"And I don't mean in the Biblical sense."

I laugh for the first time in what feels like forever. "Did anyone make love for seven days in the Bible?"

"I mean I am going to make love to every one of your senses. I am going to take you walking in the mountains where the silence is so thick it feels like velvet. I'm going to take you to eat tapas at my grandparents' tavern and make your tastebuds cry out in delight. I'm going to treat you to Romani music so uplifting your ears will jiggle for joy either side of your head. And our hearts will dance together beneath the moon just as they did in Plaza Mayor."

His words paint the most beautiful images in my mind, filling me with longing. It seems almost impossible to imagine such joyful, carefree days.

"And then we're going to take each other's hands, like this." He clasps my hands. "And we are going to leap into this thing together, OK?"

As I nod in agreement, Starkie comes into the room carrying a tray full of food.

"Have I just walked in on a marriage proposal?" he exclaims.

"No!" I cry.

"Not yet," Santiago adds with a grin.

The three of us spend the evening talking and eating and drinking, but all the time I'm painfully aware of an invisible clock ticking down the seconds until we're forced to part again, and for who knows how long.

At just before midnight, Starkie sets up a camp bed for me in the living room and says goodnight.

"Would you like me to leave?" Santiago says once he's gone.

"No," I reply instantly, trying to block out the growing fear that after tonight we may never see each other again.

"Why do you look so sad?" he asks.

"I'll probably have to leave tomorrow. It's not safe for me to be here anymore. And…" I break off, not wanting to give voice to my worst fears.

"Shhh." He gently places his finger to my lips. "We need to stay in this moment, not worry about tomorrow."

I give him a tearful smile. "That's exactly what my Grand-mère Rose used to tell me whenever I was worried about something."

"*Grand-mère*? Is she French?"

"Yes. She lives in France, but for all of my childhood she lived in America and she pretty much raised me along with my parents. She's the main reason I'm here, to help free her from the Occupation."

He nods, his expression solemn. "I shall add her to my list of reasons why too."

"Thank you." The thought of Santiago also risking his life for Grand-mère Rose fills me with gratitude. It feels so good to be able to be this honest with him.

We spend the night curled up together on the tiny camp bed. With Santiago's strong arms wrapped around me, I finally feel safe enough to let go and I drop into a fathomless sleep. But in the middle of the night, Horst appears in my dreams, looming before me, his face streaked with blood. Betty is with him. Both of them are staring at me angrily. I jolt awake, covered in a cold sweat.

"Carmen?" Santiago whispers in my ear. "Are you OK?"

"Yes," I reply, but there's no way I can hide my trembling. It might have been a nightmare, but the facts still remain—Horst is dead. And if and when the Germans find his body, I'll surely be the main suspect in his murder as the last person he was seen with.

"Hey," Santiago whispers. "Look at me."

I slowly turn over, being careful not to fall out of the narrow bed. *I don't want to leave you,* I feel like wailing as I look into his eyes. *I don't want to go back to feeling so all alone.* I bite my lip. Where's Carmen when I need her?

"Before I saw you last night, I'd become so depressed," he

says, gently stroking the side of my face. "Having to be polite to those animals, having to pretend to work for them when I know they are exterminating my people, it was making me feel ill. But now..." He gently plants a kiss on my lips and a flashback of Horst bearing down on me fills my mind. I try to push it away, to stay present in these last precious moments with Santiago. "Now I have the best reason of all to want to defeat them," he continues.

"What is it?"

"I want to create a world where we are free to be together, to be in love together."

I gulp down the sobs building in my throat. "I want that too," I whisper.

Santiago and Starkie leave shortly after breakfast, bound for the British Institute to rehearse for a show. It feels so strange to think of Carmen's old world going on without her, without me.

When Mitchell arrives, I look at him anxiously, wondering where he's going to send me and what news he might have about Betty. I pray that he's discovered she's still working for the OSS.

"So?" I look at him hopefully.

"Magnolia's not working for us anymore," he says matter-of-factly.

I swallow hard. "So they got her to turn when she was captured."

He nods.

A knot of anger tightens in my stomach. How could she? How could she betray us for them?

"We need to get to her," Mitchell continues.

"Get to her?"

"Yes. See if we can turn her back. She knows way too much about our operations here in Spain. We can't have her working against us. And if she's been hobnobbing with high-level members of the Gestapo, she could be a great source of intelligence."

"But what if she won't come back to us?" I hardly dare ask for fear of what he's going to say.

"Then she'll have to be neutralized," he replies grimly.

"I'll get to her," I say after a moment's silence. Even in the light of this terrible news, I still feel a loyalty to Betty, and a desire to try to save her.

Mitchell frowns. "You? But how? You said she's shacked up in France."

"I'll go to France," I blurt out.

"But you might be wanted there by Horst's buddies."

"No, Carmen might be. Give me a new role with a new look and a new backstory. I'm an actress, don't forget. I can do it. I knew Magnolia in training. We were... we were friends." Admitting this makes me slightly queasy. I never would have imagined Betty betraying our country and working for the Nazis. "If anyone's going to be able to turn her back it'll be me."

Mitchell frowns and for a horrible moment I think he's going to say no and tell me he's sending me back to America.

Panic courses through me. "You can't send me back home, not now, not when it isn't finished. I haven't risked everything to end up dying a soul-destroying death in a typing pool."

"Who said anything about a typing pool?" He raises his eyebrows.

"Please." Santiago's words echo in my mind. I want to create a world where we can be together, where *everyone* can live together in peace. If I can get Betty to switch allegiances again, having gotten so close to the Gestapo and with all the intelligence that would entail, then surely I'll have made a real difference.

Mitchell ponders for a moment, then nods. "OK. Let me see

what I can do." He stands up and pats me on the arm. "I'll be back soon."

It's only when I hear the apartment door softly click shut behind him that the enormity of what just happened hits me. I could be going to France to confront Betty. I could be going there to kill her—or be killed.

May 1943, France

My darling Elena,

Things are becoming so fraught here, I'm in need of an outlet once again. Today, four of my fellow townspeople were executed by the Germans for being members of the Resistance. One of them was a dear friend of mine named Jacqueline. We went to school together. We used to play together. Perhaps you remember me telling you about her when you were younger. She was the red-headed spitfire who was always up to mischief. And now she is gone—shot on the very same street we used to play hopscotch on. The Germans are really on the rampage now. Perhaps they sense that the war is lost. If this is the case, I know I should be happy, but I have a terrible sense of foreboding that the worst is yet to come. They're not going to go down without a fight. Every day brings news of another public execution. I've had to send Caleb away for his own safety. He begged me not to. It was the most heartbreaking thing I've ever had to do. What if I've made a terrible mistake? What if he'll be in even more danger now?

34

PARIS, 1943

"Name!" the German soldier barks at me, looking me up and down.

"Isabel Del Campo," I reply calmly. *Isabel Del Campo, Spanish singer, in Paris to audition for a role in a music hall,* I mentally run through my backstory.

The soldier looks at my travel papers and back at me, his cold gaze scanning my newly blond hair. As an extra precaution, I have padding inside my mouth, to fill out my cheeks. It's incredible how much it changes the shape of my face.

"Go!" he barks, shoving the papers back in my hand.

Breathing a sigh of relief, I walk through and onto the concourse of Gare de Lyon station. I'm in Paris. I'm in France. I'm in the same country as Grand-mère Rose. I'm also in a country occupied by the enemy—the realization fills me with foreboding as I see the flags bearing swastikas hung from the stone columns of the building. In her descriptions of her beloved capital city, Grand-mère Rose always painted a vibrant picture of bustling boulevards, cozy cafés and elegant museums and art galleries. As I step outside, I'm struck by how stripped of color it seems. It's not just the iron-gray clouds filling the sky.

There's a faded look to the people trudging past, their faces pale and their bodies weary and gaunt.

As a woman hurries by me, I notice that her legs have been stained brown with a thin black line neatly painted onto the backs of her calves, giving the appearance that she's wearing stockings. My heart sings at this small act of defiance. To me, those painted lines are calling out to the Germans, "You might plunder our country but you won't crush our spirit," and I feel a fresh surge of courage.

In preparation for my new role, my wardrobe has been similarly downgraded and I'm wearing a simple cotton dress, with bare legs and scuffed, cork-heeled shoes. Whereas Carmen De La Fuente needed to make a splash, Isabel Del Campo needs to sink like the plainest of pebbles.

I look along the street to get my bearings. Mitchell had me memorize several addresses before leaving Spain: 84 Avenue Foch—the Gestapo headquarters; a safe house by a cemetery named Père Lachaise, where I'm to go in the event of an emergency; and the address I'll be staying at while I'm here, close to Notre-Dame on the bank of the River Seine. "The woman who owns the house is a friend to the Allies," he told me. Being a friend to the Allies takes on a whole new level of danger here. I mustn't do anything to put her at risk.

Thankfully, the river is only a few minutes' walk from the station and I've memorized the directions so I don't look like a newcomer.

As soon as I lay eyes on the Seine, I feel a wistful pang. It's exactly how Grand-mère Rose described it in the bedtime stories she used to make up for me when I was little. In her stories, I'd been born in France—wishful thinking on Grand-mère Rose's part perhaps—and I got up to all kinds of wild adventures. One of my favorites was when I stowed away on a boat on the river and ended up thwarting a dastardly fiend who was trying to steal the *Mona Lisa* from the Louvre. As I walk over to the wall and gaze down at the water, it's easy to imagine myself back in the innocent world of the story. But then I see a sight that makes my blood turn to ice—a mother bustling two children toward me, all of them wearing bright yellow stars pinned to their ragged clothes. Of course I already knew about the Germans' hateful way of marking out the Jewish people, but it's one thing looking at a black and white photograph in a newspaper and quite another seeing it for real.

The mother catches me staring and I want to kick myself for being so insensitive. I long to pull her aside, whisper in her ear, "It's OK, there are so many people trying to bring an end to this horror." But even if I could, I feel my words would bring little consolation. I've heard the reports of the thousands of Jewish people who've been rounded up in France and taken off to God knows where. I can't begin to imagine the level of fear she must be feeling, not only for herself but for her children. When I look back at the river, all I see is a murky artery running through a poisoned city.

I keep walking until I see the turrets and thin spire of Notre-Dame, looming through the gloom ahead of me. Thankfully, my lodgings are easy to find, a narrow, three-story house tucked away down a side street just off the river. I take a breath and knock on the door. *Love your fear*, I try to remind myself, as a bead of sweat trickles down my spine. But what if this is a trap? What if this woman isn't really a friend to the Allies after all?

The door opens a fraction. A pair of big brown eyes magnified by huge round spectacles peer out at me.

"Good day, I'm looking for Aurelie Bisset. I'm Isabel Del Campo," I say cheerily in French. "I have a room booked." Isabel, I have decided, is a no-nonsense broad, not easily ruffled. The kind who has no problem loving her fear into submission.

"Yes, yes, I am Aurelie, come in." The woman opens the door just wide enough for me to slip into a narrow hallway. The walls are lined with oil paintings in bright primary colors. Aurelie is dressed as if to match the artwork, in a skirt made from a patchwork of materials in vibrant yellow, blue and green teamed with a pair of bright red clogs. Her silvery hair is piled into a messy bun and a paintbrush is tucked behind her ear. "You are Spanish, yes?" she says.

"Yes. I'm here for an audition at a music hall in Montmartre," I say for the benefit of anyone who might also be in the house and listening.

"How exciting," she replies with a knowing smile and I guess she's figured this is probably just a cover story. "Would you like something to eat or drink after your journey? A cup of tea?"

I'm painfully aware that the French have had their food rationed for years now so I'm reluctant to take anything from her but figure a drink would be all right. "A cup of tea would be lovely, thank you."

I follow her down the passageway and into a room at the back, which I assume at first must be an artist's studio—canvases are propped against all of the walls and an easel is set up in the center. But then she goes over to a far corner and removes a canvas from what turns out to be a stove. She fills an old iron kettle from a sink hiding behind another easel and places it on the hob.

"I like to work in the kitchen," she says, nodding at the easel in the center of the room. "Or rather, I don't like wasting valuable painting time having to walk back and forth to the kettle."

"That makes sense." I look at her work in progress—in contrast to the cheery pieces hanging in the hall, it's an angry swirl of black, white and red.

"Art isn't just my passion, it's my outlet," she says by way of explanation. "I have to have somewhere to channel my murderous intent." She gives me a half-smile and I nod to let her know that I understand.

Once the kettle's boiled, we take our tea and sit on a sofa at the end of the room.

"Have you been to France before?" Aurelie asks.

"No, well, only through my *grand-mère*. She's French. She used to fill my head with stories of France when I was a kid, so much so that I feel as if I've been here already, everything seems so familiar." I smile wistfully. Arriving in France has made Grand-mère Rose's presence in my heart stronger than ever.

"That's lovely. Is she still alive, your *grand-mère*?"

"Yes, I hope so... I don't know." I look down at my tea, feeling suddenly close to tears. All the time I was in another country, it was easier to keep the faith that Grand-mère Rose was still alive. But now I'm here, and I've seen the effect the Nazis have had upon France, I'm not so sure, and I'm terrified of trying to find out.

"Perhaps you will have a chance to visit her, while you are here?"

I nod. "I hope so."

Our eyes meet and I see such a genuine warmth in her gaze I know that I'll never forget this woman, with her paint-splattered shirt and her welcoming smile, and the bravery she's shown, having me stay here.

Once we've finished our tea, she shows me to my room, which is up three flights of steep stairs at the top of the house. It's barely bigger than a cupboard and made even smaller by its sloping ceilings, but I like how contained it is. It makes me feel safer.

"Thank you," I say as she hands me two door keys tied together on a piece of string.

"You are very welcome." She clasps my hands and gives them a quick squeeze and again I have the sense that so much is being said without being verbalized.

Once she's clattered back downstairs in her clogs, I sit on the bed and gaze out of the skylight. The glass is grimy, but I can just make out a patch of blue emerging from behind the clouds. I'm here. I made it. I think of Santiago and say a silent prayer that he's still safe. Then I open my case and take the assorted pistol parts from their hiding places in the lining and tucked inside my underwear. I assemble the gun quickly and load the barrel. Could one of these bullets have Betty's name on it? Would I be able to kill her if it came down to it? The question hangs heavy upon me, impossible to answer. Part of me still can't believe that she could have betrayed her country in such a horrific way. I've gone over and over it and the best I can come up with is that once she was captured in Barcelona, they threatened her with torture or death and she decided to bargain for her life. Yes, it's the coward's way out, but it means that she might just as easily flip back to the OSS. And the intelligence she'd be able to provide as the lover of a Gestapo officer would surely be invaluable. I hide the assembled pistol inside the lining of my case, praying I won't need to use it.

Exhausted from my journey, I go to bed early and fall into a fitful sleep, waking at the slightest sound. As soon as I see the sky start to lighten, I get up and get dressed, putting on a dowdy brown dress and my cork-heeled shoes. The objective today is to blend into the background *and* be able to make a hasty exit if needed.

I wipe the film of dust from the mirror on the dresser and do a double take as I catch a glimpse of my newly blond hair. Mitchell arranged for one of his hairdresser contacts in Spain to do it. She also chopped it into a short bob. There's surely no way Betty would recognize me from a distance, just as I almost didn't recognize her with her red hair. Once I've applied a quick coat of pale pink lipstick, I tuck my pistol into the lining of my purse and head out the door, trying to ignore the anxious thoughts scratching at my mind like the cawing of crows.

35

PARIS, 1943

The weather is far nicer today, the sky cornflower blue smudged with feathery clouds. The summer sunshine makes the ornate buildings lining the streets seem cleaner and whiter than yesterday and the river is sparkling. As I walk past a boulangerie, I catch a waft of bread baking and it sends my empty stomach into a frenzy. Grand-mère Rose used to make me drool with her tales of French bread shaped like sticks known as baguettes. Perhaps I could buy one for breakfast. Mitchell has provided me with some French ration coupons.

I join the queue that is trailing down the street, but when I finally have my baguette, I'm bitterly disappointed. It's so stale, I almost break my teeth biting into it and instead of the soft fluffy interior described so mouth-wateringly by Grand-mère Rose, the thing is dry as a bone. I'm so hungry, I have no choice but to keep gnawing on it.

I know from consulting my map beforehand that the walk to Avenue Foch will take over an hour. As I walk, I think of Grand-mère Rose and that final letter she wrote me, and how much her words have come to mean to me. It's as if they've been magically drawing me to her, and now, finally, I'm in her home country. I think of what Aurelie said yesterday about trying to visit her and my heart thuds. The possibility of being able to see Grand-mère Rose is too wonderful to dare contemplate. Especially as I have the small matter of finding Betty to deal with first. I quicken my pace, as if trying to shake off the dread gathering like a chill fog behind me.

When I finally arrive at Avenue Foch, I'm awestruck by the splendor on display. I'd imagined that the headquarters of the Gestapo would be bleak and soulless, but it's one of the most opulent avenues I've ever seen, lined with trees and dotted with immaculately manicured communal gardens and home to the most majestic apartment buildings. But, of course, it makes sense that the Germans would have taken over one of the finest streets in the city.

I focus on keeping an even pace. I want to look as if I'm walking with purpose but also be able to take everything in. My plan—tenuous as it is—is to case number 84 for any sign of Betty's Gestapo officer. I'm hoping to be able to tail him home from work. The thought of Betty living someplace on this street in a stolen apartment makes me feel sick. Especially when I see the swastikas on the flags outside number 84. I glance up at the building. It's seven stories tall and surrounded by a black iron railing fence. I can't believe my luck when I notice a garden directly opposite. It's the perfect place for loitering, hopefully without being spotted.

I slip into the garden and sit on one of the benches. Number 84 is now partially obscured by some shrubs, but I still have a clear line of sight to the sidewalk leading up to it. I fetch my trusty book from my purse and pretend to read. But every couple of seconds, I glance left and right, watching the comings and goings like a hawk. Soon enough, people start showing up for work. To every person going inside that godforsaken building, I utter a silent curse.

An hour passes and there's still no sign of Betty's shaven-headed lover. Doubt starts circling me like a vulture, pecking away at my plan until it's in shreds. How could I expect him to conveniently show up on my first day in Paris? He might not even be in the capital. What if he and Betty traveled further into Spain after the dinner in Canfranc? What if right now, they're in Madrid?

No, Horst told you they were just there for the dinner, I reassure myself. *And surely there's no way Betty would risk going that far into Spain. He'll show up; it just might take a bit longer than expected.*

I decide to go for a stroll and just as I leave the garden, a couple of women walk past me. They're dressed in bland gray uniforms and speaking in German. I shudder as they head toward number 84.

I spend the rest of the day walking around Paris, occasionally recognizing landmarks from Grand-mère Rose's vivid descriptions and feeling a bittersweet cocktail of love and loss. I'm sure that never in her worst nightmares would she have imagined the likes of the Louvre or the Arc de Triomphe being scarred with swastikas.

I return to Avenue Foch early evening, figuring that I might get lucky and see Betty's lover clocking off for the day. This time when I reach the garden, there's a man sitting reading a newspaper on the bench so I stroll on past. I hear the sound of women laughing and see a gaggle of them heading out of number 84, all in that same dreary gray uniform. There's something about their laughter that sets my teeth on edge. How can they be so happy and carefree after what they've done to this country?

I walk up and down the avenue several times, but to no avail and return to my lodgings as dusk falls feeling despondent. How long can I keep walking up and down the avenue without arousing suspicion? I'm going to have to come up with another plan. But what?

I go straight to my room and lie on the bed, staring through the grimy skylight at a star twinkling in the darkening sky. I wrack my brains for a way of sniffing Betty out. There's no way I can attempt to get inside number 84, that would be way too risky, and besides, she lives someplace else on the avenue.

Then I have an idea. I noticed earlier that some of the apartment buildings on Avenue Foch have doormen. Perhaps I could ask them if Betty lives in their building. I know from Horst that she's going by the name of Erika. I could tell them she's an old friend of mine and I want to leave her a message. It doesn't matter what the message is; I just need to know what building she's in. Then I can stake it out until I see her. It's surely a less dangerous option than hanging around the Gestapo headquarters.

I sigh and think of Grand-mère Rose, somewhere out there beneath the same sky and I wonder if she's looking up at the same star. I smile as I remember how I once asked her if two people in different places could pass messages to each other via the moon if they were looking at it at the same time. If only that were true.

"I love you, Grand-mère Rose," I whisper at the star before finally falling into a fitful sleep.

I wake the next morning to a sheet-white sky and the air thick as soup with humidity. I have a quick wash and put on a pale blue cotton dress. *Could this be the dress that you're captured in?* The unwelcome thought barges into my mind as I stare into the dresser mirror. *No, this will be the dress that I find Betty in,* I tell myself sternly. I apply a tiny spritz of Chanel on my wrist for courage, then I brush my hair, still finding it strange at how much less I now have. Then I check my pistol is still in the lining of my purse, although the sight does little to reassure me.

It's not much cooler outside. Banks of gray cloud are building on the horizon and the Seine glistens like an oily serpent. I'm not sure if it's the oppressive nature of the weather, but I can't shake a feeling of foreboding. By the time I reach Avenue Foch, my back is drenched in sweat and I can feel damp patches in the armpits of my dress.

You are Isabel De Campo, Spanish actress, I try to calm myself by getting into character. *You are in Paris for an audition, and you've decided to pay a visit to your long-lost friend, Erika.*

I fix a cheery smile to my face and approach the first doorman I see, standing on duty outside one of the most magnificent buildings on the street.

"Good day," I greet him in French. "I wonder if you could help me."

He nods curtly.

"I'm looking for an old friend. I understand she is living here now."

He remains silent.

"Her name is Erika and she has red hair cut short like mine."

"What is her surname?" he asks.

Damn. "I—uh—I'm not sure," I reply. "I think she might have married since I last saw her."

He shakes his head. "She doesn't live here."

"OK, thank you, good day." I hurry on my way.

This is too risky; you could blow your cover, I chide myself.

I decide to head to the garden by number 84 and regroup. As soon as I reach the cover of the trees, I slow my pace. I'll have to come up with a story that gets me access to the apartment buildings, but what? I slump down on the bench and take a few breaths, trying desperately to think of something. Could I pretend to be a cleaner, perhaps?

After a few minutes, I take my compact from my purse and reapply my lipstick whilst glancing across the street to number 84. A woman is walking toward the building, her dreary gray uniform perfectly matching the weather. But then I notice a splash of red hair beneath her peaked hat and I almost drop my compact. The woman looks to be the same height and build as Betty. I will her to turn so I can catch a glimpse of her face, but instead she turns away, heading inside number 84.

My head starts to spin. Could it be that Betty isn't just sleeping with the enemy but working for them too? *She could be working there in order to gather intelligence for the* OSS, the part of me who still wants to believe in her reasons. *She could be planning on coming back to us.* But mostly I feel dread.

I glance at my watch. It's almost nine, so if she is working there, she must be starting her shift. Now I might have located Betty, I can't afford to let her slip from my grasp. I'm going to have to stay on the avenue until she reappears. Thankfully, after about five minutes, it starts to rain, providing me with the perfect excuse to take shelter in the doorway of a building just across the street. I'm there for about an hour before the rain fades and I make my way back to the garden. Just as I get there, I see the woman with the red hair coming out of number 84. I wait a few moments, pulse racing, then begin to tail her.

The rain has thinned into a gauzy haze and it clings to my face like a sheen of sweat. *What if it isn't Betty? Surely it can't be Betty?* I don't care. After hours of waiting, it feels good to have some kind of lead. The woman hurries along in the direction of the river, then makes a right. I see the Eiffel Tower on the other side of the Seine. So many of Grand-mère Rose's bedtime stories featured the tower. Who would have guessed that I'd end up seeing it in these circumstances? I follow the woman onto a bridge directly opposite the tower. The view takes my breath away. Up this close, the Eiffel Tower is huge— the base sprawling wider than the entire width of the bridge. A huge white V has been stuck to the front of the tower and beneath it there's some kind of written sign. As I get closer, I see that it's in German: *DEUTSCHLAND SIEGT AUF ALLEN FRONTEN*. Germany is victorious on all fronts. I swallow down my fear. The Germans might be victorious here in France, but they won't be forever, and they haven't been on all fronts; they've recently lost Africa, for a start. I think of Santiago and I imagine him urging me on.

As I reach the end of the bridge, the woman walks over to the tower. If only she would turn, so I'd know whether or not I've been brought on a wild goose chase. Then she stops, still with her back to me, and a couple of moments later, I see a wafts of smoke around her head. My heart sinks. Betty didn't smoke back at The Farm. *Betty didn't work for the Germans back then either*, I remind myself. A lot has changed since.

Finally, the woman turns and takes a long drag on her cigarette. I come to an abrupt halt, my body rigid with shock and dread. She might be smoking a cigarette and she might be wearing a German uniform, but there's no doubting that she's Betty.

36

PARIS, 1943

I quickly regain my composure and pretend to look for something in my purse. When I glance up, I see that she's still standing there smoking, staring blankly ahead. She must be waiting for someone and now I'm not sure what to do. Should I confront her, or wait to see what happens next? If she's waiting for her Nazi boyfriend, I won't be able to approach her, but I could tail them and find out exactly where they live.

I turn and pretend to look down at the river. Even darker clouds are gathering overhead, giving the strange illusion that night is falling. I might not get this chance again. I need to approach her. Glancing left and right to check the coast is clear, I start walking toward her. If one of her German buddies arrives, I can slip off behind the tower. Then a much more agreeable thought occurs to me—what if Betty is working for the British? Their intelligence service has a far bigger presence here in France than the OSS. What if she's waiting to meet her contact here? Buoyed up by this possibility, I walk closer. Her gaze is still fixed firmly ahead. I stop a couple of yards from her, facing the same way, toward the bridge, and clear my throat.

"Hello, stranger." I shoot her a sideways glance, expecting

her to react in shock, but she doesn't move a muscle. Maybe she didn't hear me. "Hello, stranger," I say again, louder.

Finally, she looks at me, but instead of shock, I see sorrow on her face. "Why have you come here?" she asks me in English and I'm momentarily stumped.

"I-I've come to help you," I stammer.

"Help me? How? I don't need your help." There's a frantic tone to her voice.

I go over to her. "What's going on? Who are you really working for?" I whisper.

"Who does it look like?" She looks down at her uniform.

"But surely..." I protest.

"Surely what?" she replies, her voice tight.

"You can't really want to... Were they going to kill you, when they took you that day in Barcelona? Is that what this is about? Did you do some kind of deal to save your life?"

She finally makes eye contact with me. "My life was never in danger that day."

Her words hit me with the force of a freight train. "What do you mean?" Something about this is feeling off. Why is she showing no shock at my sudden appearance here in France? A terrible thought occurs to me: did she know I was following her? Have I walked into a trap? I take a step back and look around. A couple of guys in suits are striding toward us across the bridge. I fumble in my purse for my pistol.

"Don't!" she barks at me. Another couple of guys appear from the shadows of the tower.

"But I thought..." I stare at her.

"What?" she says sharply.

"I thought we were friends. *Beloved* friends." My words sound so pitiful.

"We were. Why do you think I warned you that day in Barcelona?" she hisses. "Why did you have to come here?"

I'm too stunned to move, not that it would do any good. The

men are closing in now and I hear one of them call something in German. Then their hands are upon me, one of them grabbing my purse, the others an arm each.

What happens next is a blur. A car screeches up alongside us and I'm bundled into the back, book-ended by two of the men. Betty betrayed me. She betrayed us all. As we speed along the street, anger begins to pierce my shocked daze. Anger at Betty, but more than that, anger at myself. I messed up. I trusted that Betty had some decency, but she lured me into a trap. And now what? She will have no doubt told her Gestapo buddies all about me. As a known American spy, who knows what they'll do to me. Then a terrible thought occurs to me. What if they know I was in Canfranc with Horst? What if they think I've got something to do with his disappearance? What if they've found his body? An image of Betty's brutish lover looms into my mind, preparing to interrogate me. Well, I won't be a cowardly traitor like her. I'd rather die a horrible death than betray the Allies.

The car pulls up outside 84 Avenue Foch and in my heightened state of fear I feel the sudden urge to laugh hysterically. Hadn't I been trying to devise a way to get inside this very building just last night? And now my wish is about to come true. Grand-mère Rose got it wrong; life isn't some kind of magical mystery, it's a cruel joke.

At the thought of Grand-mère Rose, my heart feels crushed. Have I got this far, this close to her, only to be killed?

The men bundle me out of the car and into the building. There's no sign of Betty. I picture her painting the town red, celebrating her great victory.

Don't think about that traitorous bitch, Carmen's voice echoes through my mind, as if risen from the dead. *Don't let her win!* I can get through this, I tell myself, I just need to channel the spirit of Carmen.

The men hustle me through the foyer and up a flight of stairs. I count the floors as we climb, one... two... three... four...

five. They lead me from the stairwell into a softly lit, carpeted corridor. I'm not sure what I was expecting, but it certainly wasn't this luxurious. I'm taken into a large room with three tall windows dressed with long red velvet drapes, which I recognize from the front of the building. At one end of the room, there's an ornate wooden desk with a couple of chairs placed in front of it. At the other, a cluster of armchairs are arranged around a low table in front of the fireplace. Oil paintings in gilt frames line the walls.

"Sit," one of the men says, pointing to the armchairs.

I do as I'm told, staring into my lap as I contemplate why I, a known American spy, should be brought into a place of such opulence. It's strangely unnerving. Two of the men exit the room, leaving the third standing sentry-like by the door. His shaven-headed brutish appearance is ruined slightly by the fact that he's holding my purse. I think of the pistol hidden in the lining and once again I'm swept back in time to my very first role for the war effort in the training video. Just like Steve, I'm in a very tight squeeze.

I wonder how Betty knew I was tailing her. Did the doorman tip her off? Did she notice me sitting in the garden and see straight through my disguise? I'd seen through hers after all. I should have been more careful. I was so sure I'd be able to turn her, I was so sure I was able to trust her, I forgot to picture things from her side of the board.

The door opens and a barrel-chested man with curly brown hair walks in. Like the others, he's in a suit rather than military uniform.

"Good day, Elena," he greets me in French and it's such a shock to hear him say my real name, my mouth drops open. "Or would you prefer it if I called you Carmen? And if you like, we could talk in your mother tongue," he adds in English.

How does he know my real name? Even Betty doesn't know that. Nobody does. I stay silent.

"I think Elena would be best," he continues, coming to sit in the chair opposite mine, "given that this meeting is all about being completely honest with one another."

There's a knock on the door and a young woman in a black and white maid's uniform comes in carrying a tray.

"Ah, very good," the man says with a warm smile. "Put it down here please." He points to the table in front of us.

I watch numbly as the woman places a teapot, two cups and saucers and a plate of pretty pastel-colored cookies on the table in front of us. Does she have any idea who I am and how my life is in danger? The whole thing feels surreal.

The woman scuttles from the room and the man pours the tea. I have a flashback to afternoon tea in the Embassy tearooms with Mitchell. What I wouldn't give to be back there now.

"My name is Josef Kieffer," he says, passing me a cup. My trembling fingers cause it to rattle on the saucer. I quickly set it down on the table, not wanting him to see my fear. "You're probably wondering how I know so much about you—and trust me, I know a *lot* about you. Your family home in California. Your parents' auto-mechanics business. Your younger sister, Maria."

His words are like darts piercing the carefully constructed suit of armor I've built around myself since coming to Europe. The one thing that's kept me strong all this time is the notion that I'm playing a role, and that all of this is completely separate from my real life and my loved ones. But the Gestapo know about my family. Terror courses through me as the enormity of this fact hits home.

They can't get to your family; they're nowhere near America, I remind myself. But what about Grand-mère Rose? What if they know about her? I know I didn't tell Betty she was French, but still...

My panic must be showing because he starts to smile.

"In this war, nothing is what it seems."

On that, we can definitely agree.

I swallow hard, trying to regain my composure.

"And there's no way you can know who to really trust."

I think of Betty and again I'm in agreement. But Betty never knew my real name—unless I said it in my sleep! But I couldn't have possibly blabbed about my entire family while I was sleeping.

Kieffer settles back in his chair, takes a sip from his cup. "The fact is, you Americans and us Germans have a lot more in common than you might think."

"Really?" Finally I'm able to speak.

He nods.

"Such as?"

"We have a common enemy in the communists for a start."

I think back to how Mitchell told me that Spanish communists would be our most reliable collaborators and how surprised I'd been.

"Do you really think that Russia has America's best interests at heart?" Kieffer continues, amiably. "Do you really think that the American people can trust communists? Germans have far more in common with Americans than the Russians. And we weren't the ones who bombed Pearl Harbor."

"Yes, but you declared war upon us as soon as we retaliated against Japan," I can't help reminding him. I instantly want to kick myself. I need to keep my mouth shut, try to get as much as I can from him without giving anything away.

"We are going to win this war," he says, neatly avoiding my point. "And the American people are going to be furious that so many of their lives were lost and so much money was wasted on fighting for people who don't care at all about them, thousands of miles away from home. Many British have already realized this and come over to our side."

"British?" It's becoming increasingly hard to disguise my shock.

"Yes. I assume you know all about the Special Operations Executive?"

I nod. The SOE were what inspired the US government to set up the OSS. A secret army of intelligence agents commissioned by Churchill to "set Europe ablaze" by sabotaging the Germans from behind enemy lines.

"Well, I can tell you that we have friends in very high places within the SOE." Kieffer smirks.

I bite on my lip to stop myself from reacting. He must be bluffing.

"Come." He stands and gestures at me to follow him over to the desk. As I walk behind him, my fighting training kicks in. I could take him from behind, just like I did with Teddy in the church. But his goon is still standing at the door holding my purse and who knows how many others might be stationed out in the corridor.

"This is the organizational structure of the SOE." He points to a chart on the wall, reminiscent of a family tree. "Come closer, take a look."

I lean in and see that the chart is full of names, ranks and locations. But this could be phoney for all I know, designed to demoralize people like me.

"You're probably thinking that I could have made all this up," he says, as if reading my mind. "But how would I know so much about you if I didn't have friends in the OSS too?"

"Your friend Erika," I say. Could Betty have somehow gotten access to a file on me while we were at The Farm?

He smiles and shakes his head. "Erika, or Betty as you know her, never had access to that kind of information and you know that. I'm friends with people far higher up in the organization."

I think of Mitchell, Captain Shaw, and even William Fairbairn. Is it possible that one of them could be an even bigger snake than Betty?

"Erika isn't a traitor to America," he continues, "she's trying to save America."

"From what?"

"From falling into the clutches of the communists." He leads me back over to the armchairs. "Do you know who make up the bulk of the Resistance here in France?"

I shake my head.

"Communists, with known ties to Russia. It's the same in Spain—but perhaps you already know this." As I watch him take another sip of tea, I realize that I'm in the presence of a master chess player. So calm, so polite, as he moves around the board, planting his seeds of doubt.

He nods to the goon standing at the door, who slips outside. My heart skips a beat. Is the time for tea and niceties over? Is the real interrogation about to begin?

"But I don't think you should take my word for it. I think it would be good for you to talk to someone who really knows."

The door opens.

37

PARIS, 1943

Betty walks in and Kieffer stands up and gestures at her to take his seat.

"I'll leave you two old friends to get reacquainted." He looks at me. "Hopefully you'll see that we're not so different after all."

Go to hell, I yell at him inside my head.

I watch, stony-faced, as Betty sits down opposite me. She at least has the grace to look uncomfortable, crossing her legs one way and then the other and twisting her hands in her lap. I keep my gaze firmly fixed upon her as her eyes dart about the room.

"Well?" I say, once Kieffer and his goon have left.

"I'm sorry," she whispers.

"So when exactly did you sell your soul to the devil?" I hiss. "You said your life wasn't in danger when we met in Barcelona, so you must have already been working for them. Were you working for them when we were at The Farm?" The thought that I had so blindly trusted her back then makes me feel like the world's biggest fool.

She shakes her head. "But that's when the seed was sown."

"What do you mean?"

"Do you remember the night I was in tears, one of the many

nights that bastard Teddy had spent tormenting me, and you told me that I needed to focus on the true enemy?"

"Yes."

"It made me think."

"Think what?"

"Who my true enemy really was."

"I don't understand." My mind becomes a jumble of questions. Had she already decided in training that she was going to defect? Was nothing Betty said or did real? Could I really be such a bad judge of character?

"My whole life I've had people like Teddy think they can walk all over me, speak to me like I'm a piece of dirt. Humiliate me." Her voice trembles. "Do you remember that day in the gymnasium?"

"Yes." Even now, after all she's done, I still wince at the memory of the blood on Betty's shorts and how Teddy reveled in her discomfort.

"That day, I so badly wanted to get a gun and shoot him. But then I realized there was a better way of getting revenge."

"By joining the Germans?" I spit, unable to hide my disgust.

"Why not?" Finally she meets my gaze. "What exactly are America fighting for anyways?"

"Freedom from fascism?" I offer, but she ignores me and carries on.

"Why are so many American men losing their lives fighting for countries so far from home, that mean nothing to them? And fighting alongside communists!"

Clearly she's received the Kieffer brainwashing treatment.

"Do you really want the Russians to win?" she asks.

I remain silent, barely trusting myself to breathe for fear that I might blow a gasket.

"At least now I'm somewhere my talents are appreciated," she adds.

What talents? What the hell is she talking about? Then I

remember how great she was with the wireless and coding. Is that what she's doing here, on Avenue Foch? Is she using the skills she learned against the very people who taught her? Is she intercepting messages and putting Allied agents' lives in danger?

"What do you mean?" I force the words out. "What are you doing here?"

"*Funkspiel*," she replies, a dreamy smile playing on her face.

"What does that mean?"

"Radio games. We use the radios we've captured to send messages to the British."

A chill runs right through me as I realize exactly what she means by this. "Pretending to be from captured agents?"

"Exactly!" Her eyes light up and my stomach churns. Her "games" must be leading to countless deaths. "We organize drops with London and the Brits deliver them right into our hands."

"What kind of drops?"

"Weapons, ammunition... people," she adds, softly.

"Other agents?" I don't know how I'm able to keep my voice level as I think of British agents, possibly women just like Betty and me, being parachuted straight into the hands of the Nazis.

"Sometimes, yes." She shifts in her seat, frowning as if she can't believe I've had the audacity to rain on her parade. "It's helping us to win the war, to beat the communists."

It's helping you kill people from your own side! Somehow, I manage to keep my lip zipped. She's finally letting me see her side of the board. If I have any hope of getting out of this alive, I can't let her see mine.

"I'm trying to save your life," she whispers, leaning forward, real urgency in her eyes.

"Did you find out about my family? Did you tell them my real name?" I whisper back.

She doesn't say anything, but I see a flicker of guilt on her face. So Kieffer was bluffing. He doesn't have friends in higher places in the OSS. Betty must have somehow snuck a look at my file back at The Farm.

"I told them I'd be able to turn you," she whispers.

I fight the urge to laugh at the irony. All the time I've been dreaming of turning Betty, she's been planning on recruiting me to the Gestapo.

"The guard at my apartment building notified my..." She hesitates a beat before continuing. "... notified one of my superiors that you'd been asking for me."

I wonder if she'd been going to say "my lover."

"He wanted to know who you were, so I came out to see who'd come calling—and there you were, in the garden."

"You saw me?"

She nods.

Damn, damn, damn! I curse myself for being so stupid. Just like Teddy and the other guys at The Farm, I've clearly been guilty of hugely underestimating Betty.

She leans so close, I can smell the stale cigarette smoke on her breath. "Why did you have to come here?" she whispers so quietly I have to strain to hear. "Why couldn't you have let me be?"

"I wanted to help you," I whisper back, holding her gaze. And for a moment it's as if we're back at The Farm, huddled together, trying to lift each other's spirits. "I still do," I continue. Her eyes fill with tears and I feel the faintest sliver of hope. "We could still get out of this—if we work together."

She's silent for a moment, then she wipes her eyes. "Don't you understand, there's no getting out of this. Not for you, and if you want to survive, you're going to have to comply."

"Comply with what?"

"Us. Join me."

"In your radio game?" I stare at her, stunned.

"Yes. I've told them you're a really gifted radio operator."

I can't help a wry laugh at this. "I was terrible at coding. You were the radio whizz."

She grips my arm so hard it hurts. "I don't want you to die, do you understand?" she hisses. "I'm trying to save your life." She looks so distraught, I know she's not bluffing.

"But surely you must know what your German friends are doing to the Jewish people, and to the French and the rest of the Allies," I hiss.

She sighs and shakes her head. "Do you know what the Allies did to the Germans after the last war, in the Treaty of Versailles?"

"They made them pay for the cost of the war."

Her face pinches into a frown. "They took away twelve percent of Germany's land, half of its iron and coal production, and the British blocked shipments of food and supplies from entering the country, forcing millions of people—millions of innocent women and children—into starvation."

I frown. I've never heard of this before; surely it must be more of Kieffer's brainwashing.

"It's true. The French even took all of the German livestock so the children weren't able to have milk." She looks at me earnestly. "Every government in the world has done terrible things, so why should we feel blind loyalty to any one of them?"

"But—"

She leans forward and grips my arm again. "We don't have long. If you want to survive, if you want to see your family again, you'll do as I say and join us. It's not as if you'd be the first agent to switch allegiances and work for us. They all have a very comfortable existence here."

I have the sickening feeling that she's actually being truthful. Exactly how many traitors are in this building?

"I understand that it's a lot for you to take in," she says, adjusting the collar on her hideous uniform. "Maybe you need some more time to think it all through." She stands up and smooths down her skirt. "I'll come back and see you soon."

She leaves before I'm able to respond and the goon immediately steps back in.

I slump back in my chair. *What do I do?* If only Santiago were here. Or Mitchell. But I'm all alone in the heart of the vipers' nest.

After a couple of minutes, Kieffer returns. To my surprise, he's still remarkably amiable. "I understand from Erika that you need a little more time to think about our offer."

I need no time; the answer will always be no, I want to cry, but I suppress it. The truth is, I do need some thinking time—to think of how the hell I'm going to get out of here. So I nod and bow my head.

"Franz will take you to your room," he says merrily, as if I've just checked in to his Parisian hotel. But this is no hotel. I picture a carpetless cell waiting for me, with a mattress-less bed.

Love your fear, I repeat to myself silently as I follow Franz into the corridor and up the stairs. But it's no good. It's impossible to love the terror now gripping me into submission. *Oh Grand-mère Rose, what have I done?*

We emerge onto a long corridor on the sixth floor. German guards are stationed at the end. It's quiet. Too quiet. I wonder what, or who, is behind the doors we pass. Franz unlocks a room halfway down and gestures at me to go inside. I'm surprised to see that the floor is carpeted and the single bed with its pillows and eiderdown looks surprisingly comfortable. There's a wooden bureau against one wall and a small wardrobe opposite. Rain is pounding against the barred skylight in the ceiling.

Franz leaves and I hear the door locking behind him. I perch on the end of the bed. *Think, think, think. See the board from all sides*, I hear my father urging. At the thought of Papa, I feel hollow with longing for my family. I've tried so hard to block them from my thoughts in order to stay strong, but now all

I can think is, am I going to die here, so far from home, never to see them again? Never to see Grand-mère Rose or Santiago. I put my wrist to my nose to try to inhale the last of Mom's perfume, but it's gone.

I start pacing in a small circle, trying to think of the situation from Betty's perspective. Clearly she's unbalanced, thinking that defecting to the Nazis is the right thing to do, and a way of wreaking revenge upon Teddy and all the other people who've done her wrong. But she has told me several times that she's trying to save my life, so in that regard at least, I can count on her—as long as I comply with her wishes, or appear to. Being able to turn me would no doubt earn her great kudos with Kieffer and her other Nazi buddies. If I agree too quickly though, it won't look believable, to her or to Kieffer. But what if I give them the impression that I'm considering it? Buy myself a little more time so I can try to work on Betty, get her to see sense. She still cares for me; I could see that in her eyes. *But if you comply you'd have to lure British and possibly American agents to a certain death,* I remind myself. The mere thought makes me sick to my stomach. The only solution I can think of is to make Betty think that I'm going to turn, but try to escape as soon as I can, before I have to commit any kind of treasonous act.

I stand up straight and take a deep breath. Playing the role of a defector to the Nazis is going to call upon my all of my acting skills. I only hope that I've got what it takes.

June 1943, France

My darling Elena,

I have a horrible feeling that this might be the last letter I ever write to you. All of the pain of the last three years, all of the hunger and the fear and the resentment, is hardening into a hatred the like of which I've never felt before. It's ironic to think that I always used to condemn hatred. I always urged people to love instead. But now I'm starting to realize that, for people who are being oppressed, hatred is a gift. It strengthens your resolve. It turns your fear into grit. They're not going to get away with this. I don't know how, but I'm going to do something to help make this stop. To end this barbarity, this insanity. I no longer care if I die. All I want is liberty for my country. The only defeat is to accept defeat.

If I do die, I pray that one day, when this horror is finally over, you will come to France, to this cottage, and you will find these letters hidden beneath the floorboards. Writing this secret correspondence to you these past three years has meant so much. So many times I've asked myself, what would Elena do, or what would I tell Elena to do in this situation, and it's helped me find the answers to the hardest questions.

I love you, my dear granddaughter, and I pray that you one day find these letters and discover how much you have helped me without even knowing.

All my love forever,

Grand-mère Rose

38

PARIS, 1943

I've been in my room for about an hour when there's a knock on the door and I hear the key turn in the lock. A man in a suit walks in, holding a tray.

"Good evening. I thought you might be hungry." He places the tray on the end of the bed. Even though I don't want to eat a mouthful of food stolen from the French, my stomach betrays me and rumbles in appreciation.

He chuckles. Just like Kieffer, I'm struck by how charming he seems.

"My name is Ernst Vogt. I shall be meeting with you tomorrow, but I thought it would be good to introduce myself now. I have also brought you some reading material." He nods at the tray and I notice a sheaf of papers tucked beneath the plate.

"What is it?" I ask.

"Details of the Prosper network—although the name is hardly apt." He chuckles to himself.

I look at him blankly.

"They are a network set up in and around Paris by the SOE. The papers I want to share with you contain details about their agents and operations. Details given to us by the SOE."

Given to, or stolen from? I wonder and I can't help frowning as I picture Betty playing her radio games to bring about the downfall of an entire network.

"I wanted you to see how complex this war is. And how there's no shame in switching allegiances. In fact, it is something to be proud of."

"Proud of, how?" I ask, but softly, as if I've taken his bait and I'm genuinely curious.

"It shows real intelligence and takes great courage to admit that you've been misguided."

"I think I need to see more proof of how I've been misguided," I say, hating the words as they come from my lips, but knowing that I have to string him along if I want to buy myself more time.

"Of course. That is perfectly understandable." His eyes light up and I see that he thinks he's got me. "When we meet tomorrow, I shall tell you more, but for now, enjoy your dinner and your reading." He smiles before turning to leave.

I look at the meal on the tray. There are slices of what looks like beef with potatoes, green beans and gravy. I'm so hungry, but the thought of what's on the papers tucked beneath the plate is making me nauseous.

You need to keep your strength up, I tell myself and force down a mouthful of meat.

After I've eaten, I pick up the papers and turn them over and over in my hands before I can bring myself to read. First, there's a list of names and code names. As my eyes scan the page, I feel sick, wondering what must have become of these people. Then there's a list of French names and addresses. Members of the Resistance no doubt. All of them risking their lives to try to save their country, only to be betrayed by the worst kind of traitors.

Once I've read through the names, I find transcripts of correspondence between field agents and the SOE office in

London. The thought that Betty might have had a hand in this makes my stomach churn.

Focus, I tell myself. *Getting angry is not going to help anything.* I need to figure out how I can get Betty to help me. *What is her weakness?* I ask myself. *That she has an irrational hatred of Teddy and she wants to save me.* Whatever the hell's going on in her head, my loyalty to her at The Farm has clearly counted for something. She wasn't expecting to see me in Barcelona and when she did, she tried to warn me that it was a trap. And now she wants to turn me to keep me alive. If the chips were down, would she be able to bring herself to kill me? How deep does her loyalty to me go? And would it outweigh her loyalty to the Germans? I figure if it was a choice between me and them, they would win for sure, but...

I stand up and start pacing round the small room. If I could engineer a situation where I could escape with her help, but without her getting the blame, she might possibly go for it. Could I use her hatred of Teddy to my advantage? I put the tray and the papers on the floor by the door and I get into bed fully dressed, working on my seed of an idea as if developing a movie script in my head.

I'm not sure what time it is, but the room is steeped in darkness when I'm suddenly wrenched from sleep by a terrible noise. At first, I think it's an animal howling in distress, but then the howl morphs into a word, long and strangulated: "Noooooooooo!" It's a man's voice, and this makes it all the more terrifying. I've never heard a man scream before, not like this.

I grip the edge of the quilt in fright and stare through the skylight into the darkness. Perhaps I was having a nightmare, I try to reassure myself, but then I hear him cry out again. I creep out of bed and press my ear to the door, trying to work out if the screaming is coming from somewhere along the corridor, but all falls silent. Wherever the scream was coming from it was uncomfortably close and a stark reminder that although Kieffer and Vogt might have been all tea trays and smiles so far, it was just a façade. They are still members of the Gestapo.

I think back to the conversation I had with Betty at The Farm about interrogation and torture and whether we'd use our cyanide capsules to kill ourselves. I was so gung-ho back then, insisting that I'd take whatever the Germans might throw at me and never crack. But hearing a grown man scream for mercy puts things in a whole new light.

In spite of the fact that I'm fully clothed, I start shivering violently.

Love your fear, I imagine Grand-mère Rose murmuring, in that soft melodic voice she'd use to tell me stories. I get back into bed, pulling the quilt over my head, and I picture Grand-mère Rose hugging me to her, all of my fear being absorbed into the softness of her body, being soothed away by the lilt of her voice. Then I think of everyone I love in turn, picturing my soul flying out through the skylight, flying all over the world, planting goodnight kisses on the top of their heads. Maria, my parents, Grand-mère Rose, Santiago. *Goodnight, I love you. Goodnight, I love you.* Feeling connected to them in this way is strangely comforting and I finally fall back to sleep.

The next morning, I'm brought breakfast with a cup of real coffee, which I know is harder to find than a unicorn these days in France—to the French at least. The smell is intoxicating. I gulp it down before starting on the baguette. Unlike the stick of bread I bought from the boulangerie, this one is perfectly fresh, fluffy and warm beneath the golden crust. I wolf it down, refusing to allow myself to enjoy it, seeing it purely as fuel— hopefully for my escape from this hellhole.

Once I've finished breakfast, I'm taken downstairs to the

second floor. All the way down, I desperately scan the place for a potential escape route but find none. I'm taken into an office, where Vogt greets me with a warm smile from behind his desk. A man with a shiny bald head is sitting in front of the desk. He turns and looks at me, but there's no smile, just a piercing stare from piggy little eyes set too close together.

"How did you sleep?" Vogt asks.

Oh, just great, listening to people being tortured!

I force myself to smile back. "OK, thanks."

"Good. And did you find the papers I gave you interesting?"

"Very. How on earth did you get so much intelligence?"

My flattery works and his face beams.

"We have infiltrated the SOE office in London. We know everything they're doing here in Paris—everyone who is collaborating with them."

I suppress a shudder.

"And thanks to my colleague here—" he nods to the bald man "—we are able to benefit from their very generous weapons and ammunitions deliveries." The bald man smirks. "And, of course, we have similar connections within the American intelligence service."

Even though I'm sure he's bluffing, I make myself look shocked.

"That's right." Vogt nods. "Your friend Erika is small fry compared to some of our contacts there."

Time to play it dumb. "But I don't understand. Who?"

"True Americans," he replies, "who don't want to see Europe taken over by communists."

I frown thoughtfully, as if this prospect has only just occurred to me. "Do you really think that if the Allies won the war, the communists would take over? Surely they'd only have control of Russia?"

He shakes his head, clearly excited by the fact that I appear to have fallen for his story hook, line and sinker. "No, not at all.

France is overrun with communists. They make up the majority of the Resistance. If they were to regain control of their country, it would become another Russia."

"I had no idea!" I widen my eyes, warming to my new role of dumb broad.

"Yes, I'm afraid so."

"But they didn't say anything about that in our training," I say indignantly.

"No, *they* wouldn't." Vogt sighs. "I can only assume that America has become riddled with communists too."

I gasp, just a small one, nothing too theatrical, but designed to convey my full horror at this prospect.

Vogt eyes light up, as if he's certain he's got me. "Do you see now why I said to you last night that changing allegiances was the intelligent thing to do?"

I frown. I mustn't make this look too easy. "I'm starting to. It's just hard when everything you've been told..." I break off, looking dejected.

"I know." He stands up and gestures at the bald guy to do the same. "I think perhaps it would help if you spoke to your friend Erika again. Hopefully, she can put your mind at rest."

"That would be good, thank you." Cue more doe eyes in his direction.

They leave the room and a couple of minutes later Betty comes in. *Traitor enters, stage left*, the scriptwriter in my head types. She looks at me anxiously.

Start cynical, disbelieving, I remind myself, let her think that she's convincing you.

"How are you?" she asks.

"Confused," I reply as we sit on the chairs in front of the desk.

"How so?"

"Have the Gestapo really infiltrated the SOE London office?"

"Yes." She nods vigorously.

"Wow! And is it really true that they have contacts high up in the OSS?"

Again she nods.

I truly don't understand how agents would be turned by this bullshit. Even if it were true, surely it's all the more reason to remain loyal to your cause and not add to the number of traitors. I push down my true feelings and shake my head instead, as if I'm truly demoralized by these revelations.

"Do you know what I think about every time I get one over on the British?" Betty says with a tight little smile.

"What?"

"I think of that asshole Teddy and all the others that made my life hell. Just knowing that I'm helping people like him end up on the losing side makes me feel so much better."

Even though this logic feels insane to me, I make myself nod. "Those guys really did put you through hell."

Her expression softens. "Yes. You were the only one who was there for me."

"Of course," I say, pouncing on this chink in her armor "We had to stand together. I knew from the moment we first met that we'd be friends."

Her face lights up. "Really? How?"

"When you showed me the microphones on the beds so I wouldn't say anything that might get me into trouble. I knew right then that I'd be able to trust you."

"Ah yes." She laughs. "Those microphones were crazy." She looks at me hopefully. "So what do you say? Will you join me? We don't owe those assholes like Teddy a thing."

I nod thoughtfully. "You sure gave me a lot of food for thought yesterday."

Her face beams with relief.

"I hated that asshole Teddy too." I haven't had much time to rehearse my lines; I'm going to have to improvise and hope for the best. "And speaking of which, there's something I need to share with you." *Don't share too fast, hold back a little.* "But you must promise not to say anything to *them*." I nod toward the door.

"OK." She looks at me eagerly.

I lean forward and whisper conspiratorially, "I'm supposed to be meeting with him this afternoon."

"What? Where?" Her eyes widen and the color drains from her face.

"Here in Paris. He's setting up a new network for the OSS."

I hold my breath. Will she bite or will she see through my lies?

"Where are you meeting him?"

I think of the address for the safe house that Mitchell gave me. "You have to promise you won't breathe a word first."

"I promise."

"A cemetery called Père Lachaise."

"I know it. Why are you telling me this?" she whispers.

"I thought you might like the chance to get revenge. Proper revenge." I place my hand on her arm. "I hate him for what he did to you. That day in the gym, I felt like shooting him too. I could tell you exactly where and when he's meant to be meeting me and maybe you could go pay him a surprise visit." I sit back and wait for her next move.

Her expression changes from excitement to apprehension, just as I anticipated it might. "I'd have to tell my superiors here; I wouldn't be able to capture him single-handed."

"I wasn't thinking of capturing him."

She frowns. "What were you thinking?"

"Finishing him," I whisper. "You said you wanted to shoot him that day in the gym. Well, now's your chance."

"Kill him?" She looks shocked.

"Uh-huh."

"But..."

"Surely you have access to a gun?"

"Yes, but..."

I can see self-doubt written all over her face. She's probably remembering how badly she did at the firing range and in combat training.

"But?" I echo softly.

"He's expecting to meet you; the minute he sees me he'll know something's up."

I frown as if that thought hadn't occurred to me, then feign an expression of delight, as if I've just been struck by the most wonderful idea. "What if..." I break off, not wanting to overdo it.

"Yes?"

Show a little doubt, make it look more believable. "No, I guess it would be impossible."

"What?" she hisses.

I lower my voice and stare right in her eyes. "What if I came with you? You could tail me and I could meet with him. I could lure him somewhere secluded in the cemetery and then you could..." I let her imagination do the rest.

Her smile turns to a frown. "There's no way they'd let you leave here."

"Even if I switch allegiances?"

She shakes her head. "The other agents who've turned, they aren't allowed to leave."

I feign a look of disappointment, even though, of course, I've predicted this would be the case. "What a shame."

"But what if I tell my superiors what you've told me?" She looks at me hopefully. "They could tail you and capture him."

"I don't think that's a good idea."

"Why not?"

"You know what Teddy's like. He's such a snake. He'd probably turn the second he gets here and then we'd have to live with him making our life hell all over again."

Thankfully, she looks horrified at this prospect.

"But if you were to figure out a way we could slip out of here without your superiors realizing, we could finish him and come straight back and no one would be any the wiser."

"I don't know."

As I watch her frown and wring her hands, I wonder if I've played it right. I know for sure that the Gestapo wouldn't let me gad about Paris with Betty. But how deep does her hatred for Teddy go? Would she be prepared to take the risk of sneaking me out of here?

"I need to think about it," she says, standing abruptly.

As she leaves the room, my heart sinks. Has she seen through my act? Does she know I'm trying to trick her? Have I just lost my only ally in this godforsaken place?

39

PARIS, 1943

I spend the rest of the morning locked in my room, with another folder of reading material on the SOE courtesy of Vogt. I'm far too nervous to read. All I can think is that Betty might be meeting with Kieffer right now, telling him that I tried to deceive her and can't be trusted. What was I thinking, trying to trick her like that? Why was I so impulsive? But what was the alternative? Every second in this place is a second closer to telling them that there's no way I'm going to play their radio games. I had to do something.

I'm still lost in panicked thoughts when I hear the key turning in the door. I look up expecting to see one of the men, but to my surprise it's Betty. She's holding a bag. She tips it onto my bed and a brown wig and gray uniform just like hers falls out.

"Put these on," she says, "quick."

I do as I'm told, my mind racing. Did she believe me after all? Could she really be trying to get me out of here? She helps me put the wig on and I see that her fingers are trembling.

"I'm going to distract the guard at the end of the corridor," she says once I'm ready. "Go straight to the stairs at the opposite end. They'll take you to a fire exit at the side of the building. If you make it outside without being stopped, turn right and keep walking straight down the avenue. When you get to the end, wait in the doorway of the building on the corner. The one with the red sign. I'll be right behind you."

"OK." I clasp her hands in mine, my relief tinged with anxiety at what's to come. "Thank you."

She looks ashen-faced. "Give me a few seconds, then leave. If anyone apprehends you trying to leave the building, I'm going to tell them that we were going to try to capture an OSS agent, and we'll have to let them come with us to prove that I wasn't lying."

"OK." I nod, praying that this doesn't happen as it's bound to end horribly.

She presses a key into my hand as she goes. "Lock the door behind you when you leave."

I wait a moment, then cautiously open the door a crack. I can hear Betty laughing with the guard at the end of the corridor. I step out and lock the door and hurry over to the stairwell. By the time I reach the ground floor, it feels as if my heart's in my mouth, but thankfully I don't see a soul. I slip outside and take a gulp of the warm air.

Keep walking. Keep walking. Keep walking, I tell myself as I round the building onto the avenue, keeping my gaze fixed on the floor. I'm aware of other people waking past me, but I don't look up.

Finally, I reach the building at the end of the street. I glance over my shoulder and see Betty a few yards behind me. Damn. There's no chance of giving her the slip.

"We have to get the Metro," she says as she catches up, steering me in the direction of the subway.

We breeze past the German soldiers guarding the entrance and it feels surreal to receive their nods of acknowledgment. On the train, it's a different story. French women stare at us and our gray uniforms with open hostility. I glance at Betty. She's looking really on edge, nibbling at her fingernails like a mouse gnawing on cheese. My mind whirs as I try picturing her side of the board. She could be nervous about the prospect of potentially killing Teddy, or is she worried because she could get into a whole lot of trouble for helping me leave? Or did she tell Kieffer and the Gestapo what we're up to? My "escape" did feel remarkably effortless. And how does Betty know they're not going to check on me sometime soon? If they see that my room's empty, there'll be all hell to pay—for her at least. There's no way I'm going back to that building of my own free will, that's for damn sure.

I wonder if there are Gestapo agents tailing us right now, hoping to capture Teddy. I glance along the carriage and spot a man in a suit leaning against the swaying wall at the end. Could he be Gestapo? I haven't even considered what I'll do when we get to the cemetery. How will I explain Teddy's no-show? If it's just me and Betty, I'll fess up and tell her that I want to escape. She'll no doubt try to get me to stop, possibly drawing her weapon on me, but I'm confident I'll be able to disarm her. Then I'll make a break for the safe house. But if we're being tailed by the Gestapo, it's going to be a whole lot harder. As the train rattles through the tunnel, I feel sweat trickling down my back. I'd rather die trying to escape than be a traitor, I tell myself. There's no way I'm going back to Avenue Foch.

As soon as we emerge from the Metro at Père Lachaise, I glance up and down the street. There's no obvious sign of any Germans, but if they think I'm meeting with Teddy they're going to be keeping a low profile.

"Put this on," Betty says, taking a coat from her bag and handing it to me. I don't need to be asked twice to cover up the hideous uniform, even though I'm sweltering in the heat. "You go first and I'll follow." As she puts on a coat of her own, she grabs hold of my hands. "Elena?"

I still can't get used to her using my real name. "Yes?"

"I can trust you, can't I?"

"Yes, of course." For a moment I feel a twinge of guilt at betraying her. If I do escape today and the Germans figure out she helped me, who knows what they'll do to her. But then I remember that she chose to join them and how she's been helping them capture Allied agents and my heart instantly hardens.

I walk across the street and through the ornate iron gates of the cemetery. I see an old woman in a long skirt and headscarf tending to a grave. Something about her reminds me of Esmerelda. *Someone close to you will betray you*, her growly voice echoes back to me. I never would have guessed that someone would be Betty.

I march purposefully along one of the paths between the graves. It's like a city for the dead, the mausoleums arranged like rows of ancient stone houses. I'd appreciate its beauty a whole lot more l if I wasn't feeling so scared. I follow a path toward a grassy clearing containing a cluster of trees and go and stand beneath them, figuring this would be the kind of place two agents would arrange to meet. But no one is coming to meet me and there's only so long I can stand here before Betty gets suspicious. I see her skirt around the edge of the clearing and go stand by a grave, pretending to be paying her respects. There's still no sign of any Gestapo agents tailing us—maybe they're covering the cemetery exits.

As far as I can see, I have two choices: I make a run for it now and risk her shooting at me, or I attempt to disarm Betty, then make a break for it. If I did that, at least I'd be armed if there are Gestapo tailing us. I look around again, but still see no sign of anyone. A raven swoops down onto the tree and fixes its beady eyes on me. Perhaps I could still convince Betty to come with me, to come back to the OSS.

I start walking toward her. As I get closer, she looks confused and gestures at me to back off.

"What are you doing?" she hisses. "If he sees you with me, he might leave."

"He's not coming," I say softly, adopting a square stance.

"But..." Her mouth hangs open in shock.

"I need you to give me your gun."

"No!" She clutches her purse to her chest, conveniently letting me know exactly where it is.

"Please, Betty. Do the Gestapo know we're here? Did you tell them? Did they tail us?"

"No!" She looks at me imploringly as she fumbles at the catch on her purse. "I can't let you do this."

"Come with me then. You've got the chance to put everything right."

"What do you mean? I thought you understood." She pulls the pistol from her bag and points it at me, her hands quivering.

"I'll never understand. How can you be happy, luring other agents to their deaths? How does that make up for what Teddy did to you?"

"You don't know what he did to me," she cries.

"Yes I do. I was there. And yes, he was a prize-winning asshole, but that doesn't justify you killing innocent people."

"You weren't there." Her voice breaks.

"What do you mean?"

"You weren't there when he... when he forced himself upon me."

"What?" I stare at her, feeling sick to my stomach.

"You'd been sent away for a few days."

I think of the time I was sent to Washington to be told about my posting in Spain. "But why didn't you say something when I got back?"

"Because he told me no one would believe me." Her voice becomes shrill.

"I would have believed you!"

"But the others wouldn't. He said his father was close friends with Captain Shaw. That I was just a spic piece of trash and I was no good as an agent anyways, so they'd have no problem kicking me out."

"Betty." I reach out to touch her and she points the gun at my head. "I'm so sorry." And I am, truly. I think of the night I saw Teddy at the British Institute, the way he was right up in the face of the Spanish woman. Then I have a flashback to Horst and how powerless and terrified I felt when he pinned me to the bed. The pilot spared me the horror of what could have happened that night, but no one spared Betty. Then I remember the time Teddy showed up at our room, after I'd returned from Washington, with some story about cipher training. Had he come there to threaten Betty?

"I thought today I'd finally have the chance to get my revenge, but you lied to me." Her voice rises. "You're just like all the rest."

"No, I'm not. I just wanted to escape. I want to see my family." My voice wavers. I suddenly feel so tired, so exhausted from everything. "Please come with me. We can report him. I'll stand by you, I promise. I'm your beloved friend, remember? Better than a beef tamale?" I'm hoping that this might soften her a little, but her frown deepens.

"How can I trust you after this?" She waves the gun around and my training instincts kick in and I make a grab for her wrist, but she's too quick and swipes it away. "Don't!" She stares at me, her eyes wild. "Do you have any idea what you've done? When they find out you've gone and I helped you get out. You're going to have to come back with me."

"I can't. I can't do it. I can't help them kill other agents." I pause for a moment, my breath catching in my throat. "I'd rather you killed me," I say softly. I've been hoping that she wouldn't be able to bring herself to, but to my horror, she cocks the pistol.

So this is it, this is how I'm going to die, shot in a Parisian cemetery by the one person I thought I could trust, the one person I never doubted. If someone had told me back at The Farm that this would be how things would end, I never would have believed them. But at least I won't die a traitor.

I close my eyes and I think of Grand-mère Rose and how her words have guided me all the way here, so close to saving her, yet not close enough. *Love your fear.* I focus on her words, willing them to help me one last time. *Seek the wonder. Embrace the mystery.* I see Santiago dancing, Maria on the stoop carving one of her acorn people. Papa and Mom engaged in one of their impassioned heart-to-hearts. Grand-mère Rose in her cottage writing me that final letter. And, by some miracle, my fear subsides. *I love you,* I say to them all in my mind, determined that this should be the last thought of my life.

I hear the click of the pistol, and brace myself, and I hear a gasp of pain. Is it coming from me? Has my soul left my body already?

I open my eyes and see Betty sprawled across the foot of the grave, a dark crimson stain blooming on her chest.

"What have you done?" I crouch down beside her, feeling sick with shock.

"Go," she gasps.

"But why?" I cradle her to me.

"I never could have killed you," she whispers. "But they would have killed me."

Tears fill my eyes. "I'm so sorry, Betty."

She closes her eyes and her breathing becomes shallow.

"Francisca," she whispers. "My name is Francisca."

And then, with one final gasp, her life slips from her body.

40

FRANCE, SEPTEMBER 1944

I knock at the door of the cottage, my heart in my mouth.

There's no answer. She might be out.

She might be dead, my inner voice warns.

She can't be dead.

I frantically scan the place for any recent signs of life. Clumps of moss sprout like bushy green eyebrows from the gray stone walls and the footpath leading around the building is strewn with weeds. I look up. All of the windows are shut in spite of the heat. What if I've come all this way for nothing?

It will never be for nothing, I remind myself. *I helped the Allies beat the Germans.* France is now free. I think back to the celebrations in Paris last month. Charles de Gaulle being paraded, triumphant, through the streets. After Francisca died, I made it to the safe house by Père Lachaise and the French Resistance helped me escape Paris. I spent the next few months based with the Maquis in a forest in Brittany, assisting them until the fall of Paris. And now, finally, I've been able to come find Grand-mère Rose. If she's still living here. If she's still alive... I've seen at first hand the devastation caused by the Germans, especially in the last few months leading up to their retreat. The public executions, the revenge killings, in some cases entire villages slain. Panic starts rising inside of me.

It's such a beautiful day, far too beautiful for terrible news. A bird swoops by, tweeting gaily. Then I hear someone humming. It's coming from the back of the cottage. Hardly daring to breathe, I follow the narrow footpath around the side of the building.

Please, please, please...

I peer around the wall and see a woman kneeling at one side of the garden, tending to the flower bed.

Please, please, please...

She's wearing a sun hat with such a wide brim it's impossible to see her face.

I clear my throat and she jumps, then puts down her trowel and slowly gets to her feet.

Please, please, please...

"*Bonjour,*" she calls, putting her hand up to shade her eyes from the beaming sun.

I place my hand on the wall of the cottage for support.

"Can I help you?" She starts walking up the garden toward me. Her shoulders are stooped and she's walking with a limp, but there's no denying who she is.

"You're alive," I gasp, running to meet her, tears streaming from my eyes. "You're alive!"

"*Mon Dieu!*" she cries. "Elena, please tell me I haven't been out in the sun for too long and I'm not seeing things. Please tell me it's really you."

"You're not seeing things," I sob. And neither am I. Grandmère Rose is alive. And now she's right in front of me, her hat cast to the floor, her long silver hair tumbling around her shoulders.

"Elena!" she gasps as she takes my face in her hands. "What are you doing here?"

"I-I came to help save you," I splutter, practically delirious with joy and relief.

"Oh my darling girl." She stares at me. "How are you in France? What has happened to you?" I guess almost a year of living in a forest must have taken its toll.

"I wanted to do something to help—to free France. To free you from the Germans. Do you remember the last letter you wrote me?"

She gasps. "How do you know about the letters?"

I frown. "You sent it to me, just before the Germans occupied France."

"Ah, that letter!" She nods.

"What letters were you talking about?" I ask, puzzled.

"It doesn't matter, I'll show you them later. What were you going to say?"

"In that last letter, you knew you wouldn't be able to write for a while so you sent me all of your wisdom condensed into nine words."

"I did?" She looks confused.

"Love your fear. Seek the wonder. Embrace the mystery," I repeat, parrot fashion.

"I wrote that?" Her face breaks into a smile and it's as if she's taken off a mask and I'm looking at the woman I remember, the woman she used to be.

"You sure did and I memorized it. It's helped keep me going ever since I got to Europe."

She stares at me, shaking her head. "I don't believe this."

"I even wrote back to you once, when I was in Spain."

Her dark eyes widen. "You did? You were in Spain?"

I nod. "Obviously I couldn't send it. I had to destroy it, but it really helped, just imagining I was talking to you and imagining what you might advise me to do."

To my surprise, she starts to laugh, and laugh and laugh,

tears spilling down her face. "Oh Elena," she gasps. "Isn't life the most magical thing?"

I feel a twinge of concern. Could she be traumatized by everything she's been through?

"What's so funny, Grand-mère Rose?" someone calls in French.

I spin round and see a thin boy with a thick mop of dark hair standing by the side of the cottage.

"Who's that?" I whisper. "And why is he calling you grandma?"

Again, Grand-mère Rose laughs. "Oh Elena, we have so much to talk about."

"She's Elena?" the boy cries.

"Yes," Grand-mère Rose replies. "*This* is Elena."

The boy gawps at me like she just announced I was the Queen of Sheba.

Grand-mère Rose links her arm through mine. "I think we need to go inside and have a cup of tea. Caleb, can you put the kettle on please?"

"Of course!" he replies, grinning at me before disappearing in through the back door.

As we make our way up the garden path, I think of Grand-mère Rose all those years before, at the start of the war, sitting down in this very cottage to pen me a letter. I picture the letter winging its way like a dove around the globe, all the way to me in California, and how its words embedded themselves inside of me. How they've helped me. And how they'll continue to help me after I leave here to make my way back to Santiago, waiting for me in Spain, and then home to my family.

Love your fear. Seek the wonder. Embrace the mystery. So many times I struggled to find the truth and wisdom in these words, but now, now I feel it filling the air all around me, like the sweet scent of the roses dancing in the warm breeze.

A LETTER FROM SIOBHAN

Dear reader,

Thank you so much for choosing to read *The Secret Keeper*. If you enjoyed it and want to be kept up to date with all my latest releases, just sign up at the following link. Your email address will never be shared and you can unsubscribe at any time.

www.bookouture.com/siobhan-curham

The Secret Keeper is my fourth World War Two novel and although each book focuses on a very different aspect of the war, there is one common thread: I love weaving lesser-known, fascinating historical facts into the stories. With *The Secret Keeper*, I wanted to write about a woman who joined the fore-runner to the CIA, the OSS, inspired by the true story of American model turned spy Aline Griffith. When I started my research, I came across a training video for the OSS, which made me wonder about the actors in it. Who were they? And how did they come to be in it? Down the research rabbit-hole I fell!

I had no idea that the film industry in Hollywood played such a key role in the war that they even had their own unit based in the "Fort Roach" studio. And I had no idea that major stars of the silver screen like William Holden and Ronald Reagan had performed in training and propaganda videos. I was also blown away by the discovery that one of the stars of *Gone with the Wind*, Leslie Howard, had done so much work for the war effort and was killed by the Luftwaffe. And so the idea that my heroine, Elena, should be an actor was born.

Although *The Secret Keeper* is a work of fiction, many of the characters, places and events are based in fact. The OSS training scenes at The Farm were all inspired by real-life accounts and William Fairbairn's combat manuals from the time, *Defendu* and *Shooting to Live*. Walter Starkie of the British Institute and Margaret Kearney Taylor, owner of the Embassy tearoom in Madrid, were both part of an escape network in Spain helping Jewish refugees and Allied servicemen flee Nazi-occupied Europe. Leslie Howard's welcome dinner in Madrid, during which a Romani woman foresaw his death, happened in real life, as did his romantic involvement with the owner of the Ritz salon, who was rumored to have been working for the Germans. If you want to disappear down a research rabbit-hole, I suggest you do a Google search for Leslie Howard's death. While there's no disputing he was killed by the Luftwaffe, there are various theories as to how the Germans knew he'd be on the plane they shot down. Although Santiago Lozano was a fictional creation, I found a news clipping during my research about a flamenco dancer who was a double agent, which really fired my imagination.

The station at Canfranc still exists, although it's now derelict, and in more recent years a Spanish man found buried paperwork there showing the amount of stolen gold that had passed through there during the war. Albert Le Lay, sometimes referred to as the Schindler of Canfranc, risked his life helping many people fleeing the Nazis. The events that take place in 84 Avenue Foch in the novel are also sadly rooted in truth. The Gestapo were able to turn several Allied agents in the ways depicted in the story, which led to the downfall of the Prosper network in France.

And as for Grand-mère Rose, she was inspired in part by

my love for the lost art of letter writing. My mum still has some of the letters my grandparents wrote to each other during the war and it's not hard to imagine how much those letters must have meant to them at a time when they couldn't be certain they'd ever see each other again.

I really hope you enjoyed *The Secret Keeper* and the lesser-known historical facts contained within its pages.

Siobhan

siobhancurham.com

facebook.com/Siobhan-Curham-Author

twitter.com/SiobhanCurham

instagram.com/SiobhanCurham

ACKNOWLEDGEMENTS

HUGE thanks, Kelsie Marsden, for being such a great editor and pushing me to keep raising my game with every draft. It was such a great creative experience working with you on this novel and I'm so happy you enjoyed 'the midpoint'! And it's such a great experience working with the whole team at Bookouture. I'm so grateful to be part of such a dynamic and supportive publishing family. Special thanks to Sarah Hardy (so sorry for making you cry though!), Kim Nash, Noelle Holten, Ruth Tross, Alex Crow, Alex Holmes and Alba Proko, to name but a few. Much love and thanks as always to Jane Willis at United Agents for all of your support.

I strive to make my writing as realistic as possible and as I had zero experience in being a kick-ass spy capable of killing a grown man with my bare hands hand prior to writing this novel, I knew I needed to seek expert help. I was lucky enough to receive professional guidance for the fight scenes in this book from Don Came—martial arts and self-defense expert and founder of Karate for Life—who helped me see how it would be possible for Elena to fight off and disarm her assailants and really bring those scenes to life. Thank you for being so generous with your time and wisdom, Don, and thanks also to Kayhan Etebar for repeatedly being shot, stabbed and having various limbs broken in the name of research!

I'm also hugely indebted to all of the people who took the time to review my other historical novels, *An American in Paris*, *Beyond This Broken Sky* and *The Paris Network* on their blogs,

Goodreads, NetGalley and Amazon. There are way too many of you to mention here, and I'd hate to accidentally miss someone out, but please know that I read and deeply appreciate every review, and all of the work you do to support authors and the book industry.

I'm extremely grateful to the friends and family members who have been so supportive of my foray into historical fiction. Special thanks to Lacey Jennen, Gina Ervin, Rachel Kelley, Charles Delaney, Amy Fawcett, Carolyn Miller, Sara Starbuck, Pearl Bates, Marie Hermet, Thea Bennett, Stephanie Lam, Sass Pankhurst, Linda Newman, Jan Silverman, Patricia Jacobs, Jackie Stanbridge, Lorna Read and Louise George for all of your lovely feedback on my books and for helping spread the word, I so appreciate it. And huge thanks to Linda Lloyd for patiently listening to all of my voice notes about "The Spy Novel" and for all of your love and support during the writing process.

And last but by no means least, THANK YOU to all of the readers who've taken the time to send me such lovely messages about my World War Two novels. It really means the world to me. I decided a long time ago that I would define writing success in terms of the level of connection I'm able to build with readers through my words. It's been so heart-warming to hear how the stories and characters have moved you.

Made in United States
Orlando, FL
13 August 2022

20986956R00248